THIS COVEN WON'T BREAK

ALSO BY ISABEL STERLING

This Spell Can't Last
These Witches Don't Burn
The Coldest Touch

THIS COVEN WON'T BREAK

ISABEL STERLING

RAZORBILL

RAZORBILL

An imprint of Penguin Random House LLC, New York

Visit us online at penguinrandomhouse.com

THE LIBRARY OF CONGRESS HAS CATALOGED THE HARDCOVER EDITION AS FOLLOWS:
Names: Sterling, Isabel, author.
Title: This coven won't break / Isabel Sterling.
Other titles: This coven will not break
Description: New York : Razorbill, [2020] | Sequel to: These witches don't burn. |
Audience: Ages 12+. | Summary: High school senior Hannah and
her new girlfriend, Morgan, are the Witches' best hope for stopping the
Hunters, who are now nationwide, from destroying magic for good.
Identifiers: LCCN 2020005780 | ISBN 9780451480354 (hardcover) |
ISBN 9780451480361 (ebook)
Subjects: CYAC: Witchcraft—Fiction. | Good and evil—Fiction. |
Dating (Social customs)—Fiction. | Lesbians—Fiction. | Salem (Mass.)—Fiction.
Classification: LCC PZ7.1.S7443 Thi 2020 | DDC [Fic]—dc23
LC record available at https://lccn.loc.gov/2020005780

Paperback ISBN 9780451480378

Printed in the United States of America

LSCH

1 3 5 7 9 10 8 6 4 2

Interior design by Corina Lupp

For my dear friend David.
I couldn't have done this without you.

PROLOGUE

SUMMER WAS STILL BLISTERINGLY hot when classes resumed at NYU, where a young Caster Witch named Alexis Scott was starting her sophomore year. After her final lecture of the day, Lexie gathered her things and hurried home. Her professors had wasted no time piling on assignments and complicated labs, leaving her with hours of coursework to complete. At least this year, she didn't have to learn how to navigate Manhattan on top of everything else. With her bag secure on her back, she moved confidently through the city streets.

Her life was coming together exactly as she'd hoped.

She headed east toward her apartment, weaving through the crowd of Regs as the sun warmed her brown skin. She ticked through the to-do list in her head.

Read chapters three through five for molecular and cell biology.

Finish problem sets for calculus.

Attempt the invisibility potion again and hope the new version doesn't explode.

The Regs around her—people who had no magic of their own—couldn't find out about the potions she created in her apartment. They'd never know that creating new uses for magic was her favorite part of being a Caster. She'd figure out the invisibility potion, even if it took a hundred permutations to get it right.

Halfway home, her phone rang. The number showed up as

a fire emoji, but she had no idea who it was. Someone from class? Did her roommate, Coral, mess with her contacts again?

"Hello?"

A pause on the other end. Then a sudden inhale. "Lexie?"

Lexie didn't recognize the voice. It was feminine and young, probably around her age. "Who's asking?"

"It's Veronica."

She racked her brain, trying to connect the name with the voice. She came up empty. "You must have the wrong number."

"Wait!" the voice on the other end shouted. "We met last May. I've been trying to reach Tori, but her phone is disconnected." When Lexie didn't respond right away, the girl on the other line groaned. "I'm an idiot. She blocked me, didn't she?"

A series of goose bumps rose along Lexie's arm in the wake of those words. In a flash, she remembered *exactly* who Veronica was.

It was at the end of last semester. Lexie had decided to spend the summer in the city with her Caster roommates, Tori and Coral, instead of going back home to Chicago. That particular weekend, the three of them had met a pair of Elementals who were visiting the city on a school trip. Veronica and the other girl—Heidi or Hannah or . . . something—snuck out of their hotel room to hang out Saturday night.

But the Blood Witch who had been threatening Lexie and her friends for weeks attacked again, breaking into their apartment and covering their walls with bloody runes, meant to do goddess knows what. The memory made Lexie shudder. Tori had tried to wash the blood away. She scrubbed frantically until the bucket of soapy water ran red with the other witch's blood.

When the Elementals saw what the Blood Witch had done, they wanted to protect Lexie and her friends. Tori convinced her it was a good idea to let the Salem girls help, and together, they'd captured the Blood Witch. But things got more . . . *complicated* than anyone intended.

At least the Blood Witch wasn't a problem anymore.

The Elementals made everything so much *worse* that weekend, and Lexie wanted to put the whole thing behind her. She didn't want some near-stranger dragging it up again.

"Lexie? Are you still there?"

"What do you want from us?" Her voice snapped out, harsh and bitter. She should have changed her number. She shouldn't have let Tori talk her into giving it to Veronica in the first place.

"Did you hear?"

She paused to wait for the signal to cross the busy street. Surrounded by Regs, she kept her voice low. "Hear what?"

"The Witch Hunters," the younger girl said, voice breaking. "They're back."

Lexie's entire body turned to stone right there on the Manhattan sidewalk. The signals changed. Regs pushed past her, unaware that her sense of reality was shifting. Someone bumped into Lexie's shoulder, and the touch was enough to make her legs work again.

"What do you mean *they're back*?" Lexie kept her voice low, which wasn't hard since she could barely breathe. She hurried across the street, heart slamming against her ribs, and counted the blocks until home. Only two left and then her five-story climb. "How do you know? What happened?"

"They tried to kill me. Hannah, too." A shuddered breath cut off Veronica's words, and she had to clear her throat to try again. "The Council doesn't want to cause panic, but I thought you should know. Coral didn't answer her phone, and Tori—"

"Tori isn't around anymore." The words ripped from her throat. They shredded her chest and raised an invisible flush of shame along her skin. Lexie squeezed her empty hand into a tight fist.

"Oh. Do you know where she is?"

Lexie shook her head as she reached her building, even though she knew the Elemental couldn't see her. Once she was safe behind the closed door, she started the climb. At least Tori wouldn't have to face this new horror.

"Lexie?"

Anger twisted up from Lexie's gut, but she forced her voice to remain neutral. "Don't call this number again."

She hung up before the other witch could protest.

On the fifth floor, Lexie walked down the hall and unlocked the deadbolt on her door. Inside her small, shared apartment, she let out a shaky breath and dropped her bag. The heavy textbooks thunked against the wood floor. Coral was in their kitchen-turned-Caster-workshop. She bent over a notebook, filling the page with symbols as a potion bubbled before her.

"Hey, Lex," she said, brushing a thick curl behind her ear. Coral glanced up, and something in Lexie's expression must have alarmed her, because she abandoned her notes. "What's wrong?"

Lexie picked up a bundle of dried rosemary and twirled the plant between her fingers. The herb's power hummed against her skin. It wanted to be shaped and combined and made into pure magic. There wasn't time for that.

She focused her gaze on her roommate. "We have a problem."

HIGH SCHOOL. THEY SAY it's the best time of our lives. A time of exploration and endless possibilities. We can try out for any sport, dabble in any form of artistic expression. And by the time we walk across the graduation stage, we're supposed to know exactly who we want to be.

They say a lot of things, but as I sit in my dead father's car, parked at the back of the student lot for the first day of senior year, I can't help but call bullshit.

Salem High isn't a place to discover who you are. It's a place to survive and move on. A place where the swing from celebrity to outcast is only one misstep away. Especially for a girl like me.

I cut the engine and check my hair in the visor mirror, brushing the bangs out of my eyes. Even though the local news never mentioned my name, it didn't take long before everyone figured out that their top story—*Recent Salem High graduate Benton Hall arrested on charges of attempted murder*—was about me. The entire school probably saw the gruesome re-creations of Benton's makeshift pyre, where he tied my ex-girlfriend Veronica and me to a stake and tried to burn us alive.

If any of my classmates managed to miss the news, and the social media fallout it created—which *did* mention my name—I'm sure they'll find out the second they step onto school grounds.

Not that any of them will be able to guess *why* Benton did what he did.

The only people at school who know that Veronica and I are Elemental Witches—the only ones who know about the Witch Hunters trying to kill us—are the handful of covenmates who go here, my Blood Witch girlfriend, and my best friend.

A sharp knock raps against my window. I flinch, nearly stabbing myself in the eye as my hands jolt away from the mirror.

"Sorry, Hannah!" The muffled voice of said best friend penetrates the closed window, and its familiarity calms my pounding heart. "Are you coming in?"

"Just a sec, Gemma." I grab my backpack from the passenger's seat and force out a slow breath, counting to ten as I exhale. *I can do this. I'm okay.* When my ragged heartbeat has calmed to a more normal rhythm, I leave the safety of Dad's car and lock the door behind me.

Gemma follows me toward the school, using her fluorescent pink cane to reduce some of the pressure on her leg. Veronica and I weren't the only ones the Witch Hunters hurt this summer. Gemma was with me when Benton forced my car over a bridge. He didn't know Gem was in the car, but the door crushed her leg anyway. My magic was the only thing that saved us from drowning, and there was nothing I could do to hide it from her. Gemma saw *everything*, leaving me no choice but to explain.

If the Council finds out what Gemma knows though . . . that could be the end of my magic. It could end Gemma's life, too.

Despite the danger of her knowledge, being my whole self around her has brought us closer. I wouldn't change that, even though I wish I could take away the lasting damage done to her leg. I wish I could repair her ruined dreams of a professional dance career.

It could be worse, a voice inside reminds me. *At least Gemma's still alive.* I squeeze my eyes shut and try to fight the rising panic. Fight the constant reminder whispering at the back of my head.

Dad didn't survive.

"Hannah?" Gemma's voice pulls me from the edge of drowning grief, and I focus on the aggressive pink of her cane. She doesn't use it all the time, only on her bad days. Which are usually after she pushes herself too hard in physical therapy. When I glance up, she's watching me, the space between her brows pinched with concern. "Are you sure you're ready for this?"

I flash a smile, far brighter than what I feel inside, and head toward the horde of students mingling outside the school. "I'm good, Gem. I swear." I slow to match her pace and lower my voice so no one overhears. "Besides, Mom already vetoed my plan to drop out of school and fight the Witch Hunters."

"Your mom is such a buzzkill." Gemma goes quiet as we pass through the crowd of students. Dozens of conversations dry up and turn to dust when they spot us.

When they spot *me*.

I try to smile when I see familiar faces, but there's so much pity in the rise of their brows that I have to look away. I can't stomach the obvious hunger for gossip that has infected the entire high school. Can't bear to see the glimmer of morbid curiosity shining in their eyes and the reminder of *why* they watch me like an impending car crash.

Missing Dad is too heavy. It hurts too much. I can't let myself think about it. About him.

Yet as Gemma and I move past our classmates, and whispered conversations pick up in fits and starts, some small part of me wants to know *exactly* what kind of rumors are circulating.

Everyone loved Benton. He was easily the most crushed-on senior last year. I saw at least three people cry when he signed their yearbooks back in June. No one wanted him to leave for college. But now that he's accused of attempted murder, have they turned on him? Or have they found a way to forgive the charismatic boy they used to know?

I reach for my magic, shoving past the strange barrier that's been there ever since Benton drugged me to suppress my power. My magic resists my call, and I push harder, asking the air to bring their conspiracy theories close enough to hear.

Pain lances up my spine, sharp and fast, when I reach too hard. I stumble on the steps and grab the handrail to steady myself. Tears burn, and I shut my eyes against the shame as my magic crumbles inside me. It shouldn't be this hard. Such a tiny, simple piece of magic shouldn't hurt like this. It's so small it isn't even against Council laws, since no one would ever notice.

"Hannah?"

This time, it isn't Gemma who's calling for me. It's Morgan. My girlfriend's Blood Magic vibrates deep in my bones, soothing away the sharpest parts of the pain, and then she's there, reaching for my hand. "Are you okay?"

"I'm fine," I say, but I let her thread her fingers through mine as I climb the rest of the stairs. "Between the two of you, I should get that tattooed on my forehead."

Morgan shoots me a look, one that says she's acutely aware that things are *not* as fine as I'd like to pretend they are. Once we're inside, she leads us into a still-empty classroom. "You don't have to pretend with us, Hannah. I know this summer has been hard on you."

Under the fluorescent lights, I fight to keep my eyes from shimmering with tears. I shove the grief down, down, *down* until it's so deep I can't find it. "I'm fine," I repeat, keeping my voice steady.

"No, you're not. Your heart rate shot through the roof." Morgan casts a worried look at Gem, and I get the distinct impression my best friend and my girlfriend are about to gang up on me.

This is one of the few downsides to dating a Blood Witch, besides the strange looks my fellow Elementals give me: it's impossible to hide my feelings when she can sense the literal rhythm of my heart. Morgan can't sense that for everyone, just people whose blood she's touched, and if my coven knew that I'd voluntarily given her access to mine? Well, the weird looks would be the least of my problems.

The worry on Gemma's and Morgan's faces lingers, and I shift nervously. "Really, I'm good. I tripped on the stairs. It's not a big deal." I nudge Morgan with my shoulder, aiming to distract her with flirtation. "Not all of us have impeccable grace."

Morgan flushes a satisfying shade of pink as the first warning bell clangs through the halls, effectively ending their interrogation.

We melt into the flow of student traffic and head deeper into the school. The press of shifting bodies sends a tremor of unease through me, but I do my best to keep it hidden. To bury it deep enough that Morgan won't notice. I see Benton in every tall, dark-haired figure that passes the edge of my vision and have to remind myself to breathe. The Benton I knew in these halls, the friend I joked with and confided in, is gone. The Witch Hunter he became, the boy who tried to kill me—whose parents murdered my dad—is rotting in a jail cell while he waits for his trial.

Fresh nerves turn my stomach. Jury selection begins in less than a month. Twelve strangers who will determine his fate.

And mine.

Gemma heads for her locker on the other side of the school, and I look for a distraction. "Are you nervous?" Since it's Morgan's first day at Salem High, I'm sure I'm not the only one who feels like she swallowed a migration of butterflies this morning.

Morgan shrugs, a movement so graceful that walking beside her makes me feel like a robot, all stiff limbs and mechanical expressions. "I miss my friends," she says as we turn a corner. "But it could be worse. I have Gemma and Kate and the other people from dance." Morgan tucks a red curl behind her ear. "You're not half-bad, either."

"That's the goal. A half-decent girlfriend and a not-terrible friend."

She laughs and watches the locker numbers tick up and up until we reach hers. It takes her two tries to spin the combination correctly, but soon the door pulls free with a violent shudder. "You know you're great."

"If you say so." I lean against the locker beside hers and reach for my necklace. I'm still not used to the way she tosses out compliments like she has an infinite supply. I run the bit of black tourmaline crystal along its thin silver chain. The crystal was a gift from my boss, Lauren, and Mom empowered the stone to increase its calming and protective qualities.

Before she can reply, two boys turn the corner and walk

down the hall toward us. "Did you seriously spend the whole summer doing community service? That *sucks*, dude."

Nolan Abbott, soccer star and all-around asshole, has the audacity to soak up his friend's sympathy. "It was shit. I tried to do my hours at the animal shelter, but that stupid cop wouldn't go for it. He made me pick up trash and scrub graffiti like a delinquent."

I barely suppress a laugh, and it comes out as an undignified snort. Detective Ryan Archer is not only the "stupid cop" who busted Nolan for smashing a rock through my front window, he's also the Caster Witch who helped rescue me from a fiery death. Archer denied Nolan's shelter pick on my request. Nolan didn't deserve to spend a summer walking puppies.

Unfortunately, my moment of petty satisfaction attracts Nolan's attention. He glances up, and when he spots me for the first time, his expression goes stormy. "Something funny?"

"Besides your face?"

Nolan scowls. "Sick *burn*. Did Benton teach you that when he tied you to a stake and set you on fire?"

His words drain the blood from my face and leave my knees weak.

Morgan slams the locker and props the books on her hip, pressing her free hand against the small of my back. Blood Magic floods my system, invisible to them but numbing the rising pain and panic that's threatening to swallow me whole. It blots out the memories before they can fully form, leaving nothing but wisps of smoke in their wake. "Come on, Hannah. He's not worth it."

I let her steer me away, but even with her power flowing through my veins, I can't stop my hands from shaking. *I'm okay. I'm safe.* I force myself to breathe, inhaling for five steps, exhaling for ten. *Benton's in jail. I'm okay.* By the time we make it to my locker, my fingers are steady enough to spin the combination and store my things inside.

"You can let go," I whisper as we head toward our homerooms, which are across the hall from each other. Morgan isn't touching me anymore, but she must know what I mean. Her magic falls away, leaving my jagged nerves exposed again. "Thank you."

The softest shadow of a smile graces her lips. "Are you sure you're okay?"

"I'm good. I promise." I step back toward my homeroom, the last few stragglers maneuvering around us. "I'll see you at your locker before lunch?"

She nods and slips into her class as the final bell rings. I hurry in before the clanging stops, and all eyes turn to me. The silence is heavy with expectation.

I force a smile and ease down the aisle, finding a seat near the back. My whole body is tense under the weight of their attention, but I keep my spine straight. I remind myself to breathe. Remind myself not to feel too strongly. I hide my still trembling hands under the desk.

I'm okay. I can do this.

If I can survive the Witch Hunters, I can survive high school.

2

BY THE END OF our short three-day week, I've settled back into the rhythm of school. My lack of an epic meltdown has calmed the gawking stares down to curious glances, and people stop going quiet every time I enter a room.

On Friday, while most of my classmates prepare to spend their first weekend getting wasted at Nolan's newly renovated home, I'm driving Gemma somewhere I didn't expect to visit this year: the Fly by Night Cauldron.

After everything that happened this summer, I couldn't bring myself to go back to work. As much as I love my boss, Lauren, and the freedom of having my own paycheck, I couldn't fit in Cauldron shifts *and* find a way to fight the Witch Hunters. Something had to give.

But when Gem complained at lunch that her mom couldn't drive her to the Cauldron, where she's been studying Wicca with Lauren, I saw an opportunity I couldn't miss.

Cal, my former Cauldron coworker and a junior agent for the Council, works most Fridays after his classes at Salem State. If I can convince him that I should be allowed to join the fight, maybe he can get the rest of the Council on my side, too. Mom won't be able to stop me if the entire Council wants me on board.

She won't be able to prevent me from taking down the people who hurt us—starting with Benton's parents.

The Halls have evaded capture so far, by both the police and the Council, but I intend to be there when they're finally brought in. I squeeze the necklace Lauren gave me after my dad died, trying to absorb its strength.

He didn't just die, a small voice inside corrects, *he was murdered*. Something cold slithers through my veins. Hatred, maybe. Grief.

We pull into the parking garage, and Gemma fidgets in her seat. "Are you sure you aren't mad that I'm doing this?" It's the fifth time she's asked since she started her lessons with Lauren over the summer. There's a new urgency to her tone, probably because this is the first time we'll be in the shop together.

I don't answer right away, focusing instead on backing into a spot. I'm not entirely sure how I feel about Gemma studying Wicca. It's certainly none of my business, and I'm happy that she's found a religion that speaks to her, but it's still . . . a little weird.

"I'm not mad," I say at last, when the car is parked and I don't have any more excuses to delay.

"Well, that wasn't very convincing." She grabs her bag and follows me out of the car. "If it bothers you, I could have found a different ride."

"You don't have to do that. Really, it's okay." We maneuver through narrow sidewalks packed with tourists who are already sporting black robes and pointed witch hats, even though it's almost two months until Halloween. The sun is still hot overhead, warm enough that a small bead of sweat trails down my spine.

Across the street from the shop, we pause to wait for the light to turn. I try again to convince my best friend that things are fine. "I swear I'm not mad, Gem. It's just that I had a whole church-and-state thing with this stuff. It's weird to be bringing you here instead of the dance studio."

Gemma nods and turns away without saying anything, and I mentally kick myself. She always gets like this whenever Morgan or I mention dance. Before the car crash, Gemma lived and breathed ballet and modern and tap. She had the rare combination of innate talent and the drive to work harder than everyone else anyway. She could have gotten into any dance conservatory she wanted, and her dream of dancing on Broadway always seemed a matter of when, not if. That all changed when the guardrail smashed into her door and crushed her leg. Despite her age and how hard she works in physical therapy, the doctors haven't been overly encouraging about her ability to recover in time to audition this year. If she ever does.

Before I can apologize, the lights turn and we follow the crowd across the street. I pull open the door and bells jingle above me. I smile at the familiar sound, letting the soothing lavender incense draw me into the shop.

I spot Lauren working behind the register, where she's converted the back counter into some kind of altar. Beautifully carved wooden statues of the Horned God and Triple Goddess sit at the center of the counter with large gold and silver pillar candles burning beside their respective deity.

Even from across the room, the flicker of the small flames brushes against my skin. I try to ignore the sensations, but they push and push and *push* until I can't block them out. Suddenly, I'm back in the woods again. My legs are bound to a stake. I can't move. Can't breathe. Fire presses against my skin, looking for a way past my compromised Elemental power. Smoke fills my lungs. Tears blur my vision as darkness crowds in and—

"Hannah." Gemma's urgent whisper pulls me back to the present, and I find her fingers wrapped tightly around my wrist. "Are you okay?"

"Yeah." I can barely choke the word out. It scrapes like ash and rock across my tongue as I press the heels of my hands against my eyelids. Coming here was a mistake. I need Morgan. My nerves are too raw and exposed without her.

No. I shove memories into a mental box and lock it tight. *You can do this. You have to be okay if you want to fight. Just find Cal.* Slowly, the tension leaves my body. I still step farther away from the candles though.

Lauren turns around, and her face lights up when she spots us loitering by the door. "Hannah, I wasn't expecting to see you." She's all warmth and concern as she approaches. Lauren isn't a member of the Witch Clans, but as a Wiccan high priestess, she has her own kind of power. Different from ours, less dramatic, but still real. It's that power Gem is so excited to harness for herself. "How are you?"

I shrug and find my fingers reaching for the necklace again. "I'm okay."

Her gaze drops to the tourmaline that she gifted me, a sad smile pulling at the corners of her lips. "You've been missed, Hannah. Please know you're welcome back anytime."

Warmth spreads through me, but I don't see myself coming back. Not while there are Hunters to fight. "Thank you," I say, not committing to anything.

"Now, Gemma," Lauren says, shifting her focus. "Are you ready to discuss the wheel of the year?"

Gem casts me a glance before she nods and follows Lauren to the back of the shop, where they disappear into the private reading room. It's usually occupied by tarot clients, but she uses it for her students, too.

Once they've disappeared, I go looking for Cal. I find him along the opposite wall, wearing an orange Cauldron T-shirt, dark jeans, and black-and-white Converse. He's buzzed the sides of his head since I last saw him, his blond hair still perfectly floppy on top. Cal is busy restocking the hand-packaged potion ingredients that Lauren blesses herself, but he stops to hug me tight as I approach. When he pulls away, I notice dark circles under his eyes that stand out against his pale skin.

"Are you okay?" I cringe as the question passes my lips. I know more than most how irritating it can be.

Cal reaches for another packet of dried herbs, this one labeled *To Bring Prosperity*. "I'm fine. Why?"

"You look like you haven't slept in weeks." I settle beside him and pick up a shiny black bag that promises maximum protection. I run my finger along the gold pentacle emblazoned beneath the text. "Is everything going okay with the you-know-what?"

I haven't heard much about the Council's plans, but I know they intend to destroy the drug that temporarily stole my magic, including every bit of research it took to cook it up.

Somehow.

Cal glances behind us to make sure no one is close enough to overhear. He hangs up a handful of *Opening Your Inner Eye* potions, checks over his shoulder one more time, and then leans close. "There's a raid happening tonight, actually."

"Really? Where?"

"We found out where the Hunters are manufacturing the drug. There's a team out of Boston in charge of infiltration and destruction." A shimmer of hope lights Cal's expression, and a confusing mix of excitement and disappointment floods through me. Even though I know it's an irrational hope, I wanted to be part of whatever happens next. I wanted to be the one to destroy the drug that changed my entire life.

"That's great." My enthusiasm sounds false even to my ears.

Cal nods, but his smile falters. "Archer and I wanted to go with them, but our orders are to continue watching over your coven in case of retaliation."

A shiver of fear makes my fingers tremble. I reach for another black bag, this one promising to spice up the bedroom, and squeeze tight to stop the shaking. "What happens once the drug is gone? Is there anything I can do?" I mentally cross my fingers and hope I don't sound as desperate as I feel.

But Cal shakes his head, and my chance at convincing him to talk to the Council crumbles. "The Elders are still arguing about what to do for Phase Two." He must mistake my panic at the mention of Elders for confusion, because he clarifies. "Destroying the drug is Phase One. Phase Two is neutralizing the Hunters entirely."

I nod, but I'm still shaken by the reminder that the Elders are involved in this. There are three on the Council—one from each Clan—and they have the final say on all witch matters. No one outside of Council members ever meets them, unless you've broken our most sacred law and exposed magic to Regs.

Like I did with Gemma.

A tremble of fear courses through me. Most witches who are brought before the Elders don't leave with their magic intact. I hang the bag of blessed herbs and clear my throat. "So, what's the plan for after? Do you know what options they're considering?"

"Nothing concrete. There's been talk of imprisonment.

Draining financial resources. A couple key assassinations." Cal pauses when I let out an involuntary gasp. "They're trying to wipe us out, Hannah. It's not like we can invite them to tea and ask nicely."

The tiny muscles around my eyes tighten, and I feel my expression go hard. Biting words build at the back of my throat. I swallow down the bitterness as best I can. "Trust me, Cal. I remember exactly what Benton did to me. I know they won't listen to anything we say."

I can still hear Benton's voice like it was yesterday. He called me a monster. Said he wanted to give me true humanity by taking away everything that made me an Elemental. And then he blamed me for ruining his plans and tried to burn me alive. I lean against the shelves and sigh. "I wish there was a reset button we could push and make them disappear. Or that we could go back in time and stop them from ever finding out about magic in the first place."

Cal puts an arm around my shoulders. "We'll figure something out. I promise."

I lean into his touch and will myself to believe him.

⊹ ⁕ ⊹

While I wait for Gemma to finish her lesson, the shop gets too busy to talk with Cal. I wander the aisles while he works, straightening rows of candles while I wait for another opening. I'll need to be more direct, since asking if the Council needed any help didn't have the desired effect.

But by the time Gem finishes her lesson, I still haven't found my opening. She emerges from Lauren's private room brimming with energy. Her smile dims when she spots me. "Why do you have Veronica Face?"

"I don't." I glare at her when a passing tourist gives us an odd look. "*Veronica Face* isn't a thing."

Gemma holds up her hand and ticks off each argument on her fingers. "Your brow is pinched. You're scowling. And you look like someone kicked a puppy. That's your classic post-breakup expression." My best friend gasps softly and swings closer on her crutches. "You didn't break up with Morgan, did you?"

"Morgan and I are fine," I assure her. Strangely, so are Veronica and I these days. After everything that happened with Benton this summer—him kidnapping her, me getting caught trying to rescue her, both of us nearly dying—we decided to give our friendship a clean slate. A friendship informed by the mistakes we made while dating, but not defined by them. At least, that's the goal.

"Well, it's definitely something," Gem insists. "You know you can trust me."

"I know, but I can't talk about it here." Those dual feelings of excitement and disappointment rear up again. I should be happy about the raid tonight. No other witch should have to go through what I did, but I can't stop wishing I was part of it. Wishing I could be the one to destroy the drug that stole my magic and gave it back broken and wrong.

Fresh shame claws up my chest, using my ribs like a jungle gym. The drug only affected *me* like this. Veronica's magic returned after only a few weeks. I don't understand why mine is almost impossible to reach, and when I do manage to push hard enough to touch the elements, it hurts too much to use. I don't get why three of the elements stay so far out of reach while even the

smallest fire consumes my attention and trails across my awareness like barbed wire on bare skin.

"Hannah . . ."

"Gemma . . ." I imitate her concerned tone, which only makes
her scowl at me. "We'll talk later, I promise. Are you ready to go?"

She shakes her head. "I want to get some amethyst before we
leave. Lauren said it could help enhance my tarot reading."

I glance toward the register where Lauren keeps the handmade crystal jewelry. The deity candles burn steadily, and I falter.
"I'll wait for you over here, if that's okay." I hope she can't hear the
fear that makes my voice tremble.

My best friend gives me a curious look that tells me she *definitely* noticed. "I'll be quick," she promises.

Behind me, the bells jingle as the front door swings open.
Reflexively, I turn to see who has come in. A white guy who looks
around my age, with floppy brown hair and hazel eyes behind
thick-rimmed glasses, enters the shop. He isn't the kind of guy I
normally expect to find in a place like this, dressed in crisp khakis
and a maroon polo.

He scans the room, and something flickers across his expression when he spots me. He pulls out his phone, flipping through
a few screens before settling his gaze on me again.

Nerves twist in my gut.

Cal appears from an aisle over and approaches the dark-
haired boy. "Can I help you find something?"

"Actually . . ." The guy doesn't even look at Cal, too busy
glancing from his phone to me. "I think I've found what I'm looking for."

Another customer calls for Cal, and once he's occupied, the
guy closes the space between us. "You're Hannah Walsh, right?"

I tense when my name passes his lips. "Sorry. You have the wrong girl." I brush past him and head back down the book aisle. Fucking news stories. He was probably looking at a photo from one of the articles. I wonder which channel or wannabe investigative blogger spilled that I work here.

That I *used* to work here.

The dark-haired guy appears around the other side of the aisle, an easy smile curving his lips. His posture is open and relaxed, like he's used to getting his way. "So, *Not Hannah*. I assume it wouldn't interest you to learn that Benton Hall's lawyers intend to argue self-defense." He pauses, and his words are like ice in my veins. "If you're not her, I suppose you don't care that they plan to expose every facet of Hannah's life to the public. They may even drag her new girlfriend in to testify."

I whirl on him. "What do you want from me? How do you even know about her?"

He shrugs. "I'm a reporter. It's my job to know things." He fusses with his phone again. "In fact, I'm surprised to see you here. I thought you quit."

"If you thought I quit, what are you doing here? Are you even old enough to be a reporter?"

"There isn't an age limit on talent. Besides, every good reporter knows the value of research. I was hoping to talk to your former coworkers, but since you're here . . ." He opens an audio recording app on his phone and shoves it in my direction. "Would you like to make a statement? You can get ahead of the narrative. Humanize your position before the news paints you as the *real* bad guy."

The words dry up on my tongue. I can't read this boy. I can't tell if he wants to help me or paint me as the villain himself.

There's something about him that sets me on edge. Something so assessing about his gaze, like he's piecing together an intricate puzzle, not talking to an actual person.

A shudder rattles through my bones.

"Come on, Hannah." The young reporter smirks and leans against the bookshelf. "Will you tell your side of the story? The whole world wants to know the truth of what you are."

My gaze snaps back to his. "What did you just say?"

"Okay, fine, maybe not the whole world. But my readers definitely want to know what happened to you." He holds the phone out to me. "Do you have a statement? Maybe we could set up a meeting with this new girl of yours. Morgan, right?"

But I shake my head. That's not what he said. "You want to know *what* I am?" *A witch*, I think. *A broken, grieving Elemental who can't even keep her ice water cold.* "I'm furious. I'm sick of vultures like you trying to turn my life into a soundbite for your stupid blog."

"It's not a blog—"

"Get out."

"You don't work here anymore." His voice is low, yet it curls around my spine, laced with violent intent. He stands up straighter, towering over me. "You can't throw me out."

"Then get out of my way." I shove past the boy, but he grabs my wrist, preventing my escape. I whirl on him, a fury tinged with panic climbing up my throat. "Let. Me. Go."

He squeezes tighter, twisting until he pulls a wince from my throat. "Or you'll what?"

"What the hell?" Gemma's voice cuts between us, and we both turn to find her at the end of the aisle. She must see the fear on my face, because she shouts for Lauren.

The guy unfurls a string of curses and shoves me away from him. "This isn't over," he says, tucking his phone in the pocket of his khakis. "Not even close." The rage in his expression is so severe it steals my breath. He looks at me like . . .

Like Benton did. Like I'm a monster.

I watch as he slips away, confused and disoriented by the entire interaction. I'd bet anything he's one of the Benton groupies that Gemma is always warning me to avoid online. He's gone by the time Lauren gets here.

She surveys the aisle, looking from Gemma to me. "Is everything all right?"

"Yeah," I say, rubbing my wrist. "It's fine. Just some overzealous reporter," I lie. There's no reason to worry Gemma now that he's gone.

Lauren scowls. "They should know better than to harass a minor. I've been kicking them out at least once a week. I'm sorry."

I doubt he was from a legitimate news source, but I try to smile anyway. "It's okay. I should probably go though."

"Of course." Lauren offers a hug, and I accept, soaking up her warmth. I'm surprised by how much I've missed her steady, earthy presence.

Gemma watches me with a careful expression, but she doesn't say anything while we're in the shop. I wave goodbye to Cal, who's busy at the register. "Let me know how tonight goes!"

He raises a thumbs-up in response but goes right back to work. Maybe I can text him tomorrow after the raid. If it goes well and the drug is destroyed, I can ask him to vouch for me with the Council. There *has* to be something I can do to fight back.

Outside, Gemma doesn't say anything until we're safely

closed within Dad's car, out of earshot of any nearby tourists. "What the hell was that about?"

"Just another reporter obsessed with the worst moment of my life," I say, even though there was definitely something off about the guy. If he's not part of the Benton Fan Club, he had some kind of agenda.

I turn on the car and sink deeper into the soft, warm leather. The A/C blows Dad's favorite car freshener—pine and fresh rain—into my face, and the scent transports me back in time. Dad driving Veronica and me to the mall before either of us had cars of our own. The first time he gave me the Sex Talk, the Google results for *lesbian safe sex practices* still on his phone screen for quick reference.

The memory makes me smile, even though it was absolutely mortifying at the time.

"Are you sure you're okay?"

"I'm going to start charging you a dollar every time you ask that. I'm *fine*, Gem. Some idiot boy with a recorder is the least of my concerns." I pull out of my spot and head toward Gemma's house. When we pass the cemetery, my heart clenches and I have to fight back the wave of grief that threatens to drown my vision. A chorus of *not fair, not fair, not fair* screams in my head, but I can't let the thoughts take hold. I can't let myself miss him or I'll fall apart completely.

Gemma reaches for my hand and squeezes tight. She doesn't say anything. She doesn't have to. I squeeze back, pushing the last of the tears away. But once I drop her off, I can't stop them anymore. The world turns blurry, and when I pull into my driveway, I feel lost.

This place isn't home. My home was *another* casualty of

Benton's reign of terror against my coven, burnt down by his Hunter parents. I lost my dad and everything he touched. The recliner where he used to read me stories. My childhood art that he kept plastered all over his home office. The family grimoire with his tight, cramped handwriting.

All of it's gone.

And it's never coming back.

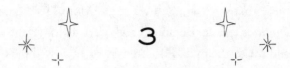

3

THE NEXT DAY, I have my first prep session with Dad's boss, district attorney Natalie Flores. She's back from maternity leave and in charge of the case against Benton. With the trial looming at the end of the month—in *twenty-four days*—we can't put off preparations any longer.

DA Flores eases me into the questioning, asking about my relationship with Benton and the events leading up to my capture. It's hard to get the words out, harder still to function with painful flashbacks overtaking my memory with each new question.

You and Veronica weren't treated for burns. Did Benton actually set fire to the wood?

Why did you go to Benton's house that night?

Did you know it was Benton you fought at Veronica's house earlier that summer?

And on and on and on. By the time the DA ends the session, I feel phantom flames pressing against my skin, and my insides are twisted into knots.

"Have you heard anything?" Mom asks as we're leaving. "About the search for the boy's parents?"

"The police are following up on every lead," DA Flores promises, but Mom and I have listened to Dad enough over the years to know that means they've got nothing.

In the car, when Mom reaches for my hand, I flinch away

before I can stop myself. "Sorry," I say, crossing my arms tightly around me. "That was just . . . It was a lot, Mom." I shudder again as the memories rise up. Benton's hands curled around my arms as he dragged me to the pyre. His strength as he tossed me over his shoulder when I tried to slow him down.

"I know, Han." The temperature in the car dips slightly. Mom starts the engine and pulls into traffic. "I wish I knew how to make it better or how to keep you from having to do this at all." When she stops at a light, Mom turns to me. "Ice cream?"

A smile pulls at my lips. "I could do ice cream." Mom turns on her blinker so we can go to my favorite ice cream stand, one of the few still open after Labor Day. "Can Morgan come over later?"

At first, Mom doesn't say anything. She still hasn't gotten over the fact that Morgan is a Blood Witch, despite my ongoing #notallBloodWitches campaign at home. Mom hasn't said anything weird to Morgan about it, and her rules are the same as they were when I was dating Veronica, but there's still this shadow of fear and doubt whenever I bring her up.

Part of me wants to believe it's her Momma Bear tendencies going into overdrive after what happened this summer, but there's another part of me that knows all the same horror stories about Blood Witches that she does. A part of me that knows those kinds of beliefs don't disappear without real work.

But then Mom slips on a bright smile. "Of course she can. She can stay for dinner, too, if you want."

I'm texting Morgan before Mom even finishes her sentence.

Morgan doesn't text back until we're done with our ice cream—mint chocolate chip for me and mocha for Mom.

MH: Sorry! Just got home from dance.

MH: How was your meeting?

HW: . . . Fine.

Three dots appear and disappear several times, and Mom is pulling into the driveway before a response comes through.

MH: I'll be over soon.

I've learned that Morgan's *soon* can mean anything from five minutes to an hour, so I frantically clean my room, tossing dirty clothes in the closet and making my bed. I consider actually throwing my clothes in the washer, but the doorbell rings.

A flutter of nerves makes my skin tingle all over as I slip into the hall.

"You two can stay in the living room," Mom yells from the kitchen. "No closed doors!"

"Why didn't you say something before I panic-cleaned my room?" I shout back.

"It's good for you!"

I groan and check my reflection in the hallway mirror. I don't know why I bother. I'm a mess. Morgan knocks again, and I open the door.

The first sight of Morgan leaves me breathless and almost giddy. She's wearing hip-hugging jeans and a floppy gray sweater. Her red hair is still wet from a shower, and she's twisted it up into a loose bun on the top of her head. Everything about her is cozy in all the ways I want to feel right now.

Her cheeks flush a gentle pink, and she glances up at me from the porch. The single step into the house makes me a few inches taller than her, and she looks through her lashes at me. "Your heart is racing," she says, her voice soft.

"Yeah?" I hadn't noticed it before, but now I feel it speed even faster. Embarrassment warms my cheeks until I'm sure they're matching hers. "What can I say?" I whisper, trying for nonchalance but failing miserably. "Seeing you does silly things to my heart."

I cringe as soon as the words pass my lips. Dating her has made me cheesier than being with Veronica ever did, but Morgan doesn't seem to mind. The right corner of her lips quirks up, and she raises a small bag. The contents clink as they shift together. "I thought a spa day was in order."

"You're brilliant." I press a quick kiss to her cheek and lead her to the living room. We start with the face masks Morgan brought and take selfies once they've dried, trying to see who can make the goofiest face with our expressions limited by the stiff clay.

I upload the best pictures to Instagram. "It's too bad I can't tag you." Morgan's parents made her delete all her accounts after everything that happened with Riley, the ex-boyfriend who turned out to be a Witch Hunter. He's the whole reason they even moved to Salem from Minnesota.

She stands and offers me a hand. "Let's wash this off before our faces turn to stone."

We spend the rest of the afternoon watching movies while we paint each other's nails. I decorate Morgan's with little flowers and tell her about my meeting with Natalie Flores. Morgan asks if Veronica is going to testify, and I have to admit I'm not entirely sure. I don't think she has a choice, so the DA must be doing some kind of video conference to prep her since Veronica disappeared off to Ithaca College back in August.

While Morgan paints my nails a shimmering sky blue, I tell her about the raid that was supposed to happen last night. How the Hunters' drug, the one that could temporarily bury a witch's magic, should be destroyed by now.

I text Cal to ask about the raid, but by the time the movie ends, he still hasn't responded. Since Mom has disappeared into her bedroom to grade papers, I turn on the news. Morgan has me sit on the floor in front of her so she can braid my hair.

As she works, her Blood Magic flows through my veins. It eases away the lingering tension from my meeting with DA Flores, but it does more than that. It steadies me. Grounds me. The air plays along my skin, and since we're alone in my house, I absently raise my hand and call to my magic. The air moves along my fingers, swirling and dancing without pain or force.

The relief of it almost makes me cry.

"Can I ask you something?" I say as Morgan secures a tie around the end of the braid.

"About what?" She shifts back into the cushions now that her work is done.

"About how your magic works." I perch on the edge of the couch beside her, weighing my words. I want so badly to know everything about her, want to understand why her magic affects mine, but I don't want to hurt her by asking the wrong way. There's still so much I don't know about Blood Witches. And the stuff I do know? It's hard to tell which parts are based on stereotypes and nothing more.

"What about it?" Morgan prompts when I've stayed quiet too long. Her expression is carefully neutral.

"Is it . . . instinctual? Like, do you hear my heartbeat whenever I'm close, or do you have to listen for it? And what about right now? Are you making me feel calm on purpose, or is it just . . . happening?"

Morgan drops her gaze. Her forehead creases. After a moment, the steady thrum of her magic disappears from inside me. A dull ache blooms in my ribs, and I hastily release my hold on the air. When I let my magic go, the pain goes with it.

"I guess it's a bit of both," Morgan says finally, looking at me again. "Sometimes I do it on purpose, like at school that first day when you were so stressed out after seeing Nolan. But I didn't realize my magic was affecting you now. I can stop if you don't like it."

"No!" I say, probably a bit too fast. "You don't have to stop. It's . . ." *The only thing that makes my magic work.* "It's nice."

"You don't think it's creepy?"

I reach for her hand and thread her fingers between mine. "Of course not."

We settle into the couch to watch the news. The meteorologist forecasts storms early next week, and Morgan leans close to rest her head on my shoulder. "I can't *hear* your heartbeat, by the way. I feel it like a second pulse next to mine. Mostly in my wrists, and only when you're close." She turns and presses a kiss to my neck, giggling when she returns to using my shoulder like a pillow. "Your heart always skips when I do that."

"Hey, that's cheating."

"What? You have more experience kissing girls than me. I'll take any advantage I can get."

I laugh and lean close to kiss her, but everything in me goes cold when Benton's picture appears on the screen. Seeing his smiling senior portrait makes my entire body recoil. I should be used to it by now. They never show his mug shot. He's always this clean-cut, grinning boy. This is why Mom tried to ban me from watching the news.

"Turn it up?" I point to the remote beside Morgan. She does.

"The court trial for local Salem High graduate Benton Hall is expected to begin with jury selection on September thirtieth," the anchor continues. "He's accused of the kidnapping and attempted murder of two local teens, fellow graduate Veronica Matthews and a current Salem High senior. Sources close to Hall indicate the young man intends to plead innocent to all charges. Jenny Cho has more of the story."

The studio fades, replaced by a shot of the courthouse where Benton's trial will take place. The image pans right, where the on-scene reporter waits with a microphone.

"Thank you, Shannon. In just a few short weeks, Salem's district attorney, Natalie Flores, will begin prosecuting the town's most unusual case since its seventeenth-century witch trials. Speculation has infiltrated legal and public circles alike, some referring to the defendant, Benton Hall, as a modern-day witch hunter."

I stiffen even though this isn't the first time I've heard this particular theory. It was popular online first—dozens of memes about burning witches filtered across my feed before Gemma blocked all the relevant terms. A few weeks ago, more legitimate news sources started pushing the theory, too.

Across the house, Mom's bedroom door squeaks open and slams closed again. I turn off the news before she can catch me watching, but she doesn't come to see us. Instead, pots and pans clang in the kitchen as she starts dinner. I'm about to ask Morgan if she wants to sneak into my room when something shatters.

"Mom?" I call from the couch. "Everything okay?" The doorbell rings, and I climb to my feet. "I'll get it." At the front door, I check the peephole before unlocking the deadbolt. "What are you two doing here?"

Detective Archer and Cal stand on my front porch. The detective is dressed in his usual crisp suit, the lack of tie the only sign that he's not on active police duty. Cal looks even more exhausted than he did last night, wearing jeans and a wrinkled T-shirt.

"We need to speak with you," Archer says, his voice tight and strained.

"Is everything okay?" I look from Archer's stony expression to Cal's fracturing calm. "What happened?"

"The raid—" Cal starts, but Archer cuts him off.

"Not out here. Hannah, can we come in?"

Archer closes the door quickly behind them. The energy in the room shifts, crackling with tension and fear. "What happened at the raid?" I ask, flinching when Morgan steps up silently behind me. I take her hand.

This time, Cal looks to Archer for approval before speaking. After a curt nod, Cal turns back to us, his face crumpling into shock and grief. "It was a trap. We lost the entire team."

"What do you mean *you lost them*? Where are they?"

"They're dead, Hannah." Cal's voice cracks. His eyes shimmer, but he doesn't let any tears fall.

Archer rests a hand on Cal's shoulder, and the younger Caster lets out a shaky sigh. "There's more," Archer says. "Is your mother home?"

"More? How can there be more?" I'm still trying to wrap my head around the Boston agents dying at the hands of the Witch

Hunters. Who were they? Who did they leave behind?

"She's in here," Morgan says, pulling me down the hall.

When we reach the kitchen, shattered glass sparkles on the floor. Mom has her phone pressed to her ear, one hand clutching Dad's ring where it hangs on a chain around her neck. She glances up at us, horror etched into her face. "Everyone?" Her voice breaks. "How is that possible?"

"The Hunters also attacked the town where your mom grew up," Archer whispers from behind me. "The entire coven lost their magic."

"What? How?" I'm trembling all over, and it's only Morgan's grip that keeps me standing upright. I know those witches. They're family. Mom's parents. Her friends. Aunt Camila and my cousin Zoë. Her little brothers. "But they'll get it back. Veronica and I got our magic back."

Except not completely, a little voice says inside. *Tell him your magic only works when you have help.*

But Archer shakes his head. "No. They won't." He steps farther into the kitchen, shoes crunching over the bits of broken glass, and reaches a steadying hand for my mother. "The Hunters perfected their drug. The effects are permanent."

4

ON THE WALL ABOVE the sink, the clock *tick-tick-tick*s, marking each second of this new, terrible reality.

The Hunters perfected their drug.

The effects are permanent.

I stand frozen in the kitchen, but inside, my mind is a whirl-wind of frantic activity. I try to piece together what this means. Hunters can erase our magic. Forever. I imagine my grandparents at the winter solstice, unable to light a candle in honor of the Middle Sister, heartbreak etched into their faces. I can picture Zoë at her swim meets. But without her connection to water, will she even want to keep swimming? The air won't whisper its secrets to any of them ever again.

Cal cleans up the shattered glass while Mom and Archer exchange hushed words that I can't hear. My mind runs through a thousand questions. How did the Hunters perfect their drug in a matter of weeks? And *why* did they kill the agents if they could just take away their power? Benton said that once they finished their drug, they wanted to save us, not kill us. Nothing makes sense anymore.

Morgan squeezes my hand and asks the questions I can't push past my lips. "How did this happen? How do you know it's permanent?"

Archer glances at us, and for a brief moment, I can see all the weight he carries with him. His shoulders slump forward. His eyes shimmer with a deep well of grief. But then he blinks and turns to lean against the counter so he can see all of us at once. He runs a hand down his face and takes a deep breath before diving in.

"A few weeks after your incident, Hannah, one of our agents was tracking the Halls." Archer pauses, and I feel myself go tense. I knew the Council was looking for Benton's parents, but this is the first time anyone's told me the specifics.

"The agent was shot," Archer continues. "The Hunters have shifted from the syringes they used on you and Veronica to a modified tranquilizer gun with their drug loaded inside the dart. The agent escaped with his life, but it's been over month and there's no sign of his magic returning."

"But it still could," I argue, desperate for my words to be true. Desperate to undermine his terrifying certainty.

"It won't." Archer looks at me, his expression sympathetic and his tone careful. "We've tested his blood. There were no markers for magic in the sample. We believe they've administered the same drug in the Washington coven."

I shake my head, fear and grief sharpening to anger inside me. I whirl on Cal. "You saw me last night! Why didn't you say anything?"

Cal shifts on his feet. "I wasn't supposed to. Besides, after the raid, it shouldn't have mattered. The drug was supposed to be destroyed."

"But it's *not*. You failed."

"*Hannah.*" Mom's voice lashes against me, shattering the anger I've been wielding as both shield and dagger. "That's enough."

"I know." My eyes burn with tears. I press the heels of my hands against my closed lids. "I'm sorry. I know. I—"

"Why don't we sit." Mom turns without waiting for a response and leads us to the dining room. I don't know how she keeps going, how she stays strong in the face of all this, but her voice is steady. "Ryan, what is this about a raid?"

Archer recaps what Cal already told me last night. That the Council figured out where the Hunters were making the drug. That a team of agents out of Boston were supposed to infiltrate the facility last night and destroy everything.

"But it was like the Hunters knew they were coming. Both Casters were shot with the drug within seconds of breaching the entrance. They were surrounded, but without their magic, the potions they brought for protection were useless," Archer finishes.

"Then why did the Hunters kill them? I thought the whole point was to get rid of our magic and make us 'human.'"

Across from me, Cal tenses and tears slip silently down his face. Suddenly, I feel like the biggest asshole in the world. Cal and Archer were from the same Clan as the agents, and they all worked for the Council. Fresh shame burns my cheeks, because it's more than just that. Cal is *from* Boston. I know Casters don't have covens the way Elementals do, but he probably knew the agents. Maybe even grew up with them.

"We don't know for sure," Archer says before I can apologize. "Cal managed to pull security footage. They fought back. That might have been enough of an excuse for the Hunters."

Silence falls over the room. Morgan reaches for me under the table. Her fingers tremble with fear, and I hold her hand in both of mine. "What happened to Mom's old coven?" I ask, making sure I keep my voice gentle now. Curious instead of accusatory. "How did they lose their magic? Were they ambushed at a coven meeting?"

"That's the worst part," Archer says. "We have no idea." The doorbell rings before I can fully process the bomb he just set off between us. He glances toward the front door. "That'll be Elder Keating. I'll be right back."

Archer slips away from the table before I can wrap my mind around the fact that there's about to be an *Elder* in my home. Beside me, Morgan tenses. I squeeze her hand tight, but I can't tell if she even feels me beside her. Can't tell if she notices that I'm panicking, too.

I flinch when the door slams closed, and I know immediately that Keating isn't the Elemental Elder. Even with my compromised magic, I can still sense Elemental power in others, and the Elder's would fill the house to bursting. Instead, I feel nothing but Mom beside me.

"Is it your Elder?" I whisper to Morgan.

Before she can respond, Cal shakes his head. "Elder Keating is a Caster." He wipes the remnants of tears from his cheeks and sits up taller in his chair.

My nerves grow.

Archer returns a moment later, followed by a woman who doesn't look nearly old enough to be an Elder. Her blonde hair, which admittedly is streaked through with bits of starlight white, is pulled into a low bun. There's hardly a wrinkle on her face. Her white linen pants, tall heels, and blue silk blouse look more suited to an executive office than our little suburban rental home. Her posture is more regal than anything I've ever seen in person. I feel childish, sitting here in my yoga pants and an oversized Salem State T-shirt.

Elder Keating's gaze is the only thing that betrays her age. As she looks at each of us in turn, I can practically see the decades of hard-earned wisdom in her glittering blue eyes. And though I can't feel her power, the way she holds herself, the soft confidence in her position, leaves no doubt in my mind that she's the most powerful Caster alive today.

"Thank you for taking the time to meet with me," Elder Keating says, like we had any choice about her arrival. Still, her gratitude seems genuine as she smiles at both Mom and me. "I'm afraid I don't know your friend, though." The Elder's gaze falls to Morgan. "Is she another Elemental from your coven?"

Morgan stands abruptly. "I'm sorry. I should go." She's more panicked than I've ever seen. I want to comfort her, but she's already pushing in her chair and backing away from the table. "Can I tell my parents?" She directs her question at Archer, and the second he nods, she's gone.

It all happens so fast, I don't have time to argue. To ask her to stay.

When the door closes at the front of the house, Archer pulls out the chair at the end of the table for Elder Keating. "That was Miss Hughes. She's part of the Blood Witch family we relocated to Salem this summer."

"Oh, of course. I'd nearly forgotten, with everything else." Keating turns to me, smiling slightly. "It's good to see you've helped her settle into town."

My cheeks flush, and it's all I can do to nod.

"Have Agents Archer and Morrissey had time to explain the events of last night?" Keating looks at me like I'm the only person in the world. When I nod, she continues. "I want you to know that we're doing everything we can to protect your coven. We're working on a barrier spell that will keep the Witch Hunters out of Salem. It will take time to complete, but I'm handling the preparations personally."

"Thank you," I say, but I can't help but feel it's not enough. There are witches all over the country. Sarah Gillow was part of a southern coven before she moved north for college and met Rachel. What about her family? What about Cal's parents in Boston? My relatives in Washington have already lost their magic. There has to be more we can do to protect everyone else.

"Is something the matter?" Elder Keating asks, her gaze penetrating. It demands answers in a way her light tone does not. It's both unnerving and inspiring, the way she commands attention with little more than the way she carries herself.

"I'm grateful, more than I can say, but . . . There has to be more we can do. Salem isn't the only place that needs protection."

The Elder Caster smiles, and I feel like I've passed some test. "That's why I'm here. I need your help."

"My help?" A surge of dangerous hope batters against my broken heart. This is it. This is my chance. "Tell me what you need. I'll do anything."

Elder Keating retrieves a thick file from her purse. She flips it open and pulls a photograph from the top. A four-story building with large glass windows stares back at me. "This is Hall Pharmaceuticals. It's where the Hunters are producing their drug."

"Is this where they had the raid last night?" I ask, pulling the photograph closer. I trace the lettering over the entrance. "Wait. *Hall* Pharmaceuticals . . . As in Benton Hall?" I trip over his name and reach for the black tourmaline hanging from my neck and squeeze tight. I need its calm now more than ever. I force myself to breathe slowly. *I'm okay. Don't let them see you crack. Don't lose your chance.*

"His grandfather owns the company, yes." Elder Keating looks to Archer, and he picks up where she left off.

"We learned last night that breaking in isn't going to work." Archer glances at Cal, a brief moment of silence for the agents they lost. "But we have a plan that will allow us to walk in the front door without suspicion."

"Except we can't do it without a couple key recruits," Cal cuts in. "Two, actually. A Blood Witch named Alice Ansley and a Caster named David O'Connell."

"That's where you come in," Keating finishes. "We believe if you met with Alice and David, if you asked them to help us, they would agree."

I trace the edge of the photograph again. Talking other witches into helping the Council isn't exactly fighting on the front lines, but it's a start. "Why me? Can't you force them to help? You're an Elder."

"We do not force our witches to do anything, Hannah. Not even when things are this desperate. It has to be their choice." She pulls another page from her folder and slides it over to me.

It's an old photo of me, one where I'm grinning at the camera while Veronica plants a kiss on my cheek. Below the photo is an article about Benton's upcoming trial.

Elder Keating rests her arms gracefully on the table. "You have been through a great ordeal, Hannah. You are the only witch who faced the Hunters, who felt the pain of losing your magic, and lived to tell the tale. Lived *and* got your magic back. There's power in that. You can use that to convince Alice and David to help us."

"No." Mom finally speaks up, and it's the first time she's ever denied a witch who outranked her. "You can't ask Hannah to do this. She's only seventeen. And she's not the only one who faced the Hunters. Veronica did, too."

"Mom, it's fine. I want to—"

"I'm not sending you across the country to recruit for the Council. You have school. You have to catch up on your lessons with Lady Ariana." Her voice breaks, and she reaches for Dad's ring. "I'm not going to lose you, too."

"You won't lose me, Mom."

But we both know it's an empty promise.

"I'm sorry, Marie," Elder Keating cuts in, "but Hannah's story *is* unique. Both girls got their magic back, but Hannah is the one who chose to go after the young Hunter on her own. She sacrificed her own safety to save her covenmate. There is no one else like her." She pulls out a calendar and slides it toward Mom. "Our plan shouldn't interfere with Hannah's schooling. Both witches will be in New York. Alice Ansley will be in Brooklyn next Saturday, and David O'Connell is a postdoc at Cornell. Hannah can go to Ithaca the following weekend."

"If he's in Ithaca, send Veronica. She's already there. She's older!"

I reach for her hand and squeeze tight. "It'll be okay, Mom. I want to help."

Elder Keating flashes me the quickest hint of a smile, there only a heartbeat before it's gone. "My decision on this matter is not up for debate. If Hannah wants to assist, you cannot stop her." All three Council members look hopefully at me. "What do you say, Hannah? Will you help us?"

In their expectant expressions, I feel the hint of desperation. The gears in my mind start to spin. They need me.

Which means I might be able to bargain for more.

I glance at my mother, and guilt worms its way around my fresh hope. I know this will break her heart, but I can't stay on the sidelines. I can't play it safe. "I'll do it. Under one condition."

Elder Keating nods. "Name it, and it's yours."

I hold the Elder's gaze so she can see how deeply I mean this. "I want to be part of the team that destroys the drug."

Mom tenses, but a slow smile spreads across the Elder's lips. "If you can recruit both witches *and* prove yourself suitable for that kind of fieldwork, we will find you a place on Archer's team."

I can feel the arguments building inside my mother without even looking at her, but she doesn't give a voice to any of them. An Elder's ruling is final and immutable. It's the highest law of our society. Only another Elder could overrule her.

"Deal."

A heady mixture of fear and anticipation flows through my veins. I promised Dad that we'd win this war.

And now I'm finally allowed to fight.

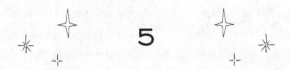

5

MOM DOESN'T SPEAK TO me the rest of the weekend. Every time I see her, I catch this moment of unguarded grief—hurt that *I* caused—before she notices me and shutters her feelings behind a scowl. I run through practice apologies, but none of them ring true.

Because I'm not sorry, I think, *because I want to fight*.

After I finish my homework on Sunday, I try texting Zoë again to learn more about what happened to her coven. She still doesn't respond, leaving my messages marked *read*, and guilt twists my insides into knots. Zo tried reaching out to me this summer, but I let all her texts go unanswered, too.

Memories I don't want to face claw their way to the front of my mind—so many tiny, imperfect moments, like Dad teaching Zo and me how to make snow when we were upset over a green winter solstice. He snuck us sweets later that night, too, after Aunt Camila kicked us out of the kitchen.

Zoë and I aren't technically related, and it's not just that we're both Elementals, either. My mom was best friends with Aunt Camila when they were growing up. Now, whenever I visit, I spend most of my time with Zo and her brothers.

Since we usually visit Mom's family around the winter solstice, I haven't seen Zoë in almost a year. Mom said Aunt Camila wanted to come to Dad's funeral, but her high priestess wouldn't let the coven anywhere near Salem. Not when Hunters could be watching for new arrivals. In the end, staying away didn't protect them, and I haven't talked to Zoë at all since Dad died . . .

I shove each memory down and drown out their voices beneath screaming vocals and angry drums. I open the sketchpad Morgan gave me, but every time I press my pencil to the soft paper, nothing comes. I can't stop thinking about Dad and Zoë and the witches Elder Keating needs me to recruit. About tomorrow's meeting with Archer to plan for my first mission. And the most terrifying question of all: How could an entire coven lose their magic without anyone knowing how it happened?

When sleep finally claims me, my subconscious supplies a highlight reel of horrifying theories. Assassins picking locks to slip into Elemental homes, armed with long-needled syringes. Snipers hiding on rooftops, tranq guns held steadily in their grip.

Benton with a warm grin as he douses me with gasoline.

That last image, more memory than dream, always sends me jolting out of sleep, gasping for breath. I can still feel the smoke choking off my lungs, the fire pressing against my skin as it searched for a way past my caged magic. His cruel smile lingers, melting into a thousand other grins, ones full of affection, ones from before he knew I was a witch. When we were friends. When I cared deeply for the boy with an artist's soul whose parents forced him into pre-med instead of letting him follow his passions.

When the alarm goes off on Monday, I have to drag myself through my morning routine. My magic still won't answer my call, and it's starting to impact every part of my life. When I turned thirteen and no longer had to wear a binding ring all the time, it was the tiny reflexive bits of magic—like drawing energy from a shower—that I loved the most. Magics so small that the Council didn't bother banning them, mostly because they come so naturally they're basically impossible to prevent. Without those daily bits of magic? I don't know who I am anymore.

And now everyone in Mom's old coven feels like this, too.

That thought follows me to school, where I wander the halls like a zombie. Morgan texted me earlier to say she wasn't coming, and by the end of homeroom, I wish I could have skipped with her. I'm so on edge that when Gemma appears beside my locker, I nearly jump out of my skin.

"Sorry!" she says, leaning on her cane. It must be another of her bad days. She never complains, but it has to be exhausting to get around school when her leg aches. "Ready for lunch?"

My startled pulse refuses to slow, but I nod and follow her to the cafeteria. As we eat, I can't help but study my classmates with new eyes. Benton hid easily among them for three years.

Are there more Hunters stalking the halls of Salem High?

The cafeteria is packed and loud and just . . . too much. Shoes squeak against the dingy linoleum floor. Chairs screech. Laughter erupts in one corner and cascades in the other. I feel everyone's eyes on the back of my neck, judging. Waiting for me to snap.

"I need to go," I say to Gem, pushing my chair back.

"But you've barely eaten."

"I'm not hungry. I'll talk to you later." I dump my tray in the trash and slip out of the cafeteria, desperate to get away from the crowded, claustrophobic room. I find myself heading to the art studio, which is where I have my next class anyway.

The room is still empty, and I take a hesitant step inside. It's blissfully quiet. The chemical tang of thick oil paints and the rich, earthy scent of clay brings back a rush of memories. Ghosts of laughter whisper in my ears as I search the cupboards for a set of brushes and watercolors.

You did not *fall off Veronica's bed.* An echo of Benton's voice rings through the room, his laughter filling the empty space. *How did her parents not catch you?*

My own laughter joins his, so loud that it hurts my chest and makes it hard to breathe. *Her parents didn't, but her little brother almost did. Thankfully, we remembered to lock the door.*

I grab a piece of thick watercolor paper and shove the memory away. I hate that he was my friend. I hate that I told him about my relationship with Veronica and my dreams of art school. I hate that he knows how I crushed on Morgan. I can't believe I trusted him with so much of myself.

The bell finally rings to signal the end of lunch. I ignore the shuffle of feet and settle at the table closest to the window, the sun warm against the back of my neck as I work. I wet the paper to make the paint glide smoothly across the surface and swirl my brush in red paint.

My classmates trickle into the room, their noise filling the space with a gentle hum as I spiral the red down my paper and add highlights of orange and gold. The second bell rings, and our teacher starts class. I ignore the scrape of chairs, the rustle of paper, and the slamming of cabinets. I block it all out. But they don't acknowledge me, either. No one sits at my table. No one asks for my permission before they steal chairs for their own groups.

The only person at my table is the fading memory of the friend who tried to kill me.

I swish my brush in a cup of water to wash away the paint. When I glance up, I can almost see Benton sitting across from me, his sleeves rolled up to his elbows and his hands buried in clay. *What do you think, Walsh? Does this cup need a lily or a rose?*

Benton leans back and tilts his head to one side, glancing from the mound of unformed clay to the half-finished cup beside it. I don't remember which flower I chose. I don't remember whether he took my suggestion or went in another direction entirely.

My hands tremble, and the brush shakes, swiping a line of blue down Morgan's emerging face. I swear under my breath. Before, when my magic was eager to answer my call, it would be risky to reach for the water's energy to undo my mistake. I might have done it on a day like today, when I was alone at my table and no one could see me. But now? When reaching for my magic is likely to send unbearable pain racing down my spine? I don't dare even try. Especially not with a Phantom Benton smiling at me from across the table. The clay is gone now, replaced by oil pastels that smudge the rainbow into his skin.

Fresh laughter, loud and raw and *real*, cuts through my thoughts and makes Benton disappear. Nolan stands beside a table of girls, bent forward so his elbows brace against the back of an empty chair. He flips his hair out of his eyes, and the movement raises his gaze enough that it finds mine. He grins and bends lower, whispering something that sends the girls into another fit of laughter.

Let them laugh. Let them stare. I crumple my ruined painting and shove my chair away from the table. The laughter dies as I throw the paper in the trash and rinse my brushes. Someone left an empty roll of paper towels beside the wide sink, so I'm forced to rummage through shelves to get a new one.

In the third cupboard, I find a row of abandoned pottery. A cup sits at the front, the sides glazed in a beautiful marble of whites and shimmering gray. On its front sits a pink lily, each petal formed and painted with care. I reach for the piece, running my fingers along the sharp lines of the delicate flower.

"Hannah?" The art teacher, Ms. Parker, approaches the sink. She's a short woman with curly black hair and pale skin. She teaches all the high school art classes, so I've known her for almost four years. Ms. Parker has a flair for bright clothing, and today's red-and-gold-patterned dress is no exception. Her thick eyebrows are raised in concern. "Is everything okay?"

I cradle the cup in my hands, feeling its weight in my palms. I trace the lines Benton so carefully created. "Why do you still have this?"

Confusion flits across her face. "It was left over from last year. I wanted to give the owner a chance to claim it before I threw it out."

"But it was *his*."

She blinks once, twice. Then a horrified expression settles over her features as she understands who I mean. "Oh, Hannah, I'm so sorry."

My fingers tighten around the cup. One of the petals snaps off.

Nolan saunters forward. "Benton made that?" He steps past Ms. Parker and reaches for the cup. "I bet it'll be worth a fortune after his trial."

The ceramic shatters before I even register the decision to throw it. Pieces skitter across the floor. Every single pair of eyes is trained on me.

The swing from celebrity to outcast is only one misstep away.

I know I should apologize. I should claim it was an accident, walk back what I did before the rumor mill starts all over again. But I can't. I *won't*.

"Benton is a *monster*." My voice carries through the room, rough with emotion. "And fuck you for thinking he's anything else."

A hushed silence settles over my classmates. Time ticks by with impossible slowness. Ms. Parker looks between Nolan and me. Finally, she nods a little to herself, curls bouncing around her shoulders. "We don't use that kind of language in my classroom, Hannah. Understood?"

"Yes. I'm sorry." I have to bite my tongue to keep from saying something else I might regret.

"Thank you." Ms. Parker turns on Nolan. "You can get a broom and clean this up."

"But—"

"I won't ask again."

Nolan mutters something that sounds suspiciously like the language Ms. Parker corrected me on, but he grabs the broom and sweeps up the shards of broken mug. The shattered pink petals wink up at me, and when the bell rings, I swear I can smell Benton's favorite cologne trailing after me in the halls.

$$-|- \quad * \quad -|-$$

The ghost of my friendship with Benton haunts me the rest of the day. He follows me to my locker, where he philosophizes about how we're destined to become our parents. He consoles me in study hall about my breakup with Veronica. When the bell rings at the end of the day, the shadow of him leans against my car with his Boston University acceptance letter clutched in his hands.

But then a cold gleam enters his gaze. The envelope dissolves into shadows, transforming into a gun as Benton raises it to my head.

I climb into the car and slam the door, burying the memories as deep as they'll go. I try to call Detective Archer to confirm our meeting tonight, but he sends me straight to voicemail. Before I can throw my phone out the window, a text comes through.

DA: In the middle of something.

DA: I'll swing by your house after to discuss the plan.

The promise of updates calms me enough to drive home, but I end up pacing the empty house. Mom won't get home from the university until after six, and there's no telling when Archer will get here. I can't sit and wait. I have to *do* something.

Zoë.

I hurry to my room and send a videochat request, crossing my fingers that she'll actually answer this time.

When my screen loads with her image, I'm so surprised that I almost don't recognize her. She's gotten into makeup since I saw her last, her dark brown skin expertly contoured and highlighted. She wears a bold lip, a vibrant red with a metallic sheen, and her eye makeup looks like the ocean at sunset.

"Hey, stranger." Zoë tries to keep her voice light, but there's tension around her eyes. Her makeup can't hide the puffiness of too many tears. When she grins, it's a half-hearted thing. "Sorry I never texted you back last night. Things here are . . ."

"Intense?" I guess.

Zo breathes out some semblance of a laugh. "That's one word for it."

Silence settles between us, and her gaze drops to her lap. I don't know how to talk about the terrible things that have happened to us. I want her to know I understand, but I can't push the truth of my own altered magic past my lips, not when she's lost hers completely.

Finally, I force myself to say *something*. "How are you holding up? I heard about what happened."

"I hate it, Hannah. All of it." Her voice catches, and she stares at the ceiling like she's trying not to cry. And Zoë *never* cries. "Everyone's miserable. The Council doesn't want us to tell anyone what happened, something about not causing mass panic. But keeping us isolated isn't helping, either. All the families are bickering. Your gran actually *yelled* at our high priestess at the coven meeting last night."

"You're kidding." The thought of my sweet Grandma Rose raising her voice doesn't compute. I can't even imagine her getting angry or upset. Unlike my other grandmother, Lady Ariana, who seems to run on a steady diet of familial disappointment and disapproval. Another wave of guilt washes through me. I should call Grandma Rose. I should have called her this weekend.

"I would never kid about Miss Rose yelling." Zo wipes at her cheeks and clears her throat. "All right, let's hear it, Hannah. I know you didn't call me, today of all days, just to ask how I'm doing. What are you really after?"

Heat creeps into my cheeks, and I hate that she's right. I hate that I have an agenda, when a good friend would simply call to tell her that she's not alone. "I know the Council is looking into what happened to the coven," I say, lowering my voice even though no one else is home. "But the last time I let them handle things on their own, it didn't go well for us."

"So, you want to play detective." She blows out a breath. "What do you want to know?"

"Everything."

We spend nearly an hour going over the details of Zoë's schedule last week. There wasn't a single moment when every member of the coven was in the same place until last night's meeting, after they'd already lost their magic. Her routine didn't change at all, except for returning to school. There were no new students in her classes. Absolutely nothing out of the ordinary.

Yet her entire coven was powerless by Saturday afternoon.

"And you can't feel *anything*?" I ask. When Benton first drugged me, I could feel the presence of the elements, but I couldn't access them.

Zoë shakes her head. "Everything is just . . . empty." She doesn't have to say what that emptiness is doing to her. The pain of it is written all over her face, a grief no amount of makeup can mask.

"I'll find a way to fix this, Zo. I promise."

A wry smile turns the corner of her lips. "Not if I fix it first. You're not the only one with skin in this game, Han."

We promise to text each other with any leads, and no sooner have I ended the call does Archer ring the doorbell. When I answer the door, he's dressed so casually I almost don't recognize him. He's actually wearing *jeans*, and there isn't a tie in sight.

I must stare at him more than I mean to, because he cocks an eyebrow at me, the expression completely bizarre on his usually stoic face. "I do have a life outside work, Hannah. Don't look so shocked."

"Shocked? Who's shocked?" I wave him inside and shut the door. "Do you need anything to drink? I'm sure Mom has coffee in there somewhere, and there's water in the fridge."

Archer walks the short hallway to the dining room and shakes his head. "This won't take long." He lifts a thin folder into my line of sight. "Shall we?"

"Right. Of course." I hurry after him and take my usual place at the table. "Has Elder Keating finished the protection spell for the town?"

"Almost. It'll be in place by tomorrow night. Anyone who tries to come into Salem to hurt your coven won't be able to step past the town line." There's this sense of . . . awe in Archer's voice as he speaks about his Elder, something that I've never heard from him before. "I'm amazed that it's even possible. Something of that scope, I wouldn't even know where to begin."

"Really?" I know so little about how Caster Magic works; the boundaries of what's possible are completely foreign to me.

"She's the Elder for a reason." Archer's phone buzzes in his pocket. He checks the screen but doesn't unlock it, setting it down on the table. "As we discussed on Saturday, the first of your two recruits is Alice Ansley. Alice rose to fame quickly over the last couple of months as an illusionist. She has a dedicated online fanbase for her impromptu street performances, which has led to a sponsored nationwide tour."

"She's the Blood Witch, right?" I'm surprised the Council lets her use magic in public like this.

"That's right." Archer ignores his phone when it buzzes again. Instead, he pulls an event flier from the folder and passes it to me. Alice is dressed all in black with an old-school magician's hat tipped forward to cover her face. The only color on the poster comes from the pink hair that cascades past her shoulders. "She doesn't use any real magic in her act, which meant we had no leverage when she refused to help with our plan."

"When did you ask her?"

"A couple weeks before the raid. We like to have several plans in motion so we're not scrambling when something falls through."

Makes sense. Though I don't want to know how far down the list of plans I am. "And our new plan is *what*, exactly?"

"One step at a time. For now, your sole focus should be on recruiting Alice." He points to the bottom of the flier and reaches for a second photo, this one of a large building. "She's performing at a hotel in Brooklyn this Saturday. The roof has an entertainment area, which is where we'll observe her show. Cal will hack into the hotel's computer system to get us Alice's room number so you can convince her to return with us to Salem."

A cold chill travels up my arms, and I press down the panic rising up my throat. The last time I ran into a Blood Witch in New York City, things didn't go well for either of us. I'm not entirely sure how I'm supposed to convince Alice to give up a national tour to help the Council. Especially since she's already refused once.

"If I'm going to recruit her, I need to know what I'm asking her to do." I glance up cautiously at Archer. "How is she supposed to help us get inside Hall Pharmaceuticals?"

Archer pulls another photo from his folder. This one is a selfie of a young white woman, probably in her early twenties. Her tan skin sports freckles across her nose and cheeks, and her long brown hair is loose around her shoulders. She has a kind smile and a pink scarf looped around her neck.

"This is Eisha Marchelle. She's a biochem senior and, more importantly for our purposes, an intern at Hall Pharmaceuticals."

"She's a Hunter?" She looks harmless enough. Although, so did Benton until he was holding a gun.

"No, actually. Most of the company does legitimate work. Vaccines and that sort of thing." Detective Archer pulls out a stack of fan forums and social media posts. "In addition to interning three days a week at the Hunters' base of operations, our intelligence indicates that Eisha is Alice's self-proclaimed biggest fan. She comments on nearly all of Alice's videos and has posted repeatedly about her disappointment in missing the live tour."

"Do I even want to know how you figured all this out?" I sift through the pages and *pages* of comments. Even though everything I'm reading was posted online for the whole world to see, it still feels weird to have it all in one place like this.

Archer grins. "Cal has some rather useful non-magical talents."

"And what about the other witch? The Caster. When are we recruiting him?" I know he said to focus on Alice, but I'm desperate to know the full picture of what I need to do.

"You'll be meeting with David the following weekend. Like Elder Keating said, we're trying to disrupt your life as little as possible. But we'll deal with that once you're back from New York." Archer's phone goes off again, and this time he punches in his passcode and reads through the messages. After a moment, his cheeks burn a bright red.

"What's that about?" I ask before I think better of it, like he's a friend instead of my boss-slash-commander-slash-bodyguard. Honestly, I'm not really sure what this new relationship between us is supposed to be. All I know is he outranks me. By a lot.

But he doesn't seem to mind. He glances up from his phone, and his cheeks grow even redder. "Nothing. Just . . . Lauren being Lauren."

Confusion settles heavily into my forehead. Who in the world is—"Oh my god, my *boss*? Are you two still a thing?" My voice squeaks on the end of my question, but I don't even care. I can't believe I forgot they were dating. Were they dating? I don't know, they were definitely flirting the last time I saw them together. But that was almost two months ago.

Archer couldn't look more like a tomato if he tried right now. "Yes, although technically she's not your boss anymore. We're getting dinner later." He clears his throat. "Now, if you don't mind, I'd like to get back on task."

I bury the urge to tease him. Archer is a Council agent, not an older brother I can harass. "Do we want Alice to convince the intern to sneak us in?"

"Not exactly." Archer shuffles his documents back into an orderly pile and slides them into the folder. "We want the intern to host Alice for a live performance *inside* Hall Pharmaceuticals. We can sneak a small team in with Alice's equipment to get past the initial alarm systems."

It's a slightly better plan than my guess, but not by much. "And when is this performance-turned-raid supposed to take place?"

Archer pauses, and all the lightness of our conversation about Lauren slips away. "September thirtieth."

The date rattles against my rib cage, a convict trying to get free. "But Benton's trial starts that day." His name is like acid on my tongue, and I want to scrape the collection of consonants and vowels out of my ears.

"I know. It's okay if you want to skip the raid so you can prepare your testimony. We can recruit another Elemental to the team. But that day is our best shot at getting into the company undetected. The Hunters will be focused on the trial, and . . ." Archer trails off.

"And what?"

"That's also our last chance to destroy the drug before you're called to the stand to testify." Archer looks at me, his expression fierce and full of worry. "Elder Keating will have to drop the protection spell for the trial. It's likely the Hunters will hire one of their own to represent Benton. If we leave the spell up, a Reg could see the Hunters get repelled by the barrier. The exposure risk is too great."

I picture Hunters bouncing off an invisible wall, and the thought makes me smile. But then the implications of what Archer's saying shatters the mental image. "Wait. If the barrier comes down and all the Hunters know when I have to testify . . ."

"We'll have no way to protect any of you," Archer finishes for me. "If this raid fails, your magic will be as good as gone."

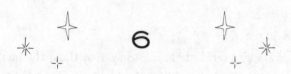

6

ARCHER'S WARNING MAKES IT impossible to sleep. I stare at the ceiling all night, desperate to find a loophole that will convince Elder Keating to keep up the barrier spell even though I know it's pointless. The safety of a single coven will never matter more than the secrecy of the Clans. They won't risk exposure to save us.

As I lie in bed, I wonder where their line is. What would make the Council decide the price to keep our secret was too steep? How many of us would have to die before they were willing to come out to the world?

I find no answers that night, and all week, as we inch closer to my first mission, I don't have time to consider it. My life is a whirlwind of school, trial prep, and rehearsals for my meeting with Alice. DA Flores teaches me how to best tell my story—sticking to the facts with just the right amount of emotion. Archer makes me practice my recruitment speech on Cal, which is seriously awkward, but at least I convince Cal to tell me more about my second recruit, David.

He won't tell me much—Archer is annoyingly fixated on the whole "one recruit at a time" thing—but Cal says the Caster Witch can develop a vaccine to protect us from the Hunters' drug.

If I can convince him to help.

By the time Friday comes, I'm as prepared as I'm going to

get for Saturday's mission, but that doesn't stop me from being a puddle of stress all morning at school. We have a pop quiz in US history, and as I look over the questions, I can't remember the last time I read for this class. There's no way I'll pass the quiz.

I'll never admit it out loud, but I don't know how long I can keep this up. There's no way I could have fit in shifts at the Cauldron, too.

"Hannah!" Gemma reaches across the lunch table and waves a hand in front of my face. "What's going on with you today?"

"Nothing. I'm fine."

"No, you're not." She looks from Morgan back to me, a grin spreading across her face. "That's it. I'm declaring girls' night. You two are coming over to my place."

"Gem, you know I can't." It's just the three of us at the table, but I lower my voice anyway. "I'm going to Brooklyn tomorrow. I can't be up all night."

My best friend rolls her eyes. "And the likelihood of you actually sleeping tonight is . . ."

"Not great," I concede. If the past four nights are any indication, I'll be up well past two rehearsing my recruitment speech. For the millionth time.

Morgan nudges my shoulder with hers. "I think it's a good idea. You can practice your arguments on me." She bats her eyelashes and sticks out her lower lip into a pout, and the resulting puppy dog look is just unfair. "Please?"

I pretend to think about it moment longer, but in the end, there's no refusing these two. Especially when they both want the same thing. "Fine. I'm in."

The promise of popcorn, pizza, and some parent-free alone time with Morgan gets me through the rest of the day. The second the final bell rings, I text Mom to let her know where I'm going, meet Gemma and Morgan at my locker, and drive the three of us to Gem's house. Both her parents are still at work when we get there, and even though we have the house to ourselves, we pile into Gem's bedroom.

Gemma maneuvers to her desk and sits in the chair. "Can I read your tarot? It could help with your mission tomorrow."

Even though tarot has always scared me a little—I've never let Lauren read for me—I'm determined to have fun tonight. "Bring it on," I say, and disappear to grab an extra chair from the dining room. When I get back, Morgan is sprawled out on Gemma's bed with her face buried in a carnation pink novel.

"You read more than anyone I know." I set the chair next to Gemma. "What's this one about?"

"International politics."

"Seriously?"

Morgan glances up, a smile quirking her lips. She looks so cute, I'm worried my heart might combust. Thankfully, her Blood Magic could probably fix that. "It's also very gay," she adds, a quality I've learned she values in books. "You can read it when I'm done."

"Come sit," Gemma says before I can reply. The cards *snick-snick-snick* together as she shuffles, a piece of amethyst sitting prominently on the desk beside her. I sink into the chair, but I can't help glancing over at Morgan. She bites her lip as she hastily turns to the next page, and a not-small part of me wants to abandon the tarot cards and curl up next to her.

"Come on, Hannah," Gemma teases, poking my shoulder. "You have to focus on the *cards*, not your girlfriend. Otherwise the reading will be about her instead of this Allison."

"It's Alice, actually," I correct after a moment of hesitation. Even after two months, it still feels weird that I can tell Gemma about Clan stuff. Secrecy is a hard habit to break. Hard, but so, so worth it. "I'm sorry, Gem. I can do this, I swear. Can we start over?"

Gemma nods and shuffles again. "Focus on your mission."

I try to do as she says, but *focus* is in short supply these days. My mind bounces from the mission to the drugged coven to how much I'd really like to kiss my girlfriend right now, even if that makes me a terrible friend.

After a few more shuffles, Gemma has me cut the deck and then she lays out three cards. A field of deep blue with flecks of gold stars stares up at us.

"Ready?" Her voice is breathless with anticipation, and when I nod, Gemma flips the first card. A figure sits below a tree, their arms crossed while a disembodied hand holds out one of four cups.

"Well, that looks cheerful," I grumble.

"Yeah . . . I don't think Alice is going to be easy to convince." Gemma examines the card more closely, and it's clear she takes this process seriously, even if it's also fun for her. "I get the feeling she has a stubborn streak. About everything."

From the bed, Morgan laughs. "Sounds like someone else I know."

"Hey! I'm not *that* stubborn." I swivel around to look at her. "Have your boys kissed yet?"

"Not yet." Morgan sighs dramatically and turns to look at me. "I'm dying."

"And card number two is . . ." Gemma says with an announcer's flair to draw back my attention. "Huh."

"What is it?" I examine the card, this one labeled *Six of*

Swords. Two people sit huddled in the boat while a third person rows them down a stream. Except it's upside down. "What's with all the swords stabbing the boat? Are we going to get a flat tire on the way or something?"

"I don't know exactly. Lauren hasn't gone over reversed cards yet. I didn't even think I had any flipped around in the deck." Gem massages her temples the same way she does whenever she gets a headache. "Something about the travel itself feels like it's going to be dangerous. I don't think it's a flat tire though. Any idea what that could be?"

"None." I stare at the card and try to concentrate, wondering what might be dangerous about traveling to New York. The city isn't exactly the best place for an Elemental, but that's not—

Realization crashes over me like a wave, and a shiver trips up my spine. Could the cards really be this accurate? "Elder Keating put up a barrier spell, but it's only big enough to keep the Hunters out of Salem. When I go to Brooklyn, I'll be outside its protection."

Morgan sits up and actually *closes* her book. "They put up a barrier?" She scowls when I nod. "Of course no one bothered to ask my parents for help."

When Gemma and I stare blankly at her, Morgan explains. "Remember the runes you found at the Witch Museum over the summer? If the Council let us, we could lock down the town in a matter of hours."

New hope sparks within me, bright and alive. Maybe Morgan's parents can protect all the witches who will be in the courthouse. Maybe they can keep the Hunters away. But then my rational mind takes over. If their barrier repelled Hunters, it would still create the same risk of non-witches seeing the magic in effect.

Gemma's hand stalls over the third card. "Why don't they let you help?"

"Because we're Blood Witches. Because they think we're creepy or monsters or goddess knows what." Morgan flops back onto the bed and drapes an arm across her face. "I'm so sick of everyone hating us."

"I don't hate you," Gemma and I say at the same time. We share a smile, but Morgan lets out an unintelligible grunt of a response.

"You've noticed it, haven't you?" Morgan peeks at us around her arm. "The way they keep to themselves? Each Clan may have representation on the Council, but they almost never work together. Cal and Archer are both Casters. The Elder who visited is a Caster, too."

Gemma abandons the final unturned card and swivels in her chair to face the bed. "But they recruited Hannah, and she's an Elemental."

"Only because they wanted something from her." Morgan's tone settles over my skin like frost. "There aren't any Casters with a story like hers. If there were, I'd bet anything they'd use the Caster Witch instead. Their Elder certainly didn't want my help, despite Alice and I being in the same Clan."

There's something bitter and hurt in her voice, and it pulls at my heart. "Do you want to help?"

"Do I want to help my girlfriend recruit another Blood Witch?" Morgan turns the intensity of her blue gaze on me. "Of course I do."

Gemma glances between Morgan and me, confused. "Why would they ignore perfectly good magic?"

Morgan waves a hand in my general direction. "You tell her.

I need more of my boys, and I'm ninety percent sure the one guy is bi, which you know I love." She reopens her book, but there's tension around her jaw as she reads now instead of the carefree expression she had before.

"It's kind of a long story, but I can give you the highlights." I glance anxiously at Morgan, but she's focused on her book. "Have I explained where witches come from yet?"

"I know how babies are made, Han."

"Where our *magic* comes from." I roll my eyes at Gemma, but I know she's only teasing. Probably to deflect from how desperately she wants to know about everything. "The Mother Goddess who guided the creation of this world has three daughters, known as the Sister Goddesses. Once humanity was well on its way, the Mother Goddess disappeared to tend to other realms and left her daughters in charge. After a few thousand years, they grew restless in their task and started issuing each other dares."

"Dares?" Gemma raises a brow at me.

"That's how my parents explained it to me. Though I was only eight at the time." I shrug. "Anyway, the Eldest Sister created the Caster Witches, and when it was the Middle Sister's turn, she wanted to create a *flashier* magic. So, she covered the world with storms. Those who danced in the rains became Elementals." I grin. "That's why we tend to see rainy days as good luck."

"Weirdos," Morgan mutters affectionately under her breath, but I'm not entirely sure if she's talking about my Clan or the guys in her book.

"So, then the last one made the Blood Witches?" Gemma guesses.

"Yes. Except the Youngest Sister wasn't strong enough to make witches on her own, so she had to break into the Mother's garden. But when she stole a rose of immortality, she pricked her finger on a thorn. She lost her immortality trying to create Morgan's Clan. When the Mother Goddess found out what happened to her youngest daughter, she punished all three sisters and banished them from Earth."

Gemma's brow furrows. "You hate Blood Witches because of a celestial game of truth or dare?"

"Not exactly."

Morgan huffs out a breath. "Close enough. And the Youngest Sister didn't accidentally touch the thorn. She meant to give up her immortality to bless us. She wanted her witches to be safe from the ones the other goddesses made."

"That's not the way Lady Ariana taught the story."

My girlfriend closes her book again. "Lady Ariana isn't a Blood Witch."

Heat blossoms in my cheeks. "Fair. But then why did the early Blood Witches use their magic to turn people into puppets?" *And not just the early ones, either* . . . But I don't mention the one who took control of my body. Morgan already knows the basics of what happened, and I'm not exactly eager to go through it all again.

Morgan sits up and swings her legs over the edge of the bed. "Your goddess had time to teach your ancestors what to do with their magic. The banishment happened before mine had a chance to learn anything. We had to figure it all out on our own." She crosses the room to us, draping her arms around my shoulders. "We figured it out eventually."

The warmth of her power hums through me, and I let my magic dance and play with the air, swirling Morgan's loose curls back behind her shoulders. I wish it could always be like this, so easy and free. But when Morgan stands, she cuts off her flow of magic and I drop mine, too.

Gemma is very purposefully staring at the final unturned card when we separate fully. "Is it safe to assume the whole turning-people-into-puppets thing had more to do with the creepy stereotype than the banishment of your goddesses?"

I look to Morgan, letting her answer. She shrugs. "Maybe a little. But that's still a shitty reason not to ask for our help. Especially when things are this bad." She shudders, and her stomach lets out a loud groan.

"Hungry?" Gemma asks. "I can grab some snacks."

"You don't have to—" Morgan starts, but Gemma is out the bedroom door before she finishes. Morgan sighs and wraps her arms around me again. "Ask me to come with you."

The whispered words play against my skin, and they simultaneously worry and warm me. I lean into her touch. "I don't want you getting hurt because of me. None of this is safe."

"I'm a Blood Witch, Hannah." Her voice is whisper soft, and I'm suddenly very aware of her warmth against my back. "I heal pretty quickly."

"I don't want to lose you."

"You won't." She presses a kiss to my cheek. "Ask me."

I bite my lip, worried despite her reassurances. But when I turn to meet her gaze, there's no hesitation. "Will you come with me to New York?"

She answers with a kiss. It's soft at first, sweet, but quickly becomes desperate and wanting, and when she threads her fingers into my hair, I forget how to breathe.

"All I could find was some white cheddar pop—" Gemma cuts off when she sees us, and her voice springs Morgan and me apart. "Popcorn," she finishes, the bag dangling from her fingers. "Should I come back later?"

"No, sorry." I stand and take the bag from her, tossing a handful of popcorn in my mouth. "Should we finish the tarot reading?" I don't particularly want to know what other bad news the cards have in store for me, but it's the least I can do for turning my best friend's room into a make-out spot.

"Next time you want to sexile me, just put a hair tie on the door."

"Gemma," I groan, even though we fully deserve her teasing. "We'll keep our hands to ourselves. Promise."

"If you say so." She takes her seat and lets out a slow breath before turning the final card. A naked figure leans over a pool of water. They hold a jug in each hand, pouring liquid into the pool and onto the ground. The script at the bottom of the card says *The Star*.

"What does that one mean?" It doesn't look too bad, but something about it pricks at my subconscious.

"I don't know. Normally it gives me really good vibes." Gemma picks up the piece of amethyst and holds it tight. "It's weird, but it doesn't feel connected to your trip tomorrow. Is it possible you were thinking about something else?"

"Maybe?" I try to remember what was in my head while Gemma shuffled, besides kissing Morgan. There was the trip tomorrow, I know I managed to think about that at least a little, and I was worried about my mom's old coven, and—

Understanding hits me with the force of a raging thunderstorm. Zoë. The drugged coven. The woman pouring something into a pool of water. My heart speeds in my chest, and I scramble away from the cards. It can't be. They're just *cards*. How could they possibly know anything about what happened to my family?

"Hannah, what's wrong?" Morgan stops my backward retreat.

"I know how they did it." I spin to face her. "I know this sounds ridiculous, but I can feel it. I know how the Hunters drugged the coven."

Morgan glances past me at the spread of tarot cards. "How?"

"They put the drug in the *water*." I pull out my phone and dial Archer. There could be a hundred other explanations, but this is the first one that makes any kind of sense, even if the inspiration doesn't. The detective answers on the third ring. "We need to talk."

7

THE CALL WITH ARCHER sets off a string of dominos. Archer promises to look into my theory about the drugged water, and within ten minutes, Mom is calling to bring me home.

She's been in full-on *Operation Never Leave Salem* mode ever since.

"I don't want you to go," Mom says Saturday morning, for what must be the hundredth time. She's standing in my doorway with her arms crossed firmly against her chest. "You're safer here behind the barrier."

"Elder Keating wants me to do this. You can't force me to stay home." Mom never stands up to Lady Ariana, but suddenly she's willing to go against an Elder?

Mom's lips press into a thin line. "I realize that, Han. But Elder Keating *also* said it was *your* choice. Which means if you back out—"

"I'm not backing out, Mom. It's just a quick trip to New York. I'll be back tomorrow." I add an extra pair of socks to my bag and zip it tight. "Archer will be with me the whole time. Besides, if I don't do this, the Council might not be able to destroy the drug before I have to testify in court."

She already knows that we'll be easy targets during the trial, yet she won't stop hovering. "I don't like this." Mom perches at the edge of my bed and reaches for my hands. "Can't someone else go? Cal seems like a persuasive guy."

"Mom . . ."

"Fine." She looks at the wall above my desk, where I've created a collage of pictures of Dad, photos I downloaded from social media and sent to the store to be printed on glossy paper. Her eyes are sparkling with tears when her gaze returns to mine. "At least promise that you'll come back in one piece."

Even though this isn't a promise I can guarantee, I swallow down the lump in my throat and nod. "Of course. Now can I finish packing?"

Mom reaches for my bag and tugs open the zipper. "Do you have enough bottled water?"

"Yes," I groan. Until we know whether my theory is right, we're using bottled water for everything, including brushing our teeth. I grab my bag and slip out of my room. "It's not like New York doesn't have more if I run out."

A car door slams. Then another. Mom follows me like a persistent shadow through the house. When I get to the living room, I check the front window. I expected Detective Archer to be here, but who's the second—

"Sarah?" I drag my suitcase down the front steps. The early morning sun is already warm on the horizon, and I'm glad I decided to wear my hair up in a ponytail. "What are you doing here?"

My covenmate Sarah Gillow leans against her car and crosses one ankle over the other. "Good morning to you, too."

"There's been a change of plan," Archer says, adjusting his tie as he approaches. "Elder Keating thinks your water theory has merit. Unfortunately, Salem's water supply doesn't come from within the town. It comes from Beverly."

"Oh." That hadn't even occurred to me. Beverly is outside the limits of Keating's barrier spell. It's completely unprotected.

"Keating needs my help to get another barrier up, so I won't be able to drive you to New York. But you can text me the entire time, and Sarah's a talented witch. You'll be in good hands."

I shake my head, still trying to adjust to the last-minute change. "I'm not worried about her magic." For as long as I've known her, Sarah has been an exceptionally gifted Elemental, particularly with air and water magics. Her strength is not at all the problem. "What about Rachel?"

Sarah doesn't move, but the line of her jaw tightens at the mention of her wife. "What about her?"

Do I seriously need to spell this out for her? "She's pregnant! You're about to be a mom. Rachel and the baby need you."

"What they *need* is a world where this drug doesn't exist. If I can help make that a reality, I will." Sarah pushes away from the car and crosses to the driver's side. "Come on, Hannah. We have a tight schedule to keep." Sarah pauses and waves at my mom, who's standing on the top step. "I'll bring her home safe, Marie!"

Mom waves back but doesn't say anything. If she could stop this day from happening, she would. But I'm the only one—besides another Elder—who could keep me from going, and I'm not sitting on the sidelines a moment longer.

I loiter outside Sarah's car and fuss with the strap of my bag. "Any final words of wisdom?" I ask Archer, turning my back on the house, turning my back on Mom's worry.

Archer takes a deep breath, like he's steeling himself before he looks at me. "Just like we practiced. State your case calmly but firmly." His gaze finally flicks up and settles on mine. There's worry in the crease of his brow, but he keeps whatever he's feeling locked up tight. "If that doesn't work, lean into the symbolism Elder Keating talked about. If you're still fighting after everything you've been through, none of the rest of us have any excuse."

A humorless laugh rumbles in my chest. "Right, so when logic fails go full-on guilt trip."

The detective flinches. It's a small thing, there one second and gone the next. "If I could take your place, I'd do it in a heartbeat." He reaches for me, and I step forward into his embrace. "You shouldn't have to do this," he whispers, hugging me tight. I never noticed before, but he must wear the same cologne as Dad. The familiarity of the scent and the strong arms around me tighten my throat. "But I have faith in you. Call me if you need anything."

"I will." My voice is watery with the tears I'm trying desperately to hide. Archer releases me, and I toss my bag into Sarah's trunk, slipping into the back seat a moment later.

The inside of Sarah's car is impeccably clean and comfortably cool. The cloth seats are still firm since no one ever sits back here with just the two of them. But with the baby coming, that'll change soon enough.

Sarah glances at me in the rearview. "You can sit in front. I don't bite."

"Morgan is coming, too," I say as she backs out of the driveway. "We're picking her up at her place."

"Ryan didn't say anything about her coming with us."

"I didn't get a chance to ask him," I admit. With all the other last-minute changes to the plan, I completely forgot. "But Morgan's a Blood Witch like Alice. She can help with the recruiting. It's this next left." I hold my breath until Sarah sighs and puts on her blinker for the turn.

"Do you want her help with the magician, or do you want to make her clothes disappear?"

"Hey!"

Sarah laughs, and the earlier tension melts away completely. "What? When I was your age, I would have done anything to sneak off to a fancy hotel with my girlfriend."

My cheeks are so hot they're in danger of spontaneous combustion, but I'm laughing, too. It feels good to have another witch tease me about Morgan, even if it's mortifying. The rest of the coven is still too weird about her being a Blood Witch to joke about anything. And as accepting as they are about us both being girls, Sarah is definitely the only one who'd ever tease me about this kind of stuff.

"We're still firmly in the *clothes on* stage, for the record. And that's not what this weekend is about." I stare out the window and direct Sarah to Morgan's house. "Promise you won't say anything in front of her?"

"You got it, kiddo."

I groan. "I'm not a kid," I say, but somehow that only makes Sarah laugh harder. I *really* hope she doesn't tell Morgan all my embarrassing childhood stories.

Thankfully, after we pick up Morgan, we spend most of our five-hour journey in silence. I try a few times to work on homework, but the closer we get to the city, the more frantic my worries become. I hated Manhattan the last time I was here, surrounded by too many bodies, with miles of concrete blocking the earth from my senses. Even the air, charged with so many people in such a small space, caused more anxiety than it soothed.

Not to mention the witches I met on those streets.

Something in my heart rate must alert Morgan to my

distress, because she reaches for my hand and squeezes, a question in her blue gaze. I nod, and her magic cascades over me, soothing the harshest edges of my stress. Guilt picks at me for still being so scared of the Blood Witch I met here, even as Morgan's magic makes my life so much better. Even as I find myself falling for Morgan more every day. Sarah glances at us in the rearview and smiles.

When we finally get to the hotel, it's far more impressive than the place I stayed on my school trip. It's a large building with geometric patterns of beige-and-gray siding around glittering glass. The lobby is all bright whites, rich blues, and a beige tile floor. It's also full of hipsters when we check in. Tourists stand beside the sign announcing Alice's show, and nerves make the little hairs on my arms stand on end. We're really here. In a few short hours, I'll begin my first real mission for the Council.

Morgan drags me over to the poster when the other tourists are done and makes me take a selfie with her and the sign. She curls her arm around my waist, and her touch makes all the worry melt away. A thrill climbs up my chest when I remember Sarah's teasing words. Morgan and I are about to have a room all to ourselves. No parents. No supervision. I press a kiss to her cheek and take another photo. I post the best few to Instagram, and my phone buzzes with at least a dozen likes by the time Sarah comes back from checking us in.

We take the elevator to the sixth floor and follow Sarah down the hall. She stops beside a room and hands me a key. "You girls will stay here. I'm the next room over. The front desk said there's a door inside that connects the two rooms. I'll leave my side unlocked in case there are any emergencies. I suggest you do the same."

"Thanks," I say, pressing the card against the lock. A light flashes green.

"We'll head to the roof at seven-thirty for the show." Sarah grins at me. "You two have fun until then." Her innuendo is clear, and my cheeks are burning by the time she disappears into the next room.

I push open our door, drop my bag on the polished wood floor, and flop onto the king-size bed. The white comforter cushions my body, and I stare up at the art behind me. It looks like a deconstructed, geometric forest.

"Are you okay?" Morgan perches on the edge of the mattress. "I know you said cities are hard on you, and the last time you were here . . ."

"I'll be fine," I say, refusing to let old memories of this city ruin the first truly private time we've had since our date in the woods back home.

"If you're sure." Morgan kicks off her shoes and stands, stretching out her long limbs. "Do you want to practice your recruitment speech, or do you want to be distracted?"

I raise an eyebrow at her. "What kind of distraction did you have in mind?"

Morgan turns slowly and raises her arms into a perfect ballet curve. "I'm auditioning for a solo in the fall recital. You could help me practice."

Her body seems to melt as she progresses through the first few combinations, and even without the music, she's mesmerizing. The arch of her back, the way her socked feet glide across the polished floor . . . I wish I had my sketchpad. I don't know if I could ever capture such elegance in still form, but goddess I want to try.

She stops suddenly, breaking the spell. "Or . . ." Morgan steps forward and bends until her face is level with mine. "Since Gemma isn't here to interrupt us, we could make out."

"Yes," I say, all thoughts of sketching gone completely. "That. I choose that."

A few hours later, we emerge onto the hotel roof. Strings of lights hang above us like little electric stars, and the rows of picnic tables are covered with soft silver-and-black cloths. At the center of each table sits a flickering candle.

My pulse lurches when I spot the flames, but Morgan is there with a squeeze of my hand. I try to breathe deep, searching for comfort in the air, but even though my magic is working with Morgan beside me, the energy is different here than in Salem. It's too busy, too full of conversation. Its vibration too quick.

I glance to Sarah to see how she's fairing under the crush of the city, especially since she normally has such a strong connection to air. There's a tension to her shoulders that isn't normally there, but otherwise she seems fine.

She catches me staring and offers a small smile. "You have to disconnect," she whispers, leaning close. "That's the only way to survive a place like this."

Morgan points to a set of tables near the middle of the rows. "There are two spots there." She frowns. "But the next closest spot is a few tables over."

"That's fine," Sarah says. "I can't believe it's this packed already." She maneuvers away from us, taking the solo space while Morgan and I hurry to the two seats at the center table.

My phone buzzes, and I pull it out to find a series of texts from Detective Archer.

DA: Good luck tonight. Try to enjoy the show.

DA: See if you can get a feel for her. If Alice seems skittish, you can have Sarah wait outside while you talk. Don't overwhelm her.

DA: Cal confirmed the room number. It's still the same.

Archer's encouragement only makes me more nervous. I know how much is riding on this, but it's clear he wanted to be here to keep an eye on me. *At least he's protecting the rest of the coven.* I type out a quick response, promising to update him as soon as I've spoken to Alice, and put the phone away.

Beside me, Morgan glances down the row to where Sarah's sitting. "I like her. She seems really cool."

"Yeah, she's pretty great," I concede, even if she sometimes treats me like a gayby, which I'm *not*. I've been out over a year. I've already been through a heartbreak and moved on. "She and her wife, Rachel, are expecting their first child in a couple months."

Morgan lights up. "That's awesome! I'm definitely up for babysitting." She bites her lower lip, still swollen from kissing. "Should I worry about the mini Elemental setting my hair on fire?"

Her question startles a laugh out of me. "Even I couldn't

do that. Not for another couple months anyway." I say it without thinking, but once the words are past my lips, I don't know if they're true. I don't know what will happen when I turn eighteen. What if I'm never ready to progress further?

And the worst of it? I don't know how I'm supposed to tell Lady Ariana any of that. Or Mom or Archer.

I know I should tell them. Anything that helps the Council learn more about the drug could be important. But if they know, will Elder Keating pull me from these missions? I still have to recruit David, and I want to help destroy the drug that did this to me. Once that's done, if it still hurts to use my magic on my own, I'll tell them.

Maybe.

Probably.

I could at least tell Cal. He and I are friends. He wouldn't look at me like I've broken his heart the way Mom might or panic about my safety as much as Archer is bound to do.

Before my thoughts can spiral any further, a soft rumble, like far-off thunder, rolls through the crowd. Silence settles over us as a dense fog billows out from some hidden machine to cover the small stage and most of the audience.

"Ladies, gentlemen, and nonbinary patrons." A deep voice booms over a speaker system. "Prepare to have your senses fooled and your minds delighted as we enter a world of illusion and misdirection, where nothing is as it seems." The announcer pauses. Anticipation electrifies the air. "Put your hands together and give a loud, proud Brooklyn welcome to Alice Ansley!"

A whoop travels through the crowd, and we all applaud.

The spotlights flick on, illuminating a shadowy figure at the center of the fog. The mist clears, and Alice steps forward. A few patrons *woo!* like they're at a concert, and the excitement spreading from table to table is infectious.

Like her show poster, Alice is dressed all in black, though she's traded out her leather jacket for a crisp three-piece suit, complete with bow tie and black-and-white wing-tipped shoes. Her old-fashioned magician's hat is tipped forward on her head while her pink hair spills down her shoulders, falling all the way to mid-back.

When she reaches the front of the stage, she flourishes a bow and removes the hat, tossing it to the side. It lands perfectly on a coat rack that I hadn't noticed before. It's an impressive shot, though I suppose any Blood Witch could master the toss after just a few tries.

"Thank you all so much for coming," Alice says, pulling a deck of cards from her pocket. She wears a tiny mic at her crisp collar, which transmits her words in surround sound. "I need a volunteer."

Hands raise all around me, each audience member eager to be chosen. I keep my hand down. Something about her voice is familiar. It picks at the back of my mind, but I can't place it. Alice selects a participant from the second row and asks the woman to choose a card.

Each time she speaks, that sense of familiarity grows stronger. I study her face, trying to see beyond the heavy contour, winged eye makeup, and shimmering highlight.

Alice places the deck between the woman's hands and presses, the cards disappearing until only one remains. The crowd gasps when Alice takes the card, and the volunteer lets out a shocked laugh, revealing that Alice has indeed found her card, the six of hearts.

"But where is the rest of the deck?" the woman asks, turning the single card over and over in her hand.

Alice scans the crowd. "You there," she calls, "in the red tie. Can you please check your jacket pocket? The inside one."

Two rows in front of me and three tables to the left, the person with the red tie checks their pocket. They laugh as they pull out a deck of cards and hold it up for everyone else to see.

The audience cheers. Victory settles over Alice's features, and an icy chill creeps up my spine. I see it now. Alice with her hair in a tight bun, blonde instead of pink. Anger and fear on her face instead of the easy smile of a performer. I feel her hand clamped tightly around my throat.

This mission is doomed.

"I know her," I whisper to Morgan. All hope of destroying the drug before the trial splinters and falls to pieces around me.

Morgan doesn't look away from the audience member searching the deck for the six of hearts. "How?"

"She's the Blood Witch I met in New York." My voice is so low that I don't know at first if Morgan hears me. But then she turns, her eyes huge. "She's the one who tried to kill me."

8

FOR THE NEXT HOUR, Alice Ansley delights and confounds her audience. Twice, I swear she looks directly at me. My palms go slick with cold sweat, but she always looks away. I can only hope that the spotlights in her eyes blur my features beyond recognition. For her final trick, Alice disappears in a puff of smoke, leaving the crowd standing and cheering in her absence.

I don't have time to be awed by her skill or to wonder how she accomplished each seemingly impossible feat. This mission is so beyond screwed.

"What do we do?" Morgan whispers as the crowd ebbs and flows around us. We lose Sarah in the rush of bodies, and Morgan keeps one hand on my elbow as we maneuver to the stairwell and slip back into the hotel. "Is there any chance she won't recognize you?"

"The Caster Witches tried to strip Alice of her magic. I'm fairly certain she'll remember me." I take the next doorway, emerging into an empty hall. This isn't our floor or Alice's, so we should have a few minutes before Sarah comes looking for us. "If the Council finds out what happened that weekend, I could lose my magic. Alice, too." Every witch who was there is guilty of using magic against another Clan. None of us would look innocent before the three Elders.

"But the Elders need you. Do you still think they'd punish you?"

"I honestly don't know."

When Veronica first invited me to hang out with the trio of Caster Witches—Tori, Lexie, and Coral—I didn't want to go. But she begged, and I thought dating her meant I had to do whatever I thought would make her happy, so I went.

That night was . . . not great, especially when a Blood Witch—when *Alice*—attacked. I managed to help run her off, but when I realized the Casters wanted to illegally strip Alice of her magic, I tried to distance myself from them and focus on the school trip.

The next day, I went to Central Park with the rest of my class. I tried to have fun with Gemma, but Veronica wanted to talk. Except talking turned into *fighting*, and the next thing I knew, I was lost and alone in the middle of the park.

I'm still not sure how exactly Alice found me there, whether she was following me or my luck was truly that terrible, but she recognized me from the Casters' apartment and attacked. She was so distracted that the Casters—who had come to the park to meet with Veronica—were able to capture us both. Alice thought I wanted to strip her magic like the rest of them, despite my protests, and there's no reason to think she'll change her mind about my guilt now.

What the three Casters tried to do is unforgivable. Even what they managed to accomplish—kidnapping Alice and binding her in potion-soaked ropes that dampened her power—is bad enough. Not to mention the fight that broke out between Tori and Veronica before we managed to escape. That kind of inter-Clan fighting is unforgivable under Council law, and I don't know if Elder Keating's plans for Alice and me are enough to save us from punishment for what we did.

But at the same time . . . I can't *not* try to recruit Alice. There's too much at stake with the Hunters' drug wiping out magic from entire covens in a single night. "We still have to talk to Alice. There has to be a way to convince her to help and not tell anyone what happened. We need her." I peer out into the hall and look at the door numbers. "She's two floors up. We stick to the plan. You and I will try to talk to her. I'll text Sarah and tell her we want to go alone so we don't overwhelm Alice."

"You don't think Sarah would get you in trouble with the Council, do you?"

"She's family, but I'd rather not put her in the position to have to choose." I lead Morgan up the stairs, texting Sarah as we climb.

When we reach Alice's floor, Morgan peers down the hall. "How are you going to get Alice to open the door? What if she recognizes you?" Doubt colors Morgan's tone, and I try not to take it personally.

Down the hall, someone left a discarded room service tray for housekeeping to collect in the morning. An empty bottle of champagne lays next to a bucket of melting ice. "I have an idea."

Two minutes later, Morgan stands outside Alice's door. The bucket is freshly stocked with ice, and the champagne bottle is tilted back to hide that it's empty. Sarah responded to my texts, giving us thirty minutes to try on our own before she shows up for reinforcement.

Morgan glances at me and smooths the skirt of her dress so

it falls effortlessly to her knees. I gesture for her to smile. She rolls her eyes and blows out a slow breath, raising her hand to knock. Time seems to slow with her fist poised to bring me face-to-face with the Blood Witch who fueled my nightmares for months.

She knocks. We wait.

A weary voice calls out. "Who is it?"

"Uh . . . room service?"

There's movement on the other side of the door. I hold my breath as Morgan raises the ice bucket so Alice can see it when she looks through the peephole.

"I didn't order anything." Alice's voice is muffled but close. So close.

A tremor of fear covers my skin in goose bumps. I remember her strength, her grip tight around my throat. The bloody runes she sketched along the Casters' walls.

I gesture for Morgan to say something. Anything.

"It's a gift," she says, scrambling. "A fan . . . from your show . . . he, um, he asked us to send it to your room."

One beat of silence. Two.

The chain lock glides free and the door swings open. Alice stands there, still in her suit, though she's discarded her tie and braided her pink hair so that it falls over one shoulder. "You can put it on the desk."

Morgan casts me a worried look, and Alice follows her gaze. Confusion creases her brow, but I see the moment she places my face, her hands curling into fists. *"You."*

"Don't freak out." I lift my arms in surrender. "We just want to talk."

"Eat shit, fire bitch." Alice slams the door.

I rush forward and shove my foot into the frame as it's

closing. Pain shoots up my leg, and I try to push my way inside. "I can't leave until you hear me out."

The door swings open, and Alice moves faster than I can track. She hauls me inside and closes her fingers around my throat. She squeezes tight, lifting me up the wall until my toes barely scrape the ground. "I have *nothing* to say to you."

The worst kind of déjà vu consumes me. Alice's grip cuts off my air, stealing my reply with no care for the consequences of using her magic against another witch.

"What are you doing?" Morgan drops the bucket of ice, and pieces slide over the wood floor. She slams the door closed behind her. "Put her down."

"Back the hell up, earth princess. Or your friend gets a broken neck." Alice's Blood Magic seizes control of my body, forcing bone and muscle to move under her direction. Pain screams through my body, and I lose contact with the floor. Lose the ability to breathe.

Morgan rushes us, twisting Alice's wrist until the pressure around my neck releases. I drop to the floor, coughing as air rushes back into my lungs.

"I don't want to hurt you." Morgan shoves Alice back a few steps and positions herself between the two of us. "But I won't let you touch her."

"Who says I have to touch her?" Alice's expression shifts, a feral flash of teeth masquerading as a grin. Then my whole body trembles as my muscles contract tighter and tighter and tighter. A scream gets trapped at the back of my throat. I shut my eyes against the pain, tiny shooting stars flying behind closed lids.

Her power is an invasion, foreign and grating against each cell of my body. I reach for the elements, trying to steal the air from her lungs. To freeze the water in her blood. Anything. But I can't find them through the agony, can't concentrate on anything, not even my own breath.

There's a scuffle above me. The crunch of bone and a sharp intake of breath. Then the pain in my body fades, replaced by the thrum of Morgan's magic. It spreads like a gentle stream, soothing the ache in my muscles, but it doesn't do anything to help with the headache already pounding at the base of my skull. When I manage to open my eyes, Alice is glaring down at me, wiping blood from beneath her nose.

"You brought a Blood Witch this time." Derision drips off her words. "Smart."

"What's *wrong* with you?" Morgan asks before I can launch into the speech I've been practicing all week. "How can you use your magic like that? That's not what our Clan is supposed to be. Not anymore."

Alice glares at Morgan and perches on the edge of her mattress. There are two large trunks beside the bed, presumably filled with supplies for her show. I can't imagine it's all clothes. "And *you're* not supposed to turn on another Blood Witch in favor of some . . ." Alice waves dismissively in my direction. "Some hotheaded flower child."

"I'm—"

"Hannah is not a hothead. You're the one who attacked *her* when all we wanted was to ask for your help." Morgan crosses her arms. She's a little scary when she's furious, but it's also kind of cute.

"My help?" Alice laughs, yet somehow even that sounds cruel. "That's perfect. Of course she wants my help. Do you have any idea what she tried to do to me? She's lucky I don't stop her heart right now."

"I—"

"She told me what happened the last time she was here. It wasn't her fault. It was the Caster Witches." Morgan doesn't even hesitate when she adds. "Hannah said she's the one who helped you escape, and then how did you repay her? You hurt her, just like you're doing now."

Alice's blue eyes turn to ice. "Letting me go was the least she could do. She's the reason I was caught in the first place."

"What?" Morgan glances back at me, where I'm still sitting against the wall. I wish I could deny Alice's claims, but they're technically true. She probably wouldn't have been caught if she hadn't seen me in Central Park.

With both Blood Witches silent for a moment, I struggle back to my feet. My body protests, every muscle sore from Alice's magical assault. "Let's back up and start over, okay? The Council sent us. We desperately need your help."

But Alice only redirects her glare at me. "I already spoke with the *Council*." She practically spits the word. "I want nothing to do with their plans."

"Staying out of it isn't going to protect you. We're *all* doomed if we don't stop the Hunters." I take a tentative step forward. My legs hold, but it hurts enough to make me wince. "If you don't help, it's only a matter of time before they dose every last one of us. And trust me, their drug fucking sucks."

Alice's expression softens into cautious curiosity, like she's seeing me for the first time. "Wait, you're not . . ." She glances between Morgan and me. "You're the girl from Salem?"

Maybe I should have led with that. I nod. "I've faced these Hunters, Alice. They're so much worse than the rogue Casters who tried to hurt you. I know you don't believe me, but as soon as I understood what they wanted to do, I tried to stop them. No innocent witch deserves to have their powers taken from them."

I squeeze my eyes against the sudden rush of emotion for Zoë and my grandparents. "Too many witches have already suffered. I'm asking for your help. Without you, it won't be long until the Witch Clans are nothing but a memory."

Alice tugs on the end of her pink braid and stares at the floor, a crease forming along her brow. She's silent for a long time, and it takes everything in me not to interrupt or push. To give her space to talk herself into helping.

Finally, she looks up.

"I can't do this. I have a tour to finish. I have sponsors to answer to." Her voice is thick with emotion, and the shift in her is so complete I hardly recognize her as the same girl who threatened to snap my neck five minutes ago. "I *finally* have my life together. I can't drop everything for some doomed mission."

"But you're our best hope to save the Clans." I approach cautiously, remembering Archer's advice. When logic fails, go for guilt. "The Hunters took everything from me. They murdered my father. They ripped away my magic, and when it *finally* came back, it wasn't the same. I can't reach the elements without pain. I don't know if it'll ever stop hurting." My voice cracks, and I don't bother trying to stop the tears. "Please, Alice. You could do something about this. You could be the one to save us."

She considers me, and I feel the weight of Morgan's gaze at my back. Feel the guilt I tried to wield as a weapon turned back at me. I let Morgan believe everything was okay. Now she knows I've kept this from her for weeks. Every time she asked if I was okay. Every time I deflected instead of telling her. But if this secures the help we need, I'll shoulder the fallout.

"Alice . . ." I reach for her hand, but she yanks away from my touch.

"Get out. Both of you." She stands abruptly and grabs me by the collar of my shirt.

I stumble behind her, and she shoves me into the hallway. Morgan follows me out.

"Find yourself another savior," Alice says, and slams the door in my face.

9

SARAH IS WAITING FOR us when we get back to our room. "How did it go?"

Her question hangs in the hallway between us, and I don't even know where to begin. Talking to Alice was a complete and total failure. I settle for a shrug, trying to crumple my emotions like an unwanted Post-it Note.

"Alice wasn't very . . . receptive to the idea," Morgan says, glancing at me. I can tell she wants to talk. Not about my failed mission, either. I can see it there in her eyes, her renewed curiosity about the first time I met Alice, but she doesn't say anything in front of Sarah. She knows the dangers of being charged with inter-Clan violence.

The Elders might offer us more leeway regarding today's violence given that we're here on their request, but I don't think that's a risk any of us wants to take.

"What do we do now?" Sarah pulls her phone out of her pocket and checks the time. "Ryan told me not to leave New York without her."

There's no way Alice is going to change her mind. A small part of me doesn't blame her. I remember the dangerous gleam in Tori's eyes all those months ago, shining as brightly as her blue hair. I remember how much she hurt Alice before I helped her get away. "Then I guess we're stuck here." I jam my keycard into the lock and shove open the door.

"Hannah—"

"Let me," Morgan says, cutting her off. "I'll talk to her. We won't try again without telling you first."

The door clicks shut, and I perch at the edge of the bed, studying the woodgrain in our polished floor. Discarded outfits still litter the room from when we changed for Alice's show, and the latch on the door to Sarah's suite is still flipped open. I consider locking it so she can't come in, but that requires finding the will to stand up when all I want to do is sink into this bed and never move again.

Morgan's shadow falls over me, her long lines lengthened by the angle of the wall-mounted lights.

"I don't want to talk about it," I say before she can ask.

Morgan sits beside me and is quiet for a long time. "I think we should," she says at last, turning to face me. "Was all of that true? Even about your magic?"

The tears I've been fighting finally break free and slip past my lashes.

"Why didn't you say anything?" Morgan reaches for me, brushing my cheeks with her thumbs. "I'm a terrible girlfriend. I should have noticed something was wrong."

"It works better when you're around." The admission dries my eyes, and I wipe my face on my sleeve. "It's best when you're using your magic, but even when you're not, being near you grounds me in a way that makes it easier to reach the elements. There was nothing for you to notice."

I don't know what it is about her presence that makes it better, but somehow, it does.

"You could have told me," she insists. "I would have—"

"What? Told my mom? Told Archer?"

"Tried to *help*. We're on the same team, Hannah, but I can't help you if I don't know what's wrong." Morgan reaches for my hand and squeezes. Her magic flows through me and eases the lingering ache from Alice's attack. "Are you okay?"

"I will be, *if* we can convince Alice to help." I didn't come this far to go back empty-handed. I didn't go through that kind of mind-numbing pain to have nothing to show for it. "But after everything that happened, I don't see how she ever will."

Morgan goes quiet again. She rubs tiny circles against my knuckles with her thumb, but her face is stormy with a hundred questions.

A long sigh makes my entire body deflate. "Go ahead. Ask."

"I'm not—"

"You practically have the questions written on your skin." I let myself lean into her, resting my head on her shoulder. The air dances playfully through my hair, and the tiny bit of magic makes my body sing. It's amazing how much closer the elements are when she's near. "You can ask."

She hesitates a moment more before resting her head on top of mine. "I don't think I understand what happened the last time you were here. Not really. You said there were Caster Witches who wanted to bind her magic?"

I close my eyes and force myself to remember that weekend. It changed everything. It was the final straw that broke Veronica and me apart.

"There were three of them," I say at last. "Tori, Coral, and Lexie." It feels strange to speak their names aloud, and I'm half expecting the words to summon them to the hotel room. "The

Casters met at college and got an apartment together off-campus. They said the dorms didn't have enough privacy for potion making."

"But why did they want to bind Alice's powers?" Morgan shifts uncomfortably beside me.

"It was mostly Tori. She lost her parents to a feud with Alice's family. They had this really intense Romeo-and-Juliet thing going on, minus the romance. I don't think Coral and Lexie realized Tori was serious about her plans." I sit up and rub the back of my neck. "Tori said Alice was the last Blood Witch in the city, and if Alice refused to leave, Tori would make her a Reg instead."

Morgan shudders. "What happened? They obviously didn't succeed." She shakes her head. "I can't believe Alice did that to you. Is that what happened last time?" Sadness and anger fight for dominance in Morgan's tone, and a tear spills over her lashes. "No wonder you blamed me for your dad when you found out who I am."

"Hey," I soothe, fighting against the pain pushing behind my eyes at the mention of Dad. "You're nothing like her. I couldn't have been more wrong to suspect you."

Someone knocks on the door before Morgan can respond. My first thought is that it's Alice, here to say she changed her mind, but she doesn't know our room number.

Morgan scrubs away her tears. "I'll get it." She answers the door, but it's not Alice on the other side.

Three people stand in the hall, two guys and a girl. They're young, maybe our age or a little older, though it's hard to tell exactly. One of the boys, the tallest of the trio, looks familiar with his blond hair, hazel eyes, and thick-rimmed glasses. Recognition rushes in all at once, and I scowl at him.

"You're that reporter from the Cauldron." I step forward, hands already squeezing into fists. "What, are you stalking me now?"

He flashes a predatory grin. "Not everything is about you, Hannah." He turns his attention to Morgan, looking her up and down.

I follow his gaze. She's frozen in place, her hands trembling. "Morgan?"

My voice seems to unlock her limbs. She tries to slam the door, but the second guy—a shorter boy with dark hair—shoves his way into the room.

Morgan stumbles back, all of her usual confidence and poise gone.

"Do you know them?" I step forward and reach for my magic, nurture its thrum in my chest just in case. I meant what I said to Morgan, that I'm stronger when she's around, but it'd be so much better if her Blood Magic was flowing through my veins.

"I'm hurt," the reporter says, theatrically pressing a hand to his chest as the girl quietly closes the door, locking the five of us inside the small room. "You didn't tell her about me?" He reaches out to brush a lock of hair behind Morgan's ear, but she flinches away.

"Don't touch me, Riley."

Riley. The name pings around in my head, and when I remember why it sounds so familiar, I lose my hold on the elements.

He's not a reporter. He's her ex.

Mine was more the show-up-at-my-house-at-all-hours type. That's what Morgan said about her ex-boyfriend the first time she mentioned him, and even before I knew he was a Witch Hunter, I could tell the guy was bad news.

And since he's a Hunter . . .

The other two probably are as well.

"What do you want from us?" I raise my voice, hoping Sarah will hear and know something's wrong.

Riley's team grabs small tranquilizer guns from the backs of their waistbands, and if they're the same guns the Hunters used at Hall Pharmaceuticals, they're filled with the drug. But Riley doesn't have a tranq gun. He pulls out a long knife. Morgan stiffens behind me.

"You really made it so easy, Hannah. All those *adorable* pictures you post with her. We tracked your phone to the city, but the photo in the hotel lobby was very helpful." He slinks forward to close the gap between us, and we match each of his steps with a retreat of our own. His focus shifts from me to his ex. "My friends and I are going to fix you, babe. You can come back to Minnesota with us. Everyone misses you."

The girl rolls her eyes. "Enough with the monologuing, Riley. We need to get back before anyone realizes we're missing." She levels her gun at me. "Let's cure these girls and go home."

I grab Morgan's hand and hope it'll be enough to tell her what I'm thinking. "As someone recently told me: eat shit."

The air responds instantly to my call with a vicious updraft that knocks the three Hunters off their feet. I scream for Sarah and tug hard on Morgan's hand. We duck behind the bed as the shorter Hunter fires his gun. A dart flies through the curtains and ricochets off the window.

Sarah bursts into the room, takes one look at the scene before her, and springs into action. The air answers her call in an instant, swirling between us with the force of a cyclone. Her hands clench, and all three Hunters drop, clutching their throats.

Morgan peers over the bed. "What is she doing?"

"Stealing their breath." I don't even try to hide the satisfaction in my voice. Some twisted part of me delights in the fear in their eyes, in the way they scramble in the face of our power. Magic like this is a perversion of our gifts, but it's one they forced on us.

The girl collapses to the floor last, her limbs sprawled. She stretches, like she can outmaneuver the need for air, like she can—

"Sarah, look out!"

The girl's fingers close around her gun, and she fires. The small cylindrical dart embeds itself in Sarah's chest.

Sarah glances down at the dart, plucks the feathered end, and lets the whole thing drop to the floor. Her pupils expand, overtaking the green of her eyes. "Run," she says, catching herself on the edge of the bed. The air stops spinning as Sarah's magic fades. "Run!"

I flinch at the ferocity in her tone, but I won't make her tell us again. I drag Morgan behind me as the Hunters reload, and we barely avoid the next round of darts. We're into the hall a second later, startling a drunk woman struggling with her keycard. I don't know where to go, don't know how many Hunters might be in the hotel. In the city.

We need reinforcements.

I tug Morgan toward the stairs, and now that Riley is out of her sight, she seems to come back to herself. She runs faster, gripping my hand to help me keep pace. We turn a corner, and there's crashing in the distance. The Hunters giving chase.

We race up two flights of stairs, my feet barely brushing each step before Morgan's hauling me up another one. The metal steps clang below us as the Hunters follow us up the stairs. Fear and adrenaline are the only things keeping my heart from shattering. Sarah just lost her magic. Because of me.

There isn't time to think about that. Not now.

At Alice's floor, we careen out of the stairwell so fast I nearly fall on my face. Morgan pulls me after her, but I can't keep my feet under me. I'm gasping for breath, silent tears streaming down my face.

"Come on," she urges as her magic flows through me. A fresh burst of energy pumps into my legs, and I run faster than I ever have before, so fast my body hardly feels like my own.

"Alice!" I shout when we reach her room, pounding on the door.

"Fuck off."

"Open the door, Alice."

"Hannah." Morgan grabs my arm, and I turn in time to see the Hunters emerge from the stairwell. They race down the hall toward us, all three of them with tranq guns raised.

Shit, shit, shit. "I need every bit of power you can spare." I reach for the place magic should pool in my chest. I'm not sure if this will work, if this is even a *thing*, but I cling to hope anyway. "Now."

Morgan does as I ask, and the power that floods my system is so strong, so intoxicating, that I can barely see. The well of magic in my chest grows so deep that I fear I'll drown in it.

I raise my hand, and the air answers my call before I'm fully aware of what I'm asking. The wind rushes to do my bidding, tossing the three Hunters back several feet, where they crumple to the floor. Behind me, I'm vaguely aware of Morgan banging on Alice's door as I follow the tendrils of breath back into each of the Hunter's lungs. I squeeze until they drop one by one into unconsciousness.

A door opens and slams shut again. "Who the hell are they?" Alice creeps toward us, her suit replaced with flannel pajama bottoms and a gray T-shirt. I realize, suddenly, that she can't be that much older than me. Nineteen, maybe twenty at most.

"Hunters," I say, breathless. Morgan's magic leaves me in a rush, and I sway on my feet, catching myself on the wall. The sudden loss of the elements leaves me dizzy and nauseated. I had only hoped her magic would keep mine stable. I had no idea it could make it stronger. Has anyone ever done this before? Do Blood Witches know they can have this effect on us? Do the Elders?

"Are they dead?" Morgan asks, her voice wavering on the edge of tears.

"No." I reach for her hand. "Not dead."

"What do we do now?" Morgan asks. "We can't leave them in the hall."

I look from the prone bodies to Alice's room. Finally, I settle my gaze on the girl I'm supposed to recruit.

"Don't look at me," she says, backing away. "I don't want *Hunters* in my room. I'm not part of this."

"You are now." I walk the short distance to the unconscious Hunters, grab Riley by the ankles, and drag him down the hall. "Please tell me you have extra room in those giant trunks."

IO

PEOPLE ARE MUCH MORE agreeable when there are unconscious bodies on their floor.

Alice doesn't try to stop us from dragging the bodies into her room—though she doesn't help carry them, either. While I bind their wrists with rope from Alice's show, Morgan shakily explains that the Hunters weren't shooting tranquilizers at us. That those darts carry a drug that will take away our magic forever.

The pink-haired illusionist turns exceptionally pale as reality sinks in.

I almost ask for Morgan's help to gather enough strength to send an air message to Sarah, but then I remember the dart in her chest. My heart breaks all over again, and I pull out my phone. She answers on the first ring, her grief covered with worry. "Are you all right? Where are you?"

"We're in Alice's room. We're okay." I squeeze my eyes shut against the guilt that wants to drown me. "What about you? Are you—"

"I'm on my way."

When Sarah arrives a few minutes later, she tries to put on a brave face, but I can see the cracks in her emotional armor. As much as she may want to, she can't hide the sheen of sweat that shines on her brow. I can only sense the tiniest bit of her Elemental magic, and it's fading with each breath.

"I'm so sorry," I say when she closes the door behind her. "This is all my fault."

Sarah winces and clutches at her side. "I knew the risks when I volunteered." She focuses on the bound and unconscious team of Hunters. "Goddess, they're so young," she says, more to herself than us. "Are you sure none of you are hurt? No one else was drugged?"

"No one *else*?" Alice's voice is pitched high.

"We're fine," I say, ignoring the panicking Blood Witch. I scrub at my eyes to stop the constant prickle of tears. "But you're not. I can feel your magic disappearing. Maybe if I'd been faster—"

"This isn't your fault, Hannah. I—" Sarah gasps and presses a hand to her chest. She stumbles and barely makes it to the edge of Alice's unmade bed before her legs give out beneath her and the last of her magic winks out of existence.

Forever.

Sarah breathes slowly, like she's trying to fight back nausea, and finally looks up at the three worried young witches before her. "We need to get them out of here before they wake up. It's Alice, right?"

Alice nods, tugging on the end of her braid.

"What kind of transportation do you have?"

Twenty minutes later, we have the Hunters locked into Alice's prop trunks and loaded in her rental. Alice refused to share a vehicle with them, leaving Sarah to drive the van. I offered to ride with Sarah, but she wanted to be alone. Said she had plenty of phone calls to make to keep her company. So, Alice, Morgan, and I piled into Sarah's car. None of us speak the entire drive to Salem. I try not to think about the night's horrors, but all I see are my failures playing over and over on an endless loop.

Once we make it back to Salem, I offer to drop Alice at a

hotel before taking Morgan home, but they both insist on coming with me to Archer's place. Lights shine in the front windows, Archer waiting for us, just like he promised when he called.

"Well, wind witch?" Alice says from the back seat, watching Archer's house with poorly masked fear. "Aren't you going in?"

I glare at her in the rearview, then cut the engine.

Archer answers the door before I even make it to the steps. "Thank the Sisters," he says in a rush, like he wasn't sure we'd make it all the way here. "Where are the others?"

"Morgan and Alice are in the car." I wave for them to join us. The doors open and slam shut again. "Sarah is on her way with the . . . cargo."

"Come in. All of you." Archer leads us into his home. "Elder Keating is in the kitchen. She's making tea."

Alice stops dead on the front porch. "There's an *Elder* here? You didn't think that was something you should tell me?" Her expression telegraphs worry, and I can understand why.

If I told Elder Keating what Alice did to me in the hotel, if I told her the way Alice contorted my body with her magic, Keating could strip Alice of her power.

"I won't tell her what happened tonight," I whisper back. "Whether or not you agree to help with the raid. Though I really, *really* hope you will." I motion for her to follow and trail after Archer through his home. As much as I want to say I'd do anything to recruit Alice, I won't threaten to have her magic bound. I won't resort to blackmail.

In the kitchen, Elder Keating stands beside the stove, pouring hot water into half a dozen mugs. She glances over her shoulder at us, giving me an approving nod when she notices Alice. "Explain everything."

I'm not sure how much of our story Archer already told her—enough for Keating to temporarily lower the protective barrier around the town so Sarah could get in with the three Hunters—but I start at the beginning anyway. I tell them about Riley coming to the Cauldron but not knowing who he was. Even though I don't want to, I admit that the photos I posted online led Riley to us.

"But why?" Elder Keating muses, looking more concerned than I've ever seen her. "Why was he so fixated on Morgan that he broke protocol?"

"Protocol?" I ask.

The Elder looks up from her tea. She clears her throat. "You said one of the Hunters was worried the others would notice they were gone. I assume it wasn't a sanctioned mission."

Oh. Right.

"So, why did this boy break protocol?" she asks again.

I look to Morgan. Her freckled cheeks flush pink. "We used to date. I didn't know he was a Hunter until he tried to hurt me. And now he—" Tears fill her eyes, and she looks to me.

"He said he wants to win her back. After he's given her the cure."

Archer's phone shakes violently on the counter, and we all jump. Well, all of us except Elder Keating. I don't think anything could startle her. "That's Sarah," Archer says, checking the message. "She needs our help with the trunks."

Morgan and Alice set their half-finished cups of tea on the counter and follow him to the door. I try to go after them, but Keating asks me to stay.

"Is everything all right? Did things go okay with the water protection?"

Elder Keating nods. "Things here are fine. There's no need to worry." She rests a hand on my shoulder. "I am so proud of you, Hannah. This mission was so much more complicated than I anticipated, and yet you still managed to recruit Alice like I asked. I hope you can take solace in a job well done."

She smiles and slips past me into the hall, but her approval leaves me unsettled. I *didn't* recruit Alice. She hasn't agreed to help us beyond getting the Hunters here. Not yet, anyway, but I don't want to admit I failed. I don't want Elder Keating to be disappointed in me.

When I make it to the hall, Alice and Morgan are dragging the trunks stuffed with screaming Hunters into the house. Even with their enhanced strength, I can see their struggle as Archer and Sarah help maneuver the luggage down the stairs into the basement.

I take a steadying breath and follow.

The basement has a basic cement floor, but otherwise it looks clean and bright. About a third of the large, open space is blocked off by metal bars that run floor to ceiling. There's a small room tucked in the corner of the cell and three mattresses strewn across the floor. The rest of the basement, the part outside the cell, is filled with shelves of potions and raw ingredients. A long table sits at the center of the room with what looks like a chemistry lab on top.

"Why do you have a cell in your basement?" Alice asks, speaking for the first time since she learned she was about to meet a Council Elder.

Archer pulls a key from a ring on the far wall. "I had it installed when we knew there were Hunters in Salem. I figured it was only a matter of time before we caught one." He unlocks the door and swings it open.

Morgan and Alice drag the trunks inside and unlock them, hurrying out with dizzying speed so Archer can secure the door before the Hunters pull themselves free of their boxes.

The girl makes it to her feet first. She kicks Riley's trunk as he's trying to pull himself out, and I notice all three managed to slip out of their rope bindings during the drive. Which is slightly terrifying. "I told you not to waste time tormenting the blood-sucker. You should have shot her first."

Beside me, Morgan goes rigid.

"Well, maybe if you were a better shot, we wouldn't be in this mess," Riley snaps back, and the exchange is so *normal*, so much like how Veronica and her brother, Gabe, fight, that it makes my skin crawl.

"Stop arguing," the shorter guy says. "I already have a migraine."

"Shut up, Wes," Riley and the girl say in unison.

The short guy, Wes, sighs. "Please tell me there's a bathroom in this stupid thing?" He looks through the bars, his gaze bouncing between the three adults like he's trying to decide who's actually in charge.

Archer points to the door in the corner of the cell, and Wes slips out of his trunk and disappears.

"This is all your fault," the girl says, shoving Riley. He trips and falls back into the trunk. "We're going to be in so much trouble when the Order realizes we're missing."

"Knock it off, Paige."

"Don't use my name in front of them." She flops onto one of the beds. "Idiots. The both of you."

"Hey," Wes says, emerging from the bathroom. "Don't

blame me for this. And you used *my* name, so don't get precious about yours."

Beside me, Elder Keating groans. "May the Mother Goddess give me strength," she mutters and pulls a vial from an inside jacket pocket. She tosses it into the cell, and blue mist rises from the concrete floor. The Hunters cover their mouths, but it's too late. In a matter of moments, they all collapse into unconsciousness.

Sarah shakes her head. "I can't believe teenagers did this to me. It would almost be funny if it wasn't so fucking awful." She approaches the cell and kneels beside the door, glancing over her shoulder at Archer and Keating. "How do you expect to get anything useful out of them?"

"Not without some magical help." Archer opens the door and drags Riley out of the cell, tossing Sarah the keys so she can relock the others inside. He props Riley up in a chair and binds him there with a length of rope. After the teenage Hunter is secure, the detective scans his shelves, selecting a gray potion and pulling the stopper out of the thin bottle.

The smoky mixture curls into the air beneath Riley's nose, and then Morgan's ex jolts awake. His eyes are wild as he searches the room and pulls against his bindings. Morgan reaches for me, her fingers digging into my arm hard enough to bruise, but I don't pull away. If she needs an anchor to weather this storm, I can do that for her.

Archer stoppers his potion and leans against the work table. "Let's start with an easy question, shall we? What's your full name?"

Riley spits in Archer's general direction.

Elder Keating scans the shelves. "We don't have time for this nonsense." She selects a shimmering white potion and grabs one of those large droppers parents use on their kids to give them medicine.

"What are you doing?" Riley asks, a mixture of fear and disgust in his tone.

"Cutting to the truth," Keating says, opening the vial and filling the dropper. She passes the rest of the vial to Archer and grabs hold of Riley's face. He struggles against her grip, but she tilts his face up and shoves the liquid into his mouth.

Riley coughs and sputters, but it's too late. The potion is already down his throat.

"Let's try this again," the Elder says. "What is your name?"

The young Hunter thrashes harder against the ropes that bind him, but he spits out the words. "Riley Martin." Sweat beads along his forehead, and he glances nervously at the assembly of witches. "What did you do to me?"

"I'll be asking the questions, Mr. Martin. And now, you have no choice but to respond truthfully." Keating pulls a chair from behind the table and positions it in front of Riley. She crosses her ankles and watches him with a level of nonchalance that I know she can't really feel. "Do you know who Ms. Ansley is?"

Though he tries not to, Riley's eyes flit over to Alice. He looks her up and down, appraising. "I've seen her picture some-where," Riley admits, brow furrowing.

"Where?" Archer presses, stepping forward until he's beside Elder Keating, slipping easily into his detective persona.

Riley presses his lips into a thin line, but he only manages to delay a few seconds before the words come spilling out. "In

Hannah's photo. She and Morgan were standing beside a poster of her."

Morgan flinches at the sound of her name, but Archer and Keating share a look. "Good," Archer says, and then continues with the interrogation, asking Riley how he followed me to New York.

I try, but I can't follow the line of questioning. My gaze is caught on Sarah, caught on all the tiny cracks in her veneer. She's fighting so hard to act fine when I know she must be falling apart inside, adrift and disoriented without her magic. Rachel is going to *kill* me when she finds out what I let happen. With all that swirling around, I can't understand why Sarah looks so relieved that Riley doesn't know who Alice—

And then it hits me. If Riley didn't know Alice was a witch before now, the rest of the Hunters probably don't know about her, either. He was there because of *me*, not Alice, which means the Hunters won't recognize Alice as an enemy when she tries to schedule the performance. The raid still has a chance of success.

If I can actually convince Alice to help us . . .

"I want to talk about the Washington coven." It's Keating speaking now, and her words capture my attention. "We have reason to believe you dosed the water supply with your drug. How?"

Riley has stopped struggling against his bonds, but he stares at Archer like he wants to tear out his heart. "I don't know. It's above my clearance level."

"But the Hunters did tamper with the water." Archer poses the question as a statement, and Riley keeps his lips sealed tight. "Mr. Martin, must we really force each of these answers from you?"

"Yes."

"Fine. Did the Hunters drug the water?"

"Yes."

"Do you intend to drug all the country's water supply?"

Riley bares his teeth, a look so violent it twists his face until he's almost unrecognizable. "No."

"Then what?" Archer's voice is pitched with desperation. "How do you intend to administer your drug?"

"We're going to make it airborne," Riley says, raising his voice and looking at Morgan while he speaks. "Soon, there will be no escaping salvation."

His laughter fills the room, and even Archer steps away from him, horror etched across his face. Morgan turns and sprints up the stairs, but whether she's fleeing Riley or the future he promises, I can't tell. But it doesn't matter. If what he says is true, the Witch Clans aren't going to survive much longer.

Magic will cease to exist.

I turn to run after Morgan, but Alice grips my wrist, holding me back.

"Wait," she says, her voice pitched low. "I'll stay in Salem. I'll help. Whatever you need, tell me and it's done."

"Really?" Surprise and gratitude lace through my tone in equal measure.

Alice's expression is unamused. "If we're all doomed anyway, I'd rather go down fighting."

―⊹― ⋇ ―⊹―

I find Morgan in the kitchen, her face buried in her hands.

"It's going to be okay." The promise passes my lips even

though I hate these kinds of platitudes. Even though absolutely nothing feels okay right now. "Riley can't hurt you anymore."

She turns and lets me swallow her up in an embrace. "I hate him so much." Her fierce whisper grazes the skin at my neck, and I squeeze her tight.

"Let's get out of here." I pull away and brush the tears from her cheeks. Her skin is warm and flushed under my fingers, the blue of her eyes glittering with unshed pain. "I'll take you home."

I find the keys on the table and borrow Alice's rental van. We leave a note on Archer's table, promising to bring it back in the morning. On the road, traffic is basically nonexistent as the clock inches toward four. Exhaustion settles into my bones, and I can barely keep my eyes open by the time we make it to Morgan's house.

"Come in with me?"

She looks so worried, the ghosts of tear tracks on her cheeks and sleep in her eyes, that I can't possibly say no. I follow her into the house, creeping quietly into her bedroom, where she shuts the door firmly behind us.

"Your parents won't mind that I'm here?" I peel out of my jacket and set it on the back of her desk chair. The collage of pictures on her wall has grown since the first time I was here, the photos with her dance class back in Duluth interspersed with shots of the two of us together, sometimes with Gemma, too. She even kept the apology card I painted for her after I bailed on our first date to rescue Veronica. That was the first time Benton broke into V's house, though we didn't know it was him at the time.

"They'll understand, especially once they know what happened with Riley." Morgan's entire body goes stiff when she says his name, fresh tears pooling in her eyes. "I can't believe he found me. That he's here, in Salem."

"Hey," I soothe, crossing to her and pulling her close. I rub circles on her back, like she did for me so many times this summer. "You're safe. He can't get you anymore. Archer has him locked up."

Morgan's muscles go rigid, and she pulls away. "I don't feel safe. Not yet." Her gaze drops to her hands, where she spins the ring on her middle finger round and round and round. "But I will be."

She pulls off the ring and removes the pin from the inside groove. Moving too fast to stop her, she pricks two of her fingers and lets blood well up on her skin. And then in a blink she's at her door, pressing her bleeding fingers into the frame.

"What are you doing?"

"Keeping him out. Keeping them all out." Shimmering, bloody runes take shape along the edge of the door. Her movements are frantic and desperate, the blood on her fingers flowing faster than she can trace the runic lines, leaving a path of blood dripping down her wrist.

"Morgan . . ."

"You don't know what he's like," she insists. "You don't know what he did."

"So talk to me. Tell me what happened." I try to reach for her, try to stop her frantic writing, but she pulls away, adding runes to the other side of the door.

"You want to know what happened? You want to know what he did when he saw the small cut on my thumb heal itself?" Tears pool in her eyes, and she hits the wall, leaving an imprint of her hand behind. "He grabbed my wrist and carved a blade across my palm."

"Fuck, Morgan."

She shakes her head and goes back to drawing runes. "That's not even the worst of it. I'm stronger than him, I *knew* I was, but I was so scared I couldn't move. He cut so deep and it hurt so much, I couldn't stop my magic. The skin stitched back together right in front of him. He called me a Blood Witch and he . . ." She swallows hard, and the tears slip down her cheeks. "He tried to slit my throat. I barely got out of there alive. We fled the state as fast as we could, and now he's back, and I—"

"And *you* are going to be okay." I grab a hand towel from the laundry basket and reach for her hand. This time, she doesn't stop me. Gently, I run the towel from the crook of her elbow to the tips of her fingers, wiping away the trail of blood. "I won't let him hurt you. I promise."

She laughs, but there isn't any humor in her voice. "I'm a *Blood Witch*, Hannah. I'm a monster, just like Alice. The same power that hurt you today runs through my veins, too. You aren't supposed to love me. You're supposed to be afraid."

The last of her blood shimmers and absorbs back through her skin. I want to tell her that I do love her, but those words are still too scary to say out loud. Instead, I bend and press a kiss to the inside of her wrist. Even though I don't feel her magic humming through my bones, my own magic stirs inside me. The air swirls around us, tossing our hair and nudging us closer together.

I let the air push me forward until there's only a breath between us. "I'm not afraid of you."

Morgan watches me with those impossibly blue eyes. Looking at her is like trying to see to the bottom of the ocean, fathomless and unknowable.

And then she's kissing me, moving so fast I don't register her touch until my back is pressed against the door and her lips are tight against mine. The runes shimmer around us like a bloody halo, but when my mind catches up to what's happening, I pull her close and feel along the wall for the light, casting us in darkness.

Morgan reaches for my shirt, slipping her hand beneath the hem. Her fingers roam over my skin, unsure where to rest or unable to choose her favorite place. There's a touch at my waist, pulling me closer. A brush of her fingers along my spine. Then her hands in my hair and her teeth grazing my bottom lip. The sensation draws a desperate, wanting sound from my throat, but before I have a second to feel embarrassed, Morgan tugs me away from the wall and guides me across her room.

The backs of my knees hit the bed, and I fall onto her mattress. I barely have time to miss the heat of her before she's lowering herself after me, leaving a trail of kisses down my neck that makes me squirm with desire.

I hook a finger in her belt loop and tug her hips to mine. She pauses for a second, braced above me on the bed, then leans down for another kiss. This one is quick and hard, and then she's trailing her lips across my collarbone, obliterating every other thought in my head.

She kisses me like she wants to remember every second.

She kisses like she wants to forget everything else.

Her hand slides beneath my T-shirt again and trails up my rib cage, stopping at the edge of my bra. I don't want her to stop. I want so much more. So when she pulls away and meets my gaze, a question in the rise of her brow, all I can manage is a broken *yes*.

And then we're in new territory, testing our boundaries to see where they match. Lips against skin usually hidden beneath our clothes. Legs tangled together, pressing our bodies as tight as they'll go. My magic is wild and free, currents of air slipping along exposed skin and getting tangled up between us.

When her fingers reach for the button of my jeans, I'm tempted. So tempted I almost beg her to keep going, but I don't know when her parents will wake up, and I don't want to rush. Not our first time.

"Soon," I promise, guiding her hands back up above my waist. "But not tonight."

We kiss until our lips are numb. Learn the places that tickle and the ones that make us shiver. We kiss until we forget what we're hiding from.

11

MY PHONE BUZZES WITH a series of texts, the vibrations against my thigh pulling me out of sleep. When I wake fully, I find myself wrapped in Morgan's arms, but I still feel cold.

My entire body is sore from the fight with Alice. It seems like weeks have passed since her fingers were around my throat, but it's been less than a day. Less than a day, and yet so much has changed.

I reach for my phone. It buzzes again as I unlock it.

GG: How'd it go?

GG: Did you recruit the vampire?

GG: Hannah? Come on. I'm freaking out over here. Are you okay? Are you still at the hotel?

GG: Did you and Morgan have fun??? 😜

Gemma's texts make me smile, and I glance at Morgan sleeping peacefully beside me. Last night wasn't the romantic hotel getaway that Gemma's implying, but it was the first night we fell asleep like this. I listen to Morgan's soft intake of breath as the early morning light highlights the dusting of freckles across her face. I want to reach out and trace each one, want to brush a finger along her full lips, but I don't.

Instead, I text Gemma and try to ignore the guilt and anger playing a percussive duet against my rib cage.

HW: Vampire?

Gem's response is swift.

GG: She needed a code name.

GG: And don't think I missed that little deflection. Can I assume you two had a good time in NYC?

HW: Not exactly. I'll fill you in later.

The only *good* thing about NYC was everything that happened before Alice's show. I still can't believe the Hunters drugged Sarah. They almost drugged Morgan and me, too, and despite what anyone says, it's my fault. I'm the one who posted the picture that led Riley right to us. And if I wasn't so reliant on Morgan's power to access the elements, I might have stopped them faster. I might have saved Sarah's magic.

I don't know how I'll explain any of this to Mom.

Fresh worry forces me to slip out of Morgan's bed. I need to get home before Archer or Sarah call my mom and she freaks out that I'm not back yet. I leave Morgan a note on her desk so she doesn't worry and try to use air magic to see if her parents are awake. The ease I felt last night is gone, and I give up when my hands start to shake. The frustration is almost enough to make me scream, and as soon as I'm in Alice's rental van, I text Cal and ask if he can meet up later.

I can't keep fighting this on my own. I can't fail anyone else the way I failed Sarah.

He doesn't answer right away, so I drive the rental back to my house. Mom wasn't expecting me home until this afternoon, so I cross everything that she's still asleep. With any luck, I can slip in, grab a quick shower, and head to Cal's before Mom wakes up.

The lock clicks, I ease open the door, and—

"Hannah? Is that you?"

Shit. "Hey, Mom." I try to inject cheer into my voice, but I don't think I succeed.

Mom appears from the kitchen with a cup of coffee. She's still in a matching set of red plaid pajamas with gray slippers on her feet. "You're home early," she says carefully, glancing out the front window. "Whose car is that? Where's Sarah?"

"Umm . . ." I glance out the window and wish, not for the first time, that I was good at lying. But since I'm not—and Mom has perfected her bullshit meter from working with college students—I sigh and settle on the truth. "There were a few complications."

"Complications," Mom echoes, raising an unamused brow. "Care to explain?"

I fidget under her attention, tracing the edge of the house key still clutched in my hand. "Not really."

Mom pulls out one of her signature glares, an expression I haven't seen leveled at me since before Dad died. "Sit," she says, pointing at the lumpy couch that came with this rental. "Explain."

So I do. I try to downplay everything that happened in Brooklyn, but it's hard to minimize a covenmate losing her magic and Hunters planning to create an airborne drug that will wipe out the entirety of the North American Witch Clans.

To her credit, Mom sits beside me on the couch and listens without interrupting. When I'm done, she's quiet for a long time. She sips her coffee and rubs her eyes like this is all a bad dream, and if she tries hard enough, it'll fade back into mist. "I think I missed something, Han. Why didn't Sarah or Ryan bring you home? Why do you have the van?"

I cringe. I was trying to avoid this part. "One of the Hunters is Morgan's ex. Seeing him really upset her, so I drove her home."

Mom nearly chokes on her coffee. She sets her cup on the side table and crosses her arms. Her expression should look ridiculous in her plaid pajamas and sleep-mussed hair, but is actually terrifying. "Why was Morgan there? That was never part of the plan."

"She went with me to New York?" I don't mean to, but my voice raises at the end, turning my words into a question. "We thought having another Blood Witch would help get Alice to agree. Which worked, by the way. Alice is going to help us."

"I really wish you had called me. I shouldn't have to wait hours to find out my daughter was attacked by Witch Hunters. Or that a covenmate lost her magic." Mom glances at the clock on the adjacent wall. Her brow furrows. "What time did you drop off Morgan?"

I swallow, glancing at my phone. It's still really early, but I spent hours with Morgan. "I don't know exactly."

Mom's glare sharpens. "Guess."

"Four?"

"Four?!" Mom lets out a slow breath, and I can feel how hard she's trying not to yell. How much effort it's taking to stay calm as she massages her temples. "Did you get *any* sleep last night?"

My blush answers for me, and Mom sighs. "Please tell me you at least used protection."

"Mom!"

"I know you girls can't accidentally get pregnant, but that doesn't mean you can't get an STI. Your dad and I looked it up. It's not impossible." She reaches for my hand, and a flicker of pain crosses her face at the mention of Dad. She plows forward anyway. "Intimacy changes things, Hannah, and you girls have only been dating a little over a month. Just because you and Veronica were having sex doesn't mean you should rush into it with Morgan."

"Oh my god, Mom. Stop." I'm dying. I am literally going to drop dead on this couch. "First of all, it's been closer to *two* months. And more importantly, we did not have sex!"

"Just because there's no penetration doesn't mean it isn't sex."

Is this hell? I'm pretty sure this is hell. I am not about to explain queer girl sex to my mom. Nope. Not going to happen. She's not *wrong*, there doesn't *have* to be penetration but—nope. Not even going there.

"Hannah—"

"We kept our pants on, okay? There was no sex. Zero kinds of sex!" Mom does not need to know about Morgan deftly removing my bra and her tongue sliding across my—nope. I shove the memories away. I refuse to blush again in front of her. Besides, I'm, like, ninety-nine percent sure none of that counts as sex all by itself. Thankfully, my phone chimes, Cal finally getting back to me.

CM: Meet me at my place in an hour. We can talk before we go to Archer's this afternoon.

His next text includes his address near the Salem State campus.

I'm about to text back and ask what he's talking about when a text from Archer comes through.

DA: We need to prep for Ithaca. My place. 2pm.

Mom sighs, which makes me look up from my phone. She reaches for her coffee. "I'm sorry, Han. Your dad was so much better at this stuff."

He still managed to make the whole conversation super embarrassing, but at least he never talked about penetration. I shudder just thinking the word, but I miss him. I miss him so much it makes me furious. "I have to go." I get up and head for the bathroom.

"Go? You just got home."

"Cal needs me."

"But—"

I slam the bathroom door and turn on the shower before she can finish. Until Cal figures out what's wrong with me, I'm not going to give her anything else to worry about.

And I'm certainly not going to give her ammunition to keep me away from the Council.

When I've showered and dressed, I slip out into the hall. Mom is nowhere to be found, and I'm still too embarrassed to go looking for her. "Bye, Mom!" I shout as I slip out the front door. I text Archer to let him know I'll be there at two, but ask if he can pick up Alice's van from my house before that. I didn't mind driving it when there were no other cars on the road, but I don't want to take it anywhere near campus traffic. Instead, I drive my car—Dad's car—to Cal's apartment.

"I was so worried about you. Archer told me what happened," Cal says and crushes me in a hug when he sees me. I squeeze back, but he winces and pulls away.

"Everything all right?" I ask, looking him over. He's wearing jeans and an oversized hoodie, his hair neatly parted to one side.

"Yeah." He groans when he rubs his side, which isn't terribly convincing. "My old binder wore out, so I had to get a new one. It's tighter than it should be though. I ordered a replacement in the next size up, but it's not in yet."

"Oh. Ouch." I follow Cal further into his apartment. It's small, but at least he's able to live alone. He converted his small eat-in kitchen into a makeshift Caster workshop. On a table that takes up most of the room, clear beakers with potions bubble gently over Bunsen burners.

"Have you thought about working with a Blood Witch?" I ask. "I know you said you were saving up for top surgery, but I bet a Blood Witch could significantly speed up the recovery. You wouldn't have to take as much time off work, so you wouldn't have to save up as much."

"Do you think they could do that?" Cal asks, still rubbing

his tender ribs. I hope the larger binder comes in soon. I hate seeing him hurt like this.

"I can ask Morgan if you want. She said they can't do much with broken bones and that sort of thing, but surgery recovery should be doable." I remember the way Morgan tried to help Dad when she found the blood clot in his brain, her eyes shimmering with magic as she worked. She's the only reason he regained consciousness one more time before we lost him.

I swallow down the rising emotion, pushing it firmly away. "You'd need a Blood Witch familiar with the surgery to do something that intricate, but I bet there's someone out there who could do it."

"Umm . . . yeah. I'll think about it," Cal says, but it's clear that he's uncomfortable with the idea of giving a Blood Witch access to his body. Part of me understands his hesitation—my first interaction with that kind of magic was the epitome of Not Great—but now that I've seen what Morgan can do? Now that I've felt the calm and peace her type of magic can provide, it's hard not to feel defensive of her Clan.

"Speaking of Morgan," he says, steering the conversation away from Blood Magic. "How is she holding up?"

"She's scared." I can still see the frantic runes she traced along her door, and I shudder, thinking of the trail of blood that went all the way down her forearm. "We're all scared, but it's so much more personal for her."

"I heard one of the Hunters is her ex. I can't even imagine." Cal pulls out the chair at the head of the table, careful not to knock into any of his actively simmering potions.

"What's all that?" I gesture to the multicolored liquids as I sit in the chair he pulled out for me.

"Just a few ideas I'm working on for after we destroy the drug."

When he doesn't elaborate, I press for more information. "They still haven't decided how to stop the Hunters?"

Cal fidgets with the ties on his hoodie. "They have . . ."

"But?"

He sighs and sits beside me. "I don't know. The plan doesn't feel right." Cal runs his hands through his hair, hesitating again.

I'm not sure if he's stalling because he's not supposed to tell me or if the plan makes him that uncomfortable. "Come on, Cal. What is it?" I stare at him until he finally relents.

"The plan relies on you recruiting David," Cal says, referring to the Caster Witch I'm supposed to meet next Saturday. "The Council is using the Hunters in Archer's basement to identify the rest of the Order. Dr. O'Connell can create a targeted potion that will poison Hunters but leave everyone else unharmed."

"What will the potion do?"

Cal doesn't look at me when he says, "Kill them."

His words ricochet inside me, battering my ribs. Too many emotions rise up inside, and I can't piece together what it is I'm feeling. Relief that we finally have a plan. Vindication that Dad's murderers will be punished for what they did. But there's also this sense of unease.

Does murdering the people who want us dead make us villains, too?

"From your expression, I'm guessing we had the same reaction," Cal says softly. "I'm working on some other ideas, and I'm sure I'm not the only one, but until we figure out a better option, that's the plan." He adjusts the intensity of the flame in front of him, dropping the liquid to a more gentle simmer. "Anyway, your text said you needed help with something. What's up?"

I hesitate. Part of me wants to know more about what kind of potions Cal is creating, but I came here for a purpose. I need to get my magic back under *my* control. "If I tell you, will you promise not to tell Archer or Elder Keating?"

Cal raises a brow at me. "Should I be worried?"

"No?" My response is more question than statement, so I try again. "Just please promise." Cal reluctantly agrees, and I force myself to admit what only Morgan and Alice know. "There's something . . . *off* . . . about my magic."

Without hesitation, Cal reaches for the leather-bound journal sitting on the table beside him. "Off how?" He flips through the book, the pages full of geometric symbols I don't recognize. "Can you reach the elements at all?"

I explain everything. How it feels like there's this invisible door locking me away from my magic, and when I manage to shove that door open, it hurts too much to actually manipulate the elements. "It's better when Morgan's around, especially if she's using her magic. She makes it feel the same as it did before he drugged me."

"That's odd," Cal muses, finally settling on a page near the middle of the thick book. He glances up at me. "I've never heard of Blood Magic doing that."

I'm not surprised Cal hasn't heard of it. I doubt our Clans have stopped hating each other long enough to try such a thing. I'm sure Morgan and I aren't the first cross-Clan relationship, but we might be the first where one lost her magic to Witch Hunters.

"Is that a grimoire?" I ask as Cal runs a finger over the page of symbols.

"Basically. It's a record of all the potions that have been

passed down to me, plus all the trial and error it took to create some of my own." There's a note of pride in his voice, and I wonder how many new spells he's perfected that never existed before. "This page has the instructions I need to test your magic and see what's going on."

"I've never seen anything like it." Which is weird. I remember the notebook Lexie had in Manhattan. It was filled with symbols, too, but it looked nothing like this. Hers were all swirls and looping circles where Cal's is harsh lines and math-like symbols.

Cal stands and pulls various ingredients from the cupboards. "That's not surprising. Casters tend to keep their spells pretty private. And the different teaching lineages all use a unique style of notation."

"Teaching lineages?"

"Yeah." He sets up four empty beakers on the table, carefully moving the other potions out of the way. "We don't have covens the way Elementals do. We don't celebrate the turn of the seasons together or form extended familial bonds. What we have is more like . . . I guess you could call it a study group. Over time, a number of different systems developed to keep track of our potions without Regs being able to read them. Can you roll up your sleeve?"

I do as he asks, and Cal puts on medical gloves. I have to look away when he preps my arm and slides a needle into the vein to take a sample of blood. "Do you and Archer use the same system?"

"No. The style tends to be fairly regional. He's from Texas originally, so his notes look nothing like mine." Cal pulls the needle from my arm and sets the vial of blood on the table while he mixes together a variety of different potions, glancing only occasionally at his notes.

"Are his all swirly?" I ask, mesmerized as I watch him work.

Cal stirs the far left potion clockwise three times and holds a hand over the open top, whispering something under his breath before turning to look at me. "No. He uses an alphanumeric code." He turns and glances over at me. "There is a style that's more looping though. How'd you know?"

"Hmm?" It takes me a second to realize what I've done. I consider telling Cal about Lexie and the other Manhattan Casters, but bringing them up risks exposing the whole inter-Clan violence thing. "It was just a guess. Yours is like anti-swirly, so I figured there'd be one that was."

I'm not sure Cal believes the rambling lie, but he's so focused on his potions that he doesn't press. I watch him work, captivated but unable to comprehend the intricacies of what he's doing. He weighs and measures herbs and whispers incantations under his breath. It reminds me of my Dad, the way he'd hum as he made pancakes from scratch, consulting his recipe every few steps.

By the time Cal sprinkles a mixture of herbs into the final potion, my throat is tight with emotion. I swallow it down while Cal whispers an incantation over the whole thing and picks up the vial of my blood. "Ready to figure out what's going on?"

A fresh flood of nerves washes through me. I nod and watch with morbid fascination as Cal pours my blood into each of the four potions. Some of them hiss and others spark with electricity, and I have zero idea what any of it means. Cal watches the process, the crease in his brow deepening. After a few minutes, each of the potions has settled and gone completely translucent, only the barest hint of their original color remaining.

"What does that mean?"

Cal shakes his head and bites the edge of his thumb. "Except for when Morgan's around, does your magic ever work on its own?"

"Not that I've noticed." I rub my arms as a chill sweeps over me. "It hurts so much each time that I've stopped trying."

Cal picks up one of the vials and swirls it round and round. This one was red to begin with, and it retained most of its color after the blood was added. "There's nothing here, Hannah. There's nothing wrong with your magic."

"What are you talking about? Of course there is." I stand quickly, my chair screeching as it slides against the floor. "Benton drugged me. He locked up my power. It hasn't been the same since."

"Veronica's magic came back." There's no judgment in Cal's tone, but I feel shame clawing into my heart anyway, infecting everything inside me. "There's no sign of the drug in your system. Your blood reacted to the four elements exactly as it should. When Archer did this with Sarah's blood, it didn't do *anything*. Whatever is causing your pain, it's not the drug. It has to be something else."

"What are you saying? That it's in my head? That it's all made up?" I'm shouting, but Cal remains infuriatingly calm.

"Your Clan has an emotional magic. Your mental state has a very real effect on that." He reaches for me, but I flinch away from his touch.

"I'm *fine*."

"I think that's the problem." Cal reaches for me again and holds tight to my hand. "You've been through an immense trauma, Hannah. You aren't fine. It takes time to heal from something like that."

"But I'm okay," I argue, even as the tears on my face make a liar out of me. Even as my voice breaks into a million pieces. "I swear."

"You have to give yourself space to grieve." Cal pulls me close, and tears spill down my cheeks. My chest tightens until it's hard to breathe. "If you don't let yourself feel all the terrible, scary, awful pieces of grief, your magic may never be yours again."

12

CAL GETS PIZZA DELIVERED to his apartment, and over lunch, he tries to convince me to test his theory.

"Just let in a little emotion and see if you can manipulate the air." Cal wipes a bit of pizza sauce from his finger. "I'll be right here the whole time. It's okay to be vulnerable."

I set my plate on the coffee table. We're sitting in the living room since the kitchen is more magical workshop than a place to eat. "I don't think I can let in a *little* grief, Cal. That isn't a thing."

"Humor me."

"Fine." I settle back into the couch and close my eyes. Cautiously, I approach the memories I've been trying for weeks to keep hidden. Dad breezing through the living room to press a kiss to Mom's cheek and ruffle my hair before he left for work. The strength of his magic at coven gatherings, solid and steady beside me.

I'm about to tell Cal this isn't going to work. That I'm *fine*, and this isn't the reason my magic is so painful, but then I remember prom.

Veronica came over to pick me up, and Dad acted like he was some undercover paparazzi guy. He kept snapping pictures at weird angles and shoving his phone around corners to take photos. He even jumped over the back of the couch to get a shot of V tying a corsage around my wrist.

The memory makes me laugh, and in my moment of distraction, that one second of letting my guard down, the grief swoops in and other memories suck the air from my lungs.

Dad in the hospital.

A young doctor holding his wedding ring and telling us he's gone.

I want to scream, but I can't breathe, can't think, can't understand how my heart is still beating.

"No." I shove away from the couch and stumble across the room, burying my face in my hands. I press hard against my closed eyes to force the tears away. All the pieces of control I'd built in the first weeks after Dad's death crumble away. I have to build them back up, have to bury the memories. Hide the hurt.

I'm fine. I'm fine. I'm fine.

"Hannah?" Cal's voice is cautious behind me. His hand a tentative presence on my back. "Are you okay?"

Deep breaths. Put up the walls. Lock the door.

I turn and force a smile. "I'm fine. It's like I told you. It doesn't work." I grab my plate from the coffee table and deposit it in the kitchen sink. "We should get to Archer's place. There's work to do."

Cal gives me a strange look, but he doesn't contradict me. We're on the road a few minutes later, driving separately to Archer's house. I keep turning Cal's theory around in my head. If he's right, how would that explain why my magic works better when Morgan's around?

By the time we get to Archer's, I haven't come up with an answer. I pull in after Cal and follow him inside, where we hear voices coming from the eat-in kitchen.

"There's no guarantee this girl will invite me to perform

where she works." It takes a second to recognize Alice's voice. She's almost timid, like she's afraid.

"All we ask is that you try," Archer says, and he sounds so normal I can picture him sitting there with one of the little notebooks he keeps in his suit jacket. "Our intel says Eisha is a devoted fan. If you ask, there's a good chance she'll say yes."

Cal and I step into the room before Alice responds. She glances up, and a hard edge flashes across her expression when she sees me. She doesn't say anything, but her face is full of insults. So that bodes really well for the rest of my afternoon.

"I didn't expect to see Alice," I say cautiously as I cross the room and take the spot opposite her. Cal sits to my left.

"Oh, good. You're here." Archer ignores Alice's intense glower and flips through the open folder on the table before him. The same photo of Eisha and the printed social media postings I saw last week are now in front of Alice. "This is your next recruit. David O'Connell."

"He's the Caster in Ithaca, right?" I pull the glossy picture Archer slides my way closer. The image shows a young white man with dark hair. It's a formal headshot, accompanied by a small-print bio. He looks innocuous enough, but according to Cal, this man is also the key to creating a targeted potion that can kill the Hunters.

Archer nods. "He's a postdoc at Cornell University, specializing in biochemical research. To the Reg world, Dr. O'Connell's research studies the long-term effects of pharmaceuticals on the body. His real area of interest is less orthodox."

I nod, scanning through David's bio. "What is he really studying?"

The detective goes silent for a moment, and when I look up, he and Cal are sharing a look.

"What is it?" I prompt.

Detective Archer clears his throat. "David has been working for years to uncover the scientific origin of Clan magic."

Alice looks up from her pages on Eisha. "Seriously?" When Archer nods, she scowls. "What the Sister Goddesses gifted us isn't science. It isn't something you can put under a microscope."

Surprisingly, I actually agree with her. Science could never explain what we do. So much of it goes against the laws of physics, and that's because it's bigger than science. It's *magic*.

But if that's the case, how can the Hunters destroy it with a drug?

Before the doubts have time to wriggle any deeper into my head, Archer continues. "When you first told me about the drug, I reached out to Elder Keating. She contacted Dr. O'Connell and asked him to work with us to find an antidote. Or, at the very least, create a vaccine to protect those not yet infected."

He doesn't mention their plans to use David to wipe out the Hunters, but I don't say anything. I don't want Cal to get in trouble for telling me. "Since she asked me to recruit him, I'm guessing that didn't go over well?"

Archer nods, and he and Cal share another strange look.

"What am I missing? Why won't he help us?"

The detective rubs the back of his neck and doesn't meet my gaze. "The Council denied his previous requests for funding. The Elders don't approve of his research, which is what sent David to Cornell in the first place. He needed resources we wouldn't give him."

I'm more surprised David bothered to ask than I am that the Council denied the request. "I assume the Council has already offered to fund his research if he agrees to help?"

"We have," Archer confirms, "but David hasn't changed his

position. He's been a bit of a sore spot for Elder Keating. So far, he's refused to share any of his research with us."

"And you think the Ice Princess can convince him?" Alice scoffs. "Good luck with that."

I cross my arms. *So much for her timid tone around Archer.* "It worked on you."

"Don't flatter yourself. The threat of an airborne drug worked on me." She examines her manicure. "I wasn't about to let *you* be the only thing keeping me alive."

Goddess, she's the worst. I want to ignore her, but her words stick in my head. "What do you mean *keeping you alive?* As far as we know, the Hunters won't kill the witches they think they've cured." *At least ones who don't fight back*, I silently correct, thinking of the agents we lost during the last raid.

Alice levels a look at me like I'm the least intelligent person she's ever met. "Our magic affects *everything* in our bodies. There's no guarantee my Clan would even survive the drug." She glances nervously at Archer. "It's why the Council binds Blood Witches who break the law. They don't strip our power." Her gaze flicks back to me. "Unless they *want* us dead."

"The Elders don't want any of their witches dead," Archer says, unamused yet unconcerned by her claim.

A sick feeling works up my throat. The Hunters found Morgan in Brooklyn because of me. They shot their drug at her, and she could have *died*. All because of me. Panic swirls inside, making my hands tremble. I hide them in my lap.

"Which reminds me," Alice says, shuffling Eisha's social media posts into a neat pile. "How exactly do you plan to protect me while I'm performing for a bunch of murderers?"

"I've got you covered on that, actually," Cal says. "I'm working on a potion that'll make the fabric of your outfit impervious to needles, so the drugged darts should bounce right off."

Alice raises an eyebrow. "Should?"

"It's a delicate balance. I still have to keep the fabric soft enough that it doesn't limit your movement."

"Your best defense, though," Archer cuts in, "is to keep the Hunters from finding out you're anything more than an illusionist." He pauses and looks at each of us in turn. "If something goes wrong, I want you to leave. Don't wait for us. Don't even look for us. You get out."

"No problem," Alice says. She's trying to be flippant, but there's a tremor of fear in her voice.

"Will we all have needle-resistant clothes?" The raid is only fifteen days away, and I'm desperate for details. "What's the plan once we're inside?"

Archer looks like he's going to protest, but Cal cuts in. "You might as well tell her. At least the big picture."

The detective sighs. "Fine. Alice will sneak the two of us inside. Cal will remain in a van just off-property to keep an eye on the surveillance footage. Once we find the lab, I'll plug Cal into their computer system while you destroy the drug."

"And how exactly am I supposed to do that?"

"We're still working on that part," Archer says cryptically. "I'll have potions with me in the event we're discovered, but that's where your Elemental magic will shine. You'll have a lot more offensive flexibility than me."

I shoot a worried look at Cal. "It . . . uh . . . it might be a good idea to have a second Elemental, if that's your plan. I'm not eighteen, so there's still a lot I can't do." Which is true, technically, but my power is so much more limited than Archer knows.

I *have* to figure out how to access my magic before then.

"I'll see who's available." Archer pulls a little notebook from the back pocket of his jeans, and the familiarity of it makes me smile. "Now we need to focus on Ithaca. Let's go over everything again."

We spend the next hour fine-tuning the plan to recruit Dr. David O'Connell.

Step one: call David and offer to be a test subject for his research.

Step two: plead my case like I did with Alice and guilt-trip the Caster if necessary.

Step three: should step two fail, distract David so Cal can look through his research for the passages relevant to making a vaccine.

And likely the poison, too, I think, but Archer never brings it up. The real gamble is which magical code David uses. He moved around a lot as a kid, so the Council isn't sure if Cal will be able to read it.

As we're getting ready to wrap up, a door opens and slams shut somewhere in the house.

"Is someone here?"

Images of escaped Hunters fill my mind, but Elder Keating steps into the kitchen before Archer can explain. I relax. A little. The Elder looks more disheveled than I've ever seen her, a few flyaway hairs sticking to her face and neck. She opens the fridge and grabs a bottle of water, downing half before she turns to face us.

There's a vulnerability to the moment that makes her seem more real. Like she actually has a past and a life like everyone else and didn't burst into existence as an Elder.

"I'm sorry," she says at last. "I've had my fill of adolescent

Witch Hunters. Ryan, would you mind bringing down their food? They're bound to start yelling about it any minute, and I don't particularly want to listen to them carry on."

"Did they give you anything?" Archer stands and motions for Cal to help him. They grab some premade sandwiches from the fridge and more of the water.

"They're basically children. They don't know nearly as much as I'd like." She watches her agents leave, then sits in Archer's vacant chair. "The young woman, Paige, reminds me of my brother's wife. Well, ex-wife. She's exhausting."

"You have a brother?" I ask, before I think better of it. She may be an Elder, but she must have had a childhood like everyone else.

"I did," she says wistfully. "He was actually the one who encouraged me to join the Council. Even among witches, the seventies weren't an easy time for a woman to be in a position of power, especially a woman in her early twenties. I was one of the first female agents on the Council, but my brother never had any doubt about my ability to succeed. He always believed I'd become an Elder one day."

"He sounds great." I fuss with the printout of David O'Connell's bio. "What happened to him?"

"Eli fell in love."

I wait for Keating to elaborate, but she doesn't. "I don't understand."

"Against my advice, my brother married a Reg woman. Like I'd warned him, she eventually came to believe he was hiding something from her and decided Eli was being unfaithful." Keating grimaces. "She wasn't wrong to suspect. He was hiding his magic from her, which is why we discourage witches from dating outside the Clans, but he was stubborn and thought their love was big enough to take the risk."

"Did he tell her the truth?" I think of Gemma, who loves me like a sister and holds the secret of my magic. Of Archer, who I caught blushing as he texted Lauren before my trip to Brooklyn.

Keating nods. "He did. His wife tried to have him committed until he showed her what his potions could do. She accused him of using magic to control her and ran off. The Council had to get involved. *I* had to get involved."

The Elder sighs, and the age she normally hides so well shows through in her exhaustion at the distant memory, heightened by a girl who reminds her of this past. "Eli didn't want me to erase her memories, and he fought back. I was only a junior agent then, and ultimately the Elders decided his fate."

"What did they do?" I'm afraid to know the answer, but I feel compelled to ask.

"They did what they had to. The Elders wiped the woman's memories and stripped Eli of his magic. My brother was stubborn to a fault, and he fought their power. He fought until it killed him." Keating shakes her head. "We had just beaten the last of the Hunters. It was supposed to be a safer time."

"I'm sorry." The words feel wholly inadequate. So many witches have lost so much. Elder Keating lost her brother. I lost Dad. Even Tori, the blue-haired Caster Witch who wanted to bind Alice's powers, lost her parents to the feud with Alice's family. When will it be enough? When will it end?

"It was a long time ago." The Elder offers a smile. Her phone rings, and she checks the caller ID. "Excuse me."

The Elder steps out of the kitchen, and Alice drapes one

arm over the back of her chair. "I don't get what she sees in you."

"Do we have to do this right now?" I rub my temples, already irritated with her.

Alice continues like I haven't spoken. "Maybe it's your self-righteous attitude. It's irritating as hell, but I guess Elders like that sort of thing." She pauses, and though I'm expecting her to gear up for bigger insults, instead, all the earlier venom leaks out of her. "But I get what it's like, losing people. You two don't have the monopoly on that, you know."

I sit silent in my chair, watching as the Alice I know fades away, revealing the real girl underneath all the bravado.

"When I was a little younger than you," she starts, fussing with the plain ring on her middle finger, "I lost both my parents." She blinks fast and stares at the ceiling like she's trying to prevent tears. "I know you think I'm a monster, but I did what I had to do to survive."

Her admission softens me, and a thread of kinship stretches between us. "Why are you telling me this?"

She shifts uncomfortably in her seat. "I got Morgan's number from Archer, but she won't return my texts. She's the only Blood Witch I've met since I lost my family. Just . . . tell her I'm sorry about what happened at the hotel, okay?"

There's something so desperate about the way Alice is looking at me that I can't help but nod. "Sure. Of course."

Down the hall, the Elder's voice rises in volume. "How could this happen?" Keating's words cut through the kitchen, and both Alice and I look toward the hallway. "How many?" There's another pause, and then Keating sighs. "Thank you for letting me know."

The clock on the wall ticks down the seconds, but eventually the Elder returns to the kitchen. Her eyes are red, and her hair is even more disheveled than before.

"Is everything okay?" It's a pointless question—something is obviously wrong—but I don't know how else to ask.

Tears shimmer unshed in the Elder's eyes. "Six of my Casters just lost their magic."

13

FEAR SETTLES OVER ARCHER'S kitchen.

"Is it too late?" Alice finds her voice first. "Is the drug airborne?"

Keating shakes her head and calls for Archer and Cal. When they arrive, she shares the update from her call. The Chicago Casters thought their water filtration system was too sophisticated to be compromised, so they were careless.

Careless, and now they've lost all connection to their power. All their potions are useless mixes of water and herbs.

I want to *do something*, to fight back, but Keating sends Alice to her hotel and me back home with instructions to prepare for the missions she's already given us. Ithaca, to recruit the Caster who may be able to give witches their magic back. Then the raid, to destroy the drug and prevent anyone else from losing their goddess-given power. Keating makes us promise to leave the rest to her.

Reluctantly, I agree.

By the time I get home, the weekend's events finally catch up to me. I'm *exhausted*. Bone weary in a way I haven't felt in ages. Everything weighs heavy on me—the fight with Alice, Riley's attack, Sarah losing her magic because of me, even the mortifying conversation with my mom. It's hard to believe it all happened over a single weekend, and each piece settles on my shoulders like a brick, compressing my spine until it's hard to walk.

And to top it all off, thanks to Cal's suggestion that I dig up my most painful emotions in an attempt to access my magic, the carefully crafted dam that kept me from drowning is now full of cracks.

I crawl into bed, desperate for sleep despite the fact that it's only seven. Unfortunately, sleep is more elusive than my magic. After staring uselessly at the ceiling for twenty minutes, I pull out my phone and pause, unsure who to call. The person I most want to talk to is Morgan, but with Riley in Salem, this weekend was harder for her than it was for me. I don't want to make things worse.

Since Gemma knows about the Clans, she's actually a viable option, but even though she *knows*, that doesn't mean she gets the danger we're facing. She won't understand how horrific it is to have your magic stripped away, how scary it is to know that people are out there, plotting how to destroy you.

So that leaves . . .

"Hey." Veronica answers on the second ring, and her voice is pitched with worry. "Is everything okay?"

"No." I tell her everything. About Riley coming into the shop. The barrier spell around the town and our water supply in Beverly. She's the only person I tell about what *really* happened when Alice saw me again for the first time, and she's the only one who understands why I feel so guilty about what happened to Sarah.

"It's awful, V. I thought capturing the three Hunters would give us an advantage, but Archer says they don't know anything useful." Riley, Wes, and Paige are all under twenty, and they're at the very bottom of the Hunters' chain of command. Archer said all they do is follow orders, but no one tells them the big picture. "Having them locked up didn't even protect the Casters in Chicago. If they didn't even know about a mission happening the same weekend they were captured, what good is having them?"

My covenmate-turned-girlfriend-turned-terrible-ex-turned-*friend* goes silent on the other line.

"Veronica?"

"Sorry," she says, but she sounds distracted now, like her thoughts have wandered elsewhere. She pauses for a long time, and I'm about to ask if she's still there when she speaks again. "Wasn't Lexie from Chicago? Do you think she knows the Casters who lost their magic?"

A flush of jealousy burns my skin, but I push down the old reflex. I hated the way Veronica fawned over the older witches in Manhattan, but that shouldn't matter now. Veronica and I have returned to our pre-dating friendship. Mostly. Who she worries about is none of my business. Besides, there's no reason to be jealous that she remembers where someone is from.

Yet that doesn't stop this weird feeling in my gut.

"Maybe I should call her again," Veronica muses. "See if she's okay."

"Wait." The weird feeling inside grows hot and angry. "What do you mean *again*?"

"Don't be mad, Han—"

"Saying that basically guarantees it's supposed to make me mad," I counter.

My ex sighs. "It's not a big deal. After everything that—" She loses her voice and has to clear her throat before she can start again. "After *everything*, I called the Casters to warn them about the Hunters. Lexie was the only one who answered."

"I'm sorry," I snap, rolling out of bed to pace the small bedroom. "After everything *they* did to us, you still have their phone numbers?!"

"They deserve to know the Hunters are back."

"Pretty sure we have a Council for that, Veronica. Or did you forget that like you forgot the rest of us when you ran away to college?"

"I haven't forgotten *anything*, Hannah." Her voice is low now, a dangerous edge to her words. "Just because I don't want to relive my trauma every day doesn't mean I don't remember. It doesn't mean my life is fucking perfect."

Her words hang between us, and the hurt in her voice deflates the righteous anger that was building inside me. We were friends a lot longer than we were girlfriends *or* exes, but it's so easy to default to the bitter, hurt feelings that consumed me after our breakup. Those emotions are more recent. Still a little raw. I perch on the edge of my bed. "You're right. I'm sorry. I just—"

"I know," she says, softening, too. "And I swear, I was just warning them to be careful. I wasn't asking to hang out or anything." She pauses, and I picture her lying back on her bed in her dorm, staring out at the moon. "You know I'm sorry for dragging you into that whole mess. And now you're stuck dealing with Alice on top of everything else."

"My life is absurd. It belongs in some modern art museum."

Veronica laughs. "Can you imagine if you had to recruit Coral or Tori to help, too?"

"Alice might actually kill me."

For the next hour, I let Veronica distract me with stories about her and Savannah. They officially started dating after V got out of the hospital over the summer, and they managed to get placed as roommates at school.

Veronica tells me about late-night walks under the stars, failed attempts to turn the dining hall into a romantic date location, and a couple of frantic all-nighters to study for tests with her new friends.

"Savannah's even planning to come out to her parents when we're home for fall break," she adds, her voice hushed. "She's been dropping little hints, and so far, they haven't said anything weird."

"That's awesome, V," I say, even as a bubble of jealousy flares up again. But then she asks about Morgan, and all that goes away. I tell her that Mom still lives by the *No Closed Doors* rule, which makes her laugh. "You should have heard the awkward Safe Sex Talk that Mom tried to give me this morning. It was *mortifying*. I'm going to have to avoid her until I leave for Ithaca on Saturday."

Veronica groans sympathetically. "You'll have to tell me all about it when you visit." But she doesn't ask why I'm coming. She doesn't want to know about my mission or *anything* about the Hunters or the Council. I want to tell her that not knowing won't protect her, but our renewed friendship is still fragile, so I don't press.

That night, Benton plagues my nightmares. Waking doesn't do me any good, either. He stalks me through the halls at school, a constant specter shadowing me through each of my classes. He leans against my locker between periods, a sketchbook clutched in one hand to ask my opinion on a logo he's designing for a friend's band. He's there in the lunch line, complaining about the soggy pizza and room-temperature ranch.

He's a thousand tiny memories built over a year of friendship. I'm already so on edge about Sarah and Alice and *everything* that each time I hear his voice, each time I remember his laugh and his smile and the nudge of his elbow at the art table, I lose a little more of myself.

My week becomes a cycle of nightmares and hallway ghosts and a half-hearted attempt to retain some semblance of normalcy. I keep my promise to explain my NYC trip to Gemma. Archer schedules meetings to practice my recruitment speech for David. We go over the blueprints for Hall Pharmaceuticals. Every day, I squeeze in as much homework as I can, but I'm slipping further and further behind.

And always there's this pain in my chest for the people we've lost. Alice's parents. Elder Keating's brother. Council agents.

My dad.

So when Mom invites me to go with her to visit Dad's grave on Friday night, I agree. There isn't much more I can do at this point to prepare for tomorrow's trip, and maybe—just maybe—visiting Dad will help with whatever is blocking my magic.

Mom drives us, and with each mile, I get more and more anxious. I haven't visited the cemetery since the burial, and by the time gravel crunches under the wheels of the car, everything inside screams at me to turn around, to beg Mom to drive away, but I can't. I don't say anything as we continue forward.

Though I haven't been here since the burial, Mom comes at least once a week. She always invites me, and I always say no. Tears threaten when I spot the crooked, gnarled tree and Mom pulls over. We sit silently in the car, Mom waiting for me to make the first move. The air is warm, her power filling the car with gentle reassurances that I'm not alone.

My fingers tremble as I reach for the handle and open my door. I step out into the mid-September sun, and the silence is suffocating. There's this awful sense of finality, and it's almost enough to send me running. Mom climbs out after me, and we both shut our doors, twin *thunks* in the silence.

Earth shifts beneath my feet, but the energy here is no different than anywhere else in Salem. The cemetery may be a place of rest for bodily remains, but there's nothing left of the energy of their lives. No spark. No pulse of power in the earth.

Not that I could feel it now anyway. Not with my magic still too painful to access.

But . . . I wish there was *something* that lingered beyond our deaths, some hint that my dad was still here, watching over me. Instead, the Middle Sister claims our souls and carries us to wherever the Mother Goddess has banished her. We're reunited with our creator in death, but she leaves nothing for those who were left behind.

Maybe that's why the Mother Goddess doesn't interfere with the happenings of earth. She's happy to let her three daughters collect us like rare dolls. I wonder, suddenly, what happens to witches whose powers have been stripped. Can the Sister Goddesses still find their souls in death?

A shudder works through me as I approach Dad's grave. I take some small comfort in knowing he was a fully powered Elemental when we lost him. At least he's safe in the next life. Even if there's a chance the rest of us won't be able to join him.

Mom and I stop before his grave, and she presses the back of her forefinger under her eyes. "What do we do now?" I ask, voice hushed.

"Sometimes I talk to him." She lays a hand on the recently installed granite headstone. "I tell him how much I miss him and how worried I am about you." Mom glances over her shoulder at me, but there isn't judgment in her tone. She's sharing a truth, even if it hurts us both.

Cautiously, I step forward and turn to sit beside the gravestone, leaning against the rough sides like I used to lean against him. I try to remember the weight of his arm slung over my shoulders or the press of a kiss to the top of my head, but it doesn't come. I want to remember his laugh and his cologne and his easy smile, but everything feels so fuzzy and wrong, like I'll never get it just right.

Tears well up, and I press down on the feelings, letting anger rise in their place. I let it consume me, wrapping it around my heart until it strangles everything good I've been trying to hold on to. "I hate that you're not here," I say, squeezing my eyes shut. "I hate that I miss you so fucking much all the time. I hate that I have to pretend that I don't miss you just to keep breathing."

It's not fair that Benton's memory follows me around like a ghost. That I see the boy who tried to kill me instead of the father who taught me how to embrace life. Where are the memories of Dad? Why can't I see him sitting across the table during meals? Why can't I remember exactly what *his* laugh sounded like?

"Do you think Dad would have liked Morgan?" The question comes out small and broken, and before Mom can even answer, I'm filled with all the things Dad will never see. He won't be there for college visits to make terrible Dad Jokes on the tours. He won't move me into my dorm or be there for either of my graduations. He won't give me advice on how to propose if I decide I want to get married. He'll never get to take his place as the high priest of our coven.

And so many tiny, fleeting moments that I will never even know to miss.

"Of course he would." Mom comes to sit beside me, and it's her arm over my shoulders that makes me fall apart. The tears come, fast and furious, shaking my entire body until I worry I might vibrate right through the earth.

I collapse against Mom, and the walls Cal made me pick apart crumble to dust. Everything comes rushing in. The pain over losing Dad. The fear and flashbacks of fire licking up my legs as I was bound to a pyre. The pressure that builds each day the drug still exists, the weight of recruitment on my shoulders.

The secrets I'm keeping from the only parent I have left.

"It doesn't work," I say, wiping tears from my face as shame crawls up my chest to burn my neck and cheeks. "My magic. It doesn't work."

Mom pulls back to look at me, a crease lining her forehead. "I don't understand."

"I can't reach the elements on my own." The admission burns in my chest, and I can't believe I'm doing this. But I'm so tired of secrets. I'm tired of fighting this alone. Maybe Cal is wrong. Maybe it's not about grief. Maybe this is something another Elemental can fix.

"How long?" Mom's voice is deceptively neutral.

For a tense moment, I consider lying. Pretending it's not that bad. But I need help. "Ever since Benton drugged me."

"What?" Mom stands and stares down at me, that crease in her forehead sharpening to anger. "Are you telling me that you went to New York powerless? That you agreed to help the Council without working magic?" Her voice goes shrill, and I cringe at the way it scrapes against the silence of the cemetery.

"It's not gone completely . . ." I pull my knees into my chest and glance up at her. "It just . . . hurts whenever I try to use it."

Mom's pacing now, which isn't a good sign. "So, let me get this straight. You went to Brooklyn without your magic, barely made it back from a mission that cost Sarah *her* magic, and you're just now telling me? I'm not letting you outside town limits like this."

A wave of guilt crashes into me. I haven't seen Sarah since we got back to Salem, haven't had the courage to face her, but I've heard plenty from Mom. Rachel was devastated when she learned the news, and the stress affected her pregnancy. Mom wouldn't tell me what's wrong exactly, except that she's on bed rest until her next checkup in two weeks.

But Sarah is all the more reason I have to do this. If David can restore Sarah's magic, I owe it to her to try. I force myself to my feet and face my mother. "You can't stop me from going to Ithaca. You can't disobey an Elder."

"Does Elder Keating know about your magic?" Mom reaches for her phone like she's ready to call the Elder Caster right now and tell her.

I can't let that happen. I can't be *benched* because I finally told the truth. "You can't tell her. We *need* David."

Mom pulls up her contacts. "The Council can find someone else."

"There isn't time." I reach for her phone, but a gust of air slams into me, knocking me back several steps. "Mom, you can't."

"I'm not going to lose you, too, Hannah. Even if that means locking you in the house."

Something angry and bitter and wicked boils over inside me. She can't do this to me. She's supposed to help me, not take away my only chance to destroy the Hunters. "Dad wouldn't do this," I say through hot, angry tears.

"Your father isn't here."

The words land like a bat to the chest, and it feels like my lungs are collapsing. Whoever Mom called must have answered, because now she's talking about meeting tonight. There are location options and times as they try to coordinate schedules. I sink back to the ground beside Dad's grave and glare up at my mother. "I hate you," I say, the words small but filling all the space between us anyway. Growing that space until it seems uncrossable.

Mom hangs up and stares down at me, her expression unreadable. "I'd rather have a daughter who hates me than a daughter who's dead." She rests her fingers on top of Dad's headstone and closes her eyes. "Come on. Ryan's waiting for us."

14

TREES WITH THE FIRST blush of their autumn colors speed by my window.

"You've been quiet."

"Hmm?" I tear my gaze away from the shifting landscape and look at Cal. Last night, Archer agreed to set up a meeting between Mom and Elder Keating. I rode in silence all the way to Archer's house, even as Mom promised she was only doing it because she loved me. But when Mom told them about my magic, something unexpected happened.

Elder Keating didn't care.

She actually *apologized* for assuming that my magic was un-affected by what happened to me. She apologized for making me feel pressured to keep my condition to myself. She even made sure I knew that struggling with my magic—or even losing it completely—would never invalidate my identity as an Elemental.

Even now, I feel the warmth of those words. The reassurance. I didn't know how much I needed someone to say that.

Mom quickly agreed with the Elder, but then Keating told her I was going to Ithaca anyway. My job as a recruiter doesn't require magic—though our strategy for contacting David is a little different now.

Mom and I haven't spoken since.

"Sorry," I say finally, shaking the memories away. "There's a lot on my mind." *Namely, that I'm a terrible daughter.* Mom might never forgive me for going to Ithaca, but I'm still mad at her, too. Instead of helping me, she tried to take away the one thing that's given me purpose.

"Me too, actually." Cal checks his rearview and glances over his shoulder before passing a semi. "I've been thinking about Morgan."

"My girlfriend? Why?"

"I keep wondering why being around her helps your magic." We pass the truck completely, and Cal slides back into the right lane. "I have a theory."

The excitement in his voice makes me want to smile and groan simultaneously. "Is it a better theory than the whole 'let in a *little* grief' thing?" I felt plenty of grief in the cemetery last night, but that didn't do shit for my magic. I grab my soda and twist open the top to take a drink.

Cal glances at me before refocusing on the road. "I think you love her."

His words catch me off guard, and I cough and sputter, soda bubbles burning my nose. "I'm sorry, what?" Embarrassment burns at my face and neck as I wipe drips of soda off my chin.

"Think about it," he says, ignoring my flustered choking. "Grief is closely tied to love. You miss your dad because you love him, but if you're closing off the bad feelings, you're probably blocking the good ones, too."

"And being around Morgan fixes that?" I don't say the *L* word. I don't know if that's what I feel when I'm around her. I know it's good and warm and safe. I know I want to see her every day, that I want to protect her and make her laugh. I want to know what she thinks and the secret hopes she holds in her heart.

But I thought I loved Veronica, and that fell to shit. I'm not ready to say those words again. To even *think* them too hard.

"It makes sense," Cal says, but he's interrupted by the GPS reminding him to take the next exit toward I-90. "If Morgan is a safe place to feel those emotions, it makes sense that you'd have more control over your power."

Mom's words from last night worm deeper into my head. "You're not worried that my messed-up magic puts you at risk? Morgan isn't here, and I—"

"Hannah." He says my name so solemnly my words dry up, and I turn to look fully at him. "I'm an agent with the Council. I'm here to protect *you*, not the other way around. We won't be defenseless if things go sideways."

I nod, but that doesn't make me worry any less.

Cal reaches across the console for my hand. "I know this mission is personal for you, but I volunteered for this trip. I don't want to live in a world where we've all lost our magic, either." He squeezes tight and then slows for the exit. "Speaking of which, you should call David soon and set up the meeting."

I'm thankful for the subject change, but I still groan at the suggestion. "Can't I text him? I hate the phone."

"You heard Elder Keating." We slow to pick up a ticket for the thruway and merge into traffic. "If David hears your voice, you'll be harder to brush off. A text is too easy to ignore."

"Why do you choose *now* to make sense?" I pull out my phone and scroll through my contacts until I get to the number Keating gave me. The phone rings three times, then cuts to voicemail, the robotic recording asking me to leave my name and number. "Should I leave a message?"

"Yeah, just remember—"

"Not to mention anything that would lead back to the Clans. I know, Cal. This isn't my first phone call with another—Hi!" I say when the voicemail beeps. "This is, uh, Hannah. Hannah Walsh? You probably don't know me, but I'm that girl from Salem, the one from the, uh, incident this summer."

I look to Cal, but he gestures for me to continue. "Anyway, I heard about your research from a . . . mutual acquaintance and thought I might be able to help. I'm going to be in Ithaca tonight to see a friend, but I thought we could meet up. Call me. Or text me. Texting is actually probably better." I repeat my number and hang up.

If I never have to leave another voicemail, it'll be too soon.

"Wow. That was—"

"I know. I told you I suck on the phone." I focus on the road, watching the trees zip by. The hints of orange in the leaves make me miss home. The coven is probably at Lady Ariana's house right now to celebrate the equinox. For generations, Elementals have ushered in the changing of the leaves. Lady Ariana leads the ceremony, and by the time we're finished, all the trees in the woods behind her house have leaves like sunset. An ache settles in my chest. That ceremony is another thing Dad will never do again.

Tears prickle at my eyes, and I reach desperately for a new subject. "How are classes going?"

"Actually, I turned in paperwork last week for a leave of absence." Cal rubs the back of his neck. "I couldn't justify spending the money on this semester. I've missed half my evening classes, and I'm behind in all the others."

"Shit. I'm sorry, Cal. Did you at least get your money back?"

"Not all of it, but yeah. Some." He sighs, and it's like a mask shifts and I can finally see how exhausted he is. Between school, his shifts at the Cauldron, and all the stuff for the Council, no wonder something had to give. He rubs a thumb into his left temple. "So much for my three-year plan."

"Don't be too hard on yourself. It's not like you're taking a semester off because you were partying too hard and failed all your classes."

Cal laughs. "Very true."

The rest of the way to Ithaca we chat about life and love and a Hunter-less future. Cal and his boyfriend are trying to make things work, but all the secrets Cal has to keep are causing tension. I want to warn him about what happened to Elder Keating's brother, but I don't think that's my story to tell. Maybe Cal's boyfriend will forgive the secrets. Or maybe Cal will tell him like I told Gemma. Maybe that's more common than I thought, especially since the Council doesn't outright forbid dating non-witches. It's certainly not encouraged, but it isn't against our laws.

"I wonder how Veronica's pulling it off," I muse after we've refueled the car and merged back onto the thruway. "Her girlfriend, Savannah, isn't a witch, and they see each other all the time at college now." A prickle of jealousy dances along my arms, but not because I want V back. I just wish I had the freedom to hang out with Morgan whenever I wanted.

I wish I could so easily forget the threats against us.

"What about you?" he asks. "And Veronica, I mean. I remember things were pretty tense between you when we first met."

"Things are . . . better." Out my window, the sky grows grayer as we creep closer to the central part of New York. A place Veronica says is all cows and cornfields. "We're finding our way back to being friends. I don't think it'll ever be exactly like it was, but it's mostly good now. She doesn't want any part of what's going on with the Council, though, which makes it hard to talk to her."

"So, what do you talk about?"

"Our new girlfriends?"

Cal laughs so hard he nearly misses our exit, and I pretend to be annoyed at his amusement, staring out the window as we travel the rest of the way to Ithaca.

When we finally make it to the college, Veronica is waiting for us in the parking lot nearest her dorm. Despite the warm weather, she's wearing full-length sleeves. I wonder if she's actually cold or if she's hiding the scar from where Benton shot her. Morgan's parents had offered to heal the wound, but she turned them down.

I never found out if she wanted the scar as a reminder or if she was too creeped out to let the Blood Witches help.

We pull to a stop, and I slip out of the car, standing awkwardly beside the door until Veronica rolls her eyes and hugs me tight. Her embrace doesn't spark any lingering romantic feelings, and I settle a little more comfortably into her touch.

"You two must be starving!" Veronica says when she slips into the back seat with me. "What are you in the mood for?"

Cal pulls out of the parking lot and drives around the edge of campus. "Something we can take back to the hotel?"

"You did not drive all this way to sit in a hotel room." Veronica taps at her phone. "I know this great Thai place. We'll eat there."

"But—"

"It's perfectly safe," she says, cutting Cal off. "I've been here for weeks. I don't want to hear any 'it's too dangerous' nonsense."

Cal meets my gaze in the rearview. I roll my eyes, hoping he can read the meaning there. Same old Veronica, always pushing until she gets her way. He must take my meaning, because he glances over his shoulder at her and asks, "Directions?"

To Veronica's credit, the food is *fantastic*, and we manage to have a good time. She tells us all about life as a first-year college student and her surprise at the constantly gray sky. "I don't know how I'm going to do all these hills in the winter," she says as Cal picks up the cost of our food with a card sanctioned by the Council. "They're ridiculous."

After dinner, Veronica isn't ready to go back to her dorm room. She drags us to the Ithaca Commons, a pedestrian area downtown with all sorts of locally owned shops and restaurants.

"This is cute," I admit as we walk down the blocked-off street.

Veronica glances over her shoulder at Cal, who's following at a respectable distance so we can chat in relative privacy. "So, what's the deal with this Caster they sent you to fetch?"

I bristle at her flippant tone. "I thought you didn't want anything to do with the Council's plans."

She raises an eyebrow at my bitter tone. "Excuse me for trying to have a life outside the shit that happened this summer. Not everyone wants to bathe in their trauma every day."

"That sounds disgusting."

Veronica pulls me under a small tree that's draped with twinkling lights. "I'm trying to be here for you as much as I can, but I have limits. You need them, too. No one will blame you if you take time to heal from what happened. You should be allowed to recover instead of letting the Council appropriate your pain."

"Appropriate my pain? What does that even mean? Who are you and what have you done with Veronica?"

"I'm serious, Han." She brushes her fingers against the bark of the tree beside us. "I've been going to therapy. They have a counseling center at school and . . . Well, I didn't want to make the same mistakes with Savannah."

"That's great, V."

"It's not just about the relationship stuff," she admits slowly. Carefully. "My therapist says I have PTSD from this summer. I've been too afraid to create fire since that night, not that I've told her that part."

The breeze kicks up around us, and I pull my sleeves over my hands. "I can't be near it, either. And I see him everywhere. At school. When I'm asleep. I hate it." My voice breaks, and Veronica reaches out and squeezes my hand in hers.

"You should talk to someone." She keeps her voice low and makes sure no one is close enough to overhear before she continues. "I thought it wouldn't help, since we can't mention any of the Clan stuff, but so much of what happened is public knowledge. You don't have to explain why he hurt us to get help."

"Really?" I always thought you had to explain *everything* for therapy to make a difference. That's why I turned down Mom's offer to schedule an appointment. None of the Elementals in my coven are psychologists or social workers, which meant if I wanted to see someone in person, I'd have to talk to a non-witch. And how could a counselor like that help someone like me? But if it's working for Veronica . . . maybe I should try, too.

After the raid, I add, solidifying the promise to myself. I don't have time for anything else until then.

"Really," Veronica promises. "Now come on, there's this shop with handmade gifts I want to show you." She tugs on my arm until I'm following her down the street again. V casts me a conspiratorial glance. "How awkward is it to work with her? The Blood Witch we met in the city?"

"Alice? I think it's safe to say she hates me." My phone buzzes against my leg, cutting off any further explanation. I pull it out and see David O'Connell's name on the screen. "Hello?"

"Hi, this is David. Is this Hannah?"

I turn and scan the street for Cal, waving him over. "Yes, this is her. She? I mean—" I take a deep breath. "Yes, I'm Hannah. Did you get my message? Can we meet?"

"Not tonight," he says, sounding breathless, like he just ran up a flight of stairs. "Can you come by tomorrow? I'll have every-thing set up by then."

"Tomorrow?" I ask, and Cal nods vigorously. "Yes. Yeah, I can do that. Text me the address and time. I'll be there."

15

MORNING DAWNS IN ITHACA gray and drizzling.

I shower and dress quickly, wearing the same black slacks I wore to Dad's funeral. I've paired them with a soft gray cardigan over a light blue button-down. Even though it might not make any difference, I want to give Dr. O'Connell every reason to take me seriously when I ask him to help the Council.

Outside Cal's door, I pause before knocking. Part of me wants to leave without him. He'll be safer here, and I don't want to risk him being drugged like Sarah was. But this time will be different. The Hunters don't know we're in Ithaca. I haven't posted anything online, and I've changed all my accounts to private. According to Wes and Paige, they were the only Hunters tracking my phone, and only because of Riley's obsession with Morgan.

An obsession the rest of their Order doesn't share.

Before I can sneak away, the door swings wide. Cal, who looks like my twin today in dark jeans, a navy dress shirt, and a soft cream sweater, startles when he sees me. "Oh. You're already up." He adjusts the messenger bag slung over one shoulder. "Ready to go?"

"Yeah." I fidget with my phone since there aren't any pockets in these pants. David said there's only street parking by his house—which is on one of the town's ridiculous hills—so last night we decided to walk the near mile from the hotel.

My legs are screaming by the time we make it to David's, and the place looks like it's ready to fall down. Half the shutters are missing, the paint has faded to gray where it isn't peeling off completely, and the back steps are dangerously uneven.

I climb the stairs, the wood creaking under my weight, and find the door unlatched. "Hello?" I expect the Caster Witch to be waiting for me inside with a blood-collection kit like the one Cal used a few days ago, but he's not in the small foyer. "David? Dr. O'Connell?"

"Did we get the address wrong?" Cal steps back and checks the number on the house. "One sixteen, apartment B?"

"Hang on." I double-check the address David texted me. "Yeah, this is it." I push open the door and step inside. Even without my magic, there's this feeling of *wrongness* to the air. I pause in the living room, unsure if I should venture any farther into the small space.

The apartment shows signs of rushed, late-night cleaning, but it's still hopelessly cluttered. There are stacks of papers on nearly every surface. A spilled pile of what looks like half-graded chemistry assignments sits beside a short stack of thick leather notebooks.

Cautiously, I crack open the top journal. I'm greeted by page after page of tight swirls and methodical loops. "Do you think this is his research?" I ask Cal, keeping my voice low.

Cal peers around me at the pages of coded notes. He lets out a low whistle. "Looks like it. Are all three journals full?"

I quickly flip through the two other books—careful not to make too much noise so David doesn't catch us going through his things—and find them similarly packed. "There's so much. Can you read any of it?"

"With time to properly learn this style? Probably. But right now, it's as meaningless to me as it is to you."

"Well then," I say, closing the books and making sure they're in the same order I found them, "we'd better make sure David agrees to help." I continue deeper into the apartment. "Dr. O'Connell? It's Hannah Walsh. We were supposed to meet here this morning." I'm practically shouting now, but I still get no response.

The small kitchen is clean except for a pan of burnt eggs on the stove and a plate of cold toast beside it. Smoke lingers in the air, but it's taken on a stale edge. Is David running late? Did he give up on his sad attempt at breakfast and run out for something to eat?

Deeper in the apartment, I hear the steady spray of water and trace it to a bathroom. *Thank the Middle Sister*. I cast my eyes to the sky, even though I know the Sister Goddesses don't have any say over what happens here.

"Excuse me?" I knock on the bathroom door. "I don't mean to disturb you, but—" The door swings open, and steam escapes into the hall. I avert my eyes, heat warming my face. "Shit. I'm sorry. I didn't mean to open the door."

The spray of the shower against the tub is his only answer.

"Dr. O'Connell? Are you okay?" Cal steps closer and peers into the steam-filled room. "Dr. O'Connell?" Worry pitches his tone, and when the Caster still doesn't respond, Cal turns to me. "Hannah, can you?"

"I'll try." I reach for the particles of water in the air, let their power hum in my chest. Magic prickles along my skin, and I think of Morgan. Of the way her smile lights up my insides. The heavy door that blocks my power feels more like a sheer curtain, and I reach through and grasp hold of the steam.

The air whispers danger across my skin, and the sudden fear cuts the tether to my power. Pain strikes hot and fast down my spine, and my knees buckle. I hit the floor, and something wet seeps into my pants.

"No. No, no, no." I scramble forward to David's still body and put pressure on the small hole in his chest. Blood coats my fingers. It soaks deeper into my clothes. I shut my eyes, desperate to block the horror of his vacant expression. "Please don't be dead. *Please* don't be dead."

Behind my eyes, a parade of horrors crashes through my memory. Gemma bleeding out in my car, her injury turning the water pink then red as we sank farther beneath the surface. A pool of blood on Veronica's floor. Savannah tied to a chair, telling me my ex had been shot. Dad's eyes rolling back in his head, his body beginning to shake.

My throat closes, and I press harder on David's chest. No one else is going to die. The Hunters can't take any more of us.

But then I register the cold against my skin. The stillness of his chest. The warm hand tugging hard on my arm. I force myself to look at the scientist—to *really* look. His eyes are glazed and unseeing. Behind me, Cal is trying to pull me back to my feet.

"Hannah, come on," he urges, and his panic makes me wonder how many times he's said my name. "We have to get out of here."

I nod and stumble to my feet, grabbing the wall for balance when I slip in blood. Cal's right. We can't stay here. The Hunters could come back. Who knows if they've already called the police, hoping we'll get caught inside with blood on our hands.

My stomach clenches, and when we hit the kitchen, I glance

back. There are bloody footprints following me everywhere I go. Handprints on everything I touch. I hurry to the sink, scrubbing my skin raw, scraping under my fingernails.

"Hannah, we have to go."

"I need him off me." I scrub until my skin is burning under the water. "We need to call the police. We need to tell Archer."

"We have to get out of here first." Cal shuts off the water and grabs my arm, dragging me toward the door, past the table with Dr. O'Connell's research.

I lunge for the three leather-bound books, but Cal holds me back. "What are you doing? We need those!"

"You're dripping wet and covered in blood." He says it so matter-of-fact he might as well have reminded me the sky is blue. "Let me take them."

Cal releases me and stashes the books in his messenger bag. "All right, let's go."

When I don't move, he grabs hold of my arm and tugs. I stumble forward, and the window I was standing in front of shatters. The wall behind me sprays bits of plaster into the air.

"What was that?" I cling to Cal as he guides us into a crouch. The junior agent tightens his grip. "Don't panic."

"I'm not panicking."

"You are, and I need you to focus." Cal waits until I meet his eye. Another window shatters. A pile of chemistry homework scatters into the air. "They're shooting at us, but we're going to be okay."

"In what world is this okay?" I reach for my magic, but I can't find anything. Not even pain. Another window shatters as the Hunters—I assume they're Hunters—try different angles. A tall shelf to my right breaks and falls over, spilling books across the floor. "Are those bullets? Why aren't they shooting the cure at us? Why are they trying to kill us?"

Cal reaches into his messenger bag and pulls out two vials, one with an off-white color and the other pitch-black. He pours the white potion over both of us, and it settles against my skin like sand.

"What is that? What did you do?"

"I told you I would protect you." He stoppers the white potion and puts it back in his bag. "Light will refract around us. It isn't true invisibility, but it'll make us harder to see."

Another bullet ricochets past us.

"And that one?" I point to the black vial, my hands shaking.

"It'll help us disappear." Cal puts the messenger bag back over his shoulder and reaches out a hand. "Do not let go, no matter what. Understood?"

I grasp his outstretched hand tightly with mine and nod.

"Okay. Things are about to get really dark in here. Hold on."

"What are you—"

A series of bullets rains into the house. Cal shatters the vial. Darkness blooms, spreading like ink through the air until the entire floor is filled with impenetrable shadows and there's nothing left to see.

With only Cal's touch to guide me, we escape the dead Caster's house and disappear into the winding streets.

⊹　✳　⊹

Why do they keep killing us?

It's the only coherent thought running through my head. The only thing that isn't a loop of blood and death and pain. Between his two potions, Cal manages to get us back to the hotel unseen, and while I shower and scrub every last bit of David's blood from my skin, he calls Archer to explain what happened. I dress in fresh clothes in the steamy bathroom—hazy and opaque, just like the one where we found David—and Cal calls my mom to explain that I'm safe and that we'll return soon.

What did we ever do to them?

Why do they hate us so much?

The questions swirl like twin cyclones as I climb into the too-soft bed and pull the covers all the way to my chin. I am untethered and barely clinging to the edge of a mental cliff, but Cal is focused. He paces the room as he waits for Archer's instructions, and when the call finally comes, Cal leaves to handle things with Dr. O'Connell's body.

I don't emerge from the safety of the bed or ask to go with him. I don't know what he's going to do or how he'll stay safe if the Hunters come back. It's not that I don't care—of course I care—but I can't stomach the stress or the worry. Can't let myself entertain the thought that he'll be anything other than okay.

Maybe Veronica had the right idea. Maybe I *should* run away and let someone else deal with all of this. Let the fate of the Clans rest on someone else's shoulders. Someone like Cal and Archer and Elder Keating. Someone who knows what the fuck they're doing.

Someone who isn't me.

When Cal comes back, there's a hint of smoke on his clothes that neither of us acknowledges, but he's not alone. This time, Veronica is with him. She kicks off her shoes and climbs into bed, wrapping me in her embrace. Her touch carries the support of the entire coven, and in that moment of perfect love and perfect trust, I shatter. My defenses shred into a thousand tiny pieces, and I cry until I can't breathe.

She holds me until every last tear is wrung from my body, leaving me aching and raw and fragile. I must fall asleep, because when I open my eyes, Veronica is kneeling beside the bed.

"We have to leave." Her voice is soft but demanding, giving me no room to negotiate. "I'm coming with you. Let's go."

Veronica drags me out of bed, and I find Cal waiting by the door, all my things already packed in my suitcase. Cal hands his keys to V so we can wait in the car while he checks us out of our rooms.

And then we're on the road, heading back to Salem.

"How did this happen?" Veronica asks when we're stuck in traffic near Albany. She's sitting in the back of the car with me, and though it's not strictly safe, she's letting me lie across the seat with my head nestled on the sweater in her lap. She plays with my hair, brushing it back out of my face. The soothing gesture reminds me so much of her mother. Mrs. Matthews does the same thing whenever a coven kid is sick, and it makes me miss my own mom so much it physically hurts.

I can't believe I said such awful things to her before I left.

"I don't know." Cal sounds as exhausted as I am, energy drained from too many feelings and too much horror and just Too Much. "The Hunters shouldn't have known anything about him or our trip. Unless David said something, I have no idea."

"What if he did?" Veronica straightens in her seat, forcing me to sit up, too. "Hannah said you were recruiting him because he's working on the science behind magic. What if he helped the Hunters create the drug?"

"Why would he—"

"The funding," I say, cutting Cal off. "David was upset with the Council for not funding his research. What if he turned to the Hunters for help?"

Cal has to slam on his brakes when the car in front of us makes a sudden stop. "If that's true, why kill him now?"

"A loose end?" I guess. "Or maybe my phone call made David change his mind? He might regret creating the drug now that he knows what the Hunters are doing with it."

My suggestion hangs in the air as cars on either side inch past our window.

"I really don't want to believe a Caster did this to us . . ." Cal eases into the middle lane, which is moving a fraction faster than ours. "At least when we get back to Salem, we'll be safe."

A familiar chill ruins the calm he tried to provide. I run the countdown in my head. "For the next seven days anyway."

"Seven days?" Veronica asks. "Why only a week?"

"That's when jury selection starts." Now that I'm sitting up, I buckle my seat belt and stare out the window. "Elder Keating needs to lower the barrier for the trial. We can't risk someone seeing Hunters trapped outside the town's border."

My covenmate tenses, her knuckles turning white. "But if there's no barrier . . ."

"We'll be sitting ducks inside the courthouse. Yeah. I know." I lean my head against the window. The last bit of fight drains away. It's too much. Hunters and potential betrayals and all the Council's hopes tied up in three journals of notes that neither Cal nor Archer can read.

I watch the world creep past, inch by careful inch, and I can't conjure up the energy to *care* anymore. So what if the Hunters take my magic? It's not like it works anymore anyway.

None of it matters.

Veronica tips her head back against the headrest, and a tear spills down her cheek. "When will it stop? Will we ever be safe again?"

"We won't stop trying," Cal promises. "Alice is making progress with Eisha. We're close to breaching the company. There's still hope."

"A man is dead, Cal." I raise my head away from the cool glass, and the lack of emotion in my voice is unsettling, even to me. But I can't inject any more life into my tone. I don't have any left. "Hope isn't going to bring him back. It's not going to translate his spells, either. It's over."

"David isn't the only Caster who uses that system," Cal says.

"Are any of the others scientists?" I counter. "Being able to read his notes doesn't guarantee they'll understand what they mean."

"Elder Keating will find someone." But Cal doesn't sound so sure anymore.

Traffic picks up, and no one speaks for a long time. Not until we leave New York behind. Veronica reaches for my hand. "Don't be mad, Hannah."

I tear my gaze away from the scenery and find her biting her lip, like she's nervous. I raise an eyebrow in response.

She turns to Cal. "We might know someone who can help. Another Caster scientist. She's a bio major at NYU."

"Who?"

Veronica shoots me a worried look again, and I sigh, answering for her. "Lexie." I picture the Caster Witch in her Manhattan apartment, swirling notes like the ones in O'Connell's journals laid out before her. Hope tries to restart my heart. "Actually, I think she uses the same writing system as David, too. She might be able to translate his notes."

Cal and Veronica make plans to call Lexie as soon as they get Archer's approval. I listen to them work, but that empty feeling hollows me out again. I should warn Alice that the Casters who tried to hurt her might be coming to Salem, but I can't make myself reach for my phone. Every plan we put together falls apart. Every time we think we're making progress against the Hunters, they're still one step ahead. Even if we get Lexie to Salem, there's no guarantee she'll actually be any help.

And what good am I against all of that? An Elemental who can't even use her magic. A girl who can't even recruit other witches without someone ending up drugged or dead.

I'm only making things worse.

What if I ruin everything?

Sleep must come for me, dragging me from despair into unconsciousness, because I see Dad. He doesn't want me to give up, but what am I supposed to do? You can't fight a hurricane with half an umbrella.

I jolt awake when someone opens my door. My head jerks forward, and my body floods with adrenaline. But then I see Mom standing in the dark, bathed by the motion-sensing lights in our driveway. Every horrible thing I said to her comes rushing in.

"Mom?"

She reaches for me and pulls me out of the car. "It's okay, Han. I'm here."

"You were right." I bury my face in her neck and don't even try to fight the tears. "I can't do this. I'm done."

"Oh, sweetie," she says, holding me fiercely. "I didn't want to be right."

16

I SPEND THE REST of the night catching up on homework.

This is my life now, I guess. Discovering murdered witches
in the morning and reading Shakespeare after dinner. I dodge
Archer's calls, and on Monday morning, when Cal stops by before
school, I ask Mom to lie and tell him I already left. Cal tells her
Archer is looking into David's death and asks if I'll call him.

From my hiding spot around the corner, guilt worms into my
chest, but I can't call. I won't.

At school, the halls are hazy with wisps of memories. I walk
through Benton's form twice before homeroom, but I don't acknowledge him. He isn't part of my life anymore. I'm embracing
my future as a Reg. It's only a matter of time before the drug is
airborne and everything I've spent my entire life working toward
won't matter.

I'll never learn to create fire with nothing more than my
own magic.

I'll never inherit my grandmother's coven.

Even though part of me remembers what Elder Keating
said—that I'll always be an Elemental, no matter what happens
to my magic—it's hard to believe her right now.

On Wednesday morning, Morgan meets me by my locker
before homeroom with a mischievous smile on her face. I've spent

the last two days distracting her with kisses whenever she asks how I'm feeling, and I spent an hour last night sketching her as she practiced for her dance solo.

She glances over her shoulder to make sure no one is in the hall before she plants a kiss on my cheek. "So . . . my dad wanted me to invite you over for dinner."

I raise an eyebrow at her. "Why is your dad inviting me? Isn't that your job?"

"Well, I *was* trying to spare you from my parents' interrogation, but now they've got this whole *Meet the Girlfriend* dinner planned." She sighs dramatically and leans her head on my shoulder. "Any chance you're up for an awkward night meeting my family?"

"Honestly? That sounds perfect."

The bell rings, and Morgan hugs me tight. "Thank you, thank you, thank you!" She slips away to her first class, leaving me a smiling mess in her wake.

But when we get to Morgan's house after school, she shuffles me off to her bedroom, calling to her parents that we'll see them when dinner is ready.

"So, are you embarrassed of me or them?" I ask when the door closes behind us.

My girlfriend freezes halfway across the room. She glances back at me, a mixture of shock and embarrassment on her face. "What? No, not you. Never you. My mom and dad are just . . . super dorky. I'm trying to spare you their weird parent humor. Especially Dad's. That's the one downside to having a bisexual dad. You get Dad Jokes *and* bi puns."

I laugh, and it might be the first real one since Ithaca. "Do I look like someone who minds?" I gesture to my T-shirt and the

LET ME BE PERFECTLY QUEER slogan across the front. I spin to show her the back, which reads I'M SUPER GAY.

"Well, when you put it that way." Morgan reaches for my hands and draws me closer. "Maybe I wanted an excuse to make out with you."

"Now *that* is a plan I can get behind."

She's still in her jeans and a flowy sleeveless shirt from school, and her exposed skin is warm against mine when I trail my fingers up her arms. My lips meet hers, a soft, barely there kiss. "But all of this stays on with your parents home." I gesture to our clothes.

Morgan blushes and bites her lip. "Deal."

It's a delicate dance, this thing between us. We collapse into her bed together, and with her legs interlocked with mine and her lips warm against my neck it's hard not to get carried away. I want to lose myself in her. I want to replace all the bad memories with new imprints of joy on my skin. But when we're both breathless and desperate to do things we know we shouldn't without more privacy, we force ourselves to slow down. And when we start to get carried away again, we stop.

I grab the sketchpad from my bag and find a new spot on her bed, my back against the wall. Morgan lounges with her legs draped over mine as she reads another book. This one has armored hands grasping a glowing pink sword on the cover. I flip to a fresh page and sketch her as she reads, trying to capture the focused, earnest attention she gives the characters inside.

"Have you thought about homecoming on Friday?" Morgan asks, flipping to the next page in her book.

"What about it?" I sketch the basic shape of her face and focus in on her eyes.

Morgan lays her book down on her stomach. "Should we go?"

"Should we go to the aggressively hetero school dance when the world is falling down around us?" I ask, lowering my graphite pencil.

"Umm, yeah?"

I bounce the unsharpened end of the pencil against her knee. "If you want to go, then yes. We definitely should."

She grins and dives back into her book. Homecoming is the last thing I want to do this week, but if it'll make her happy, I can put on a smile and dance. I go back to my drawing, and once I've finished her expression, I move down to sketch the lines of her shoulders and forearms. I'm working on her delicate fingers when there's a knock on the door.

"You girls decent?" her dad asks. The ten-day-old runes still mark the frame, and I have to suppress a shudder remembering Morgan's panic and fear as she drew them in her own blood. Mr. Hughes waits for Morgan to call out an annoyed *yes* before he comes in.

Her dad has the same coloring as her, vivid red hair and a neatly trimmed red beard. He's wearing jeans and a blue-and-white-checkered dress shirt, the sleeves rolled up to his elbows. "Excuse me for not wanting to break up true love."

Morgan rolls her eyes. "What's up, Dad?"

"Besides my blood pressure?" He chuckles to himself, clearly amused.

I'm . . . confused. "Is that supposed to be a Blood Witch joke?" I whisper to Morgan. I'm fairly certain their magic would prevent those kinds of medical conditions.

"Yeah. It's easier if you ignore him."

"Hey now, don't sass your elders." Mr. Hughes props his hands on his hips and gives Morgan what from my mom would be A Look, but from him makes me think I'm missing out on some inside joke.

"Oh, are we admitting you're old now?" she asks, all innocent charm.

"Keep it up, missy, and you'll be banned from reading."

Morgan fakes a gasp. "Never!"

Her dad laughs and approaches the bed, his attention turning to me. "Since my daughter has failed to introduce us, I thought I'd say hello myself. I respond to Fitz, Mr. Hughes, Morgan's dad, or Hey, You."

"It's nice to meet you, Mr. Hughes," I say as Morgan groans like her dad is the most embarrassing person she's ever met. It makes my heart ache in a way I can't afford to indulge in, not in front of them. Not if I want to keep functioning. "Do you need help with anything in the kitchen before dinner?"

"Eleanor and I are all set, but thank you." Mr. Hughes turns back to Morgan and ruffles her hair. "Twenty minutes, kiddo. We'll see you out there. It's nice to officially meet you, Hannah." He slips out the door, leaving it open behind him.

"I'm sorry about that," Morgan says when he's gone. "He's extra weird when there are new people around."

"No, I like him." I tip my head back against the wall and lose the fight against the sting in my eyes. "He reminds me a little of my dad. I bet they would have gotten along well."

Morgan reaches for my hand and squeezes tight. Before she can say anything, the doorbell rings and one of her parents answers the door.

"Are you expecting someone?" I ask.

"No, I—"

"Morgan!" A woman's voice calls through the house, presumably Morgan's mother. "It's for you!"

We share a glance, and she looks as confused as I feel. She slips out of the bed and motions for me to come with her. Morgan closes her bedroom door behind us, and I wonder if she's thinking of the runes. If she wants to hide them from whoever has come to see her.

When we get to the foyer, Alice is standing inside the door, looking smaller than I've ever seen her. She's wearing jeans and an oversized hoodie, her hair up in a simple ponytail. She scowls when she sees me.

"Alice, what are you doing here?" Worry makes my nerves brittle and rough. "How do you even know where Morgan lives?"

"My parents have been teaching Alice healing techniques." Morgan steps forward and puts an arm around Alice's shoulders, guiding her farther inside. "What happened? Is everything okay?"

The pink-haired Blood Witch doesn't say anything until she's seated on the couch in the living room, her forearms resting against her thighs. "They drugged the first Blood Witch."

Morgan tenses beside me. "Mom? Dad?" The panic in her voice brings her parents running. Their magic makes them so fast, it's like they simply appear in the room. "How do you know?" Morgan asks Alice. "What happened?"

"I overheard the Elder telling Mr. Tiny Notebook about it at our meeting today. The meeting *you* skipped." Yet the venom in her voice cracks, and she shudders. "He's just a kid. Some boy in Texas. His parents swear they've been careful. They don't use any tap water at home."

"What happened to him?" Fear curls around my heart. Alice said their power controlled everything, that without it they couldn't survive. "Is he okay?"

Alice shakes her head, and actual tears spill over her cheeks. "He's in the hospital. He collapsed on a school trip last Friday and hasn't woken up since. He's only fourteen." She buries her face in her hands, and Mrs. Hughes goes to sit beside her.

"We're safe here, Alice. You're okay." Morgan's mom rubs Alice's back and glances to her husband. Some silent understanding passes between them.

"I'm sorry to do this, Hannah," Mr. Hughes says, resting a hand on my shoulder, "but I think we need some family time tonight. Can we raincheck?"

"Oh, uh, sure," I say, realizing he's already managed to steer me out of the room. I glance back over my shoulder, but Morgan and her mom are sitting on the couch now, Alice sandwiched between them. Morgan glances up at me, and an apologetic smile flashes briefly across her worried face.

I try not to take their dismissal personally, but it still hurts more than I want it to. I'm the only witch in this house who has actually felt the effects of the Hunters' drug. If anyone can relate to what they're going through right now, it's me.

But maybe . . .

Maybe there is something about being a Blood Witch that makes this different. That makes my experience not as relevant as it feels. The Blood Witch boy is in the hospital, unable to wake up. Sarah was physically fine after her magic left her.

So I don't argue to stay when Mr. Hughes asks me to gather my things. I don't say anything when he promises that Morgan will call to reschedule dinner soon.

But when the door slams closed behind me, their rejection hurts.

Knowing that they're in there, hurting even more than I am right now, hardens the rejection into rage. There's somewhere I need to be. Someone who owes us answers no one else seems willing to get.

I climb into the car and grip the steering wheel, squeezing until my knuckles are white.

It's time I paid Riley a visit.

-¦- ✳ -¦-

Voices trickle through Archer's house when I sneak in the front door. Elder Keating's voice isn't loud enough for me to make out the words, but I recognize Archer's murmured disagreement. If I had access to my power, I could use the air to draw their conversation closer. I could dampen the sound of my creeping footsteps so they wouldn't hear them as I inch across the floor toward the basement.

Thankfully neither of them are Elementals. If they were, they'd sense my breath on the air the moment I entered.

At the basement door, I check the handle and find it unlocked. Gently, I pull it open, cringing when the hinges whine, and stand frozen in the entrance. When no one comes to yell at me for sneaking through the house, I descend.

The basement looks the same as it did a week and a half ago, though there are more empty vials sitting on the work table, the potions within already used up. When I reach the bottom stair, I spot the Hunters.

Riley stands with his back to the cell door while Wes

perches at the edge of one mattress and Paige stands facing them both. They're eating sandwiches, bottles of water scattered around the cell. Riley says something that makes Wes chuckle before taking another bite of his dinner.

Ice crackles around my heart, the shards piercing the fragile muscle. I step farther into the room.

Paige spots me first, her face contorting into a scowl. She presses her lips into a thin line but doesn't say anything.

Riley notices Paige's expression and turns. "What do we have here?" He cocks his head to one side and lets his gaze roam all over me. His attention travels over my body like pawing, unwanted hands. He saunters to the edge of the cell and rests his forearms on the horizontal bar. "How's it hanging, Not Hannah?" he says, playing the role of the intrepid reporter I met nearly three weeks ago.

I don't waste time with pleasantries. "Did you know?" I demand, clenching my fists.

"You'll have to be more specific," he says lazily. He takes a large bite of his sandwich, lettuce crunching as he chews.

"The drug," I say, torn between holding my ground and rushing the cell to punch that fucking confidence off his face. How? How does he look so at ease and in charge when he's the one behind bars? "Did you know the drug would kill Morgan?"

Riley freezes. His entire body goes rigid, and then his brows arch up his forehead as concern settles over his features. But then he blinks, and all that falls away. He takes another bite of his sandwich, chewing slowly.

His silence chips away at my composure. I feel like a string pulled too tight, on the verge of snapping. I close the distance between us. "You didn't know, did you? They didn't tell you the drug could kill a Blood Witch."

He shrugs off the accusation, but when he glances at me, there's nothing casual about his expression. It's hard and cold and devoid of humanity. "If those monsters can't survive the cure, they don't deserve to live."

Pain explodes across my knuckles as my fist connects with his face. "Say it again." The words come out a growl, and I reach through the bars, gripping the fabric of his collar. With all the strength I can summon, I yank him forward and slam his face against the bars. "Say it!"

"Riley . . ." Wes stands from his mattress. "Enough, man." The other Hunter steps toward us, but Paige holds up a hand. Wes backs off and Paige crosses her arms, shooting an irritated look into the back of Riley's head.

"I hope I'm the one who gets to do it." Riley doesn't blink. His voice is steady. "I hope it hurts when she dies."

With a speed I don't expect, he reaches through the bars and slams two fingers into my throat. I choke, coughing as I lose the grip on his shirt and fall to the floor. My elbow scrapes against cement, and hot blood slides down the torn skin. Riley laughs and steps away from the bars until he's level with Wes.

Paige sneers at me. "Pathetic." She turns to the boys like I'm not even here. "I can't believe *she's* the one who captured us. It's embarrassing."

Trembling, I pull myself back to my feet. These kids, with their hatred and their cult-like obedience, are the real monsters. Hunters who want to kill us for no other reason than we exist. For the first time, I understand why the Council wants to kill them all. Even if we showed every kindness, they would never acknowledge our humanity.

It would be so much easier if we could turn their techniques against them.

I stumble back and bump into the worktable. I glance over my shoulder at the wall of completed potions. There are fewer than last time, and I don't know what any of them do, but I find myself reaching for them anyway.

"What are you doing?" Wes actually sounds nervous.

Arms full of glass vials, I whirl back at them. "If you can kill us, if you can shoot David and drug little kids and try to kill someone you used to love, then fine. You win. We'll be just as horrible as you."

Paige and Riley share a worried look. Wes crinkles his brow. "Who's David?"

I set the potion on the table and select a red one. "He was a Caster Witch. One of your fellow Hunters murdered him last weekend. He was going to create a potion that could kill every last one of you." Their shocked, worried expressions light up all the brittle, angry parts inside me. I raise my arm. "But I'm sure one of these potions will do the job just fine."

"*Hannah.*"

Archer's voice whips across the room, and I lower my arm. Slowly, shame already creeping up my chest, I turn around. His disappointment nearly breaks me. He takes the potion gently from my hand, setting it on the table beside the others.

"Upstairs," he says, his voice soft but full of command. "Now."

17

DETECTIVE ARCHER LEADS ME upstairs, and worry builds with each step. I can already hear the lecture. Can already picture him bringing me before Elder Keating. Is it against our laws to touch a Caster's potions without permission? That never came up at coven meetings.

What will the Council do to me?

My breath comes in short, panicked inhales as we emerge into the hall. Murmured conversation still rumbles from the kitchen. I don't recognize the voice of the woman speaking with Elder Keating, and I brace myself to face them. Instead, Archer presses a finger to his lips and closes the basement door with a barely audible *snick*.

I follow him to a part of his house I've never been before. We pass through the living room and down another hallway. Archer opens a door and leads me into a small office. The walls are the same soft cream as the rest of the house, and there's an open laptop sitting on the desk against the far wall.

Archer gestures for me to enter and closes us both inside.

We stand in the fading natural light that streams in through the windows. Neither of us says anything for a long time. I get the sense that he's waiting for me to speak, that he wants me to apologize, but I don't know where I'm supposed to start.

Finally, the detective runs a hand through his hair, his posture deflating, making him look much shorter than he is. "What's going on, Hannah? This isn't like you."

There isn't any judgment in his tone, only curiosity, but I feel myself tense anyway. Feel myself grow bitter and sharp. "Alice came to Morgan's. She told us about the Blood Witch. She told us what happened to him." My throat closes, and everything the anger was trying to hide comes rushing forward. "Why did you let the Elder recruit me? Why didn't you force me to stay out of this?" Tears turn the room into a blur of soft colors, but I press on, unable to stop.

"I've fucked it up at every step. I let Morgan come with me to Brooklyn, and she could have *died*. Sarah lost her magic. Cal and I were almost shot. The Hunters *murdered* David, and I can still feel his blood on my skin. I can still see him whenever I close my eyes." Hiccupping sobs steal my words, and I bury my face in my hands. "We're out of time to set up the raid, and the Hunters are still killing us. They're going to keep killing us until we're all gone, aren't they?"

Archer doesn't tell me I'm wrong. He doesn't tell me that everything will be okay. I glance up when the silence stretches on. He looks sad. Impossibly sad and lost and scared.

The tears start all over again. "I'm right, aren't I? We're fucked."

He shakes his head and buries all the naked worry behind a composed mask. "There isn't an easy solution," he says, confidence infused through his tone. I don't trust it. Not after I saw the feelings he's trying to hide. "But we're not giving up. We're making progress. Progress that wouldn't be possible without *you*."

I wipe my face dry and sit in his desk chair. "You're just saying that so I'll stop crying."

"No, Hannah, I'm not." He crosses the room and kneels so we're eye-to-eye. "I know what happened at the hotel was awful, but if Riley hadn't followed you and Morgan there, we wouldn't know about their plans for an airborne drug. Alice might not have agreed to help us without that."

"But Eisha—"

"Eisha Marchelle contacted Alice earlier tonight. Her supervisors approved the magic show for Monday. We're in, Hannah. We're going to destroy the drug. We're going to strike our first major blow against the Hunters."

A tiny, withered stem of hope tries to break the surface, but it's been beaten down so many times, I don't think it'll ever fully rise again.

"And Elder Keating reached out to the Casters you told us about. They'll be here tomorrow. They're going to help us." Archer rises to his full height and reaches out a hand, helping me to my feet, too. "You did that, Hannah. *You.* Don't discount the impact you've made. Don't let the Hunters turn you into someone you're not."

"I don't—"

"The Hannah I know wouldn't threaten to murder someone or throw random potions into their cell. You're better than that."

"But are we really?" I feel it again, the desperation that sent me into the basement in the first place, the realization that I have no fucking clue how to stop the Hunters without turning their own methods against them. "The Council is planning to kill them. How does that make us any better?"

"It doesn't," Archer says, which surprises me. I can't read his expression. "I don't like the Elders' plan, because you're right. Killing them would make us just as bad as they are. I hope it won't come to that." He knits his brows and tilts his head to one side. "How did you even know about that part of David's research?"

"Umm . . ." I don't want to lie, but I don't want to get Cal in trouble, either.

The detective sighs and shakes his head. "Cal. Of course."

"He didn't—"

"Cal and I are the only ones who know besides the Elders. He also told me that he's working on alternative plans, so I'm not surprised he shared his thoughts with you. I know you two are close." Archer turns and leans against the windowsill, staring out at the backyard. "I also know you decided to drop out of the raid."

"Are you mad?"

"No." He glances over his shoulder. "Even with Alice getting us in, it's still a risky operation. You've dealt with enough danger to last a lifetime. I'm glad you'll be here."

"Then why do I feel like I'm letting everyone down?" Even though the raid will probably go better without me there to screw it up, I can't stop the guilt that whispers in my ear, telling me that I'm letting the Hunters win by taking myself out of the fight.

Archer's right, though. We can't let them corrupt who we are, even if I have no idea how to do that without leaving the front lines.

"You're not, Hannah. I promise." Archer crosses the room to the computer. "I do have a little good news, though, if that helps. It took some creative wording, but we got more answers out of the Hunters." He taps on the keyboard and inputs a password. "According to Wes, there are roughly a hundred Hunters across the US."

"Only a hundred?" That doesn't seem possible.

He nods and pulls up a map. "Hall Pharmaceuticals is their

base of operations, but they have families stationed across the country. They're obscenely well-funded, so they have easy access to travel and can relocate entire families within a week."

"Do you know their names? Where they are?" I can't believe there are so few of them. How can such a small group inflict so much damage?

Because they train for it. Because they're fed on hate.

They've spent generations on this quest, keeping their network small and contained, raising everyone with perfect devotion to the cause. Benton's entire family is in the medical field. He was heading down the same path. He'd been trained to fight since he could walk.

And with enough money, they could hire whoever they needed to fill in the gaps.

"The Hunters we've captured only know a few families each. It will take time to get a full picture of who they are. They move frequently, which makes things more challenging." Archer closes the computer and swivels to face me. "I need to get back to my meeting. You should go home."

"You're not taking me to Elder Keating?"

Archer raises one eyebrow. "Do you want me to?"

"No. No, I'm good." I follow him out into the hall. "Wait. How did you even know I was in the basement?"

"Our potions are an extension of ourselves." When we reach the front door, the detective holds it open for me. "We know if they're being mishandled."

"Oh." My cheeks burn hot. "Sorry."

He flips on the front porch light. The sun has disappeared behind the tree line across the street, casting the front of the house in shadows. "I'll see you tomorrow."

"Tomorrow?" I ask, pausing halfway to my car.

"Elder Keating is calling all the witches here for a meeting. Your Caster friends should be here by then, too."

A fresh sense of dread weighs heavy in my stomach, but I force a smile. "See you then."

$$-\!\!\!\mid \quad \ast \quad \mid\!\!\!-$$

GG: Wanna come over? I haven't seen you in forever.

HW: I can't tonight.

GG: 😣 Please? Mom bought more of that popcorn you love.

The popcorn is seriously tempting, and I do miss Gem. I could use some non-witchy time, a reminder that I have a life outside of the nightmare my coven is going through. It feels like ages since the girls' night we had with Morgan.

HW: Maybe this weekend? Or after homecoming? I have family stuff tonight.

GG: "Family stuff" aka gardening?

HW: Gardening?

GG: It's a code word. Like vampire.

HW: 😳

"Ready, Han?"

Mom knocks on my open doorframe. I glance up from my phone, which is resting in the book I'm supposed to be reading for English. Mom smiles when she spots me doing homework, and the relief transforms her face. I can't remember the last time she looked so at ease.

As hard as everything has been for me, I never stopped to consider what Mom must have been going through. Not really. It must have been terrible, watching me rush again and again into harm's way. No wonder she was always badgering me to quit.

I send Gem a quick text telling her I have to go and set my bookmark between the pages of the paperback. Tonight will be the first time I've seen the entire coven since Dad died. The first time I've seen Sarah since she lost her magic. At first, I missed lessons because I was recovering from my head injuries. Later, I avoided the coven because I didn't want anyone to find out about the issues I was having with my magic. Between working with DA Flores to prepare my testimony and helping the Council, I had plenty of excuses to stay away.

But there's no getting out of this one. All the witches are going, including Morgan's family *and* Alice. I'm not sure which of the NYC Casters are coming—all of them? Just Lexie?—but they're expected sometime today, and I *still* haven't warned Alice. I keep typing out texts and deleting them. How do you tell someone the people who tried to hurt them are coming to visit?

"Hannah?" Mom prompts when I haven't moved.

"Sorry, yes. I'm good. I'm coming." I set the book on my pillow and climb off the bed. It still feels too lumpy, but I'm starting to get used to it. Mom says the contractors are hoping to finish rebuilding the home we lost around the new year, but I haven't had the courage to visit and see the progress for myself.

Mom stops me before I slip out of the room, catching me in a hug. "You can stay home if you have more work to do. I can pass along whatever Ryan has to say." She kisses the top of my head, and my heart squeezes tight. I close my eyes and wish for a vision of Dad, who always dropped a kiss there.

But when I open my eyes, there's nothing.

"It's fine, Mom. I'm sure it won't take long." I breathe deep and square my shoulders. "Besides . . . I have to stop avoiding Sarah."

"She doesn't blame you, sweetie." Mom brushes my hair out of my face. "I promise."

I shrug and slip past her, staring up at the ceiling to stop the sting in my eyes. I am *sick* of crying all the damn time.

Mom drives us to Archer's house, and she tells me about her new batch of students at the university. She teaches a lot of first-year classes, and she swears each group has their own collective personality. Apparently, the new one is especially active on campus, which she says is fun to see.

Most of the coven is already at Archer's when we arrive. Mom leaves me to chat with Margaret Lesko, and I scan the yard, looking for Lexie and the other Manhattan Casters. I don't see them among the crowd, but I do spot Sarah. She's standing at the edge of the crowd with her arms crossed tightly around her. Ellen Watson—who's a few years older than I am—stands beside her, and I get the impression Ellen's trying to get her to mingle with the rest of the coven.

Sarah isn't having it, and it feels so much like my fault.

Finally, Ellen gives up and sulks back toward the main

part of the yard. She notices me and adjusts her course. "This is bullshit," she says, her words hushed but no less fierce. "I fucking hate them."

I'm not sure what startles me more, her profanity or her willingness to say what everyone else is thinking. "The Hunters?" I clarify, just in case.

She nods. "Why aren't we storming their headquarters and dropping every last one of them to their knees?" She glares at me when I try to respond. "That's a rhetorical question, Han. I know why, but it's bullshit. Look how freaked out everyone is, always glancing over their shoulder to make sure we're not under attack. I still can't believe the Council put you in danger like that. You're a kid!"

"We're only three years apart."

Ellen waves my words away. "I'm just glad they're not making you take part in the raid on Monday."

I raise an eyebrow. "How do you know about that?"

With a snap of her fingers, flames burst into existence between us. "I volunteered to be the fire power."

The heat of the flames licks across my skin, and I flinch away. "But it's dangerous." I thought Archer would recruit a Council agent, not another one of my covenmates. "You could lose your magic!"

At that, we both glance over at Sarah, who's still standing on the edge of the yard, watching the rest of the coven. "It'll be worth it," Ellen says, a stubborn fierceness creeping into her voice. "Archer is confident we'll succeed, and I'll do whatever I can to protect our coven."

Ellen nudges me with her shoulder and slips back into the crowd. I watch her leave, and I have to admit that she isn't wrong about the coven. There's a tension to the gathering that isn't usually here. Even the children are quiet and still. The younger kids should be running around the yard, tossing balls of air at each other, enjoying one of the few spaces where they're allowed to remove their binding charms and let their magic roam free.

Instead, they're clustered in a small group on the other side of the yard. One of the kids shifts to the side and reveals a flash of pink hair. Of course. *Alice.*

The Blood-Witch-turned-illusionist has a large, shiny coin in her hands. She waves it before the crowd of small children, and in the next moment, it vanishes. The kids gasp.

"I don't get how she's the same Blood Witch we met in New York." Veronica sidles up beside me and crosses her arms. "She looks harmless."

I consider Alice. Her pink hair flows in soft curls past her shoulders today, and though she's forgone the full three-piece suit, she's still rocking a teal-and-white-striped blazer over a white button-down and dark-wash jeans. There's something about her that draws my eye like a magnet. She's so full of contradictions that I can't tell what's real and what's not.

She's an orphan desperate for connection with her Clan.

An abrasive bully who refuses to call me by my name.

A girl on the edge of fame who still makes time to delight nervous children.

But then I remember her fingers closing around my throat, her Blood Magic scorching through my body, and I shudder. "She's far from harmless, V. Be careful around her."

"You don't have to tell me twice. I have no intention of speaking to her." Veronica nudges me with her shoulder. "Wanna help me harass Gabe? Mom let slip that he has a crush on a girl in his math class, and it's my duty as the older sister to pester him until he dies of embarrassment."

"I'm good. You go ahead." I don't have the energy to tease her brother tonight. "But go easy on him. He was always cool about us."

"Only when *you* were around." Veronica tosses her hair over one shoulder. "He was a little shit whenever you weren't. It's payback time."

She gives my hand a squeeze, then weaves through the crowd of witches to her brother, slow and methodical like a lioness stalking her prey. I catch myself laughing, but when I notice Sarah at the edge of the yard, avoiding the rest of the coven, everything inside me goes cold. Not even the warm sun can dispel the deep-seated ice in my heart.

Delighted squeals startle at least half the adults—myself included—then children go scattering in a million directions, their unfocused magic rippling through the earth. The ground trembles until my grandmother shifts her attention and steals the element back from the kids, leaving them with only the air to play with. They shout for Alice to watch, but when I turn to look, her gaze is focused on me.

A sudden touch at my back sends me whirling around. Morgan raises her hands. "Sorry! I didn't mean to sneak up on you."

"It's okay." I focus on her smile and let it erase all the worries in my head. "I may have to get you jewelry with thousands of tiny bells for the solstice though. You are way too quiet."

Morgan laughs. "Any idea what Archer wants with all of us?"

Before I can answer, the ground ripples with power. I turn toward the source, and Lady Ariana stands beside Archer, calling us to order. "I think we're about to find out."

We gather close, and Archer goes over all the things I already know. That the barrier is coming down. That we'll need to take extra precautions. That there will be extra security for Veronica and me, including needle-resistant potion on the clothes we'll wear in court. When Archer mentions the added danger of testifying, Mom shoots me a concerned look from across the yard.

"Excuse me?" A voice interrupts Archer as he's asking if anyone has questions. The assembled witches turn toward the sound. "Are we in the right place?"

Lexie, a petite Black girl, cautiously approaches from the side of the house. She's changed her hair since I saw her last—she has long braids now, which she's wearing in a bun on top of her head—but I'd recognize those sharp, inquisitive brown eyes anywhere. She's traded the stud in her nose for a thin hoop, and she's dressed in jeans, red sandals, and an NYU T-shirt.

"Lexie Scott?" Archer asks, crossing the yard to her.

"Yeah. And this is Coral." She gestures behind her at Coral, a Latinx girl with shoulder-length curls and pink glasses. I hold my breath, waiting for the moment Tori appears behind them. She never comes.

Archer greets them both, and the three speak too quietly to hear. Coral scans the crowd, and her eyes grow wide when she recognizes me.

A hand closes around my arm and squeezes tight. "Are you *fucking* kidding me?" Alice's sudden appearance startles me, her voice quiet in my ear. "What the hell are *they* doing here?"

Around me, the coven grows restless as Archer speaks to the newcomers. The kids run off to play. Adults break into small groups to discuss schedules. Morgan's parents wave her over, and Alice takes her place beside me. As soon as we're alone, her magic tears through my body. "Well, Tree Hugger?" An ache spreads through my bones, and it's hard to stay on my feet. "I'm waiting."

"I'm sorry. I—"

"You knew?!" She releases my arm, but the pain only builds as her temper flares. My knees buckle, and her Blood Magic takes control of my body, forcing my legs to stay standing. "Why the fuck didn't you say something? Why weren't you at the meeting last night?"

At first, I don't know what meeting she's talking about, but then I remember where she heard about the drugged Blood Witch. I remember the voices in Archer's kitchen. Alice must have been there with Ellen and Elder Keating before she escaped to Morgan's house.

"Archer didn't tell me you were meeting."

"Bullshit." Her magic makes the muscles around my ribs constrict. "He wouldn't forget to invite you. The raid is in four fucking days, Snow Queen."

"Alice," I say, gasping for breath. "I can't breathe."

She scowls at me, then shuts her eyes. Her power leaks out of me, and though she doesn't say anything, the way she forces herself to breathe more deeply makes me think the pain wasn't intentional. Her eyes open slowly, and she trains her hard, blue gaze on me. In it, I see the fear she's channeling into rage. The betrayal she must feel at Lexie and Coral's unannounced arrival.

"He didn't forget to invite me," I admit when I can't stand her intense glower a second longer. "I'm not part of the raid anymore."

"Yes. You are," Alice says, and it sounds more like a threat than a statement.

"I'm not, Alice. I can't—"

"The hell you can't." She steps closer, and this time, the pain that travels down my spine feels *very* intentional. "I don't know what kind of trap you've set by bringing those Casters here, but I am *not* waltzing into the Hunter headquarters alone. No fucking way. You want my help? You better get some skin in the game, Cyclone."

"Alice—"

"Save it. If you're not here for the meeting on Saturday, I'm calling my sponsors and going back on tour." She squeezes her fists, and the pain flares bright. My knees buckle, and she grabs my arm, holding me upright. "And if those Casters do anything to hurt me," she says, her whispered words curled around my brain like barbed wire, "I'll stop your heart."

18

ALICE'S THREATS FOLLOW ME home that night. Mom talks about how good it was to see everyone and then reviews the plans to keep me safe in the courthouse. I listen as best I can, but I don't know how to tell her about Alice's ultimatum: if I don't go on the raid, it won't happen at all.

It's going to break Mom's heart.

All night, I try to find a way out of this. But no one can force Alice to go through with the raid, not even Elder Keating. Her words from the night we met play on a loop in my head. *We do not force our witches to do anything, Hannah. Not even when things are this desperate. It has to be their choice.*

If I don't agree to go with Alice, we're fucked. I should have warned her about Lexie and Coral. I should have done *something* besides write and delete the same texts over and over.

At school, I'm reminded by painted banners that homecoming is tonight, which is . . . *unfortunate*. I don't have anything to wear, but Morgan is so excited, and I'd like to keep at least *one* promise this year.

Thankfully, Gemma comes through for me. After she takes care of my hair and makeup, she lets me wriggle into the dress she wore last year. The flowing red fabric hit her at mid-thigh, but it falls to my knees. Her own dress, pale blue this year, goes all the way to her ankles. When she changed, I noticed the patchwork of angry scars on her right thigh.

"Not a word, Han," she says when she sees me looking.

I mime zipping my lips and fight the urge to ask if she's okay. To apologize for her getting hurt in the first place. Instead, I let her lead me out of the house. We pick up Morgan, and her enthusiasm about the dance is infectious. By the time we get to school, I've committed to having the best night of my life.

An hour later, I've let homecoming erase all the stress that's been dragging me down for weeks.

Morgan grabs my hand and spins into me, pressing her body against mine as we move to the pounding bass of the maxed-out speakers. My hands slide across the fabric of her black dress, finding a resting place at her waist, tugging her closer. She's gorgeous tonight. She's always beautiful, but something about the flush of her cheeks and the way she let a couple strands of hair fall out of her bun sets my pulse on fire. She tilts her head back and presses a kiss to my cheek.

Gemma tried rocking the dance floor without her cane, but it's clear her leg is still giving her trouble. She sat out the last few songs, and though she played it off by doing tarot readings for some of our classmates, I noticed the way she massaged her thigh. Noticed the crease of pain above her brow.

But she's back, putting the rest of us to shame as she swivels her hips and moves like her body is made of rhythm and melody instead of muscle and bone. She has her cane now, and she incorporates it into her dancing to take some of the pressure off her leg.

"Hey now, get a room!" Gemma shouts when Morgan tips her head back for a kiss.

"This is a room!" Morgan says, but she slips away from me,

taking Gemma's hand and spinning her twice. I watch them, my heart full and my mind lighter than it's been in a long, long time.

Morgan dances back over to me. "We're going to get a drink!" She has to shout to be heard over the music, even though she's close enough now that I could kiss her if I leaned forward a little. "Come with?"

Rather than shouting over the noise, I nod and follow her and Gem out into the hall, where there are long tables filled with punch bowls and trays of snacks. I grab a handful of chocolate-covered pretzels and follow Gemma down the line of tables to the drinks.

She grabs a bottle of water, drains half, and tries to hand it to Morgan.

But Morgan shakes her head. "I'm good. I'm actually going to go to the bathroom. Hannah?"

I glance up at the sound of my name, finishing the last of my pretzels. "Yeah?"

"Keep me company?"

"Yeah, sure. You good, Gem?" I look to my best friend, but she rolls her eyes and shoves me after Morgan. We bypass the main hallway bathroom, slipping instead around the corner unseen.

"Where are we going?" I whisper as Morgan takes my hand and pulls me into a vacant classroom, the rows of desks illuminated by the streetlights outside.

Morgan closes the blinds. "Somewhere we won't be interrupted." She smiles shyly and lets her fingers trail up and down my exposed arms. "I thought you might like a moment alone."

I grin. "That sounds like a brilliant—"

Her kiss cuts off the rest of my sentence. I freeze at first, caught off guard, but then I melt into her embrace, wrapped in the quiet cocoon of the empty room. "What was that for?" I ask when she pulls back.

"Have I told you yet how beautiful you are?" She wraps her arms around my waist, pulling me closer.

"At least twice," I say, "but a third time doesn't hurt. You look pretty great yourself."

"Yeah?" The smile on her face says she already knows. I nod anyway, and then we're kissing again, flying really, her magic tingling across my skin, making my whole body warm. She steps forward until I'm pressed against the wall, her hips on mine, fingers tangled in my hair.

Locked in our own world, I forget the dance down the hall. Forget the trial starting on Monday. Forget Alice's ultimatum. I forget *everything* but the parting of her lips and the graze of her teeth against my skin. I want her hands everywhere, and as if she can hear the thought in my head, she deepens the kiss, her tongue slipping into my mouth.

But then Morgan pulls away, her fingers warm against the back of my neck. She smiles, suddenly shy, and kisses me briefly on the lips before dipping her head lower, her breath tickling my neck as she presses the first kiss against the sensitive skin.

I shiver beneath her touch, her hands sliding down my arms, coming to rest at my hips. She trails kisses down my throat, and my eyes flutter shut. I want to tug her closer, but my hands press against the wall as she moves lower, trailing the neckline of my borrowed dress. Her fingers brush against the hem of the skirt, slipping under the fabric.

Morgan's touch travels up only an inch before going back down again. She rubs tiny, electrifying circles along my outer thigh. The sensation is so intense, the desire to go further so strong, that I squeeze my eyes shut, unable to process any other input.

"Wait," I say as her lips graze my collarbone. "We need to slow down." My heart is pounding in my throat, my breathing coming too fast. The air swirls through the classroom, spinning around our bodies, spurred on by my subconscious magic.

I rest my hands on her shoulders and create space between us. My skin is flushed with heat, and goddess, there's still a part of me that wants to damn the consequences and kiss her again. "We probably don't want our first time to be at school, right?"

Morgan bites her lip, and for a second, I wonder if she wants to risk it, but she shakes her head. "No, you're right." She lifts my hand from her shoulder and presses a kiss to my knuckles. "I'm sorry I got carried away."

"It wasn't just you," I admit, thinking of the air I accidentally spun around us. "But we should probably hold out for a room with a bed. Deal?"

"Deal." She holds out her pinky, and I loop mine with hers, sealing the promise with a kiss that quickly heats up the room. Literally. My magic is still buzzing and alive, the air warming around us.

"We should go." I force myself to pull back. "Gemma's probably waiting for us." We walk back into the hall, hand in hand, but Morgan stops me before we turn the final corner back to the gym.

"Let me fix your hair." Her fingers move deftly, smoothing out the places where she crushed my curls. She kisses me gently. "Perfect."

When we turn the corner, Gemma nearly crashes into us.

The blood has drained completely from her face, leaving her pale and wide-eyed.

"What is it?" I ask, glancing behind her at the chaos of the dance, which seems to be breaking up even though there's another hour left. "What's wrong?"

Gemma holds tight to my upper arm, but whether to steady herself or me, I'm not sure. "Benton," she says, his name landing like a brick on my heart.

"What about him?"

"He broke out of jail. He's free."

19

BENTON.

He broke out of jail.

He's free.

The words echo in my head, accompanied by the *whoosh-whoosh-whoosh* of blood pulsing through my body. He can't be out. His trial starts in three days. He can't—

"How do you know?" My voice is harsh and unrecognizable. The world spins, and I stumble. Morgan keeps a hand on my elbow to hold me steady. "It has to be some kind of trick."

But Gemma's eyes glitter with tears. "It's all over the news." She presses something on the screen and holds out her phone.

A video reloads to reveal a reporter standing in front of the prison gates. "We've received word of a disturbance at the prison tonight. Tensions have been high as we near Monday's jury selection for the trial of Benton Hall. A small riot broke out at approximately seven o'clock tonight, and sources inside—" She pauses, touching one hand to her ear.

The reporter looks up, past the lens, like she's staring at her camera operator. After a beat, she focuses on her audience. "I've just received an update from inside the prison. Benton Hall has escaped. I repeat, Benton Hall has escaped from prison. Though he was not armed at the time, officials warn that he is extremely dangerous and should not be approached by civilians."

Before the video ends, I reach for my phone, dialing Archer. He answers on the second ring. "Have you seen the news?"

"I'm on my way to the precinct now. They called in all off-duty personnel to help with the search."

"What do we do?" I lean against the wall for support, Morgan and Gemma a shield against our classmates as they stream out of the gym. Teachers usher them toward the doors, and they must know. All of them. Which means it's only a matter of time before they're looking for me.

A door slams on Archer's side of the line and his car rumbles to life. "You don't do anything, Hannah. I want you home. I'm sending Ellen and Cal to watch over your place."

"You don't have to do that. The barrier is still—"

"I'm not taking any chances, Hannah. Go home. I need to know you're safe."

"The raid," I say before he can hang up. "I'm going with you." Alice's threat is meaningless now. No one could keep me away from the Hunters, not with Benton loose. My heart beats with the raging fire of a thousand suns. If the Hunters think they can take Benton back without consequences, they're sorely mistaken.

"Hannah . . ."

"Elder Keating said I can still go with you. I'm coming."

Archer sighs. "Is Morgan there? Give her the phone."

I do as I'm asked, passing my cell to Morgan. The initial surge of adrenaline is already fading, and I slide down the wall, tucking my knees to my chest. My body trembles, but my mind is made up. Benton being free changes everything. If anyone is going to bring him down, it's going to be me.

He will regret ever crossing us.

"Yes, sir." Morgan glances down at me. "Of course, sir." She nods once more and hangs up the phone. "Come on, Hannah." She pulls me up from the floor and wipes tears from my face. I didn't even realize I was crying. "Let's get you out of here."

Morgan calls her parents and comes home with me. She explains everything to my mom so I don't have to, sending me to wash the makeup from my face and change into fuzzy pajamas. They take my silence for shock, and I let them assume. Instead, my mind is whirring with all the things I remember about the raid despite the meeting I missed.

Alice got Eisha to agree to the show. That's our way in.

Cal will loop the security footage to keep us off their screens and serve as our digital lookout.

But then . . . what? I don't know how we're supposed to neutralize the drug without David's research. I know Lexie's good, but I doubt she had enough time to translate his work in just a few short days.

When I can't stall in the bathroom any longer, I emerge to find Morgan's parents in the dining room with my mom.

She crushes me in another hug. "It's going to be okay," Mom whispers into my hair. "Morgan's parents agreed to stay with us tonight to keep an eye on you."

Mr. Hughes offers me a smile. "We'll spell the doors to keep the Hunters out."

"What about the Elders' border? Won't that keep them out?" I ask.

"It doesn't hurt to take extra precaution," Mrs. Hughes says. She spins a ring on her right middle finger, a simple band that matches the one Morgan wears.

"Thank you," Mom says, "I can't tell you how much we appreciate your help."

We watch Morgan's parents draw bloody runes around every door and window. Out front, Cal and Ellen keep watch in Ellen's car. It feels like overkill to have five witches watching over Morgan and me, but it's also a special kind of magic to have all three Clans here like this.

It takes some negotiating with our parents, but Morgan ends up sleeping in my room with me. She holds me close, and I tuck my head under her chin, let my arms drape across her stomach. Her fingers smooth tiny circles on my back, and as the calming influence of her magic settles over me, I fall into the deepest, most restful sleep I've had since the bonfire last June that put this entire horror show into motion.

On Saturday, I'm itching to get back to planning the raid, but Archer is tied up with the search for Benton and has to cancel the morning meeting Alice mentioned. Morgan and her parents leave after breakfast, and Mom and I spend the next several hours fighting. She wants to lock me in our basement until the raid is over. I threaten to tell Elder Keating she's trying to stop me.

Around three that afternoon, the police chief decides I need a protection detail since I was one of Benton's victims. Archer gets himself assigned to the case—whether through magical or mundane means, I'm not sure—which gives us the time we need to prepare for Monday.

Everyone else is already at his house when Archer brings me over.

"Great, the other glorified gardener is here." Alice glares at me, but the hurt-fueled rage from the other night is gone. It probably helps that the Casters haven't attacked her since then. "I was beginning to worry you wouldn't come."

"Don't worry." I take a seat opposite her. "I wouldn't miss it."

Archer stands at the head of the table. "We have a lot to cover and not a lot of time, so let's get to work. The general mechanics of the plan haven't changed much."

And then we're in the thick of it. Cal and Alice have rigged false bottoms in her trunks. Archer and I practice getting in and out of them—we're the only ones who have to hide, since our faces are too likely to be recognized. Ellen, who hasn't had any contact with the Hunters, will go in as Alice's assistant so she can push the second trunk.

We have lightweight gas masks to wear in case the drug is airborne. Jackets that Cal has already soaked in his needle-repelling potion. Archer will have a handful of other potions on him, liquids that can eat through metal and knock the Hunters out cold, but we'll rely on Ellen's magic if things get really dicey. We'll also have communication devices—Archer calls them *comms*—that we'll wear in our ears. They'll allow us to talk, since we'll be separated for most of the raid.

Cal will wait in the van to keep an eye on the security footage. Alice will have to stay and go through with her performance to prevent suspicion while Ellen, Archer, and I handle the drug.

"How are we supposed to destroy their supply? Has Lexie made any progress with David's notes?" I reach for another slice of the pizza that was delivered half an hour ago while Alice glares daggers at me. I ignore her. "Where are Lexie and Coral, by the way?"

"We've got them set up in a short-term rental a few miles from here." Archer rubs the back of his neck and makes a notation on his list of preparations. "Lexie is doing the best she can, but it's slow going. David was a brilliant Caster and an incredible scientist. I think she'll get there, but not before Monday. Elder Keating is working on a plan B. She said she'd stop by later tonight with the finished potion."

"And what about Benton?" I ask cautiously, trying to keep my voice as neutral as possible. "Do we think he'll be there?"

The four of them share a worried look.

"I'm not going to fall apart. I'm well aware that he's out there somewhere." I pause, and when no one challenges my claim, I continue. "Did Riley or the other two know anything?"

Alice leans back in her chair. "Those three might as well be feral kittens for all the good they've done."

A bell chimes throughout the house. "That'll be Elder Keating," Archer says, and leaves to answer the door. With Benton loose, he stopped leaving it unlocked.

When he returns with Elder Keating, the atmosphere in the dining room shifts. I sit up a little taller, but I notice Alice lowers her gaze to the table.

Elder Keating beams when she sees me. "Good to have you back on board, Hannah."

Before I can thank her, she reaches into her oversized purse and pulls out a vial of potion. Inside the crystal container, the liquid is as dark as night. It seems to absorb the light around it, like some kind of miniature black hole.

She hands the vial to me. "Be very careful with this. It'll destroy any liquid, including the drug. Unfortunately, it's extremely volatile. Don't let it come in contact with broken skin. It'll burn up your blood as easily as it'll destroy the cure."

"Are you sure I should be the one handling this?"

"Would you prefer to burn the paper copies of their research or help Cal establish access to their digital files?" Keating asks, but she doesn't give me time to answer. "You've earned the right to destroy the thing that has taken so much from you."

I cradle the vial gingerly in my hands. "Thank you." The words aren't big enough for what this means to me, but I hope she understands anyway.

"You're welcome." Elder Keating smiles softly and bids us goodnight. When she's gone, Archer clears his throat. "All right then. From the top."

—+—   —✳—   —+—

By Sunday night, the plan has ingrained itself into my brain, running on a constant loop.

Get in.

Destroy the drug.

Get out.

Three simple steps. None of them easy.

I lie in bed, staring at the ceiling while my mind spins all the ways our mission could go wrong. All the ways we could fail. When the clock hits four in the morning, I give up on sleep and drag myself out of bed. Within an hour, I'm showered and dressed and moving through the house on silent feet. I don't want to wake Mom. I'm afraid to say goodbye. Afraid to fight one more time before I leave.

I'm not sure what I'm supposed to bring with me, so I only slip my phone in my back pocket and grab my keys. At the front door, my fingers curl around the deadbolt, my keys jingling in my other hand, when someone clears their throat behind me.

"No goodbye?"

Everything inside me freezes. I turn slowly. "Hey, Mom."

She stands in the hallway, still dressed in the clothes she

wore last night. The dark circles under her eyes confirm that she never went to bed.

I fidget with the keys in my hands. "Go ahead. Tell me not to go."

The corner of Mom's lips quirks up, but there's only defeat in her eyes. "Would you listen if I did?" She sighs when I shake my head. "That's what I thought."

"I'm sorry, Mom, but I have to—"

"You have to go. I know." Mom wraps her arms tightly around herself. "I'd tell you to be careful, but I don't think you know how to do that."

"I'll be back soon." I hate making promises I can't keep, but I slip out of the house before either of us can say anything else.

Despite the obscene hour, I'm the last to arrive at Archer's house. Cal passes me one of the needle-repellant jackets. The fabric is stiff against my skin when I slide it on over my plain black T-shirt. They've already loaded Alice's trunks into one van and fitted another with Cal's tech gear, so we don't waste any time heading out. The hour-long journey passes too quickly, and then we're pulling over to get ready.

Cal slips into the back of the second van, where his computer equipment is already set up. "Good luck," he says, passing Archer a thumb drive. "Don't lose this."

Archer stores the drive in the small pocket at the front of his jacket. "We'll see you on the other side."

We leave our phones with Cal and pile into the main van. Archer and I hide inside Alice's two supply trunks. The spaces are barely big enough, and panic rises in my chest when the door clicks shut behind me. Locked in a world of darkness, claustrophobia clawing at my throat, I force myself to breathe. To press down the swell of nausea as the van lurches forward to drive us the rest of the way to our destination.

When we finally arrive, my muscles cramp and spasm. The pain spreads as Alice, or maybe Ellen, rolls the trunk down a sidewalk. The *thud-thud-thud* against the lines in the cement makes my teeth ache.

Get in. Destroy the drug. Get out. I repeat the steps like a mantra, let it consume my thoughts so I don't scream and give us away.

We come to a stop, and muffled voices filter through the thick casing of the trunk.

"I told you, they're supplies for my act." Alice's voice comes into focus when someone opens the top of my trunk. Her haughty, sarcastic tone doesn't betray any of the fear I saw on the ride here. "Be careful with that. It's expensive," she snaps.

Above me, separated by a thin piece of particleboard and fabric, someone rifles through Alice's things. I hold my breath, wishing I could still my heart until they leave, afraid the erratic pounding against my ribs will give us away.

Something heavy bangs on the space above my head, and I stifle a gasp. I close my eyes and pray to the Mother Goddess. Her daughters may be banned from watching over earth, but maybe she's there. Maybe she's listening. *Please protect us.* I send the plea skyward, tears prickling my eyes. *If you have any love at all for the sisters' creations, please help us get in.*

The noise continues, and I worry it might be rude to bargain with a deity. Ruder still to wonder if the family of goddesses is even real.

"Are you satisfied?" Alice's tone is so quintessentially her—well, the stage version of her—that I can practically see her scowl and her hand propped on her hip.

The lid closes, muffling the security guard's reply. I release the breath I was holding. A few heartbeats later, we're moving again, the wheels gliding smoothly across the polished floor. It feels like an eternity until the trunk stops. Another millennia until Alice taps out our secret code.

I feel around the side of the case, looking for the latch that'll release the bottom and—

My fingers hit the trigger and I fall out of the trunk, landing hard on my back. I contain a groan as I shimmy out from under the wheeled case and sit up. Archer and Ellen are already on their feet, positioning the slender gas masks on their faces.

Archer touches the comms in his ear. Ellen and I echo the movement.

"Can everyone hear me?" Archer grabs a holster from his box and secures it around his waist. Instead of his police weapons, there are vials of potions strapped to the belt.

Loud and clear, boss. Cal's disembodied voice is crystal clear in my ear, even from his position a mile away. *I'm compiling footage for loops now. Most of the building looks empty. Almost everyone is gathered for Alice's show.*

"Wonderful," Alice mutters, adjusting her earpiece. She's already dressed in her signature three-piece suit, and she pulls the hat from one of her trunks, placing it at a precise angle on her head. She straightened her hair today, the vibrant pink running in sleek lines down her back. She moves quickly, pulling the supplies she needs from the trunks and setting them up by the door that'll take her to the awaiting crowd.

I grab the holster from my trunk and secure it around my hips, the potion Elder Keating gave me settling at the edge of my thigh. I double- and triple-check that it's secure. "How much longer until we can go?"

Almost there, Cal says, computer keys clacking in the background. *All right. Footage is ready to go. Hallways are clear.*

"Ellen. Hannah. With me." Archer waves for us to follow, but I hesitate. It feels wrong to leave Alice. She's both the safest of us and the one most in danger, and I don't know how to pull those realities apart. "Hannah," he prompts.

"Be careful," I tell Alice, stepping toward the door.

She rolls her eyes, but it doesn't have her usual level of enthusiasm. "Get out of here, pyro. Go save the world."

"Hannah, now," Archer says, opening the back door.

I hold Alice's gaze a second longer, then turn, following Archer deeper into Hall Pharmaceuticals. Ellen hands me a gas mask, and I slip it over my face. It makes my breath too loud in my ears, but it must not be that noticeable, since I don't hear Archer's or Ellen's breathing in the comms. Only Cal's instructions.

Follow the hallway. You'll find a stairwell behind the third door on your left. Take it to the basement.

Even though we studied the building's blueprints for hours, we have to follow Cal's instructions through the mazelike basement. With each corner we turn, I expect to see a battalion of Hunters waiting for us. But there never is. The halls are empty, just like Cal promises again and again. Yet the lack of guards makes me nervous. The Hunters wouldn't leave their secret lab completely unguarded, even with an event happening on the main level, would they?

Wait. Cal's voice comes out rushed. *There are two guards around the next corner.*

"Can you route us around them?" Archer holds up a hand. Ellen and I stop behind him.

They're guarding the lab. It's the only entrance.

Archer reaches for the vials hooked to his belt, pulling out one with a gray, swirling potion inside. He unstoppers the top. Gray smoke slithers up the sides of the bottle and pools on the floor.

Archer glances at me. "Hannah, can you—" But he falters, and heat burns my face. "Ellen, can you push the potion around the corner?"

My covenmate nods, and her magic permeates the air. A gentle breeze picks up the gray smoke and whisks it down the hall. After a beat, there are two soft *thump*s.

"What was that?" My question earns me a look from Archer, who presses a finger to his mask. He waves us forward, and we find a pair of guards slumped on either side of a thick metal door with a wide glass window.

"I guess we don't need these." Archer rests one hand against the potions at his hips—potions that, once combined, would have eaten through the metal door.

"Why not?"

It's a bio scan, Cal says through the comms. *You just need to press their thumbs to the scanners.*

Ellen and I dart forward and grab hold of the unconscious Hunters. The dead weight of my guard is almost impossible to lift. I have to tug his arm over my shoulders and use the strength in my legs to drag him to the door.

"Three," Ellen says, looking to me.

"Two."

"One," we say together, pressing the unconscious men's thumbs to the panel.

At first, nothing happens. I panic, convinced with each beat of my heart that an alarm is about to sound. But then the system beeps and the door slides open. "Finally," Ellen whispers, dropping her guard to the floor with little ceremony.

"Drag them inside. We need to bind them." Archer leads us into the lab, which must double as an armory if the wall of drug-filled darts is any indication. At first, I think Archer wants to give them a binding potion like the one he gave Benton when he was arrested, something that will prevent them from speaking about the Clans. Instead, he pulls lengths of rope from the bag on his back and ties the guards together.

While he works, I take in the room that created so many of my nightmares. It's all stainless steel and glittering white tile floors. There's a computer station on one wall and rows and rows of filing cabinets on the other. The center of the room boasts a series of lab tables covered in beakers and vials of liquid.

It's finally time to destroy the drug.

I can't do much until you plug me in, Cal reminds us.

Archer hurries over to the computer. He slips in the thumb drive and lets our resident hacker take over. "Ellen, help me with the paper files. Hannah, you know what to do."

While they work on prying open the filing cabinets and setting the papers inside ablaze, I pull the glass vial from my bag. At the table in the center of the room, I add a drop of the thick, almost gelatinous potion to the largest beaker.

The Elder's potion vibrates inside the glass, absorbing the thin liquid that has destroyed covens, sent a young Blood Witch to the hospital, and ripped my own magic away. When there's nothing more to consume, the remaining potion bursts into a tiny flame that leaves behind no trace.

A thrill of something that might be vengeance burns hot in my chest. We're *finally* doing something real.

I move as quickly as I can, but my progress is slower than Ellen's fire. I scan the room, looking for a better way to do this . . . *There.* I grab the metal trash can and toss vial after vial inside. The glass shatters on impact, the drug pooling at the bottom. When I've tossed in every last beaker and tranq dart, I dump the rest of Elder Keating's potion inside.

It sizzles and shifts through the shattered glass, until finally, it's gone.

That warm feeling in my chest withers away. My part of this mission is done, but it doesn't feel like enough. It feels like barely anything at all.

Ellen slams the last of the filing cabinets, ash littering the floor around her. "Are we good?"

I'm almost done, Cal says. *I still have to purge the external emails. Another sixty seconds. Two minutes, tops.*

"Is that it? Is it over?" I glance around the destroyed room. Ellen is dampening the last of the flames, ash on her cheeks. She slams the final drawer closed, and a strange emptiness yawns open inside my chest. Shouldn't there be more to it than this? Could it really be as simple as finding a way inside?

"We have a lot more to do before this is over." Archer touches his comms unit. "Are you good, Cal?"

Almost . . . there. *Grab the drive and head out. The hallways are clear.*

Ellen crosses the room and wraps me in a tight hug. "I can't believe we actually did it!"

"We still have to get out," Archer reminds us, pulling the thumb drive from the computer and pouring a red, squirming potion over the entire system. The metal whines as it collapses in on itself. "Are we still clear, Cal?"

Yes, but you should hurry. The security at Alice's show is looking restless.

"Understood." Archer opens the door and steps out. He stops short, grabbing his neck.

When he pulls his hand away, there's a small dart pinched between his fingers.

20

THE METAL DART DROPS to the floor. A hollow echo rattles around me as the drug-dispensing needle bounces off the tile. Archer sways on his feet, grabbing the doorframe for balance. I catch him as he slips and get my first glimpse of the Hunters in the hallway. Of the tranq guns trained on us.

"Freeze!" A man stalks closer, three more Hunters on his heels. "Hands in the air."

Ellen steps past us into the hall. "I'm pretty sure those are contradictory commands." She raises her hands anyway, her power surging with the motion. The air pressure in the hall drops so fast my ears pop, and with a flick of her wrist, gale-force winds whip toward the guards. The Hunters fall back like rag dolls, and Ellen grabs my hand. "Let's go."

We run, Ellen dragging me while Archer staggers after us. It takes him a few strides to get his feet under him while the drug courses through his system, tearing apart his Caster magic. Tearing apart the constant connection he has to his potions.

"What the hell, Cal?" Ellen yells and drops my hand. "I thought you said the hallway was clear!"

It was! It is! He types frantically on his computer. *They must have noticed the looped footage and overwritten the live feed. I don't see you anywhere.*

"Argue about it later," I say, my lungs protesting each word. "Get us out of here!"

I'm working on it. A second later, the Hunters are shouting behind us. Alarms scream through the halls, and angry red lights flash warnings from every side. *Do you still have a smoke screen?*

"No." Archer's voice comes out rough and broken. He pushes more speed into his legs and closes the gap between us. "I mean, I do. But none of it will work."

But why— Cal's voice dies. He must realize what Archer means. *Oh my god. Ryan . . .*

We reach the same stairwell we came down earlier, and Archer yanks open the door. "We'll deal with that later. Can you tell if the stairwell is clear?"

As far as I—

"Everyone up," Archer says, not waiting for him to finish. Another round of darts flies past as we slip through the door. The Hunters are almost on us.

We're at least three stories beneath the lobby, and my legs are screaming after the first staircase. Below, the door slams against the wall, and heavy footsteps follow.

Cal shouts something unintelligible, and the van door slams shut.

Calm down, hacker bro. It's me. Alice's voice sounds far away, but it's unmistakably her. She must have taken the don't-wait-for-us rule seriously. *Please tell me this is a fire alarm.*

"Unfortunately not." Archer surges past me as the second subfloor door swings open. He smashes his elbow into the side of the Hunter's head, and the man collapses to the ground. "Deep breaths, Hannah. Keep going."

I nod, but my thighs are screaming. Why does there always have to be so much *running* with these Hunters?

The air fills with the soft *pop* of the Hunters' tranq guns as they gain on us. Drug-filled darts bounce off handrails and the backs of our spelled jackets, and I'm so grateful Cal is the one who made that particular potion. But there has to be more I can do. I can't let them drug Ellen, too. I can't let anyone else I love lose their magic. Not when we already destroyed their main supply.

I reach for the thrum of magic in my chest, crossing my fingers that it'll heed my call. Pain ripples up my back, and I trip on the edge of the stair, smashing my shin. I turn until I'm facing the Hunters racing up behind us. I raise my hands, searching for the thread of air in their lungs or the water in their blood.

Nothing.

"Alice!" I shout. "Alice, can you hear me?"

I'm here. What do you need? Her voice is closer now. She must have turned on her own comms device.

Doubt stalls my tongue, but the Hunters are still coming. Above me, Ellen sends another rush of air to slow them. I grip the handrail to keep from falling. "Can you control my blood from that far away?"

I don't know.

"Try. Please." I push deeper, searching for the well of power inside my chest. "Hurry!"

A moment later, Alice's magic tingles up my spine. It's sharper than Morgan's, elbowing its way through my body, foreign and grating. But in the next moment, my own power explodes inside me, a vast pool that's all mine for the taking. I grab hold of the first element I can reach. Water. *Blood*. I infuse the water with my will and let it crackle with cold.

The closest Hunter drops first, screaming as his blood starts to freeze. His comrades leap over him, and I push harder, grabbing their breaths with one hand and their blood with the other.

They drop. Screaming. Blood drips from their eyes.

"Hannah, come on." Ellen grips my arms and hauls me upright. "We have to go."

I follow, but I don't let go of my grip on their air. I hold tight, denying them their next breath. Keeping them down. With Alice's power flowing through me, the exhaustion in my limbs falls away, and I race up to the main floor.

We spill out onto the ground level. People are heading lazily for the exit, more irritated than worried by the disruption of the alarm. Archer tries to blend us into the flow of traffic, but I pull away when I see *him*.

Benton stands in the hallway. I blink hard—once, twice—trying to make him disappear. I've seen him everywhere for weeks. I can't afford to get distracted by lookalikes or ghosts of memory that don't want to die. We have to go. We have to—

"Hannah?"

His voice knocks the wind from my lungs. It knocks the elements out of my control. "Benton." I look closer. He's thinner than I remember. Paler. He's dressed in dark-wash jeans and the same black jacket as the Hunters chasing us up the stairs. This isn't a memory. He's here. He's *alive*.

For now.

I'm running before I realize I've made the decision to move. There's only enough time for Benton to register surprise before I'm on him, lunging, catching him around the chest. We go down hard, but I'm scrambling the second we hit the floor. My nails dig into his flesh. I pull myself up until I've got him pinned beneath me, knees pressed into his chest.

The first punch catches him on the side of the face. Pain blooms across my knuckles, but I don't care. I swing again, but he's still stronger than me, better trained. He catches my fist and throws me off. My elbow slams into the floor, pain radiating up my arm, but I won't let him get away. I can't.

Alice's magic is still mixed with mine, and it takes next to nothing to reach for the thread of air flowing into his lungs. I squeeze tight, holding the air hostage. He falls back, clutching at his neck, nails scraping against skin until they draw blood. His panic only makes me hold tighter. I dig my knees into his chest and wrap my hands around his throat, reaching for the water in his body, just like I did with the Hunters on the stairs. I plummet the temperature until everything is freezing. The tiniest blood vessels burst first, spiderwebbing around his eyes.

He tries to scream, and I drink in the choked sound.

Everything that's wrong and broken inside me is his fault. He did this to me. He tore apart my magic, made me rely on Blood Witches to access my powers. And with Alice's magic flowing through my veins, I'm stronger than I was before he drugged me. Before he and his parents ruined my life. Before they destroyed *everything*.

Hands grip my shoulders and try to pull me away.

"No." The word is a growl in my throat. "Not until he's dead. Not until he pays for what he's done."

"We have to go, Hannah. Please." Ellen tugs at me again.

"I said no." Pressure builds inside my chest, and I lash out, wind tearing through the hall. Ellen falls back, crashing into

Archer, who pushes her toward the exit. But I can't leave. "We don't go until he's gone."

Archer raises a hand to his ear. "Alice," he says, voice steady. "Release Hannah."

"No!" But it's too late. Her power disappears, leaving me hollowed out and raw. My hands tremble, and Benton finally throws me off. I hit the floor hard, and my breath violently escapes my lungs.

"Hannah, come on." Archer is reaching for me now, his grip tight on my upper arm. "We have to go."

A metal cylinder slides across the floor. It bursts into an explosion of light and sound. My vision goes spotty. My ears ring. Six Hunters carrying tactical rifles surround us, weapons raised. They scream at us to raise our hands. Archer moves protectively in front of me, but the men carrying guns don't care. They grab us both, dragging us farther down the hall. I catch a brief glimpse of Ellen by the exit, staring after us.

"Get out of here," I scream as the man behind me pulls the comms device from my ear. "Go!"

She hesitates, but the last thing I see before a dark hood covers my face is my covenmate following the crowd out the door.

21

I'M DRAGGED DOWN THE hall and shoved into an elevator, my vision cut off by the hood over my face. My stomach swoops as we rise several floors. My knees buckle, and fingers dig into my arms to hold me upright. With a shudder, we come to a stop. The door dings open, and we're moving again. Another beep, and metal scrapes on metal. I'm shoved forward and pressed into a chair, my limbs bound tight to the wooden arms and legs. Another length of rope secures my torso.

My entire body convulses as the memories come bursting in.

Benton's expression in the rearview mirror, hard and unfeeling. The confusion on his face moments ago in the hall. My legs bound from ankle to knee, tied to a pyre, the fire licking at my skin. Smoke choking my lungs.

It's happening again. Except this time, Archer is caught, too. He won't be able to save me. We're both going to die, and it's all my fault.

The black hood is ripped off, and I blink against the brightness. When my vision adjusts, I'm surprised to find myself sitting in a large office. Huge windows let in the early afternoon light, and the space feels warm and inviting. A large wooden desk is covered with picture frames, and a slim laptop sits at its center. Archer's belt of potions is laid out before us.

"Hannah." Archer's voice comes from my left. I turn and

find him strapped to a wooden armchair like the one I'm in. The office is empty except for the man standing watch by the door. "Are you okay?"

I shake my head. How is any of this okay? "This is all my fault." Tears spill down my cheeks. "If I hadn't gone after him, we could have gotten out. And now we're trapped. They're going to kill us like they killed the other Casters and—"

"Hannah," he says urgently. "We cannot panic. If they wanted us dead, we'd already be dead." He speaks with such calm that I almost believe him, but I remember how well he can mask his fear. I don't trust his confidence for a second. I've ruined us like I ruined Sarah and David and nearly Ellen, too.

Please, Ellen. Please be safe.

"Why didn't they kill us? What do they want?"

"That is a very astute question, Miss Walsh." The presence of the deep voice makes me jump, and the door slams shut. A man dressed in a well-tailored suit approaches the desk. A woman follows after him, similarly dressed like she's late for a board meeting. She wears a navy pencil skirt and crisp, white blouse with her dark hair pulled into a neat bun at the nape of her neck.

The woman leans against the edge of the desk and looks me up and down, assessing. "I'm disappointed," she says to someone behind me. "We trained you better than to be caught off guard."

Her gaze tracks movement that stops to my right. I risk a glance and find Benton leaning against the wall. His neck is still covered with red scratches, and he doesn't meet either of our gazes. He keeps his attention fixed to the floor.

"I'm sorry, Mother."

Mother? I turn sharply back to the pair of Hunters in front of me. The woman—who must be Mrs. Hall—smiles coldly at me. And the man . . . Now that I'm looking for it, I can see Benton in him, can see the future Benton might grow into. The same dark hair and hazel eyes. The same nose and jawline.

These are the Hunters who murdered my dad.

I struggle against the ropes that bind me. I'm not sure if I'm desperate to escape or to finally hurt them like they've hurt me, but the chair doesn't even shake. "What do you want with us?"

"We'll be asking the questions," Benton's father says. He reaches for his pocket and pulls out a slim, silver lighter while Benton's mom walks around the desk and opens the laptop. "Let's start with how you managed to break in. We haven't found you on any of our entrance footage."

"You don't need Hannah for this," Archer says, still infuriatingly calm. "I have all the answers you need and more. She's just a child."

"A child who sent our *son* to prison," Mrs. Hall says, glancing up from the computer. There's a cold glint to her eyes now, an edge of poorly concealed hatred creeping in. "She's not going anywhere."

Benton's father flicks open the lighter and toys with the striking mechanism. He rests his hip against the desk. "You destroyed *years* of careful research. We sunk millions into the development of the cure, and you ruined it!"

His temper boils over and he turns, knocking the vials of Archer's magic-less potions to the floor. The glass shatters, but that's not enough for the man's rage. He pockets the lighter and lunges for Archer, hitting him hard across the face. Once. Twice. Three times, and I'm screaming for him to stop and there's blood dripping from Archer's nose and I want my reality to be anything but this.

"There's also the matter of our missing children," Mrs. Hall cuts in, and her voice finally stops the assault. "We lost contact with three of our young agents two weeks ago. We have reason to believe *you* are responsible for their disappearance."

I struggle against the bindings, anger mixing with terror. I reach for my magic, but it's even harder to find with panic and fear clouding my senses.

"Well?" Benton's mom prompts. "Where are they?"

"Where they belong," I snap, the anger winning over.

Mr. Hall glares at me, and I flinch when he moves, but he heads for the desk and rummages through the top drawer. When he turns back to face me, there's a syringe in his hand. My entire body goes cold. "Let's try this again." He stalks slowly toward me. "Where are our missing agents?"

"Hannah doesn't know anything." Archer struggles against his restraints. "You don't need her."

But the Hunter doesn't care. He grabs hold of my chin and tilts my head to one side, exposing my neck. "Where are they?" His voice scrapes against my skin like broken glass. When I don't answer, even as Archer begs him to let me go, I feel the bite of the needle and—

"James, wait." Mrs. Hall crosses the room and eases the needle from my neck. "We don't have much left." She steps back, and I expect to see compassion in her features despite everything I know she's done. Instead, she looks at me like I'm an experiment. "Besides, she's already been dosed with a previous version. Her biology could be useful."

"She still has her magic," Mr. Hall argues. "She's dangerous until she's either drugged or put down."

"No, she's not," Archer says, his voice steady again. "Hannah can't access her magic. She hasn't been able to since she was drugged."

Mrs. Hall sets the syringe gently on the table. "The agents in the stairwell—"

"Were attacked by another Elemental. Not Hannah," Archer says, and I can't tell if he's lying or truly thinks it was Ellen who dropped those men. "You don't need her biology, either. I was drugged today, too. You can use me."

"Archer . . ." I won't abandon him here. I won't let him sacrifice himself.

Mr. Hall hits him again, and Archer stifles a groan, his face contorted with pain. "You are not in a position to *bargain* with us. Neither of you are leaving this building alive." Benton's dad pulls out the lighter again and flicks it open. "Let's see how powerless your fire demon is."

For the first time since the Hunters shot at us in the basement, I see real fear flicker across Archer's face. Mr. Hall sparks the lighter, and a tiny flame bursts forth. Archer sits impossibly still, but his hands curl into fists as the Hunter approaches. Mr. Hall runs the flame along Archer's knuckles, and I reach desperately for my power.

A scream tears from Archer's throat, and I push as hard as I can past the barrier around my magic. Pain explodes up my spine, and I try to push. I try to keep going, try to grab hold of the fire's will and bend it to my own. But the harder I reach for the flame, the more it hurts, and I can't focus through the pain and Archer's screams and I can't, I can't, I can't . . .

"Dad, that's enough." Benton crosses the room toward us. "You heard him. He was cured. He's human now and—"

Mr. Hall catches Benton across the side of the face with a

vicious right hook. The impact sends Benton to his knees, and a bone-deep terror settles over me as blood drips from Benton's nose. *If the Hunters will do this to their own children, what will they do to us?*

Benton's father looks down at him, disdain written all over his face. "Don't forget your place. They *destroyed* the cure. This is the least they deserve."

He turns back to Archer, repositioning the lighter in his hand as Benton pulls himself to his feet.

"Wait!" I shout when Mr. Hall relights the flame. Fear shakes my voice, but I can't let this continue. Even if they know where we hid the teens, they won't be able to get past the barrier. With Benton out of jail and the trial on hold, there's no reason for Elder Keating to put the town at risk. "Riley and the others are in Salem. They haven't been hurt. They're fine."

Mrs. Hall closes her laptop and stands. "We'll need an exact address."

I glance at Archer, but I can't tell if that's disappointment or gratitude on his pain-stricken face. I rattle off the address.

"Good." Mrs. Hall grabs hold of my chin and forces it left until I can't see anything but Archer. "Now pay close attention," she whispers as her husband pockets the lighter and smashes his knuckles against Archer's face.

Again.

And again.

"We decide when this stops. Not you." Her grip on my chin tightens. "And once we've re-created our cure, we will decide how and when you die."

22

WHEN BENTON'S PARENTS GROW bored, they call for guards to bring us back to the basement. I know I should try to keep track of the twists and turns through the halls, but I can't focus on anything but Archer's slumped body as they drag him in front of me. Benton leads our group and stops before a cell. He pulls a key from his pocket and unlocks the door, swinging the creaking metal wide.

Archer's guards drop him in a heap in the center of the small room, and large hands shove me hard from behind. I stumble forward, and the door slams shut by the time I can whirl around. One of the guards spits at us before he leaves. Benton is the last to go, his jaw still red from where his father hit him.

And then we're alone.

I spin and drop to my knees before Archer. The backs of his hands are angry and blistered, and blood flecks the front of his jacket. Shame twists my insides into knots. I should have been able to protect him from the flames. If I could just—

Archer sucks in a deep breath, surfacing out of unconsciousness. He groans as he tries to pull himself into a seated position.

"Let me help. Hang on." I move him toward the edge of the room so he can lean against the wall for support. Once he's up, I can see more of the damage. His left eye is already swollen shut. Benton's dad split his lip, and the blisters on his hands are starting to ooze. "I'm so sorry, Archer. I tried to stop him, but I couldn't . . ." Tears cut off the rest of my apology. I felt so fucking helpless, watching them hurt him, unable to do anything but scream.

Archer clutches his ribs and gingerly turns his head until I'm within range of his right eye, the one that isn't swollen shut. "This isn't your fault, Hannah. You didn't do this."

"But I did! I'm the one who went after Benton. I'm the one who gave up your address and couldn't stop the flame from the lighter and—"

"Hannah." His voice is slow and thick with pain. "Blaming yourself isn't going to help us get out of here."

He may believe we have a chance at escape, but I know better. We're outnumbered and outgunned. Neither of us have access to magic, and the only one of us trained for this sort of thing can barely sit up, even with a wall to lean on. We're going to be lab rats, and the second the Hunters don't need us anymore, we'll be dead.

Will Mom even have a body to bury?

Archer reaches out and grips my wrist with surprising strength. "You have to stop, Hannah. If you give up on us now, we won't stand a chance."

Tears slip down my face, and I wipe them away with my free hand. "How can you possibly believe we'll get out of here?"

"Because I believe in you."

I scoff and roll my eyes. The normalcy of the reaction makes me feel a fraction better, but Archer doesn't relent. "I'm serious," he says, his grip on my wrist urgent now. "You are resourceful and driven. You've been through so, *so* much the past few months, and you just need to push a little further."

He lets go of my wrist, and I sigh, turning to sit against the wall beside him. I still don't believe we can escape, but I'm not going to go out without a fight, either. "So, what's the plan then?"

I think Archer tries to smile, but his whole face is swollen and bruised, and he just ends up wincing instead. "It sounds like they'll draw our blood as part of their research for the drug. That might give us an opportunity." He turns his head a little more in my direction. "We need to get your magic back before then."

"But I've tried. The only thing that works is Blood Magic."

"If Blood Magic can help," Archer insists, "that means it's in there. You just need to figure out how to access it." He tips his head back, staring at the dark ceiling. He's quiet a long time, and I don't interrupt his thought process. My mind is busy with its own wandering, parsing through all the things Cal said about my magic, about what it means that just being near Morgan, even when she's not using her power, makes it better.

How am I supposed to embrace grief in a place like this without getting lost in it?

"I don't think fear will help," he says at last. "If it did, I think it's safe to say you would have found your magic in that office." His burnt hands are proof enough that fear is not the emotion I've been avoiding.

"I am so, so sorry about that."

He shakes his head. "Don't blame yourself for a *second* of what's happened here." He goes quiet, his eyes shut against his pain. "I don't want you to feel pressured, but if you can't find a way back to your magic . . ." He lets the sentence trail off, and my mind is happy to fill in the horrifying gaps.

"I'll try," I promise. "I'll do whatever it takes."

And I do try. Long after Archer has fallen asleep, I try to reach my magic. I force myself to pull down the walls around my heart. I push against every emotional bruise until I'm aching and raw and so scared and miserable I can't breathe.

Time has no meaning in this windowless cell, but it feels like hours have passed. I'm exhausted, but my mind won't stop spinning. I don't understand how this happened—how this *keeps* happening. Going after Benton was my fault, but the Hunters finding us and drugging Archer? That wasn't me.

David's death wasn't on me, either. The Hunters *always* seem to be a step ahead, almost like . . .

Nope. I don't even want to *think* it. But no matter how many times I push it away, the thought comes back. Each time, it's more insistent, it brings more clues and theories.

What if someone betrayed us?

What if someone told the Hunters we were recruiting David? What if the Hunters knew we were coming to raid their facility? Once the thoughts lodge in my brain, a list of suspects comes racing through.

Maybe Veronica, Cal, and I were right before. Maybe David helped the Hunters create the drug, then thought better of it and tried to change his allegiances. Except . . . he didn't know anything about the raid, which means it was probably someone else. Someone who tipped off the Hunters and got David killed, so he couldn't create the potion to destroy them.

What if it's Lexie and Coral? They weren't thrilled that I let Alice escape, and Veronica did call them long before they were recruited. Plus, Lexie made those charms that could detect other Clan Witches. That could explain how the Hunters knew where to find us.

Or maybe it's Tori. I didn't get a chance to talk to Lexie or Coral, so I don't know where Tori is or what happened to her. She was the one who wanted to bind Alice's magic. Maybe she helped the Hunters make the drug as a way to get back at the Blood Witches and didn't realize the Hunters would target all three Clans.

But how would the Casters have known about the Council's other plans for Dr. O'Connell's research?

Then it hits me. *Alice*.

Alice, who acted like she didn't want any part of this. Alice, who was furious at me for inviting the Casters to Salem without warning. Who was furious that I dropped out of the raid. She threatened to back out unless I helped, and then less than a day later, Benton was out of jail.

I must finally fall asleep, because the next thing I remember is waking up to the sound of metal scraping against the stone floor. I scramble to my feet, disoriented and sore from sleeping on the ground.

Benton stands on the other side of the cell. A deep purple bruise blooms across his right jaw, and dark crescents sit under his eyes like he slept worse than I did. There's a tray of food on the floor of the cell where he must have pushed it through, and he holds a cloth bag in his hands.

He glances from me to Archer, who is awake but still leaning against the wall, and then shoves the cloth bag through the bars, tossing it in my direction. "There are clothes and soap and toothbrushes in there. You should eat the food before it goes cold."

I glance behind me at the door to the little bathroom, the one piece of dignity this awful cell provides. "I bet you love this." I grab the tray and take it to Archer. I won't eat until Benton's gone, even though my stomach is begging for food. "I bet you dreamed of this while you were in jail."

"My parents are gone for the day," he says, ignoring my accusations. "You should rest while you can."

"Why? So we can be *fresh* for their experiments? Do they have more fun torturing us if we can stay conscious?" My words are bitter and angry, but Benton won't even meet my gaze. He stares at the floor, his fingers pressed against the metal bars, and I can't help but remember the way he asked his father to stop. His father's wrath so swift and vicious that it knocked Benton to his knees.

I don't understand how he can win, how he can see us locked in a cell, and still look so miserable.

"It wasn't supposed to be like this," he murmurs to himself, but the empty hallway echoes his words back to me.

"Why?" I try and fail to inject the same level of acid as I did into my earlier words. "Upset your parents get to kill me instead of you?" My voice trembles as the reality of it crashes in. They're really going to kill us, once they've used us for all we have.

Finally, Benton glances up to meet my eye. He stares at me like he's trying to peer into my soul, and when he finally turns around to leave, he looks impossibly sad and alone.

-|-   *   -|-

Benton's expression haunts me the rest of the day.

At least, I think it's been a day. It's impossible to tell without the sun or clocks to mark the time. My empty stomach grumbles, but then even hunger gets tired of spending time with me and abandons me to my thoughts. Archer, who is in even more pain than yesterday, tries to coach my magic into existence. We strategize how to escape. He tells me how to hold on to my sense of self, but Benton's expression lingers in my mind. He should be happy that I'm caught, that I'm going to die, and yet . . .

And yet.

Every time I hear a door close out of sight, I expect the Hunters to come back. I expect to see Benton's father with his cold eyes and shiny silver lighter. I expect someone to draw our blood to begin their tests, but it's like something else has captured their attention. No one comes for us. Not until the tide of hunger has come in and out at least three times.

Then finally *he* is here again.

Benton is back with another tray of food. His face is different now, a mask composed of plaster and ice. Emotionless. He slides the food through the space at the bottom of the cell and leaves without a word. I help Archer eat—he can't bear to use his hands—and after I've finished what's left of our food, I curl into a corner and reach for my magic again and again until my entire body aches and unconsciousness consumes me.

Metal crashes against metal, and the sound jolts me out of uneasy sleep. I flinch away from the sound, slamming my elbow against the wall.

"Now, what do we have here?" A familiar voice asks, but I can't place it right away.

I force myself to sit up, squinting until I can make out the shapes in the light. My heart stops.

Riley.

Morgan's ex holds a crowbar in one hand, and he hits it against the cell bars again. "I'm sorry, did I wake you?" He sneers at me, and I notice the bruising around his eye. His jaw. He carries himself gingerly, like there are injuries I can't see.

The coven didn't do that to him. Did the Hunters?

"How are you here?" I rise to my feet, legs stiff to the point of pain. "You were locked up. You were behind the barrier."

Riley shrugs and glances over his shoulder. The other boy he was with—Wes, I think—steps into view. He's sporting a split lip, a large keyring gripped in his hand. Riley puts his free arm around the other boy's shoulders. "It's a beautiful sight, isn't it?" he asks, his voice almost dreamy.

Wes nods. "Monsters in cages. There's definitely something right about it."

"How did you get out?" I demand again, ignoring their taunts. "How are you even *here* right now?"

"Do you want to tell her?" Riley asks, looking to Wes. "Or shall I?"

"After you."

Riley taps the crowbar against the cell. "Your directions were *very* helpful. The Order brought us home this morning." He turns to Wes. "How many witches do you think we killed on our way out? Four? Five?"

"At least."

The boys laugh, but the world trembles around me. This can't be happening. The Hunters shouldn't have been able to get through the barrier. The town was supposed to be safe. How—

No. Not how. How doesn't matter. *Who* was it? Who did the Hunters take from us? Cal? Ellen?

Mom?

My lungs constrict and won't let anything else back in. I can't breathe. I can't—

"Hannah." Archer's voice barely carries over the Hunters' laughter, but even his presence can't stop the panic that's tearing me apart inside. I'm a spool of ribbon that's been sliced down the center, every seam fraying and coming undone. Archer drags himself to his feet, and he closes the space between us. "Hannah, you have to breathe."

But I can't. I can't, I can't, I can't—

The air around us turns cold.

It's freezing.

My magic is a wild and untamed thing inside me, and it spills past the careful boundaries I spent the last day trying to pull apart. The temperature continues to plummet until I'm shaking with cold. The laughter dies away.

"They said your magic was gone." An edge of fear creeps into Riley's voice.

"Is it back?" Archer whispers as his body trembles.

I reach for the air as frost crackles along my lashes. I shake my head. "I can't stop it. I can't control it."

Riley curses and drops the crowbar before the metal sticks to his skin.

"What the hell is going on?" Benton turns the corner, tugging his arms tightly around himself. "Riley? Wes? What are you doing here? I thought Dad—"

"Shut up, Hall," Riley snaps. He wraps his sleeve around his hand and bends to retrieve the crowbar. "Unlock the door."

Wes hurries forward to do what he was asked, his hands trembling with cold. I try to pull my magic in, try to contain it beneath my skin, but all I can see is my mom covered in blood and she's dead and Dad's dead and I'm all alone.

The air gets even colder.

"What are you doing?" Benton demands, more authority in his voice now.

"Knocking the witches out before they kill us." Riley adjusts his covered grip on the cold metal and waits for the door to swing open. I share a worried look with Archer. He pulls me into an embrace I know must hurt him more than it could possibly soothe me.

"No. You're not." Benton tries to grab the crowbar from Riley, but he flinches away when the cold bites into his bare skin. "The detective is human now. We can't hurt him."

"The fuck we can't." Riley motions for Wes to hurry with the lock, but the other boy looks from Riley to Benton and back again, unsure. "Open the door, Wes."

Benton grabs Riley's wrist and twists. The crowbar clatters against the floor. "I said *no*, Riley. Our directives are clear. We don't hurt them once they're human. My parents need samples anyway."

"Screw that." Riley adjusts his sleeve over his palm and grabs the crowbar from the floor. But this time, when he swings, the metal connects with Benton's side.

Benton doubles over, and Riley kicks him until he's sprawled on his back. "Fucking witch sympathizer." Riley drops the bar and nods for Wes to open the door.

This time, the other Hunter obeys.

I know I should try to run, but Archer is still holding tight, our combined warmth keeping us standing. Riley drags Benton into the cell and hurries out, slamming the door just as Benton makes it to the bars.

"Maybe this time, you'll manage to kill the witch." Riley sneers at Benton, already backing away from us, away from the cold. "Unless she kills you first."

Then they're gone.

And the temperature continues to drop.

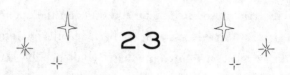

23

BENTON STANDS WITH HIS back against the cell door, his arms crossed tightly against his chest. He watches us, his expression streaked through with worry as he shivers uncontrollably. His breaths come out in little white puffs.

"They're gone, Hannah." Archer pulls away and bends until our faces are level. "We're okay."

I shake my head, magic still rushing out like water through a broken dam. Tears freeze against my cheeks. "I can't. Not if Mom . . . Not if she—"

"We don't know it was her. There was no reason for her to be at my house." He tucks his arms around his chest, careful not to scrape the blisters on the backs of his hands. "Hannah, please. You have to try."

Cautiously, Benton approaches us. "What happened? What did Riley do to her?"

"Your people murdered more of her family," Archer snaps at the young Hunter. "We don't know which ones, but—"

"What are you talking about? No one died." Benton looks past Archer, and realization softens his features. He steps closer. "Riley lied, Hannah. The house was empty when the team rescued him. The team freed them and came straight home."

"Riley lied." I repeat his words, stack them into a wall to close off my power. *Mom is alive. She's fine. She's okay.* I try to be-

lieve the words, but the relief is slow to come. My brain hesitant
to accept yet another new reality, the grief unwilling to release its
grip on my heart.

"Your mom is safe," Archer says, but his swollen eye and
chattering teeth ruin the soothing effect I know he must be going
for. He lays assurances at my feet, and piece by piece I come back
to myself. The magic fades until his words can no longer be seen
in the air as tiny puffs of white in the cold.

"Don't lock it all away," Archer warns as he releases me.
"Your magic is our best chance at getting out of here."

"I'll try," I promise, and when I've removed the last of the
cold from the air, we stand frozen in the cell. Two witches face a
forsaken Hunter, and none of us seem to know what to do. I rub
my arms, trying to get feeling back into my limbs.

Benton turns and leans his forehead against the bars. "It
wasn't supposed to be like this," he murmurs to himself, but it's so
quiet in the cell that his words are crystal clear. He screams curses
into the empty hallway and shakes the door, but it holds tight. He
hits the bars again and again with the side of his fist before turning and sliding defeated to the cold floor. "Go ahead." He wraps
his arms around his knees. "Kill me."

"We're not going to hurt you," Archer says while I stare at
the boy who tried to kill *me* two months ago. He's broken and
bruised, and my mind plays a loop of his father's fist cracking
against his face because he told the older man to stop.

Why did he tell him to stop?

"I don't understand what changed." Benton runs a hand
through his hair, making it stand on end before it flops back into
place. "My parents raised me to hunt witches, but we only killed
them because we had no other option. We have a cure now. We're

supposed to save you. We're supposed to make you human, and we *protect* humans." He goes silent and glances up at us. "Well, we *had* a cure until you two destroyed most of it."

The reminder that there's any left turns my stomach, but at least we have time before they can make more. Hopefully enough time for Lexie to translate David's notes and create an antidote.

Or create a weapon against the Hunters.

But the thought of killing them makes me uneasy, despite everything they've done. If someone like Benton wants to save us, as twisted as his version of *saved* is, can't we do something similar to the Hunters? Can't we cure them of their hatred instead of killing them off?

"What do we do now?" I direct my question at Archer, but it's Benton who says, "I don't know." He sounds miserable and lost and alone. I can't stop looking at the bruising on his face. Was his entire life like that? Or did his time in jail change how his parents see him?

"What will happen when your parents find out Riley put you in here?"

The last bit of color drains from Benton's face. "We need to get out before they do."

"Okay then." I force myself to breathe deep, and the air sings through my lungs. I don't dare reach for the elements, but they're calling to me for the first time since Benton took them away. With the air playing along my skin, I manage to find focus. "How do we get out of here?"

Benton pats at his pockets and pulls out a phone. He stares at the screen, and a flash of the date and time is visible. October 1. 7:57 P.M. It's hard to believe the raid was only yesterday morning.

"Is there anyone you trust?" Archer asks, walking over to

the wall to lean against the rough stone for support. "Anyone who would let you out?"

"After this?" Benton raises his shoulders in a noncommittal shrug. "I honestly don't know."

Trust is a funny thing. Benton doesn't trust the Hunters who raised him. He doesn't trust us. I don't trust him *or* the Hunters, and if a witch has betrayed us . . .

I leave Benton to wallow in his identity crisis and approach Archer, keeping my voice low. "Even if we get out, I don't know if we'll be safe. The Hunters shouldn't have been able to get past Keating's barrier. Not unless someone helped them."

Archer looks up from his injured hands and fixes me with a suspicious stare. "Who exactly are you accusing?"

Even with everything at stake, a thread of nervousness stitches through me. Accusing a witch of treason isn't something to do lightly. It carries a weight I'm not sure I want to bear, but I tell him my suspects anyway. I tell him everything.

Lexie and Coral working with Tori to bind Alice's magic this spring. How they could have worked with the Hunters to develop the drug, how the Hunters never used their cure until after that fateful encounter. And being Caster Witches themselves, they could have let the Hunters past the barrier.

And then there's Alice, who's attacked me more than once and was furious when I backed out of the raid. How she got away and made it to Cal's van before the rest of us even got to the main floor. I tell him what Morgan told me about Blood Witches being masters of barrier spells.

He listens through it all, alarm widening his eyes every time I mention another violation of Council laws. When I'm done, he tips his head back against the wall and stares at the ceiling. "Fuck,

Hannah." His profanity startles me, and it's like his entire persona as a detective, as an agent for the Council, crumbles away. He looks at me like I'm a kid sister he wants desperately to protect. "Why didn't you say something?"

The emotion in his voice tightens my throat. "I was scared."

"Of what?"

"The Council," I admit, trembling too much to keep my voice low. "Lady Ariana always warned us that if we stepped out of line, if we broke the laws, the Council would come and take away our magic."

"I have an idea," Benton says, interrupting before Archer can respond. But not before I notice the deepening sadness in his eyes. "I know someone who might let me out."

"Good for you," I snap. "That doesn't exactly keep us alive."

But Benton shakes his head. "I'll take you with me."

The absurdity of his promise makes me roll my eyes. "In what world do you expect me to believe that? You hate us." *Even if he did stand up for us twice . . .*

"I swore an oath to protect humans from harm, and I paid for that when Gemma got hurt." With his free hand, Benton gingerly touches his abdomen where Riley hit him. "I don't know what happened to the Order while I was away, but former witch or not, the detective is human now. I won't let anyone hurt him." He leans heavily against the door, the phone clutched in his hand. "Not even my parents."

Despite what Benton thinks, Archer is still a Caster. He'll *always* be a Caster, but I don't bother arguing the point. "What about me? I'm still an Elemental." I gently reach for the air, but my intentional magic is weak and out of practice.

Benton falters. He may honestly believe that it's his duty to protect Archer, but it's pretty clear what he's supposed to do with someone like me.

"Well?" I prompt when he still hasn't come up with anything.

"You won't like it," he warns, rubbing the back of his neck. I cross my arms and glare at him until he continues. "I don't want you to die," he admits slowly, watching my reaction. "You deserve to be cured, but if I leave you here, they'll just kill you."

His obsession with curing something that isn't broken or bad or wrong makes my skin crawl. Even after everything I've been through, even with the months of friendship in our past, he still can't see my humanity, and that breaks my heart more than I thought it could.

"And you're willing to risk yourself to help us?" I ask, unable to keep the emotion out of my voice.

Benton shrugs. "They already think I'm a witch sympathizer. At least, Riley does. Breaking the detective out is bad enough. They can't exactly kill me twice if I break you out, too."

If I don't kill you, the Order will.

They'll kill me for being too weak to do my job.

A strange feeling tugs at my heart. Kill or be killed. What kind of family raises their kids like that?

Before I can say anything, Benton's thumbs are flying across his screen as he taps out a text. He hits send and slips the phone back into his pocket. He looks up and meets my eye. "Now we wait."

24

IT FEELS LIKE FOREVER before Benton gets a response. His brows knit as he reads the text, which isn't the encouraging sign I was hoping for.

"What did they say?" I ask, my heart lodged in my throat.

He glances up from his phone. "All she sent was an eye roll emoji. No, wait." The phone buzzes again. "She's on her way."

I stand from the cold stone floor and stretch my legs in case this escape—or trap or whatever it actually is—involves more running. "And who is 'she,' exactly?"

"Someone likely to assume Riley was being an ass. She'll let me out," he says evasively. I want to push the issue, but I don't want to give him any reason to leave me behind. Especially when there's already a solid chance he's only pretending to rescue us so I don't freeze him to death.

If I thought the text took forever, that's nothing compared to waiting for the mysterious sender to arrive. I jump at every tiny sound as I strain to hear the moment someone comes to the basement level. Finally, a door creaks open down the hall. I stop pacing, and I'm not even sure when I started walking the length of the small cell.

"Stand in the back with me," Archer whispers urgently. "It'll look more realistic if we keep our distance."

I do as Archer says, anticipation making me jumpy. Footsteps approach and pause, metal sliding against stone, then the visitor approaches again. Paige, the third Hunter from Brooklyn, steps into view.

She raises a single eyebrow at Benton and leans her forearm against the horizontal bar in the door. "What happened, Hall?" She looks amused, and I take that as a good sign.

"Did Riley say anything?" Benton asks, sighing dramatically like this whole thing is nothing more than a ridiculous prank. Paige shakes her head, and Benton glances over his shoulder at us. "Ri thought it'd be funny to lock me in here with *them*."

"Boys," Paige grumbles, looking fully irritated with both Benton and Riley.

"Let me out?" Benton bats his lashes and gives her puppy eyes. I want to vomit and maybe punch him one more time.

Paige rolls her eyes again and slips the key into the lock. She looks past Benton to where Archer and I are standing at the back of the cell. "If either of you moves, you'll regret it," she says, and turns the key.

The door swings open, and my heart soars with the chance for freedom. Benton steps through the door, but Paige closes the cell again. My hopes sink, and I reach for my magic. If I can drop them both before she locks the door, then maybe—

Benton lunges forward and wraps his arm tight around Paige's throat, pressing his forearm against the side of her neck. The keys fall with a clang to the floor. She braces her feet against the door and *shoves*. Both Hunters slam against the opposite wall, but Benton doesn't relent. Paige scratches his face, and he only tightens his hold.

She fights until her limbs fall to her sides and her eyes roll back in her head, unconscious. Benton catches her before she falls, scooping one hand under her knees until she's cradled in his arms.

"Get the door." His voice is choked with emotion as he steps toward us. I rush forward and push open the still unlocked cell door. "Move." He shoves by me and gently lays Paige inside the cell, swiping the back of his hand over his cheeks before grabbing the gun from her waist.

I've seen this Benton before. Cold and unfeeling with a gun held firmly in his hand. My throat closes, and it's like I'm back in his bedroom. But he tucks the gun in his waistband and strides through the cell door.

"Come on. We want as much distance from here as possible before anyone notices we're gone." Benton leads us out of the cell, and then the race is on.

I want to know where we're going. I want to know what the plan is, but I force myself to trust the boy who just knocked a fellow Hunter unconscious to protect Archer.

To protect me.

Benton uses his thumbprint to open a door to a stairwell that wasn't on any of the plans we studied and heads upstairs. I still don't understand why he's doing this, why he isn't falling in line like Riley and the others did. But with my heart hammering in my ears and our footsteps too loud around us, I can't concentrate on anything but running to safety. Running home to my mom.

"We're almost there," Benton says, pausing us before the next turn. "Once we're clear of the building, we'll be in a rear parking lot. It's late, so it should be pretty empty. There won't be much cover, so we'll need to move fast."

"Do you have keys to any of the vehicles?" Archer asks, breathing hard.

"Not on me," Benton admits. "We'll have to run as far as we can and figure it out from there."

"If we can get out unseen, how long do you think we'll have?" Archer glances around the corner. "If there are any older cars in the lot, I can have one hot-wired in a couple minutes."

Benton shakes his head. "I don't know. We—"

"Hall? Is that you?" Riley's voice washes over us, and I tense. We turn and see the Hunter approaching from the way we'd just come. "What are you doing?"

"Not another step." Benton raises the gun, his voice trembling but his aim steady.

Riley freezes, but even from twenty paces away, I can see the hatred burning in his eyes. "You're making a huge mistake. Do this and you're as good as dead, Hall."

"The Order has lost its way, Ri." Benton lowers the gun a fraction. "The detective is cured now. He's *human*. We're supposed to protect him."

His words grate against my soul—the Hunters' drug didn't *cure* anything—but Benton is helping us, and for now, that has to be enough.

"*She* isn't human," Riley argues. "Leave the witch, and I'll let you go." He bares his teeth. "For now."

Benton glances back at me, and I can tell he's considering the offer. That he's weighing his options. His brows crease, and he closes his eyes tight before shaking his head. "Please, Hannah," he whispers. "Don't make me shoot him."

"I won't stay here."

"I'm not asking you to." Tears spill down his cheeks. "But I don't want to shoot him. Can't you do something?"

Understanding blooms in my chest, but before I can reach

for my power, Riley rushes forward. "Look out!" I shout, and then everything happens too fast.

Benton turns.

The gun goes off.

Someone cries out.

And then Riley's on the ground, clutching his lower leg. He's screaming and cursing but still very much alive. Benton backs away, pale and shaking. The gun slips from his grip and clatters to the ground.

"Come on." Archer pulls us both away, his face swollen and contorted with pain.

We stumble after him.

And then we run.

25

WITH THE GUNSHOT ALERTING the rest of the Hunters to our escape, we run into the trees and don't stop until we can't breathe. Then we walk until our legs are ready to give out. When we're about to collapse, Archer slips into an abandoned parking garage and comes out ten minutes later driving an old sedan.

We ride in silence back to Salem, Archer and I in the front with Benton curled up in the back, his knees pulled up to his chest as he stares out at the speeding scenery. He let me borrow his phone to call Mom. She didn't answer the unknown number, but I left a message and she called back in less than a minute. Hearing her voice, hearing her alive and simultaneously furious and relieved, was enough to soothe the last of the tension from my heart. I doze off and on the entire hour back to Salem.

"Are we taking him to the police station or the jail?" I ask as we near the town line.

Though he doesn't say anything, Benton tenses.

"Neither," Archer says, surprising me. "Without the three Hunters we lost, he's our last connection to the Order." He doesn't say it's my fault that Riley and the others got away, but he doesn't have to. It was. "He could be useful."

I glance at Benton in the rearview. He looks just as uneasy with the plan as I feel, but I imagine for opposite reasons.

When we finally pull into the driveway at my house, the lights are all on inside. The curtains rustle as Archer cuts the engine, and then Mom comes tearing out the front door. She squeezes the breath from my lungs. "I will never, ever let you go." She tightens the hug. "You are never leaving this house again."

Archer clears his throat. "We should go inside."

Mom releases me, but when she spots Benton, the air around us crackles with cold. "What is *he* doing here?"

"Inside," Archer says again, more command than question now. He steers Benton toward the house without waiting for an answer. When Mom notices the injuries on Archer's face and hands, she sucks in a worried breath and ushers me after them.

In the bright, artificial light of the house, Benton looks even worse than I feel. It's hard to imagine he was ever the smiling boy I knew in school. Harder still to picture his currently bruised and swollen face contorted with disgust like the night he tried to burn me alive. I can't believe he protected us. I can't believe he shot Riley to help us get away.

He looks like he can't believe it, either.

I try to squash any softness I feel toward him, but my stupid heart constricts as he moves gingerly through the house. His ribs are likely bruised from where Riley hit him, and his hands haven't stopped shaking.

Mom reluctantly, and after several thinly veiled threats against Benton, leaves us in the kitchen to talk to Archer in the hall. I pull two cups from the cupboard, fill them with water, and pass one to Benton.

"Thanks." We drink our water, and the air grows heavy with unsaid things. I wonder if he remembers all the times we laughed and joked in art class. If he remembers how much we cared for each other before we learned that we stood on opposite sides of a deadly feud.

I drain my cup and reach for the faucet to fill it again. While my back is turned, his voice catches me around the chest.

"I'm sorry about my parents. They're . . . I don't know. They've changed so much since this summer." He runs his free hand through his hair and finishes the water.

Anger hardens around my heart. "But you said you'd still drug us if you could, right? You'd still strip away our magic if you had the choice."

"That doesn't mean I want you dead."

"It doesn't make it *right*, either."

My raised tone draws Mom and Archer back into the kitchen. The room crackles with cold, but it's Mom manipulating the air, not me. Every time she looks at Benton, the temperature dips another degree.

"The Elders will be here soon," Archer announces, looking between the pair of us. "Cal, the New York Casters, and Alice, too. We'll figure out how the Hunters made it through the barrier, and then we'll plan our next move."

"You should clean up," Mom says to me. "Archer and I will secure him downstairs." She still won't say Benton's name, and I don't blame her. It's a miracle she's even letting him breathe right now, so I don't say anything as they escort him to the basement.

When they're gone, I grab fresh clothes from my bedroom and take the hottest shower I can stand. The water pelts against my skin, and maybe it's wishful thinking, but I swear the water bleeds energy back into my body. After I dress, I slip back into my room to handle my hair and steal a few minutes to myself before I'm forced to relive everything that happened for the Council.

Outside my bedroom, the front door opens and slams shut.

An intense power washes through the house, and the scent of wildflowers and cut grass drifts through my room. There's a new Elemental in the house. Someone with immense power. Archer mentioned the Elders were coming, but I didn't stop to think the Elemental Elder might be among them.

The air buzzes encouragingly around me, and I leave the relative safety of my room. Archer and Cal are talking in hushed voices in the kitchen while Archer holds an icepack to his bruised face. Someone also bandaged his hands since I saw him last. The men fall silent when they see me, and Cal offers a smile. "How are you holding up?"

I shrug. "I feel ready to collapse."

Cal crosses the room to hug me. "I'd be worried if you weren't."

"We should go," Archer says. "The Elders are waiting for us."

In the small living room, Mom stands beside my grandmother, whose harsh exterior is more cracked than I've ever seen it before. Her lips are pressed into a thin line, but her arms are crossed defensively against her chest.

When Lady Ariana sees me, something in her breaks. Her posture deflates, and she rushes over. I have to stop myself from stepping back. My grandmother has *never* rushed in my entire life. She hugs me tight, and I feel myself go stiff before I force my arms around her.

"Thank the Middle Sister," she whispers into my hair before she finally steps back, revealing the rest of the room.

Now that I'm here, I'm positive the older Black man standing beside Elder Keating is the Elemental Elder. The air seems to gather around him, and there's this crackling of power that makes me want to speak in hushed tones. He's wearing a tailored charcoal suit, crisp white shirt, and deep green tie. His neatly trimmed beard is flecked with white, and his head is shaved. Despite the bits of gray, it's hard to guess his age. His warm brown skin boasts only the beginnings of laugh lines, but his dark eyes are deep wells of wisdom. Archer confirms my assumption when he introduces the man as Elder Hudson.

Behind the pair of Elders are the witches I've accused of treason.

Well, almost all of them.

Alice is sprawled out across the couch. She examines her nails like this whole thing bores her, but when her gaze flicks up to mine, it's murderous.

Since Alice is taking up the entire couch, the two Caster Witches share the armchair. Coral sits in the chair itself, dressed in an orange-and-yellow knitted sweater, while Lexie sits perched on the arm, carefully surveying the room of witches. She's wearing jeans, maroon wedge boots, and a long-sleeve T-shirt with some kind of chemical symbol on the front. Lexie catches me staring and raises one eyebrow. "It's the chemical makeup of caffeine."

"Is anyone going to tell us why we're here?" Alice sighs dramatically. "I've done my part. My sponsors are threatening to cancel the tour if my mysterious 'illness' doesn't end soon."

Coral shifts uncomfortably as Alice speaks, but Lexie actually agrees with her. "I need to get back to school. I can't keep missing classes."

"You're here," Elder Keating cuts in, giving her Caster Witches a stern look, "because someone has betrayed the Clans." Archer must have updated her on my theories while I showered, and it's terrifying to hear those words from her. It makes them more real now that she believes, too.

"What are you talking about?" Coral shifts forward, perching on the edge of the chair, like she's ready to bolt at a moment's notice. "Why would anyone do that? What proof do you have?"

Elder Keating turns to me. "Care to explain?"

"Umm . . ." I've tried to avoid outright accusations ever since I thought a classmate—who was dabbling in dark pagan magic to get back at his shitty dad—was a Blood Witch. But now isn't the time to lose my nerve. "We don't know *why*, exactly, but the Hunters have been a step ahead of us this entire time. They couldn't have done all this on their own. Someone had to help them past the barrier last night."

Alice sits up, her nonchalance completely erased. "And what? You think one of us did it?"

"That's ridiculous," Coral adds, adjusting her pink-framed glasses. Lexie presses her lips into a thin line.

"It's offensive is what it is. What the hell are you thinking, wind witch?"

"You've already called me that," I say, which earns me an eye roll from Alice. "If it's not one of you, it has to be Tori. She *hated* Alice. She hated me, too, by the end. She could have helped the Hunters create their drug."

But Coral shakes her head. "It's not Tori." She glances up at Lexie and continues when the other girl gives her an encouraging nod. "Tori was out of control after you left. Always ranting about how it was our fault that her plan failed. We turned her in to the Council."

The Elemental Elder's forehead creases with thought. "Tori

Whitman?" He turns to Keating. "We sentenced her back in June, didn't we?"

After a beat, Elder Keating nods. "I remember her. She couldn't be reasoned with, so we stripped her magic and took her memories. She was reunited with a parent, wasn't she?"

"Hannah?!" The front door slams, and Gemma's voice rings through the house.

A sinking feeling pulls at my heart.

Morgan appears a second later, Gemma a moment behind. They stop short when they see the assembly of witches. My best friend and my girlfriend share a worried look.

And then all hell breaks loose.

26

ALICE IS ON HER feet first, color rising in her cheeks. "Who the hell is that?" She shifts her attention from Gemma to me. "Is *she* another one of your suspects?"

"Gemma's not—" The words die on my lips, and my skin crawls under the attention of every witch in the room. There's no way to finish that sentence without creating more questions.

Gemma's not a witch.

Gemma's not part of this.

Except . . . she is.

I look to Mom, but her expression is guarded and suspicious. I can't even look at Lady Ariana. They're both going to kill me when they realize what Gem knows. Across the room, Gemma's eyes are wide with fear, but she tips her head into a shallow nod.

She's in this with me.

No more secrets.

Elder Keating steps forward, her face completely neutral. "What's going on, Hannah?"

"Gemma would never betray us, but she . . . she does know. About me. About the Clans."

"Hannah." Mom's shocked voice stills the rest of the room into silence. It steals all the warmth from the air, but Lady Ariana or Elder Hudson must take back control, because it doesn't stay

cold long. I feel the weight of their stares, the weight of their anger and betrayal and mistrust.

"This is just perfect," Alice mocks. "How can you sit there and accuse us of being traitors when *you're* the one who already spilled everything to a Reg?"

"Gemma hasn't told anyone," I argue, but the excuse sounds weak, even to my ears. I look to Mom for support, but her disappointment is too much to bear. "I didn't mean to tell her, Mom. I didn't have a choice. When Benton pushed my car into the river, I had to use magic to survive. We would've drowned without it."

Mom shakes her head. "But you said Gemma lost consciousness once you were in the water."

"I'm sorry." My voice cracks, and tears threaten. "I should have told you the truth, but I was scared." I search for Archer and Cal and find only cautious interest. "I swear I never told her about anyone else in the coven. I never even intended to tell her about Blood Witches, except—"

"Except she overheard me and Hannah talking about it at the hospital," Morgan cuts in. "Gemma has always been there for us. She wouldn't do anything to hurt the Clans."

From her perch on the chair, Lexie pinches the bridge of her nose. "Witches in this town are out of control." She looks over at Archer. "Can we get back to work now?"

There's this beat in the room, a second of silence when I think maybe this will all be okay. Maybe there's enough going on that Gemma knowing about us will be too small of an issue to worry about. I let myself believe in a world where Gemma could come to coven meetings and hang out around my mom without me having to hide that she knows.

"No one is leaving until we untangle this mess," Elder

Hudson says, his voice rich and resonating. "Your friend will not be harmed, Miss Walsh, but her memories must be erased."

His words cut like a blade, and my knees go weak. Morgan reaches for me, but I force myself to rally. He's not the only Elder here. Keating can help. She can fix this. "Please don't do this. Gemma won't tell anyone. She could help us."

"Hannah . . ." The way Elder Keating says my name is part warning, part understanding, and I grasp on to the chance.

"Please," I beg. "Gemma isn't like your brother's wife. She doesn't hate us. She won't do anything to hurt us."

Something flickers across Elder Keating's features, something soft and victorious and longing. For a brief moment, I feel bad for invoking the brother she lost, but Gemma and I shouldn't have to share their fate. Things can be different this time.

Elder Keating glances over her shoulder at her colleague. "She might have a point, John. Maybe it's time we step out of the shadows completely. The Hunters won't be able to kill us with impunity if the world knows who we are."

But the other Elder shakes his head. "Secrecy is the only thing that keeps us safe. We cannot afford to create more enemies for ourselves."

"Open your eyes! We are not *safe*. Look at what the Hunters have done to us, pitting witches against each other. Stealing our magic and torturing us. We have the power to change the future of our Clans. All we have to do is get off our asses instead of clinging to outdated laws."

Elder Hudson exhales slowly, like he's had this argument a thousand times. "Katherine—"

"No, John. You can't keep pushing this off. What is it going to take to convince you? We are under attack from all sides.

Dozens of your Elementals have lost their magic. If there has ever been a time to change our laws, it's now." Elder Keating gestures to Gemma. "Sharing our secret with trusted Regs is the least we could do."

"Maybe that day is coming," Elder Hudson says, keeping his voice infuriatingly calm, "but we cannot let our enemies force that decision."

"Excuse me?" Gemma asks softly, interrupting the Elders' argument. She raises her hand like we're in class and she has a point she'd like to add. She waits patiently for the Elders to acknowledge her before she speaks. "Am I allowed a say in what happens to me?"

"I suppose," Elder Hudson says, a hint of amusement in his voice. "I assume you agree with my Caster counterpart?"

Gemma reaches for my hand and squeezes tight. "Do you really think the witches will be safer if I don't remember anything?"

Elder Hudson nods. "Yes, child. I do."

"Does everyone?" Gemma looks around the room, each witch nodding in turn. Cal casts me an apologetic glance before agreeing, too.

Keating crosses her arms and shakes her head. "This is a mistake." Her voice is bitter and angry, and I wonder how many times since her brother's death she's fought to change our laws. Fought to make what Gemma knows okay.

Gem worries at her lower lip, but after a moment, she nods, too. "Then that's what I want," she says, reaching out and squeezing my hand. "If it'll keep Hannah safer, I want you to take away my memories."

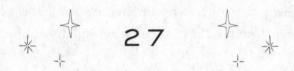

27

THE WORLD SPINS OUT of control around me. "Gemma, you can't." I won't let them strip away this new piece of her. I won't go back into hiding. Not with her. Not again. "Please," I beg, but I'm not sure who I expect to save me from this. "There has to be another way. I don't want to lose Gemma, too."

Gem turns and places her hands on my shoulders, staring down at me. "You're not going to lose me. It'll be fine." She glances over her shoulder at Elder Keating. "It won't hurt, will it?"

But the Elder Caster doesn't acknowledge her question. She turns on the rest of the Council. "If you want to do this, fine. But don't expect me to participate in any more of your regressive decrees. I'm going back to my hotel."

The door slams on her way out.

"Don't worry, Miss Goodwin," Archer says in the wake of his Elder's loud exit. "It won't hurt. Cal will take good care of you."

"We can help," Coral says, standing up from her chair. "Unless Lexie wants to keep working on the journal."

Lexie shrugs. "Wherever you need me. I'm game."

"Does this mean we're not suspects anymore?" Alice flops back onto the couch. "Or is all this traitor business on pause while we deal with Miss Savior's No-Big-Deal Betrayal?"

Everyone ignores Alice, and the Casters shuffle Gemma into the kitchen. I try to go after her, but Archer puts a bandaged hand on my shoulder. "They just need a few minutes to calibrate the potion to your friend. After that, you'll have a few hours before it's ready. She can wait with you until it is."

"I hate this," I say, my voice broken and full of petulance I wish I could take back.

Archer doesn't seem to take any offense at my tone. "I know."

We wait there together, Mom and Lady Ariana coming to stand on my other side. Morgan fidgets nervously at the edge of the room, under the archway that leads to the hall. None of us speak. I feel my mother's support and my grandmother's disappointment, and I can't face either of them.

Finally, Cal brings Gemma back to us.

"Why don't you girls take a moment for yourselves," Archer suggests. "I'll supervise the Casters."

"What about me?" Alice asks.

Lady Ariana levels her cold glare at the flippant Blood Witch. "You can stay here." She speaks the words with a quiet coolness that drains the color from Alice's pale face.

"Come on," Morgan prompts, something catching in her voice. Gemma and I follow her to my room, and the moment the door closes behind us, tears spill over Morgan's face. "This is all my fault. My mom wouldn't let me come see you, but I had to know if you were really okay." She wipes the tears off her cheeks. "I was so scared."

"We both were," Gemma says. "And it's just as much my fault. I'm the one who convinced you to sneak out so we could come see her."

I don't blame either of them, but my lips won't form those

words. "I hate this," I say again. Apparently, it's the only thing I can say anymore.

I hate that I'm losing my best friend.

I hate that it's *my* Elder taking Gem from me when Keating seems so ready to make a change.

I hate that every time I think I've reached the limits of how awful my life can get, the universe laughs in my face and makes everything so much worse.

"It's going to be okay," Gemma soothes. "I'm not going anywhere. I'll still be your best friend."

"But I hated hiding things from you." My voice catches, and this shouldn't be the thing that breaks me, but it is. It's a loss I never prepared for. "I can't go back to that."

"You can and you will."

"Gemma . . ."

"Hannah . . ." She mimics my whining tone, drawing out the final *ah* sound. "You are going to be fine. I will always love you, whether I know you're a witch or not."

"Promise?"

"Obviously."

"Well," I say, trying to get a grip on my emotions, "since it's your last day knowing about witches, is there anything you wanted to ask?"

"Besides everything?"

I laugh. It's a sad, wilted thing, and then I spend the next two hours telling Gemma absolutely everything about my Clan. The stories and beliefs of how we came to be, the years of practice, wearing binding rings until we're thirteen. Morgan does an impressive one-handed push-up and admits that Blood Witches can regulate their periods, even skip them altogether if they want, which draws serious jealousy from both Gem and me.

But we laugh. We get to forget—if only for a few minutes at a time—what's waiting for us on the other side of the door.

"Girls?" A knock interrupts Morgan mid-handstand, and she nearly falls. Mom's voice penetrates the door, but she at least doesn't try to barge her way in. "We're ready for you."

Gem blows out a slow breath. "I guess this is it."

"I'll be right there the whole time," I promise, even though I don't know if Archer will let me. "I'll never forget how great you've been. I'll never forget what you're doing for me today."

Gemma crushes me in a hug, her long arms wrapped tightly around me. "I'll be okay, Hannah." But she sounds less sure of herself, and when she pulls away, there are tears in her eyes. "And even if you forget, it's not like I'll remember to be mad at you."

A laugh catches in my throat, and it takes all of my strength not to burst into tears right there in my room. "At least with this, you'll have met someone from all three Clans. You're probably the only non-witch who's seen all our magics."

"You'll have to remember for me." She smiles, but it's a sad thing. A curve of the lip that doesn't fully hide the pain in her eyes.

Gemma and Morgan leave first, but Mom stops me from following them.

"Mom, I need to be there."

"I know, baby." She reaches out, and I step into her hug. "I need you to know I'm not angry with you. Gemma is such a good friend, and I'm so glad you have her. She's still welcome here anytime."

"Thanks, Mom." I squeeze back, but I have to pull away first. When we get to the dining room, only Archer, Cal, and Elder

Hudson are waiting for us. A glass of shimmering opalescent liquid, like melted pearls, sits on the table.

Archer must see my confusion. "Your grandmother took the others back to her place. We still need to question them about their involvement with the Hunters."

Cal pulls out a chair for Gem. "The potion will feel a little weird going down, but it won't hurt."

"Will I know why you're all here?" Gemma asks, peering into the glass and sniffing its contents. "If I don't know about magic, will I even know . . . I'm sorry, I didn't actually get your name."

The Elder smiles at her. "It's John Hudson, and no, you won't remember how I'm connected to Hannah. I'm leaving to join Lady Ariana, but I wanted to thank you for doing this. This is always easier when it's done willingly." Elder Hudson excuses himself, and when the front door closes behind him, Cal slides the pearl-like liquid closer to Gem.

"You'll feel disoriented when you wake up, but it'll pass quickly. Your mind will need to smooth the frayed edges of memory where magic used to be." Cal smiles encouragingly at her. "The human mind does a pretty great job protecting itself from that kind of dissonance. You'll be okay. Archer and I will wait in the kitchen until you leave."

"Well, I guess this is it." Gemma raises the glass like a toast. "Here's to no longer knowing I'm the only muggle in the room." She downs the shimmering liquid in one long gulp and grimaces when she sets the empty glass on the table. "Wow, that shit is weird. What the heck is in—" Gemma's eyes flutter rapidly and then close completely, her entire body going slack in her chair.

"Gemma? Gemma, are you okay?" I reach for her, but Morgan holds me back.

"Cal said to let the potion run its course."

"But—"

As quickly as unconsciousness took her, it subsides. Gemma stirs slowly, like she's waking up from a simple nap. When her eyes flutter open, she stares blankly at me, completely dazed. Her pupils are dilated, covering the blue of her irises, but then she blinks and she's herself again.

"Hannah? Oh my god, Hannah! You're okay!" She leaps out of the chair and crushes me in a hug. "I've been so worried about you! What happened? Why weren't you at school the past two days?"

I have to fight tears. "I'm fine. I'm okay." I pull back and look her over. She seems like herself. "What do you remember?"

Confusion crosses her face like a cloud. "We were at homecoming when we found out Benton escaped from jail. And then you didn't come to school on Monday, which I expected, but then you weren't there again today and no one would tell me what was going on and—" She shakes her head, like she's trying to dispel something confusing. "I was so worried, and Morgan texted me that you were home and—oh my god! Did Benton kidnap you? I will *kill* him if he hurt you."

"The police have us in protective custody," Mom says, sitting in the seat beside Gem. "We aren't supposed to be seen until that boy is back in jail."

Gemma looks from Mom to me and back again. Hurt crosses her face, but eventually she nods. "Why are you home, then? Are you safe now?"

"Safer," Mom says. "The detective is in the other room.

I'm really sorry, Gemma, but we aren't supposed to have any visitors yet."

"Oh." Her face falls. "I'm sorry, Mrs. Walsh." Gemma stands and squeezes my hand. "Text me later?"

"Of course."

"Are you coming, Morgan?" Gem asks.

Morgan looks at me, but I don't know how to explain why it'd be okay for her to stay if Gemma has to go. My girlfriend forces a smile. "We're right behind you!"

We follow Gem to the front door. "Are you sure everything's all right?" she asks.

I hug her tight, one more time, before I let her and Morgan leave. "Yeah. It's good. I'll call you later." I watch until Gemma's car rumbles to life and rolls out of view.

When they're gone, Archer approaches, one hand pressed to his ribs.

"I hate this," I tell him, promising myself it'll be the last time I say those words out loud. They aren't going to help me fix any of it.

"I know. Maybe one day you'll be able to tell her again. Maybe our laws will evolve, but we can't make those kinds of decisions for all witches. We can't let the Hunters force this on us."

We fall silent for a long time. I hear Cal talking quietly with my mother in the kitchen.

"Can I ask you something?" I wait for Archer to nod and try to form the question in a way that makes sense. "If Casters have the power to erase memories, why haven't they done that with the Hunters? Why not wipe their memories of magic and move on with our lives?"

"Gemma only knew about magic for a couple months. It's harder when the knowledge is so deeply embedded in their minds." Archer heads back to the dining room and sits in one of the chairs, resting his bandaged hands on the glossy wooden surface. "Even if we managed to wipe all their memories of magic, the remaining Hunters would re-indoctrinate them."

"But we have Benton now. We could test the potion and make sure you get it right." If we could erase the memory of magic from every Hunter, we could end this. Our secret would be safe. No one else would have to die.

"Cal's been working on something like that for weeks, but creating a potion broad enough to affect everyone is almost impossible."

"I got the idea from you, Hannah," Cal says, coming into the room with my mom. He sits across from Archer. "That day in the Cauldron when you wanted to go back in time and stop the Hunters from ever finding out about magic in the first place. I think I'm close to a breakthrough."

"Really?" Archer's voice is infused with so much hope it makes me want to burst. "I thought you were having trouble with it."

"Lexie has been helping. If she's still allowed to, it shouldn't take much longer. A week. Maybe two." Cal drums his fingers against the table and glances up at Archer. "I haven't figured out how to prevent it from working on the witches who have been drugged though."

"We might not have time to wait for that," Archer says. "And we'd still need a way to disperse the potion that would cover all the Hunters at once. As long as even one remembers, we're still at risk."

"We could put it in the water supply," I say. "We could use their methods against them."

But Archer shakes his head. "There's too much room for error. They could already be avoiding tap water, given their own pursuits."

"Then we do what they couldn't." A smile blooms as the idea takes root. "We make it airborne."

28

THE REST OF THE week is a whirlwind of investigations, magic lessons, and potion making.

And homework. So much homework.

Archer keeps me out of school under the guise that I need to stay out of sight while the police are hunting for Benton, but that doesn't stop Mom from contacting my teachers to get homework sent to the house. While the Elders question Lexie, Coral, and Alice about their connections to the Hunters, I'm writing essays and solving for *x*.

I'm also working with Lady Ariana to regain control of my magic. I have access to the elements again, and the pain is finally gone, but it still feels . . . different. There's a chance my power will never be the same as it was before, but I think I'm okay with that. It's slow, and my endurance right now kind of sucks, but it's still *mine*.

While I'm busy working with my grandmother and catching up on school stuff, the Elders focus on the witches I've accused. They interrogate Lexie first, then Coral, and finally Alice. Each one is cleared of the charges I made against them, and by some miracle, they don't leave Salem out of spite.

Probably because they believe I'm right. *Someone* betrayed the Clans.

It just wasn't any of them.

Archer continues his search for the mole—questioning everyone who might have had access to our plans, including my entire coven. Alice works with Morgan's parents to learn more of the healing techniques she missed by being orphaned so young. Coral and Lexie return to helping Cal with the memory potion, Lexie even incorporating some of Dr. O'Connell's research into their task.

I don't hear from any of them until Sunday, when we learn that the Casters were successful: they've created a version that should work on anyone without Clan magic flowing through their veins. Archer calls while I'm in the middle of calculating the velocity of a falling object and invites me to the testing—he wants me to be the one to make the potion airborne.

Technically, any Elemental could do this, but Archer must know what it means for me to finish what I helped start. Mom drives, and between our combined anxiety, the car is freezing. When we get to Archer's house, the cool October breeze is a warm relief.

Behind me, a vehicle slows and crunches over gravel. I turn and find Morgan and her parents pulling in behind us.

"I didn't know you were coming," I say when Morgan steps out of the car.

She pulls her sweater tightly around her and reaches for my hand. "Cal thought you'd want me here."

Her fingers slide between mine, and though her presence warms my heart, it doesn't stop the thoughts running through my head. It was easy enough to guess that we'd be testing the potion on Benton, but I don't know how I feel about taking away his memory. I don't know what that will mean for the emotions battling inside my chest.

Benton tried to kill me.

He rescued me from his family.

And though he doesn't want me dead like the rest of the Hunters do, he'd still take my magic if he had the chance.

"It'll be okay," Morgan says, tugging me toward the house. "If it doesn't work, Cal can try again."

I follow her to the porch, where our parents are waiting. "Ready?" Mom asks, reaching for the front door.

"As much as I can be." I squeeze Morgan's hand and step inside.

We find Archer in the foyer, his expression grim. "Alice is watching over Benton. This way." He leads us to his living room, where Benton is sitting alone on the couch. He looks like he hasn't slept much since we came back to Salem, but I'm sure that has more to do with his tormented conscience than anything the Council has done. Alice hovers at the edge of the room, her hair in loose waves around her shoulders and her arms crossed. She glances at me briefly but keeps a tight watch over the unbound Hunter.

Benton looks up when we come in, and I catch a glimmer of fear in his eyes. "Hannah." He stands and steps toward us.

"Sit down, asshole." Alice squeezes her hands into fists, and she must have taken a sample of Benton's blood, because he winces as his body bends awkwardly back into a seated position.

"I wasn't going to hurt anyone," Benton says, the fear more pronounced now. Power like Alice is using is the epitome of everything he was taught to hate, yet he doesn't hurl insults at her. "What's happening? What are you going to do to me?"

The tremor in his voice does strange things to my heart. *He tried to kill you*, I remind myself, but another voice says, *He saved you, too. He's lost.*

Suddenly, I wish I hadn't agreed to this.

Before I can back out, Cal comes into the room carrying the potion in one hand and a gas mask in the other. He passes the mask to Archer, who accepts it with a tight nod.

"What's that for?" I ask.

Hopelessness carves across Archer's expression, there only a second before he hides it away. "It's like we discussed. Anyone without Clan magic will be affected." He slips the mask over his head, but he must see my regret, because he tips it back so it isn't covering his face yet. "This was still a smart plan, Hannah. It'll buy us the time we need to translate David's work and create an antidote. The Elders were impressed."

"That we were." Elder Keating steps into the room. "Let's hope our enthusiasm was well placed. Agents." She nods to Archer and Cal in turn. "Let's begin."

"Begin what?" Benton tries to get up again, but he grimaces when Alice's magic keeps him in place. "What are you going to do to me?"

"Don't worry, Mr. Hall, this won't hurt." Archer turns to me. "Once Cal removes the stopper, I need you to vaporize the potion and ensure he inhales it. You shouldn't need to use much."

I nod and reach for the hum of magic in my chest. It still feels like a miracle that it's working again. The air responds to my call, swirling between us and tossing my hair. "Ready."

"Here goes nothing," Cal whispers and pulls the cork loose.

Inside the vial, the potion's energy is unlike anything I've felt before. I worry my power will separate the water base from everything that went into it, like the paint that stained my old bedroom carpet this summer, but the Caster potion hums in tune with my magic and answers my call. I pull a small portion of the liquid out of the glass vial, and it's like an amorphous, floating pearl. My hands shake, but I bend the air to my will, blending and mixing the elements until it becomes fine mist.

Benton squirms as the airborne potion closes in on him. "Please don't. Hannah, please." His voice shakes, but he has no-where to run. For once, he's the one being hunted. He tries to hold his breath to escape the spell, but he can't hold it forever. Eventually, he's forced to inhale, and I plunge the potion deep into his lungs.

His whole body goes slack, and his eyelids slide shut.

Cal stoppers the vial. "You can let go of his blood. That should be all he needs."

Alice steps back, and as her control leaves Benton's body, his closed eyes shift from side to side. His body trembles like he's plagued by nightmares.

When he finally falls still, I cautiously step forward and kneel in front of the couch. "Benton? Are you awake?" I poke him in the shoulder.

"Don't touch him," Mom says, like I'm playing with a poi-sonous snake.

"We need to know if it worked." I shake his knee. *"Benton."*

His eyes flutter open, and he startles away from me. He looks around the room, pupils blown wide. "Where am I? What's hap-pening?" He searches the room, and when his gaze finally settles on me, for a second, I see him. The old him. The Benton from art class. The boy whose laugh always made me smile.

The boy I ran into a burning building to save.

His betrayal breaks my heart all over again.

"Hannah? What's happening. Where am I?" He reaches for my hand, but I flinch away. "What's wrong?"

Tears slip past my lashes, and I step away from him. "What do you remember?"

Benton's forehead creases, but then horror whitens his face. He looks up, his hazel eyes glittering with tears. "Oh my god, Hannah, I'm so sorry. I don't understand what happened. I would *never* hurt you, but I . . . I—" He buries his misery behind his hands.

Something heavy and sad presses hard on my chest, but I don't know what to do with that feeling. I don't know how to handle any of this. Behind me, I hear Archer praising Cal on his hard work, telling him we'll need as much of the potion as he can make. As quickly as possible.

I watch Benton fall apart. My heart breaks again and again.

But this isn't over for me. This is about more than how this broken boy hurt me. "Please, Benton," I say, forcing myself to speak his name. "You have to tell the police what you know. You have to tell them what happened to my dad."

"Your dad?" Benton looks up, and confusion creases his face. Another breath and his eyes go wide. "Oh my god, my parents . . . They—"

"I know, Benton. I know." But then he's crying, and I can't breathe. I can't even *look* at him. I didn't think it'd be like this. I didn't think winning would feel so hollow. Behind me everyone is celebrating. Morgan reaches for me, her fingers brushing along my back.

And I. Just. Can't.

So I run.

-|-   ✱   -|-

When Morgan finds me at the edge of Archer's property, where the neatly trimmed lawn gives way to wild grasses and the beginnings of a patch of woods, I'm clinging to a low branch for support. I grasp at every element I can touch, begging for their solace, their support. The sky above us is stormy and gray, the air heavy with the promise of rain.

"Hannah?" Morgan approaches cautiously, like she's worried I might take off again. It wouldn't matter if I did. With her speed, she'd catch up in an instant.

I stare into the quiet woods, hating myself. It's stupid to be this miserable. We finally have a way to eliminate the Hunters, a plan that doesn't lower us to their level of violence. I should be glad. Instead, I'm hiding outside, wiping tears from my face.

Morgan places a gentle hand on the small of my back. "What's wrong?"

"Besides everything?" I laugh, and it's a bitter, broken sound. Goddess, I hate this so much. I don't want to snap at her. She's done nothing but love me.

The word catches in my mind, the truth of it heavy and scary. I lean my forehead against the tree for support.

"I can't imagine how hard it is to see him at all, let alone like that, but it worked, Hannah. Your plan worked. He doesn't remember anything about the Clans, and he was *raised* to hate us. He saw you, and he *apologized*." She gently turns me to face her and wipes away the tears I missed. "He's telling Archer everything. He'll testify against his parents. You did it."

The sky rumbles with rolling thunder. Around us, the wind picks up and tosses leaves across the yard. They skitter past in flashes of yellow and red, a whirlwind of fallen sunset. "Then why does it feel so shitty?" I ask, leaning forward into her embrace. "Why can't I be happier about this?"

"Because it still sucks," she says, rubbing my back until goose bumps prickle up and down my arms. "And because we still have a long way to go before it's really over."

She's right. Having a working potion is not the same as having a plan to make sure *every single Hunter* is exposed to it. If it were that simple, the Council would have done this years ago.

Lightning flashes across the sky, and the heavens open. Rain falls in heavy sheets, soaking me in a single breath.

"Come on," Morgan says, "we should go in."

But I'm stuck rooted to the now-muddy earth.

"Hannah, let's go."

"How were they going to do it?"

Morgan sighs, shivering in the rain. "Who? Do what?"

"The Hunters." Lightning flashes above us. I flinch and follow Morgan back toward the house. "How were they going to make sure every single witch was exposed to their drug? We know they wanted to make it airborne, so they must have had a plan."

"I don't know. Maybe they were going to drop it from the sky?"

A thousand tiny threads unspool in my mind. "But nothing they've done makes any sense. Why did they attack Mom's old coven first when they *knew* there was a coven in Salem? Why give us time to defend ourselves?" There's no reason the Hunters wouldn't try to take me out. I was already slated for death, so why avoid me? A sick feeling works through my gut. "What if this goes back further than David's murder? What if someone has been helping the Hunters the whole time?"

"The Council already cleared Alice and the others. It wasn't any of them." Morgan catches me when I nearly slip and fall on my face in the mud. "Why would a witch help the Hunters destroy us? What could they possibly hope to gain by hurting the Clans?"

What is it going to take to convince you?

Dozens of your Elementals have lost their magic.

If there has ever been a time to change our laws, it's now.

My hands tremble as the Caster's words ring loudly in my ears. "Elder Keating."

Morgan pauses beside me, halfway back to Archer's house. "The Elder?"

With horrifying clarity, all the pieces click into place. "Think about it. The Hunters attacked the only family I have outside Salem the same day she showed up to recruit me. She acted shocked when Riley went after us in Brooklyn, but that's because he wasn't *supposed* to go. The Hunters went after the Chicago Casters, and that's where David was from. She must have been trying to hit close to home for him just like she did for me."

"And then what? When he still refused her, she had him killed?" Morgan sounds skeptical, but there's a thread of fear in her voice as thunder rumbles again overhead.

"Maybe. It makes as much sense as anything else."

Morgan glances nervously at the house. "I don't know, Hannah. That seems so . . ."

"Evil?" I supply, fury rising. My magic joins the already howling wind, and it tears at my clothes. "When I dropped out of the raid, she must have broken Benton out of jail to make sure I'd go." My breaths go shallow, and my heart beats too fast. Too hard. My knees go weak.

She wanted me captured.

She probably wanted me dead.

"Hannah, you have to breathe." Morgan's magic floods through me, settling my panic enough so I can grab hold of the threads we've started to weave.

"It was her, Morgan. All of it. She's the reason Archer lost his magic. I'm supposed to be dead right now."

"But why? What could she possibly gain from doing all this?"

"You heard her. She's been fighting with the Council about going public. She's trying to force their hand. I bet she wanted to use my death to rally the Clans together."

Lightning flashes above us, and the thunder comes less than a second behind. The storm is directly above us now.

"It's more complicated than that, Hannah."

I whirl around and find Elder Keating standing beneath a wide umbrella, her clothes completely dry while we're soaked through.

"Stay away from us."

Elder Keating shakes her head. "We want the same things. Your friend only knew about your magic for a couple months. I've been dreaming of a world where we could live openly for longer than you've been alive. We can still make that happen."

"You can't make that decision for everyone." I step forward, blocking Morgan from the Elder's attentions. "You can't *murder* witches to get your way."

"I already told you. It's more complicated than that. We're already losing witches. For decades, I've stripped witches of their magic for doing what you did with your friend. It has to stop. Sacrifices had to be made."

A small part of me feels the pull of her words like a siren's call. I think of Gemma knowing all of who I am. I think of assholes like Nolan finally knowing that *they* should be afraid of *me*, not the other way around. But then I think of David's lifeless face. I think of Sarah and Archer without their magic, and I reach for my own power.

"How long?" I ask, threading my magic through the storm, grabbing hold of the water so I can bend it to my will. "How long have you been helping the Hunters?"

Elder Keating smirks. "I've been guiding the Hunters since before you were born. For decades, I've tried to nudge the Council in the right direction." Frustration streaks across her features. "They refuse to be led into the future."

The temperature plummets around us. The rain turns to ice as it falls. It pings uselessly against the Elder's umbrella. "And when, exactly, did you decide you were willing to kill us?"

"It's interesting, really, how it all comes full circle." Keating steps forward, the muddy ground now cold enough that it's gone solid again. "I decided the day I met the Caster you betrayed. Tori hated you so much when she was brought before me. I tried to spare her, but the other Elders voted against me. Taking away her magic, I decided she would be the last witch our laws failed. I knew I had to make the other Elders desperate, and I vowed to do whatever it took."

The timeline clicks into place. Tori being brought before the Elders in early June, not long after Veronica and I had our run-in with her and the others. Elder Keating reaching her breaking point. I bet she created the first version of the Hunters' cure. The version Benton used to drug me.

She gave the Hunters the confidence to attack us.

She's the reason Benton's parents killed my dad.

It's all because of *her*.

"You can still join me, Hannah. I'm going to change the world. You can change it with me."

"You can eat ice." I reach into the sky and grab hold of the wind and the rain and the rage boiling inside me. I freeze the rain and shape it into a spear.

Elder Keating's face contorts with anger. She reaches for something at her hip and flings it toward us.

Lightning brightens the sky, glinting off the silver dagger speeding through the air, and then Morgan is a blur of color as she pushes in front of me.

Warmth splashes my face and shirt, and I startle, the ice melting through my fingers. Morgan falls. A flicker of regret passes Elder Keating's face before she turns. Before she climbs into her car and pulls away. I drag my gaze away from her tail-lights and find Morgan at my feet.

There's a blade sunk deep in her chest.

And a pool of blood growing around her.

29

I COLLAPSE TO MY knees beside Morgan. Cold mud soaks through my clothes. Hot blood covers my hands. "You're going to be okay. You're going to be fine," I promise, but I don't believe the words.

She's a Blood Witch. She'll heal.

But her face is twisted with pain and the blood is still pouring out and I don't know what to do.

"Help!" The word tears from my throat, carried farther by the wind. "Someone, please!"

Morgan winces and reaches for the hilt of the knife.

"No, don't pull it out."

She keeps reaching. "I have to. I won't heal."

"Then let me." I reach for the handle as the back door bursts open.

Archer rushes into the storm after us, and he falls to his knees opposite me. His eyes are wild with concern, but his jaw is set. "What happened?" He takes the hilt in his hands and yanks the blade from Morgan's chest in a single, fluid motion. "Who did this?"

I press my hand against the wound, but blood continues to pour out. "Why isn't it healing? Morgan, why isn't it getting better?"

Her eyelids flutter. Lightning brightens the sky. Thunder

rumbles the ground beneath me. The earth keeps shaking, on and on and on, but it's not the thunder. It's me. My power is wild and uncontrolled without Morgan to anchor me. She always knows when I'm panicking. She always makes it better.

"Morgan?" I press harder against the wound, but her body's gone slack. "Morgan!"

Archer loops one arm underneath her knees. "We need to get her inside." He stands and lifts her, despite his injuries, and races back into the house. I chase after them. My shoes, soaking wet and covered in blood, slip on the wood floors.

I follow him into the living room, where he's laying Morgan on the couch. He shouts for Morgan's parents, and they arrive a second later, Mom and Cal coming in behind them.

"What happened?" Mrs. Hughes kneels on the floor beside her daughter. Archer backs away, but he looks at me. Mrs. Hughes follows his gaze. "Hannah, what happened?"

"Elder Keating . . ." I fight the emotion that wants to close my throat, that wants to seal off my lungs until I can never breathe again. "She's the one who betrayed us. There was a knife—"

It's enough for Morgan's dad to kneel beside his wife. They reach for their daughter, blood coating their hands. Their eyes glow blue as magic unfurls within them.

"Hannah." It's Archer calling my name now. I pass him again and again as I frantically pace the living room. "Hannah, we need to know more. Where's the Elder?"

"I don't know! She drove off somewhere. But she's the one who betrayed us. She's the puppet master behind all of this." I turn to pace across the room again, but I slam into Archer.

He winces. "Once more." He places his bandaged hands on my shoulders, forcing me to stop. "Slowly."

"She made the Hunters' drug. She's the reason my dad is dead."

Archer whispers something gentle and urgent to me, but I don't hear him. All I hear is the crash of thunder and the echoing *my fault, my fault, my fault* screaming in my head.

If I hadn't helped Alice escape from the Manhattan apartment all those months ago, Tori would have taken her magic like she'd wanted to. She wouldn't have blamed Lexie and Coral, and they wouldn't have turned her into the Council. Without Tori, Elder Keating wouldn't have taken drastic measures. Dad would still be alive.

"We have to stop her." I look up at Archer, cutting off whatever useless reassurances he was saying. "Before she remakes the drug. We have to stop the Hunters before she sends them after us."

Mom, who's been lingering at the head of the couch, watching over Morgan, looks at Archer. "But I thought she helped you destroy the drug? Why would she create it again now?"

I answer before he can. "Maybe she didn't mean for so many of us to die. Maybe some part of her regrets what she—" Another crack of thunder makes me jump, cutting off the rest of my sentence. "God, enough!"

I storm over to the window and throw it open wide. Wind and rain spill into the room.

"Hannah, what are you doing?" Mom asks.

"Making it quiet enough to *think*." I reach for the storm's power, but it's vast. So much bigger than I could ever control alone. "Alice!" I shout her name, and a second later, the pink-haired Blood Witch appears from the hallway.

She takes in the scene in the room, and her face drains of color. "What—"

"You want to help?" I ask, and she nods. "Then help."

Mom starts toward us. "Hannah, it's too big. You can't—"

But Alice's power floods my body, and magic explodes within me. This time, when I reach for the heart of the storm, I'm able to grab hold. My awareness shatters across the sky, but I'm still not strong enough to push it away. I glance to the Blood Witch, her pink hair flowing down her shoulders. She presses her lips into a thin line and grabs hold of my wrist.

Together, our combined magic is enough to call a swell of wind that pushes the storm west.

Alice releases me, and I collapse onto the floor. The next rumble of thunder is far off, barely audible from here, but Gemma's voice is loud in my head.

Controlling the weather would be a handy trick.

I told her we couldn't. That it was impossible.

Maybe we don't know anything about the limits of Clan magic. Not when we work together.

"Hannah?" Mom rushes to my side. Static shocks us when she touches me, but she holds tight and helps me to my feet. "What the hell were you thinking?"

"How is that even possible?" Archer is staring at me now. "Elementals can't do that."

Beside me, Alice is breathing hard, but she grins. "Apparently with a little help, they can."

"Such a badass." Morgan's voice is quiet, but it spins me around. She's lying on the couch, her clothes still soaked in blood, but there's fresh color in her cheeks.

"Are you okay?" I want to run to her, but her parents are sitting protectively on the edge of the couch.

The corner of her lips quirks up, but she doesn't make any move to sit. "Never better."

Cal looks between Alice and me. "Imagine what an entire coven could do with Blood Magic on their side."

"We could spread the potion for miles."

"And we could coordinate with other covens across the country," Cal says. "I can send instructions to all the Casters we know. If we can get a list of all the Hunter locations, we could launch from strategic points. We'd still have to destroy any new research they've started this week though."

"What if we borrow from Keating's playbook?" A plan comes together piece by piece in my mind. "We'll need the Council's permission, and we'll need most of the coven's help, but I might have an idea."

30

THANKS TO THE SUCCESS of Cal's potion, we manage to convince Elder Hudson to approve my plan. Most of the coven adults agree to join us, leaving Veronica, Sarah, Rachel, and Mrs. and Mr. Blaise behind to keep an eye on the children.

It takes three more days to lay the groundwork, and by Wednesday, we're ready to go. The Casters have made more of the memory-altering potion. Cal, Lexie, and Coral are also bringing smoke screen and knockout potions with them. Morgan wanted to come, but her parents have her on bedrest for another week until she's fully healed. Her mom is staying home with her, but her dad is part of the team.

My mom is coming, too.

The large van jostles over the uneven pavement as we near the drop-off point. Mom sits beside me, and I catch myself shooting nervous glances at her. I finally understand why she hated me being involved with the Council so much. Watching her run toward danger feels terrible.

The only thing stranger than Mom being here is the fact that Archer is *not*.

But that's part of the plan, too. When we left for Hall Pharmaceuticals, Archer was walking a handcuffed Benton back into the police station. Other detectives should be questioning the escaped convict now, while Archer pulls together his piece of the puzzle.

"Nervous?" Mom rests a hand on my knee, stopping it from bouncing.

"It's going to work," I say, and I feel it in my bones. This is it. The calm before we unleash the storm. Before we take back our lives.

"You can still be nervous." Mom puts an arm around my shoulder. "I am. A little," she whispers just for me. Ellen is here with us, sitting on the other side of the van. She flashes me a smile. She's maybe a little too excited for this.

My magic hums in my chest. I'm excited, too.

I'm finally keeping my promise to Dad. We're finally going to win.

Margaret Lesko, who is driving our van, follows the vehicle in front of her and pulls off the main road. Soon, over a dozen Elementals, three Caster Witches, and two Blood Witches— Alice and Mr. Hughes—stand huddled in the woods.

And all eyes are on me.

"Not everyone inside the company is a Hunter," I remind the group of assembled witches, "and the actual Hunters won't necessarily be marked. There shouldn't be much of the drug left, but they may still have one or two darts. They also won't hesitate to use force."

The group around me shifts, and a tremor works through the ground.

"Forget everything you've been taught about secrecy. This needs to be big." I scan the group, Elementals I've known all my life and new witches I've only just begun to trust. "We want to embody everything these Hunters fear we are. We need to embrace Keating's vision of a world where we don't have to hide anything."

"Go big or go home," Ellen says, igniting fire in each hand.

I roll my eyes at her. "That's the gist of it, yeah. Everyone ready?" Nods all around. "Let's go."

The group splits off into two teams, Ellen leading the rest of the Elementals and our Blood Witches toward the front of Hall Pharmaceuticals. I stay behind with Cal and the other Casters. We're needed elsewhere. Before we can pick our way around to the back parking lot, Mom pulls me in for a quick hug.

"Be careful," we say at the same time, and she presses a kiss to my head. "When this is over, we need to have a serious talk about your tendency to walk right into danger." But she turns and hurries after the rest of her group before I can respond.

I wait until she disappears through the trees, then lead the team of Casters to the rear parking lot where Benton helped us escape eight days ago. Cal wanted to bring the light-refracting potion he used in Ithaca, but Lexie surprised him with an invisibility potion that works even better.

He fanboyed over it for an entire day. I did, too, once Lexie assured me this version wouldn't explode. She hadn't quite cracked that code the first time we met.

Lexie covers us in a fine, shimmering mist, and by the time she's done, I can't see any of them.

"It won't last long," she says, somewhere on my right. "Fifteen minutes, tops."

"Then we'd better hurry." I step out from the cover of the trees and cross the open parking lot, the potion tingling against my skin.

Everyone in position? Ellen's voice crackles in my comms.

On my left, a handheld video device appears. Cal must have pulled it from his bag, where it wasn't exposed to the mist. Soon, the company's security feeds are on his screen. "We're a go. Commence Operation Fire Starter."

The words barely leave Cal's lips before the first tremor shakes the ground. Fire shoots into the air, visible even over the top of the building. Alarms scream from inside the lab, and I watch the security feeds, even as I'm disoriented by the way Cal's screen seems to float in midair. We watch scientists glance up at the alarm and leave their stations, walking calmly toward the exit. But some— the Hunters—are panicking, running with weapons drawn.

"We've got Hunters exiting the building," Coral says into the comms. Then to me, "I hope you're right about this, Hannah."

"Me too," I admit, keeping an eye on the door. We're only a few feet away now, and even though I know the Hunters can't see us, I still crouch behind the closest car to the door.

Cal flips through another couple camera angles until we're looking at the front lawn. The screen is full of Elementals wielding fire and tornados that tear up the ground. Their power is incredible to see. Alice and Mr. Hughes trace bloody runes on the grass, creating a barrier that will keep bullets from hitting the witches behind the line.

But there isn't time to linger over their part of the mission. The back door bangs open, and Hunters come streaming out.

One of the Casters hurls a glass vial at the entrance. It shatters against the side of the building, and a plume of lavender smoke settles over the Hunters. One by one, they drop into unconsciousness.

I reach for the air and disperse the knockout potion away from the door. One of the Hunters fell partially inside, so it's still propped open.

The door swings wide. "I've got this. Drag them away from the building," Cal says, and we do as he asks. By the time we're done, the invisibility potion is already wearing thin, and we follow Cal inside.

Our paths are predetermined by the updated building schematics Benton gave Archer before we took his memory, and we race through the halls. At the split, Coral and Lexie—who are little more than glittering shadows—head downstairs to destroy whatever makeshift lab the Hunters have created since the last time I was here. Cal and I continue on to the security room.

There aren't any cameras inside—at least none Cal has been able to tap into—and when we come flying around the final corner, our shadowy figures must catch someone's attention because the door bursts open and Hunters come spilling out. Cal is faster, though, pulling another purple vial from his belt and hurling it at the wall beside the Hunters. The smoke engulfs them, and the men fall in heaps on the ground.

"Let me know when the air is clear," Cal says, checking his device to make sure no one else is sneaking up on us.

I send a gust of air down the hall, moving the potion away from the door. "We're good."

Cal doesn't waste a second. He hurries into the security room. I watch, useless, as he takes over the feeds, spreading the relevant ones across several screens.

Lexie and Coral are in the lab, mostly visible now, destroying what little of the drug the Hunters have started to re-create.

In the siege at the front of the building, Elementals are making a lot of noise and flash but not hurting anyone. Hunters and scientists are being dropped into unconsciousness so they can't escape before we deploy the memory potion.

And then Cal's real work begins, disconnecting the feeds and erasing all previous footage. He plugs in a thumb drive and downloads all personnel files to sift through later. I watch anxiously as he works, aware of the witches risking their lives to be our distraction.

How much longer, hacker bro? Alice's voice crackles through the comms, and I flinch at the sound.

"Almost there," Cal says. He glances at the far-right screen, where the other Casters are exiting the lab. "We need an extraction outside security. Lexie? Coral?"

Coral looks up into the security camera and gives us a thumbs-up. *On our way.*

By the time the other witches make it to our floor, Cal is nearly finished. "Take them out with the others," he says. "I'll be right behind you."

"*We'll* be right behind you," I say as the girls grab hold of the guards. "I'm not leaving you alone in here, Cal."

Lexie shifts her grip on a Hunter's legs. "See you on the other side."

And then they're gone, taking the unconscious men with them.

I pace the small room, ready to be out of here. Ready to initiate the final phase of my plan. "What's left?" I ask when Cal is *still* typing away minutes later.

"Just doing a final sweep of the building to make sure there's no one inside." He types the entire time he speaks, his fingers flying over the keys as the main screen flips through each camera in the building. Empty room after empty room after—

"Wait. Go back." I step closer and peer at the screen. Cal tabs back, and two figures slip around a corner. "Where is that?"

The security door beeps as the locks disengage. The door swings open.

And Benton's parents raise their guns.

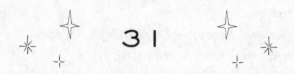

31

MRS. HALL ENTERS THE room first, heels clicking against the polished stone floor. "What have you done with my son?" She trains her weapon at my heart.

Her husband follows her inside, his expression contorted with rage. The same rage that flashed across his features before he burned Archer. Before he struck the son they now claim to worry about.

I fall back a step as they approach, Lexie's potion completely worn off now, and force my chin up. "Benton is where he belongs."

Mrs. Hall closes the distance between us and presses the barrel of the gun under my chin. "If you hurt so much as a hair on his head—"

"What do you care?" I wince when she jabs the gun harder against my neck. "You let his father beat the shit out of him. He's better off where he is."

Pain ignites across my temple. Bright lights explode in my vision, and I stumble. Cal catches me by the elbow and slips something cold and metallic into my hand. Mr. Hall grabs Cal and pulls him away, separating us.

"Hands up, both of you." He shoves Cal into one of the desk chairs. "Undo whatever you did. Now."

"I can't type if my hands are in the—"

Benton's dad hits Cal before he can finish, and Cal spits

blood at the older man's feet before glaring up at him. There's this moment of tension before Cal flicks his gaze to me. I swear I see him nod before he turns around and starts typing into the computer.

"You heard him," Mrs. Hall says, tearing her attention away from the computer screens. "Hands. Up."

"Whatever you say." I raise my hands and adjust the metal contraption in my palm, sliding my thumb down the striking mechanism. A tiny flame emerges from the lighter, and though it still makes me shudder, I grab hold of my magic and throw everything I have into the fire.

There's only a fraction of a second to enjoy the flash of fear on the Hunters' faces, and then their guns are raising and I'm pushing the flames forward and down. A wall of fire cuts the room in half, and I press forward, forcing Benton's parents back a step.

One of the guns goes off. I duck instinctively, and the bullet goes wide. Mr. Hall spews profanity as I raise the fire higher, blocking their line of sight.

Sweat prickles along my brow, the heat pressing in. Smoke fills the room. Behind me, Cal is typing away on the computer, and then suddenly he stands and pulls one of the vials from his hip, dumping the potion over the controls. The metal twists in on itself, an ear-shattering whine splitting through the room.

The guns go off again, a rapid fire of shots that blankets the computers. Cal drags me into a crouch and pulls the final potion from his hip. "On the count of three," he says, losing his voice to a series of coughs as the smoke around us thickens. "Drop the flames and make sure they breathe this in."

Metal clangs in the hallway, then the spray of a fire extinguisher suffocates the first section of flames.

"Or now works," Cal says, uncorking the vial.

I tighten my hold on the flame's power and press it as low to the ground as I can. Cal shifts his weight and hurls the vial across the room. It cracks against the wall, and the pearlescent liquid spills out onto the floor.

The Hunters glance back at the vial, and I take advantage of their distraction, releasing my hold on the fire and mixing the air with the spilling liquid, vaporizing it. Mr. Hall covers his mouth and nose. "Don't breathe it in. Don't—" But his words only help me guide the mist into his lungs. He collapses as the memory-erasing potion takes hold.

"James!" Benton's mom rushes to her husband, but then Cal's magic is in her lungs, too, and she crumbles to the floor.

Cal rubs his jaw where Mr. Hall hit him. "Let's get them out of here."

I nod, but kick Benton's dad—just once—before I grab his wrists to drag him away. Halfway to the exit, Ellen's voice is in our comms.

The police are seven minutes out. If we're going to do this, it has to be quick.

"We're almost there," I say through gritted teeth. Mr. Hall is heavy and almost impossible to drag, but despite everything he's done, I know Dad wouldn't want me to leave him to die.

As soon as we exit the final doorway and step into the chilly October afternoon, I look to Cal for the signal. He nods.

"The building is clear." With a final heave, I drop Mr. Hall unceremoniously against the parking lot pavement. "Light it up."

32

HALL PHARMACEUTICALS IS CONSUMED by flames.

Fire licks up the sides. Windows burst and shatter glass into the parking lot. Cal and I painstakingly drag the Halls to the pile of unconscious Hunters and then join my coven at the edge of the tree line. A few of the Elementals are focused on growing the fire as fast as possible while the rest stand huddled around Alice and Morgan's dad.

I allow myself a moment to watch the flames tear apart the headquarters. Smoke billows into the sky, and the wail of approaching sirens can be heard above the roar of fire.

My comm crackles in my ear. *You have two minutes*, Archer says. *I'm almost there.*

"Stay in your car until we give you the all clear," Cal reminds him as we all slip more fully past the tree line. We can't leave yet. Not until the final phase of this mission is complete. Lexie sets a large metal container on the ground, and Coral pries off the top with a crowbar.

"Ready for this, snowflake?" Alice's magic zips through my veins until my insides are crackling with static. Behind her, Mr. Hughes pricks Mom's finger and presses her blood against his palm. Mom shifts uncomfortably as the Blood Magic mixes with her Elemental power, and the rest of the coven looks similarly unnerved.

But they're doing it. They're trying.

"Ready or not, we're running out of time." I join the circle of witches gathering around the metal container. The white, shimmering potion winks up at me, and the sirens grow closer.

Cal approaches from behind, worry etched across his brow. "We need to hurry. The potion needs to be dispersed before Archer gets here."

Lady Ariana takes her place in the circle. "Then let's begin."

The coven joins hands around the potion, and I scan the ring of witches. Ellen. Mom. Lady Ariana and Margaret Lesko and so many more. All people I love, a family bound by magic and generations of history, all working toward the same purpose.

"As one," our high priestess says, the tiniest hint of fear in her voice.

We close our eyes, and the Blood Witches at the edge of our circle allow their power to mingle with ours. As Alice's magic ignites like fire inside me, I'm overcome by the gravity of a moment like this. It's not just that we're about to wipe the memories of all the Hunters and scientists lying before the burning laboratory. For the first time since the very creation of witches, the three Clans are working together. Our magics blending into something greater than their individual parts.

Lady Ariana directs the combined power of the coven, and we reach as one for the potion at the center of our circle. The liquid bubbles, and I open my eyes in time to see it burst into the air. As the sirens close in and the first emergency vehicles skid to a stop, we blanket the compound in the Casters' potion.

Something electric and wild zings through me as the potion curls in on itself, shimmering tendrils collapsing on a single point, and then it bursts wide, exploding outward like a million microscopic shooting stars, covering a five-mile radius in every direction in case any Hunters slipped past us.

It'll cover anyone we missed . . . including Detective Archer if he's too close too soon.

Alice's magic leaves my body in a rush, and my knees give out beneath me. I fall to the soft ground and glance up in time to see more police arrive. Fire trucks connect to the hydrant, dousing the flames. Lady Ariana, Ellen, and a few others provide the fire enough strength to resist the onslaught of water.

But I lose track of their fight when a dark sedan turns off the road and makes its way toward the front of the building. No. It's too soon. "Not yet!" I yell into the comms. "It's not safe."

I've been thinking . . .

Archer goes quiet on the line, and I turn, searching the woods for Cal. Is he hearing this, too? He must be, but I can't find him in the crowd, and there isn't time.

"Whatever it is, Archer, don't. You'll lose your memories. *We'll* lose you."

You won't need me after today. His car stops behind the line of fire trucks, but the air is still saturated with the potion. *I promised that we wouldn't give in to the Hunters without a fight, but that fight is over.*

Cal appears at my side, searching through the trees for Archer. His face has gone ghostly white. He's heard everything. "Ryan, please. Don't do this," he says, voice thick with emotion.

It'll be nice to stop hiding things from Lauren, he says, almost wistful. Then he clears his throat. *It's been an honor working with both of you. Now I have some Hunters to arrest.*

"Archer, no!" But it's too late. The detective steps out of his car and pulls the comms from his ear, letting it drop to the ground and crushing it under his heel so no one else will notice it. He turns toward the stirring Hunters, focused and unafraid, but then he stumbles, catching himself on the front hood of his car.

He presses the heel of his still-injured hand into his temple and falls to his knees as the potion strips away a lifetime of magic.

I start forward, but Mom grabs my hand. "You can't," she says, her voice thick with emotion. "We can't be seen."

"But Archer—"

"Made his choice." Mom turns to Cal, who also looks ready to bolt. "Ryan has been considering this since you finished the potion. It wasn't a snap decision."

"You knew?" I ask, feeling fragile and heartbroken. "We could have stopped him."

Mom soothes away the hair stuck to my face. "It was his choice, Hannah. We have to respect that."

A loud *boom* cuts off my reply. The pharmaceutical company collapses in on itself. Dirt and debris fly in every direction, but a gust of wind—Elemental-enhanced wind—keeps the shrapnel from hurting anyone.

When the dust settles, another officer kneels before Archer and helps him back to his feet. When he stands, confusion creases his brow. He looks from the collapsed building to the dozens and dozens of employees sitting up in the lawn, watching with horrified expressions as their work falls down before them.

Then Archer's gaze narrows, and he calls for backup. He races toward the Hunters on the front lawn, shouting for someone to freeze.

He and another officer haul Benton's parents to their feet.

Their wrists are handcuffed behind their backs, and Mom pulls Cal and I close, wrapping an arm around our shoulders.

"Ryan is a good man," she says. "He'll be okay."

My heart breaks all over again. Even without his memories of magic, he still kept his promise. He stopped the people who took my dad from me.

"I can't believe it's over," I say, and Mom presses a kiss to the top of my head.

Cal stares into the sky, a failed attempt to keep the tears at bay. I reach for his hand, and he squeezes tight. "We can't let Keating get away with this."

I watch as Archer guides Mr. Hall into the back of his car and slams the door shut. A thrill of victory washes over me, but Cal is right. This isn't over.

Not yet.

33

THE NEXT FEW DAYS go by in a blur.

Cal and the rest of the Council don't get a minute to relax. Several teams are tracking Elder Keating—the *former* Elder— while several others analyze the personnel files Cal managed to steal from Hall Pharmaceuticals. They identify every possible Hunter, and just like Wes admitted to Archer, there were fewer than a hundred in all.

Now, none of them remember magic exists.

After their initial arrests, it didn't take long before Benton's parents were officially charged with Dad's murder, and the news is *everywhere*. Fresh whispers start up at school, and though this time the air is eager and willing to bring the gossip close enough to hear, I let it go. I try to focus on classes, even though I'm on edge waiting for updates about Keating.

The following Saturday, Archer stops by the house to visit Mom and me. He's Detective Archer to us again, not Archer or Ryan. Without his memory, he's no longer a Council agent. It's strange to see him, to talk to him and wonder how the potion has changed his understanding of our relationship. I wonder how the potion altered his perception of all the time we spent together this fall, all the hours of preparation to recruit Alice and David. How does he think he got the injuries on his hands?

I wish he'd let us remind him of the magic he lost, but Mom

is helping me accept that this is the life he chose for himself. Even if I don't fully understand, I have to respect that.

"Is everything okay, Miss Walsh?" Detective Archer looks up from his little notebook.

His caring tugs at my heart, and I press the heels of my hands against my eyes to push back the tears. "I'm fine," I say finally. Mom slipped away to get us drinks, and I glance toward the kitchen. "You said you had updates?"

"I do. Mr. Hall—the younger one, Benton—struck a deal with DA Flores as part of his agreement to testify against his parents." Archer flips back a page in his notebook, and I can't tell whether he's afraid of my reaction or simply wants to get his facts exactly right. "He'll plead guilty to aggravated assault and spend the next five years in prison."

A few weeks ago, learning that Benton wasn't going to spend the rest of his life behind bars would have sent me spiraling into despair. But now? With the threat of the Hunters gone and Benton's only reason to hate me erased from his memory? I can live with five years.

"Miss Walsh?"

"I'm okay," I say quickly. "Did he ever say why he did it?"

Detective Archer closes his notebook and pockets it. "He says his parents made him do it, but he hasn't been able to explain how."

I nod. Benton isn't entirely wrong. His parents raised him to hate us. They raised him to expect violence for his failures. And though I'll never forget what he did to me, maybe someday . . . Maybe someday I could forgive him.

But today is not that day.

Mom appears in the doorway, a cup of tea in each hand. "I'm

sorry to rush you out, Detective, but I just heard from my mother-in-law. We have a family thing to take care of this evening." She shoots me a meaningful look, and my heart skips a beat.

Elder Keating.

They must have finally found her.

"Of course, Mrs. Walsh. I'm finished." He stands and pulls a card from his wallet. "If you or Hannah ever need anything, please don't hesitate to call."

We wait for Archer to leave, and as soon as his taillights have disappeared, I turn to Mom. "Where is she?"

Mom grabs her coat and keys. "They're bringing her to Lady Ariana's house. The other Elders will be there."

I zip my sweater and slip into my shoes. "Let's go."

-|- * -|-

Elder Keating is a witch of great power.

But now, she stands alone.

Without the support of her Clan, and without the power of the Council, it didn't take long for the agents she betrayed to find her. It seemed only fitting that they dragged her back to Salem to stand trial for her crimes.

The entire coven is here, even the youngest children, and there's this hush in the air. Mom and I pause at the altar, adding our magic to the Middle Sister's flame, before continuing toward the gathered witnesses. Morgan and her parents are here, too. Though her injuries have fully healed, I catch Morgan tracing her thumb over the spot where Keating's knife pierced her chest. Where it narrowly missed her heart.

"You okay?" I ask when we reach where they're standing.

Morgan drops her hand and smiles. "I guess so." She reaches out and threads her warm fingers through my freezing ones. "She looks so different now."

I follow her gaze and examine the fallen Elder.

Keating stands alone, her arms secured tight behind her back with a binding cord that severs the connection to her power. One of the Elementals—Lady Ariana or perhaps Elder Hudson—coaxed the earth into holding her still, the ground rising up to her knees to pin her in place. Her mascara runs in streaks down her face, with small flecks of black on her muddy shirt. Even her hair looks different, more white than blonde now.

Morgan leans her head against my shoulder. "I still can't believe Riley got to go home like he did nothing wrong."

After our final mission, the police questioned everyone outside Hall Pharmaceuticals. One of the Hunters, overcome with guilt, confessed to shooting David O'Connell in Ithaca, but when the fire marshal ruled the building's demise accidental, no one else besides Benton's parents was arrested. According to Riley's social media feed, he's been back in Minnesota for a few days now. The only consolation—besides the gunshot wound I like to imagine still hurts—is that he missed so many classes that they kicked him out for the semester.

"I'm sorry we couldn't do more." I rest my head on top of hers.

She shrugs. "It sucks, but at least he's out of my life. My parents like it here. They don't have any plans to take me back to Minnesota."

"Good," I say, squeezing her tight, "because I'm not letting you go."

"Am I interrupting?" Veronica asks, eyebrow raised. My

cheeks flush hot, but she smiles and nods over her shoulder to where Cal is standing alone, glaring at his former Elder. "He wanted to talk to you before we start."

"Of course," I say, but Veronica shakes her head.

"Not you, Han. Your girlfriend." Veronica watches Morgan leave, and when we're alone, V bumps her hip against mine. "She makes you happy."

"She does."

"I guess that means I'm not allowed to hate her anymore." Veronica smirks at me.

Though I roll my eyes, thoroughly, I appreciate a bit of lightness before what's about to be a very heavy day.

Lady Ariana, Elder Hudson, and a woman I don't recognize exit my grandmother's home. A shudder travels through the earth, silencing conversation.

When Elder Hudson finally speaks, his voice fills the air with the energy of a storm. "Katherine Keating, you have been found guilty of breaking the highest laws of this Council. You have torn magic from innocent witches and instigated the death of others. For these crimes, your magic will be stripped away and you will be banished from our community."

The other woman, who I assume is the Blood Witch Elder, steps forward and pulls a long knife from a hilt around her waist.

Keating's wild blue eyes catch in the fading sunlight. "I only did what had to be done. I tried for *decades* to push us into the future, but you were too weak to do anything about it."

If not for the earth slithering higher up Keating's legs, I might have thought the other Elders hadn't heard her at all. Their expressions remain unmoved by her pleas.

"Secrecy has cost us more good witches than anything I've

done." Keating is trembling now, the other Elders nearly upon her. "It's not too late. There's still time to fix this. We can step out of the shadows. We shouldn't have to hide from *Regs*."

The Blood Witch Elder cuts the binding cord from Keating's wrists and pulls one arm forward, forcing her palm up.

"No." Keating tries to pull away, voice breaking. "Don't do this. Please don't do this. You know me, Christine. I've only ever wanted what was best for our Clans. We can still fix this."

"You cannot replace the lives you took, Katherine." The Blood Witch drags the blade smoothly across Keating's palm, and there's an edge to her voice. I think of the Blood Witch boy, who died in the hospital the day we burned Hall Pharmaceuticals to the ground. "And now, you'll never hurt us again." She presses her palm against Keating's bleeding one.

Keating screams as Blood Magic tears through her system, and I force myself to watch as Elder Hudson steps forward with a potion clutched in his hand. He tips the vial against Keating's lips, and the mixture of magics tears her power apart piece by piece.

Her agony, her grief, does little to numb the hurt she caused. Dad's death. Sarah and Archer and Zoë and my grandparents and so many others without the magic they spent lives mastering. It's fitting that she should lose her own magic now, too.

Yet no matter her crimes, it's hard to watch the unmaking of a witch.

When the ritual is complete, when Keating collapses to the ground, shaking and shuddering, Council agents collect her. They give her another potion that will bind her from ever speaking about magic or the Clans again.

We talked at length about whether to take her memory but

ultimately decided the more appropriate punishment was to let her live out her days knowing what she lost.

Though she will also spend those days locked up in a secure Council facility.

After she's gone, there is no celebration. No laughter or overwhelming sense of victory. Instead, there's pain. Lingering echoes of hurt and grief. There's the remembrance of all we've lost. I text Zoë and tell her it's over, that we did it. A few minutes later, she reminds me that it isn't over. That we still need to find a way to restore the magic that was lost.

That the hard part—the after—has only just begun.

34

LIFE SETTLES INTO A new normal.

Mom has me on Operation Salvage Senior Year, which means I have zero social life until I'm caught up on all my missed assignments. My teachers are mostly accommodating given everything in the news about Benton and his parents, but that doesn't lighten the workload.

Getting back on track is about more than school, though. I finally take Veronica's advice and agree to let Mom find me a therapist. I've only been to a few sessions, but so far, so good. I always leave feeling lighter than when I arrive, but if I decide later that I want to talk to someone who understands *everything* I've been through, the Council says they can locate an Elemental qualified to help, even if it's only over the phone.

On a Thursday night late in October, my old boss Lauren calls and asks if there's any chance I could help cover a few shifts during the Halloween rush. Since I'm finally caught up on school— and since I blew through a good portion of my cash on new paint supplies—I agree.

Which is how I find myself spending the last Friday night in October at the Fly by Night Cauldron. The shop is *packed* with tourists. It's all hands on deck, and between the tourists and the full staff of employees, there's barely any room to maneuver. Quinn, a genderqueer first-year student at Salem State, helps me at the register. In the two months they've worked here, Quinn is already a faster cashier and bagger than I am, and I've worked at the Cauldron *forever*.

I ring up our current customer's final item—an exceptionally creepy dried scorpion—and pass it to Quinn. They wrap it in protective paper before sliding the crunchy creature in the bag. "That'll be sixty-two thirty-nine," I say, and the young woman dressed in black and copious amounts of dark silver jewelry swipes her card.

"Thanks for shopping at the Fly by Night Cauldron," Quinn says, flashing a bright smile that would make Lauren proud. "Come again soon!"

We continue to ring up the line, but one customer in particular keeps catching my attention. Detective Archer has been in the shop for an hour, and Quinn says he's in here all the time now.

I'm sure he's mostly here to see Lauren, but I keep catching him looking at books on the magical properties of herbs and spinning bundles of rosemary between his fingers, like there's some small part of him that aches for the magic he lost.

Seeing him here breaks my heart. It's the same heartache that echoes in my chest whenever Gemma talks about coming here for her lessons, still thoroughly invested in her new path despite not remembering what first sparked her interest. I hate not being able to tell her. I hate that we have secrets again, but she chose this, and until I can convince the restructuring Council to let me tell her—and I *will* convince them—I won't betray that trust.

Quinn and I send another customer on their way, and the person who steps up next has their collar flipped up, a hat on their head, and dark sunglasses covering most of their face.

They don't seem to have any purchases, either.

"Can I help you?" Before they respond, I notice a loose section of pink hair that has fallen out from under their cap. "Alice?"

"Keep it down, crystal witch. Do you want to cause a scene?"

I roll my eyes as Alice glances over each shoulder and pulls the brim of her hat lower. "What are you doing back here? Do you need to test-drive a few more insults?"

"There's a tour stop in Boston tonight, but I have been playing with one about grass. It keeps coming out like you're a stoner though."

Quinn clears their throat and glances between us. "Do you know her or something?"

"Unfortunately." The rest of the line is currently only a couple people deep. "Can you cover for me?"

"Sure." Quinn punches in their code on the register. "Do you know if Cal is coming in tonight?"

"I'm not sure," I lie. I know exactly where Cal is, but I've been sworn to secrecy.

When Cal spoke with Morgan that day at Lady Ariana's house, he wanted to know how Blood Magic might affect surgery recovery. Morgan's dad overheard them and helped Cal connect with a Blood Witch friend in LA who's a plastic surgeon. Thanks to the mix of Blood Magic and modern medicine, Cal will be back in two weeks, fully healed from top surgery.

He was still nervous about letting a Blood Witch control his healing when he left for California, though. Nervous, but excited, too. I think watching Blood Witches control my coven outside Hall Pharmaceuticals helped him make the final decision.

"I'll be right back," I promise Quinn, and lead Alice through the Staff Only door. In the break room, where we'll have a little privacy, Alice pulls off her hat. Her pink hair flows down her shoulders, and she props the sunglasses on the top of her head.

"What brings you to the Cauldron, Alice?"

"You." She pulls a ring from her middle finger and removes the thin needle from along the inner part of the band. "Like I said, I'm in Boston for my show, but I've also been training with Fitz and Ellie. Morgan's parents."

"I know who they are."

Alice rolls her eyes. "Anyway, they taught me how to unbind blood from our magic." She pricks the pad of her finger and winces when the little bead of red wells up. "Give me your hand."

Reluctantly, I do. Alice swipes the blood across my palm, and by the time she's done, her magic has already healed the tiny puncture. The smear of red against my hand burns hot, but then it soaks in, slipping beneath my skin.

"What was that?" I rub my thumb over the place the blood disappeared.

"That's me letting you go. That's me saying I forgive you for what happened in New York. I hope you can do the same for me." Alice's cheeks flush red, and she tucks her hair behind her ears. "I know I play a tough game, but I honestly think what we did together—what *you* did to protect not just your coven but all of us—is pretty great."

Her words are unexpectedly warm and genuine, and I find myself smiling at her. "Thanks, Alice. Really."

"Don't mention it." Alice slides the sunglasses back down. "Besides, I think your girlfriend should be the only one allowed to make your heart race." From behind her glasses, Alice waggles her eyebrows at me, and my entire face goes hot.

"Is this where we hug and promise to be friends forever?"

"Witch, please. That would be gross." Alice shudders, but the elaborate show makes me laugh. "See you around."

"Don't be a stranger!"

Alice flips me off as she walks away, and somehow that's more perfect than anything she could have said.

On the screen, a vampire confesses her love for a mortal girl, but Morgan and I aren't paying attention at all.

It's the first time we've been alone without adult supervision in *forever*, and her hands are all tangled up in my hair. We're supposed to be passing out Halloween candy while Mom teaches an evening class, but we turned off the porch light as soon as Mom's car was out of view.

When Gemma got up to make more popcorn, Morgan pulled me into her lap and drew my lips to hers. She releases her hold on my hair and lets her hands slide down my back, slipping her fingers under the hem of my shirt, pressing her palms against my warm skin.

She pulls away to press fresh kisses along my neck. Her Blood Magic soars through my body, and goddess, I cannot get enough of her. My magic swirls the air in the room into a frenzy, buffeting against our hair. When she notices the wind, Morgan leans back.

"We can't let Gemma see," she whispers.

"I can't help it." I cover my burning face with my hands, pushing down on my magic. The air slowly stills. "When you kiss me there, it gets all tingly and then the air just kinda . . . reacts."

Morgan brushes my hair back into place. Her expression

goes serious, all flirting gone. "Have you made a decision?"

"About?"

She worries at her lower lip. "Benton."

I scowl. "No."

Benton's been sending almost daily letters since he returned to jail. He wants to see me, wants to apologize in person, but I don't know what *I* want yet. I don't know if I can handle seeing him. When it counted most, he came through for me. And this new version of Benton, the boy without all his Hunter memories, has no idea why he hurt me in the first place.

"You don't have to decide right away," she says, brushing one final stubborn section of hair back into place. "But I have a feeling the letters will keep coming until you make a decision."

"I don't want to talk about him." I lean close, my lips a breath from hers. "Not tonight."

"Who's ready for popcorn!" Gemma's voice fills the room, and we spring apart. "Gah! It's every time with you two!" She sets the bowl of buttered popcorn on the coffee table. "Should I go? I should go."

I scramble off Morgan's lap and grab the popcorn from the table, tossing a piece into my mouth. "Don't be silly. Come on." I scoot over so there's room for Gem on the couch with us. "We've been having movie marathons since our parents decided we were too old to beg for candy. We're not about to skip our last Halloween in Salem."

"Oh, I hate that," Gemma says, letting her head rest on my shoulder. "I don't want to think about next year yet. I'm not ready to leave you."

"Like you could get rid of me that easily anyway."

The doorbell rings, and Gemma jumps up. "I'll get the pizza, but I swear, if you two are naked when I get back, I will lock you in a room until you're sick of each other."

Morgan kisses my cheek. "I don't think that's possible, Gem. Sorry."

"You're hopeless," she grumbles as she heads for the front door.

"Jealous!" Morgan calls back, teasing, but in Gemma's absence, I reach for Morgan's hand.

"Maybe we should," I say, watching the screen instead of looking at my girlfriend. "After Gemma goes home, of course."

"What? Get naked and lock ourselves in your room?" That teasing note is still in her voice, but my face burns anyway and I nod. "Wait, really?"

I finally look at her. "I'm ready if you are."

Morgan bites her lip. "Any chance we could fast forward through this thing?"

"Be careful. If Gem catches you talking like that, she might stay all night."

Gemma returns with the pizza, and we spend the next hour yelling at the screen, debating whether or not we'd date vampires if they were real.

I laugh along with them and let myself imagine a future of my own. One where witches can come out of the shadows. Where we can give back the magic that was stolen. Where we can tell the people we trust—people like Gemma—who we are without fear.

But until then, I will grieve the ones we lost and love the ones who are left as hard as I can.

And hope that Dad would count that as a win.

EIGHT MONTHS LATER

35

"HANNAH, COME ON! WE'RE going to be late." Gemma shouts at me from the bottom of the stairs. "It's our last bonfire before graduation. Hurry up!"

"Just a second," I call from my bedroom. My *real* bedroom. Construction took a little longer than expected, but Mom and I moved into the new house, built in the same spot as the one we lost, a little over three months ago.

Mom and I are making new memories here, and I think Dad would like that. And if we're wrong about the afterlife, if our spirits do linger on earth after death, it feels good to know we'll be in a familiar place, somewhere Dad can find us.

Beside me, Morgan is practically buzzing with excitement. "How long do you think it'll take her to run up here to yell at us?"

"Less than a minute," I say without hesitation. Gemma is not about to let us miss the end-of-school-year bonfire. Thankfully, this one should be free of animal sacrifices.

Although . . . she may be less interested in the party once we show her what I *finally* convinced the Council to let me share.

After Cal returned from top surgery, I wasn't sure if he'd stay on with the Council without Archer. He wasn't sure at first, either, but he couldn't pass up the opportunity to study the combination of different Clan magics. The boundaries of our powers are so much blurrier now, and he wanted to be part of all of it.

Still, even with Cal's help, it took months of discussions and committees and cowritten proposals to win the Council's approval. We're still years, maybe decades, away from the Clans coming out to the world. Even so, the restructured Council—now with better inter-Clan relations and more input from younger witches—agreed that telling trusted friends about our power is an acceptable first step.

There's still an obscene number of hoops to jump through to get a non-witch approved before telling them, but Cal was able to rush my application. It helped that Gemma willingly gave up her memories to protect us.

Downstairs, Gemma grumbles. A beat later, she's climbing the stairs. "I am not going to be late to another party because you two are busy making out." She stops outside. "Please tell me you're dressed at least?"

"Fully clothed," I promise as I pull open the door. I can't keep the grin off my face. "We do have something to show you though."

Gemma looks cautiously from me to Morgan and back again. "Okay . . ." She steps into the bedroom and looks for what the surprise might be.

"You may want to sit down." I lead her to my bed and wait for her to perch on the edge of the mattress.

"What's going on?" Gemma glances up at me. "You're freaking me out. If I didn't know better, I'd worry one of you was pregnant."

"No one's pregnant," Morgan says, grinning. "We do have a secret though. Hannah?"

I raise my right hand to chest height, palm up. "Ready?"

Gem gives me a skeptical look and shrugs. "I guess so."

"Don't freak out," I warn, and wait for Gem to agree. Then I snap my fingers, and a small flame bursts forth. I've been perfecting this skill with my grandmother for weeks now, and I feed the tiny fire more of my power until it's the size of a golf ball.

"What the hell?" Gemma stands abruptly, and she has to grab the bedpost for balance. Her eyes are alight with curiosity. "How are you doing that?"

Saying this to her again is all the excitement of that first time without the worry that twisted my stomach into knots. "I'm a witch. An Elemental, to be specific." I extinguish the flame and reach for the bottle on my desk, freezing the water to solid ice.

Gemma curses appreciatively under her breath. "What about Morgan? Are you one, too?"

"Also a witch," Morgan confirms, "but a different kind." We decided to ease into the whole Blood Witch thing, since Gemma was slightly grossed out last time.

"Seriously? Who else knows about this? How long has this been a thing?" Gemma falls back onto the bed, like she's overwhelmed by all the possibilities. "Wait. I'm not your token muggle friend, am I?" I laugh, and Gemma sits back up. "What's so funny?"

"You said that the first time I told you, too."

"The first time?"

"We . . . have a lot to talk about." I check my phone and slide it into my back pocket. "But I know you don't want to be late to the bonfire."

"Screw the bonfire." She drags me and Morgan onto the bed with her. "Tell me everything."

ACKNOWLEDGMENTS

This Coven Won't Break was the most difficult book I'd ever writ-ten, and I couldn't have done it without the support of some incredible people. First, my brilliant and insightful editor, Julie Rosenberg, who helped me see past all the wrong turns and dead ends to find the heart of Hannah's story. Thank you for guiding the way and trusting me to get it right. To my incredible agent, Kathleen Rushall, who has the rare and treasured ability to keep me grounded in reality even as we weave dreams for the future. A huge thank-you to the teams at Penguin and Razor-bill: Alex, Bree, Casey, Jayne, Abigail, Bri, Christina, Felicity, and Shannon—books really are a team effort, and I'm forever grateful for all you do.

To the talented people responsible for the cover—Travis Commeau, Amy Blackwell, and Dana Li—thank you, thank you, thank you! I feel so lucky to have such beautiful art representing this book.

Thank you to Dill Werner, Kate, and Eisha, who provided feedback and guidance at various stages of *Coven*'s development, and a second thank-you to Eisha for letting me borrow your name. Look, you're famous!

On the days I feared I'd never finish this book, I was lucky to have wonderful friends who kept me going. To Jaimee, who let me spoil the entire plot of this book, in all its different iterations.

To David, who never had any doubt, even when I did. And to my wonderful writing coven, Jenn Dugan and Karen Strong: I can't imagine navigating this industry without you. Here's to many more years of licorice candy.

I've been blessed with a family that champions my books but won't let me forget my roots. Love always to Mom, Chris, Cameron, Taylor, and Tristan. Kim, Rod, and Pat. My grandmothers, who both read my very first novel and encouraged me to keep writing. My dad and all my amazing aunts, uncles, and cousins. Y'all are seriously the best.

To my wife, Megan: there is no one in this world that I'd rather have on this journey. You always see the best in me, even when I'm grumpy about deadlines. I feel so lucky that I get to spend the rest of my life with you.

Finally, to my readers. Thank you for letting Hannah into your hearts. This one's for you.

KEEP READING FOR AN EXCERPT
FROM ISABEL STERLING'S
STEAMY, COMPELLING NEW
PARANORMAL ROMANCE

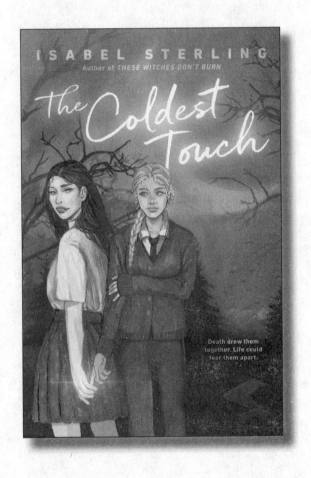

Prologue

A girl made of stone and masks and broken glass sits alone at her desk. In her new apartment. In a town far from home. The girl is used to being alone. Used to wanting things she cannot have. A family. Friends who care about *her* more than the favors they request.

Love.

But she doesn't have those things, doesn't remember if she ever did. She's been lonely longer than she's been seventeen.

And she's been seventeen for so many years she's lost count.

The girl ignores her silent heart and focuses on the task at hand. On her laptop, she opens a secure link and flips through the file of a girl who has everything. Photo Girl stands among her family with a bright smile and laughter in her eyes. She's victorious atop a podium with wet hair and a gold medal around her neck. She kisses a boy on the cheek while his arms wrap tight around her. Comments under the post declare them #RelationshipGoals. She's with him again, glittering crowns on their heads and a flower pinned to his suit. Photo Girl's life is everything the lonely girl wants for herself.

But then the family photos and smiling selfies cease, and a series of newspaper clippings follows.

SUDDEN STORM SENDS LOCAL MAN OVER BRIDGE

CAR PULLED FROM RIVER, BODY STILL MISSING

MEMORIAL SERVICE FOR NICHOLAS BEAUMONT, 21

The next images make her recoil, but she carefully commits each one to memory. A grieving family greets mourners beside a closed casket. A twisted, broken guardrail and muddy tire tracks. Photo Girl on her knees beside the river, hair stuck to her face as she screams.

The smiling portrait of a young man no longer among the living.

She didn't know about the dead brother, not until she'd already accepted the case. The death doesn't change her mission. Even so, seeing the stories in black and white makes something uncomfortable shift and knot inside her.

But there isn't time to care about the people in these photographs. She has a job to do.

So, she tries on an array of personalities. Becomes a dozen funhouse versions of herself until she forgets who she is inside. She'll wield her charm as a weapon and her smile as her shield.

And when she meets Photo Girl, when she sets eyes on this creature with hair the color of sunlight and eyes like the ocean, she will be ready.

1

Elise

*I*don't belong here.

Though I've visited three times in as many days, I still feel like an intruder as I maneuver through the tiny shop's narrow aisles. Heart & Stone Metaphysical is located in downtown Elmsbrook, where stores shorten their hours and sit mostly vacant while the local university is closed for the summer. I wish I'd known about this place then. Now, in the early days of September, the shop is full. The new college students are only two years older than me, but it feels like a lifetime.

Their gazes linger as I pass shelves of carefully wrapped lies and impossible promises, like they know I'm trespassing in their world of magic and make-believe. The two white men who work here seem nice enough. Over the course of a few visits, I've overheard enough conversations—and asked enough questions—to know they believe in the hope they're peddling.

So far, I've avoided knowing their deaths.

In the center of the long, rectangular store, one of the men offers advice to a young woman on the best stones to banish unwanted attention at work. He rattles off a list of black rocks: tourmaline, onyx, and smoky quartz. He seems at home in this world of magic and make-believe. He chose this life.

I was cursed into it.

At least, that's the only logical conclusion after a summer of medical tests and therapy appointments didn't solve anything. When I turned sixteen last April, I lost *everything*—my brother, my spot on the swim team, and eventually, my friends. My heart clenches as the memories try to surface, but I force them under. I won't fall apart in public, not again.

Tugging the sleeves of my sweater down far enough to cover my palms, I check the list of supplies on my phone. As much as my rational mind wants to deny everything this shop stands for, science failed to uncover the source of my problem. I have no choice but to test the magical, the paranormal, the strange.

With the help of the internet, and a couple awkward conversations with the men who work here, I've cobbled together the best of what the metaphysical world has to offer. Bay, fennel, and nettles to break hexes. Selenite to cleanse my so-called *energy field*. Plus five different kinds of salt, and enough candles to burn down the house if I'm not careful. All of that, yet each time I review and refine my plan, there's something else I need. Buying supplies for the ritual has already used up most of my savings, but I'm afraid to leave anything out. If I'm going to do this, I'm doing it right.

As if there's a *right* way to dabble in make-believe.

Careful not to get too close to the woman scanning the bookshelves, I approach the back counter. Beneath the glass sits an assortment of handmade jewelry, but I'm not interested in a necklace or a hunk of sparkly rock. Instead, I focus on the display of pendulums swinging from a wooden stand.

Except . . . the list on my phone doesn't specify what kind of pendulum to get. Would it make a difference if I used an amethyst pendulum instead of one carved from wood? I bite back a sigh.

Why can't one part of this process be simple? My frustration almost sends me sulking out of the shop, but I have to try. I already tried faking migraines, but the X-rays and MRIs I had this summer found nothing.

They couldn't explain why I see death everywhere I go.

"Trouble making decisions?"

I flinch away from the soft voice and turn to find a white girl standing close beside me. *Too close.* She's wearing jeans and a plaid shirt rolled up to her elbows, the pale skin of her forearms flawless beside the green fabric. I pocket my phone and tug my sleeves all the way to the base of my fingers.

"What?" I finally ask, heart beating too fast as I put more space between us. I didn't hear her, didn't notice her get so close. She could have touched me. She could have—

The girl points to the display of pendulums, cutting off my panicked thoughts. "These are great for making decisions." She smiles, but the quick sweep of her gaze contradicts that warmth. It feels calculated, like she's examining me.

I return her stare, cataloguing the soft cascade of brown hair that falls past her shoulders and the deep black sunglasses perched on top of her head. She seems about my age, but I've never seen her around town before.

"They can also help find what you've lost," she offers, still smiling. Still standing too close.

"I know." The words come out stiff and harsh, and my cheeks flush with heat. "They supposedly do a lot of things."

I pluck one of the clear quartz pendulums from the rack. Based on my few weeks of intense research, colorless stones are supposed to work for most rituals, sort of like a universal blood donor. Except . . . for magic. The quartz should work well enough to open chakras, and—more importantly—close them.

"Supposedly," the brunette echoes, and follows me away from the display case. I can't read her tone, can't tell if she's agreeing with me or mocking me.

At the wall of bulk herbs, where dried plants are stored in large glass jars, I pause. The girl stops, too, lingering beside me. With the pendulum clutched tight in one hand, I try to focus on something other than my new shadow. Soft instrumental music filters through the store, and there's enough incense in this place that it's nearly a breathing hazard. But I can still sense her standing beside me. *Just get the supplies and get out.*

I scan the labels and grab the jar of dried witch hazel.

"Interesting choice," the girl says, leaning over my shoulder and making me flinch. She must notice my discomfort, though, because she steps away. "Are you looking for protection or divining for true love?" A conspiratorial grin tugs at her blood-red lips.

Something about the easy way she smiles picks at my defenses. In another life, one where this curse hadn't destroyed everything, I might have returned her grin. Now I just want her to leave me alone. "How is that any of your business?"

She glances at the floor like she's embarrassed. "Sorry. I don't mean to be nosy." When she looks up again, her expression is softer and less teasing. "I'm Claire," she says, and holds out a hand.

"Elise." I ignore her outstretched palm and adjust my grip on the supplies. She doesn't leave, and I don't know what she wants from me. I don't have time for whatever this is. The new moon is tomorrow, and it's my chance to fix everything. The friendships I smashed to pieces this summer. The distance I have to keep from my family. The terrible curse ruining my life.

"Nice to meet you." Claire drops her hand, and the smile finally slips away, uncertainty taking its place.

Guilt tugs at my heart, which makes no sense. I don't know this girl. I don't owe her anything.

"All set?" One of the shopkeepers suddenly appears beside me, hands reaching for the jar. "I can take that to the front for you." His fingers slide against mine as he takes the pendulum and witch hazel.

Pain and fatigue crash into me, and I squeeze my eyes tight. In my mind, I see an older version of him, gray hair clinging in thin wisps to his head. It's hard to breathe. Impossible. Each gasping inhale refuses to fill my lungs, and my brain gets fuzzy. Then everything is cold, and the hospital machines are screeching that he's gone.

When he finishes collecting my things, his fingers slip away from mine. The moment the contact is gone, the vision fades. I gasp for air, lungs expanding again the way they should, but I can't stop my hands from shaking. I didn't want to see him die. I didn't want to know, didn't want to *feel* it.

"Another small bag for the herbs?" he calls on his way to the register, and it's all I can do to nod. My voice is trapped in my throat, tears threatening behind my eyes.

I remind myself to breathe, forcing one deep inhale then another. It takes every bit of control not to cry, not to think about all the other deaths I've seen. The lives I've failed to save. My heart clenches tight, and I see my brother's face.

Nick is gone, and it's all my fault.

"Are you okay?" Claire reaches for me, face etched with concern.

"Don't touch me." I jolt away from her approaching fingers and knock into the shelves. Jars rattle dangerously, but none of them fall. "I have to go." My tone is harsh, but I don't apologize. I'll never see this girl again, anyway.

I leave her standing beside the herbs and hurry to the counter to pay for my things. I slide over exact change, grab the small bag of supplies, and head for the door.

Before I can escape, there's this tightening in my chest. A prickle of cold against the back of my neck. I glance over my shoulder and find Claire watching me. Studying me. A shudder trembles across my skin, and I push open the door, slipping into the warm afternoon.

I have a ritual to prepare.

2

Claire

The moment Elise slips out of the store, I dissect our interaction. I don't know what to make of her presence in a place like this. Nothing in her dossier pointed to an interest in the paranormal. Yet given her reaction to the scrawny man who touched her—and the way she kept a deliberate distance between us—I'm positive the witches found the right person.

But what was she doing *here*? Has she embraced her gift? Does she think other types of magic are at her fingertips, waiting to be discovered?

When the lead shepherd talked me into rejoining their team, when they talked me into taking *one last case*, I thought I'd find the grieving girl from the file. I was wrong. Elise isn't the same girl she was before, smiling and aloof, but there's a spark in her I didn't expect. A fire in her ocean eyes.

And she's getting away.

I move silently through the shop and slip behind the counter where the owners are bundling dried herbs. It would be easier if I could corner each of them alone, but I'm strong enough to handle two humans at once.

The paler one notices me first. "You can't be back here." His tone is kind but unapologetic.

"Oh, I'm sorry." A flutter of guilt moves where my heart does not, but I ignore it. I grab each man's forearm and stare into their eyes, waiting for the moment their minds belong to me. When I feel the familiar pressure in my head, I hold tight to the sensation. "Do you know that girl?" I keep my voice low so I don't alarm the mortals shopping in the aisles.

"Not well."

"She's come in a few times."

"If she ever visits again, call me immediately." I make the men memorize my number. "What is she trying to do?"

"She's been asking about chakras and how to close them."

"She asked me about curses."

"Is there anything else?" Impatience tightens my grip. The longer I delay, the harder it'll be to track Elise. The men shake their heads, so I release them. The compulsion will settle into the back of their minds, only activating if Elise steps into the shop.

If she doesn't, these men will never feel my influence again.

Outside, the bright afternoon sun assaults my senses, weakening my muscles and blurring my vision. A dull ache blossoms at the back of my skull. With a groan, I slide the sunglasses onto my face. The witches on our research team developed special lenses that block the worst of the sun's effects, but this pair is getting old. I haven't worked a daylight shift in ages, so I didn't realize their strength had faded.

There's no time to get a replacement pair, so I turn left and stalk through the busy streets. At first, I'm surprised by the amount of traffic on a Monday afternoon, but then I pass a bookshop with a large LABOR DAY SALE! banner in the window. It explains the crowd, but that doesn't help with the growing headache or the pressure throbbing along my gums. I mentally flip off the blazing sun and consider telling Wyn to give this assignment to someone else.

But then I remember Wyn's final argument. *You know what this girl means to the Veil, Claire. If you succeed, Tagliaferro and Guillebeaux will owe you for a change.*

Wyn made it seem simple, but shepherding is never easy. Not everyone takes well to the rules of our world, and unlike the men in the shop, I won't be able to compel Elise. Her gift makes her immune to paranormal manipulations, but that's not even the worst part of this case. Infiltrating her world means going back to high school. I'd rather die.

Again.

Ahead, I finally spot Elise, her blonde braid swinging in a gentle arc across her back. She slips through the crowd, careful not to brush into anyone. Splotches of sweat speckle her thin gray cardigan, yet she keeps the sleeves pulled all the way to her fingers.

Part of me wants to sprint after her and explain everything— she clearly has no idea how to control her rare gift—but she was more guarded than I expected. I'll need to go slow, build at least a little trust, before I explain the paranormal world and her place within it.

Still, as I watch Elise dodge around a small child with tiny pigtails on top of her head, I can't help but feel a twinge of sympathy. I remember the bone-deep fear that flooded my newly heightened senses when I realized humanity was my past, not my present. I'll never forget the dead girl on the floor, the taste of blood in my mouth, the panic that drove Rose away.

Rose, who stole my life and never bothered to explain what I'd become.

The ache in my jaw intensifies, and I squeeze my hands into

fists so tight each of my knuckles pops. *Rose*. I've been chasing her for so many years I've lost count, but she's always one step ahead. Every time I think I've found a new lead, the trail disappears like smoke in the night.

You know what this girl means to the Veil.

Wyn's words are in my head again, and I remember the panic at headquarters when Elise's predecessor went missing. When it became clear she had died and passed the gift to someone new. Convincing Elise to embrace her power, convincing her to serve the Veil, is vital to our continued survival. Wyn was right about the reward, too. If I succeed, Tagliaferro and Guillebeaux, the Veil's leaders, will finally owe *me*. They'll have to help me find Rose.

I smile despite the pain pulsing through bone and muscle and marrow. I'll find her.

And then I'll tear out her slender throat.

Up ahead, Elise turns west, away from the downtown area. I keep plenty of space between us, but I don't let myself lose sight of her golden braid for more than a second or two. When we pass into a residential community, the sidewalk traffic thins to nothing. Storefronts give way to green lawns, and the scent of sweat and exhaust fades to burning charcoal and sizzling burgers.

Now that we're alone, now that it's clear Elise is simply headed home, I let more space stretch between us. I lose sight of her when she turns north into an even more expensive neighborhood, where she lives with her surgeon father and real estate agent mother. The moment she's out of sight, my phone buzzes against my leg. I ignore it, since the only creature who bothers to call me is Wyn.

Despite their centuries of experience, Wyn never cultivated a sense of patience.

The buzzing eventually stops, and I silently thank whoever

planned this neighborhood for the tree cover. Though shade is a poor substitute for the dark of night, it's better than facing the direct assault of the sun. The pounding in my head relents. A little.

My phone buzzes again, and this time, I pull it out. As expected, Wyn's name glows in the middle of the screen. I consider ignoring them, but apparently, they'll just keep calling.

"I've been in Elmsbrook less than a day. What could you possibly want?" Even though there's more than enough space between Elise and me, I keep my voice low. She can't know I'm here until I *want* her to know.

"You were supposed to call after you settled into your apartment." Wyn's voice sounds far away, like they have me on speaker. "You promised not to miss check-ins."

"And before that, I promised I'd never shepherd again." I'd meant it, too, when I left Wyn's team ten years ago. I didn't expect them to lure me back with promises of revenge. "If you don't trust me, why the hell did you beg me to do this?" My voice is harsh, but they deserve it.

Wyn sighs. "You're the only one young enough to pass as a student."

"So glad you believe in me."

"You're also one of the best damn shepherds the Veil ever had," Wyn adds, albeit begrudgingly.

Down the street, Elise turns off the sidewalk and approaches a two-story house with gray siding and white trim. The shrubbery out front is carefully sculpted, the grass as neat as all its neighbors'. She punches a code into the lock, opens the door, and slips inside. I'm vaguely aware of Wyn rambling on about protocol and precautions as I slip closer to the house and pause across the street.

The navy-blue front door is fitted with panes of glass, and

through them I spot Elise darting up a staircase with the supplies she bought at the occult shop. I wonder again what she plans to do with the pendulum and witch hazel, and I kick myself for not asking the shop owners if she'd purchased anything else.

I'm tempted to knock on the door when I notice more movement inside. A white woman with dark red hair follows Elise up the stairs. Her mother, probably, though she's dyed her hair since the funeral.

"Are you even listening to me? Dammit, Claire. You can't—"

"I found her," I say, cutting off Wyn mid-rant. "She's not alone, though." I run through a dozen different scenarios, ways to show up at her house uninvited and ditch the mom long enough to tell Elise everything she needs to know. None of them work. Trust takes time. Patience. Setting the right foundation is essential.

"And?" Wyn prompts. "Have you made contact?"

A plan comes together piece by piece. "Tomorrow," I say as I start the trek back to my apartment. "I'll make contact at the academy."

3

Elise

Mom is in the kitchen when I get home.

I slip inside, close the front door as quietly as I can, and race to the stairs with my supplies. I only make it three steps before Mom calls out. The downside of the *open-floor plan* she loves so much.

"Elise? Is that you?"

"I'll be down in a minute!" I hurry up the rest of the stairs, no longer quieting my steps. My parents aren't particularly religious, but I'd rather shave my head than explain the magical properties of witch hazel to my mom. She would only worry, and she's had enough of that.

At the top of the stairs, I turn right down the hall. My chest constricts as I pass Nick's room. It's unavoidable, just like the way my fingers brush against his door. The habit started when Nick left for college three years ago, and it didn't stop when he—

My throat closes, as if my body thinks that will stop the words in my head. I missed Nick so much when he left for college, but that was nothing compared to this new crater in my chest. It's been five months since we lost him—since *I* failed to save him—and the pain only grows and grows, like a black hole slowly consuming my life.

Inside my room, I lock the door and go to my closet. Mom usually doesn't snoop, but I don't want to risk it. Not with the collection of herbs, crystals, and candles I'm hiding. Reaching for the box under the pile of discarded jeans—

Merrrrowww!

I jolt back and swallow a scream. "Damn it, Richard!" The three-year-old calico saunters out of the corner. She meows more politely and tries to nibble on my fingers. "Why are you such a jerk? I'm the one who feeds you." I scratch under her chin with one hand and lay the witch hazel and pendulum inside the box with the other supplies.

Just one more day.

The thought soothes some of the ache in my chest. I spent all of August researching for this ritual. It's going to work. It has to.

"I don't suppose you could help?" I ask the fuzz ball, petting the patchwork of orange, gray, and white fur along her back. In response, Richard turns and nips at my fingers hard enough to hurt. When I wince, she jumps over my lap and scratches at the bedroom door.

"You are such a traitor, Richie." I stand and strip out of my sweat-slicked shirt and sweater, ignoring the cat's pleas to escape. Mom has the air conditioning cranked, and the cool air kisses my skin until I shiver.

Though it's a tiny problem compared to the weight of this curse, I'm tired of dressing in soft cotton armor, with sleeves pulled down to my fingers. Central New York summers are muggy and hot and terrible, especially stuck in sweaters all the time. I never thought I'd say this, but I'm actually looking forward to winter.

But tomorrow . . . Tomorrow everything will be different. I'll be free of this curse, free to wear my favorite T-shirts again without fear.

"Elise? Dinner's ready." Mom shows impressive restraint by knocking instead of barging in. "That cat better not be scratching my carpet."

"I'll be right there!" I grab the nearest long-sleeve shirt and tug it on. In the mirror, I find my hair a mess, flyaways that Mom will definitely try to smooth against my head. With quick fingers, I undo my braid and grab the brush from the top of my dresser.

The door handle jiggles. "Why is this locked?" Mom's voice is tight with worry. "Elise Beaumont, what are you doing in there?"

"Getting changed. Hang on." I adjust the pile of clothes covering my magic supplies.

"Open the door right now, young lady. Or I'll—"

I reach the door and pull it open before Mom can finish. Despite the cat's earlier whining, she lingers in the open doorway like she can't decide if she actually wants to leave. Mom, on the other hand, looks pissed. She's still wearing work clothes, a charcoal pencil skirt and white blouse, and her face is nearly as red as her salon-colored hair. I toss my brush on the bed. "See? I was just changing. Nothing scandalous, I promise."

Mom narrows her eyes at me, the same blue-green eyes Nick and I share. *Shared.* The correction churns like acid in my stomach. We both looked a lot like Mom, with golden hair and thin noses. After the accident, after we lost Nick, Mom started dyeing her hair a fiery red. She claimed it was to make herself more memorable with clients, but I think it was too hard to see Nick in the mirror. It's a miracle she can still look at me.

Dad doesn't.

Mom props one hand on her hip. "If you're doing drugs again, so help me." She stalks into the room and sniffs the air. "I'm not afraid to get you tested."

"I'm not doing *drugs*."

"Funny. That's what you said right before we found your vape pen."

Shame burns my cheeks. There wasn't *supposed* to be anything illegal in the cartridge. The seller said it was an herbal mixture meant to cure visions, not create them, but there was definitely something medically—not magically—mind-altering about that stuff.

"Don't worry, I learned my lesson." I reach up and start working my hair into a tight braid. "I was hot from my walk and needed to change. That's it, I swear."

She studies me a second, but then her posture softens. "Here, let me help with that."

"It's fine, Mom. I got it."

"Don't be ridiculous." Mom reaches for me, but I flinch away. Pain flashes in her eyes, which makes me feel like shit. I don't want to hurt her more than I already have.

"Sorry," I say, sitting at my desk. "I'm just nervous about school tomorrow." It's a dangerous kind of lie, the type that skirts too close to the truth, and I brace myself for the hurt of her touch.

"I know last year ended on a sour note." Mom runs her fingers through my hair and starts on the French braid. I try not to tense, but between the thickness of my hair and the length of Mom's fake nails, her skin doesn't touch mine.

A relieved sigh escapes my lips, but then I really hear her words. "Sour? Dean Albro threatened to expel me." Which was bullshit, honestly. After Nick . . . School didn't seem that important. I was seeing death everywhere, and I needed to find a way to fix it. I couldn't tell my parents—they'd never believe me—so I cut a few classes. Got behind on homework so I could research. Faked terrible migraines to convince doctors to order all sorts of scans. I scowl at the wall while Mom works on my hair. "He said if I couldn't 'get over it' and 'focus on my classes,' I should drop out and go to Elmsbrook High instead."

"I'm sorry, baby. I know you don't want to switch schools." Mom pauses, my hair held tight in her fingers, but then she's working again. "Dean Albro promised to give you a clean slate this year, but he emphasized that Elmsbrook Academy doesn't alter their standards of achievement, no matter how real the reason you're struggling."

I suppress a bitter laugh. *Struggling.* As if that could explain the horror of seeing Nick die. His was the first death I felt unspool inside my head, and I was there, hours later, when he actually drowned. Every agonizing second of his death is seared into my brain.

It was the world's worst sixteenth birthday.

"All set," Mom says, and I carefully pass her the hair tie around my wrist. She secures the end, and I have to smile. This is the closest we've been in months, the closest I've been to anyone without pain tearing through me. "Come on." She bends forward and wraps me in a hug, pressing her cheek against mine.

Images unfurl like a poisonous flower, vivid and painful, inside my head. Every part of me freezes up, and then I see her. Mom. Wrinkled and gray and alone in a hospital bed. Her weakness is echoed inside me, limbs heavy and going numb. My heart rate slows, each beat a struggle. Finally, hers stops altogether.

And then so does mine.

Panic tears at my chest as the seconds pass and my heart doesn't beat. But then Mom stands and pulls away, taking her touch with her. I gasp as my heart starts again, racing to make up for the beats it missed.

"You okay, Ellie?"

"I'm fine." I stand quickly, pain and grief intertwining inside me, making my body tremble. It's always like this. Every single time. I've tried to focus on the good things—that she's old, that she gets to live a long life—but Mom is always *touching*, and every time it's the same. Her heart gives out while she sleeps. Alone in a hospital bed. Dad nowhere in sight.

Probably because he dies first.

I hate the thought the second it arrives, but I can't push it away. I don't know for sure—Dad hasn't touched me, hasn't hugged me, since we lost Nick—but I looked up the statistics. Husbands usually go before their wives. Not knowing is the only good thing about him hating me. He hasn't said it, but I know he blames me for Nick.

Which is fine. I blame me, too.

"Come on," Mom says. "Your dad and I grilled burgers." She turns and steps into the hall, leaving me standing by my desk, the fatigue in my muscles still fading. Her death lingers like a fog, and every time I blink, all I see is her dying in that bed.

Just one more day, I remind myself. *One more day until the ritual that fixes everything.*

I raise my chin and follow Mom down the stairs, trying very hard not to cry.